Dedalus Europe
General Editor:Timothy Lane

The Prepper Room

Karen Duve

The Prepper Room

Translated by Mike Mitchell

Dedalus

The translation of this work was supported by a grant given by the Goethe-Institut London.

Published in the UK by Dedalus Limited
24-26, St Judith's Lane, Sawtry, Cambs, PE28 5XE
email: info@dedalusbooks.com
www.dedalusbooks.com

ISBN printed book 978 1 910213 72 8
ISBN ebook 978 1 910213 85 8

Dedalus is distributed in the USA & Canada by SCB Distributors
15608 South New Century Drive, Gardena, CA 90248
email: info@scbdistributors.com web: www.scbdistributors.com

Dedalus is distributed in Australia by Peribo Pty Ltd
58, Beaumont Road, Mount Kuring-gai, N.S.W. 2080
email: info@peribo.com.au

First published in German as *Macht* by Karen Duve in 2016 by the imprint Galiani Berlin
First published by Dedalus in 2018

Printed and bound in Great Britain by Clays Ltd, St Ives plc
Typeset by Marie Lane

A C.I.P. listing for this book is available on request.

The Author

Born in Hamburg in 1961, Karen Duve is one of Germany's leading contemporary writers. She has won eight literary prizes, the latest being the Kassel Literature Prize for Grotesque Humour. While working on her book *Anständig essen* (*Eating Responsibly*), in which she tried out a number of ethically based forms of eating, she became a committed vegetarian and a well-known figure on German television arguing, for example, with representatives of the agricultural industry. As well as polemics, short stories and children's books, she has written five novels, one of which, *Taxi*, has been made into a film. *The Prepper Room* is her most recent novel.

The Translator

Mike Mitchell has been a freelance literary translator since 1995 and has published over eighty translations from German and French, including Gustav Meyrink's five novels and *The Dedalus Book of Austrian Fantasy*. His translation of Rosendorfer's *Letters Back to Ancient China* won the 1998 Schlegel-Tieck Translation Prize after he had been shortlisted in previous years for his translations of *Stephanie* by Herbert Rosendorfer and *The Golem* by Gustav Meyrink.

His translations have been shortlisted four times for The Oxford Weidenfeld Translation Prize: *Simplicissimus* by Johann Grimmelshausen in 1999, *The Other Side* by Alfred Kubin in 2000, *The Bells of Bruges* by Georges Rodenbach in 2008 and *The Lairds of Cromarty* by Jean-Pierre Ohl in 2013.

Step one: 'Seize the victim and spirit her away.'

Step two: 'Isolate the victim and make her totally dependent on you for survival.'

Step three: 'Dominate the victim and encourage her to seek your recognition and approval.'

Step four: 'Instruct the victim and re-educate her to think and act in terms of your ideology.'

Step five: 'Seduce the victim and provide her with a new sexual value system.'

"Brainwashing: How to Fold, Spindle and Mutilate the Human Mind in Five Easy Steps," an article from the June 1976 edition of the men's magazine *Oui*, quoted in *Perfect Victim* by Christine McGuire and Carla Norton, William Morrow, 1988.

"Women and people of low birth are hard to deal with."

Confucius

1

I've just installed the telephone I found up in the loft, a simple, light-grey device with a dial and no technical frippery – no stand-by mode, no screen, no integrated photocopier with ink cartridges that can only be changed following instructions in pictures, and, above all, no answerphone. Just a big, old-fashioned receiver on a sturdy base that can be opened and repaired by any layman with a simple screwdriver.

But when there's a ring, it's not this epitome of durability and recyclability, that connected my parents to the world in the '60s, but the snazzy, slim, sightly concave egosmart in my pocket, of course, that curse on humanity that forces us to be available anywhere, anytime, if we still want to be involved in things. The fact that it emits the same old-fashioned ringtone as my parents' phone merely adds insult to injury.

I'm worried it might be someone from the Community Association. I made the mistake of volunteering to join in the local campaign to eradicate the invasive 'killer rape' that's growing rampant everywhere. But I know the face on the display from somewhere – the profile of a bird of prey with receding, greying hair and pouches under his unshaven chin – though I can't at first remember from where.

"Hi, Basti," the face shouts, "it's time again. You coming?"

Hardly anyone gives their name on the telephone any more. The more tedious the person, the more they're convinced that their ugly mug has made an indelible impression everywhere.

I shuggle the image over to the eighty-inch compunicator over the sideboard, hoping that at least the caller's name will display, but nothing doing.

"It's me – Norbert! Don't tell me you didn't recognise me? Norbert Lanschick. Don't you remember me?"

"Yes… of course… but you've…"

I leave long pauses between the words in the hope that Norbert Lanschick will fill them.

"Ohlstedt School! Graduation 1981. Has the penny dropped now?"

It has. Norbert – Nobby – Lanschick, in those days a spindleshanks so skinny the girls all shouted "Biafra" when he went past; above average marks in physics, below average, if any at all, in sport; a bit childish as well, never a girlfriend. Today: marathon runner, lawyer, husband, father, drives a BMW, still boring, still thin, balding. Every five years he organises a reunion for our year in Gasthof Ehrlich in order to allow the witnesses of his wretched youth to become witnesses of his wonderful transformation. Which doesn't work, of course. You can't pull the wool over your classmates' eyes any more than you can over your brothers' and sisters'. Even though Biafra Lanschik brings his very presentable wife, no one can forget how he used to wrap those incredibly long, thin legs sticking out of his shorts round the asymmetrical bars and hung there for ages between the upper and lower bars, head down like some bizarre insect, trying to heave himself up with his stick arms, all the while slipping down to the floor inch by inch.

"And there was me thinking you'd given them up…" I said. Five years ago there hadn't been a reunion. He must have had a setback in his career. What's he got to show us this time? A new wife, a new car?

"I couldn't manage last time," Lanschick says with a quiver

in his voice, "my partner died. It really hit me. We'd had the chambers together for thirty years, you understand? I spent more time with him than with my wife. Since then I've had to do everything myself."

The vulture face, blown up to four times life-size on the compunicator screen, tries to hide a self-satisfied grin. A complexion like the skin on porridge. He looks old – old, old, old. How can a man let himself go like that?

"But this time I'm doing it again. If I don't, nobody will. Do you realise this is the fiftieth anniversary class reunion? Should I book a room for you?"

"No, I don't need a room," I say. "I'm back in Wellingstedt."

"Wellingstedt? Where? Surely not with your parents?" Lanschick makes his braying laugh. "Since when?"

"I've been here four years now," I say. "And my parents are dead. I'm just living here in the house."

When things around me started to disintegrate, my wife left me and took the children away, when it became clear that global warming had already passed every tipping point and the official state feminism wouldn't make any difference to that, when my favourite pub burnt down and my vision became so poor I could only read the newspaper holding it at arm's length – which didn't really matter because the last quality printed newspaper closed down – when first my mother and then my father died out of pure wilfulness, and my brother and sister kept going on at me to hand over the house in which we'd grown up to an incredibly oily estate agent, I sold everything that was at all saleable, took out a loan, paid off my brother, had laser treatment for my eyes and let my hair grow again, packed my toothbrush and a couple of pairs of underpants in a sports bag and went back to the place where I'd spent the happiest years of my life.

"Actually it's not a bad location at all," Lanschick says patronisingly, "I've even thought about it myself."

By now Wellingstedt is regarded as a superior residential area for young families with a high income and poseurs like Lanschick. A low crime rate, only two asylum-seekers' hostels – and very well integrated ones at that – green woods, a brown river winding its way through the terminal moraine and only twenty kilometres from the centre of Hamburg.

In the late fifties tradesmen and clerks had built their houses on plots which a not very farsighted farmer had let them have for an incredibly low life annuity. Among them were my parents, who mixed concrete and brought in bricks in a wheelbarrow after work. Once all the access roads had been tarmacked, better-off people moved in and built their spacious flat-roofed bungalows right next to the red-brick hipped-roof houses with the coloured glass bricks. And naturally we, the children of electricians and detergent salesmen, went to school together with the children of bank managers and directors of insurance companies, paddled with them in the Alster in the summer and fought battles in which often-repaired inflatable dinghies faced canoes of Canadian cedar. As a matter of course we finished our schooling together under a social-liberal coalition – a brief window of social justice had opened up, an anomaly of history that had never before existed and presumably never will again.

In those days there were toads there, kingfishers and otters, and even today you might, if you're lucky, catch a glimpse of a sparrow or a rabbit. Wellingstedt has undergone great changes, of course. The conifers planted in the gardens in the sixties have grown so tall that now the gardens look like Böcklin's Isles of the Dead. Moreover the place is gradually but inevitably being gentrified. Estate agents are prowling up and down outside the last little houses where the remaining indigenous population is quietly muddling along. And whenever one of those houses is free, it's torn down and replaced with a monstrosity of a Tuscan-style villa on the site that is too small for it, because for some reason or other a Tuscan villa can be built with two stories without contravening the building regulations that only allow one-storied buildings.

"The building itself isn't worth anything at all," said the estate agent my brother had engaged to put a value on our parents house that was to his own advantage. "On the contrary, you have to deduct the demolition costs from the value of the land – but that's still five hundred thousand euros cash down, north euros, of course."

Property prices have gone through the roof. Which is why the wool shop and the barn I used to pass on my way to school have long since disappeared. The rather grubby riding stables are now a sports hotel and the strawberry fields, where decades ago I used to gather little sandy fruits, warm from the sun, in a wicker basket, have been transformed into a twenty-seven-hole golf course. In the next village a koi-breeder has set up business. And on top of that there's a Michelin-starred restaurant there and two 'design for living' shops. My past is disintegrating like a sugar cube in the rain.

"Did your wife move with you?" Lanschick's huge face asks. "I mean, she must have to be there in Berlin, she can't keep commuting back and forth. How are you managing that?"

I don't reply. I decide to leave him on tenterhooks for a while until the truth dawns on him.

"Oh my God," Lanschick says. "How stupid can I be! You must excuse me, I'd just forgotten. What a blundering oaf I am. Has there been any news, a clue, I mean? I'm sorry, I really am sorry."

"That's okay," I say, "it's more than two years ago. Anyway, we'd already separated. The divorce had come through ages ago."

Lanschick mumbles several times what an idiot he is and doesn't stop apologising.

"Right then," I say, to try and cut things short. "Now tell me who's going to be there at the reunion. Have many confirmed they're coming? Will Bernie and Rolf be there?"

"Yes, both of them. They always come."

"And the women? Kiki Vollert and Elisabeth Westphal, are they coming?" I ask in as casual a tone as I can manage. Elisabeth Westphal is the woman I've never had. Elisabeth Westphal is the reason why I go to the class reunions. I spent half my young days longing for her. Today I still miss her, even though by now I've become so accustomed to her absence, that I mostly don't notice it. Until the sight of a woman who has a similar laugh or movements as Elli used to have brings it all back to me.

"I've not got that far yet. I'm only at 'L'. But Birgit Lammert's coming," Lanschick replies.

"Good," I say. "Great."

I give him the number of my landline.

"Ring me on that number in future, not my mobile" – I deliberately say mobile even though it's only the real oldies who say that now – "I'm going to deregister my mobile in a few weeks."

"You can't mean that seriously," Lanschick says. "How are people going to get in touch with you then? I couldn't find your email address. Fortunately Holger Hasselbladt had your mobile number."

"I've had my email address deleted," I say. "In three or four months I'm going to throw my computer out and then I won't be using any technology that was invented after 1980. If you want to get in touch with me, there's the landline or you can write me a letter. Or you can come round. The old address: 12 Redderstieg. Same as before."

"That's crazy!" Lanschick says. "You can't do that."

He sounds outraged, but at the same time he also sounds impressed.

"Of course I can," I say. "And don't get the idea of sending me letters with one of those cheap firms that pay their employees four westos an hour – on zero-hours contracts as well. If you want to send me something, then use the post, otherwise I'll refuse to accept it."

Lanschick just can't believe me, he thinks I'm having him on, and when he realises I'm serious about it, he says it's probably just a phase I'm going through because everything's a bit too much for me at the moment.

"It happens to all of us," he says.

But it isn't a phase, it's self-defence. And unless I'm very wrong, self-defence is recognised in all the social systems around the world as an exceptional situation justifying actions that are otherwise not condoned. When it's a matter of them or us everything is permitted. Sometimes you just have to ask other people to put up with a few inconveniences if you don't want to end up as a slave carrying out the orders of a tyrannical machine dictatorship. And sometimes you have to destroy a woman if you don't want to be destroyed by her yourself.

And no, none of the neighbours has noticed anything.

2

I'm taking the kids back to their grandmother. About time too. Over the weekend they've spread their sticky little fingerprints all over the house. The 1950s lacquered chest of drawers, where I was unthinking enough to keep their hologram games, is so dull and greasy that from a distance it looks furry. Ploughing its way across the box with pot plants is a whole train of bizarre model covered wagons made of rubber. Driving them are green, yellow and red lumps with pug noses, cowboy hats, and holsters round their non-existent hips which, according to the children, are meant to represent some kind of vitamins or other nutrients – Sheriff Fatty, Vitamity Jane, the Mineral Kid and so on.

We're out on our bikes because it's such lovely weather. Lovely? It's as hot as hellfire every day! Never below thirty-five degrees, yesterday it was thirty-seven, once last week even forty-one, and they say it's going to get even hotter. For the last eight weeks the sky's been as blue as a picture-postcard – and not a drop of rain. The leaves on the trees have rolled up, the gorse is bowed down under the weight of dust and the grass in the meadows looks the way it does at the end of summer, brown and withered as it rustles away to itself. And it's only April. What's the summer going to be like? Even without water the killer rape is flourishing, spreading its heavy, sweet smell everywhere. It's in the gardens, even on the footpaths, in the meadows, in the woods, in the shade, behind the dustbins, simply everywhere – apart from on the golf course where they're employing two assistant greenkeepers just to pull up the rape. The whole area's glowing yellow. If, for a moment, you forget what a noxious, genetically manipulated pest it is – blossoming four times a year and growing faster than it can be pulled up, resistant to every known weed killer and surviving in any kind of soil and almost any kind of climate – it's incredibly beautiful. As long as you're not too bothered about the diversity of plant life.

My son Racke is riding along in front of me on his BMX, slewing and swerving wildly. He's wearing a red-check shirt and a greasy pair of short lederhosen with a white heart made of horn on the strap between the braces – just like the ones I wore when I was his age – and his bronzed, rather chubby legs are going up and down like pistons. When he turns to look at me, the airstream catches the back of his head, making his fine flaxen hair stand up straight. His sunglasses with the drop-shaped pilot's lenses slip down onto the tip of his nose.

"Look," he screeches, and his milk-white teeth glint as he makes such a sharp swerve that the sprung frame of his bicycle goes right down and the red pennant on a flexible stick attached to the luggage rack almost touches the road surface.

"Very nice," I shout back, "and now would you be so good as to look in front."

The warm airstream caresses my temples, the parakeets twitter in the trees and the rape-bugs clatter into our sunglasses. I feel like one of those endangered great whales ploughing its way through a yellow sea with its young.

My daughter's a few metres behind us. Binya-Bathsheba's in a huff. Actually that's where she is most of the time. She's not particularly pretty anyway, her face is rather round, and then this permanent sulky pout – she's sulking for the second time already today. The first time she stopped speaking to me when I took the pROJEKTas away from her and Racke and locked them up, which meant that the pair of them would have to spend a whole afternoon without their 3D friends. I could perhaps have put up with Racke's Destroyer, it's the slightly tamer version for kids between seven and ten. That means the projection is only one and a half metres tall, a robot with a crocodile's head, a loincloth that looks ancient Egyptian and a gigantic hammer, that keeps on rasping, "I want to be your friend," or suggests, "Let's make a rumpus." If Racke, speaking slowly and clearly, says,"Yes, let's make a rumpus," which amounts to permission to start, then the tin lizard stomps over to the nearest item in the house and thumps it with the hammer and the pROJEKTa loudspeaker emits remarkably realistic noises, as if it wasn't a projection but a real sledgehammer causing real damage – a sharp clinking for glass, a softer sound for china, crashing and splintering for the coffee table. For the Destroyer you need nerves as strong as a ship's rigging but at least it's cured Racke of his mumbling. The commands have to be given with exaggerated clarity. What really drove me mad was Binya-Bathsheba's lisping unicorn, that was all the colours of the rainbow. It's about the size of a pony with twenty-centimetre-long eyelashes and it would lounge around on my couch, fluttering its eyelids and had something to say about everything because the language unit in its pROJEKTa is programmed to respond to particular key words.

"I am Shangri-La, the last living unicorn," it would coo in its telephone-sex voice. "Come with me to the woods, where the butterflies sing, and become part of the whole." Or, "Life is a river, build a boat so you don't get wet."

It said the stuff about the boat when there was a special programme on TV about the flood wave that swept a coach off the wall of a dam and flattened two villages farther down in the valley, after several million tons of rock and ice had broken off from a melting glacier and slid into the reservoir. When I took their pROJEKTas away, Racke threw himself on the floor and howled until he was starting to go blue in the face. Binya, arms folded and legs crossed, sat on a chair but the wrong way round, her face covered in tears and pressed against the chair back; she hissed 'fascist' and then kept her lips pressed tightly together. That's something that has always bothered me about children – their low frustration threshold, their inability to keep their pain or fury at a level appropriate to the cause. At the least thing they go off at the deep end. How loud are they going to bawl when they have a real reason to? What kind of a rage are they going to work themselves up into when, in the near future, the arctic tundra and seas will have released their millions of tons of methane into the atmosphere and there'll be nowhere on this bloody planet where it's not either burning, or flooded or there's a drought or such a gale-force wind you have to cling on to the nearest lamp post? Half an hour later they were playing with their Lego, as calm as zen monks.

Now B's in a huff again because Racke and I aren't wearing helmets, even though, in her self-important and bossy way, she'd trotted out a fifteen-minute lecture on the dangers in traffic that was probably given to them at school a week ago. "It's the law," she said, as if that settled the matter and then, when Racke and I just pulled silly faces, she brought out the clincher, "And Mama wants us to wear helmets."

That's correct. My wife had even threatened to stop me seeing the children again, if I were to insist on continuing to subvert their education.

"You go ahead, then," I said to my daughter, "no one's going to stop you sticking that stupid plastic bowl on your head. But do stop bugging your brother and me about it. And, anyway, you may not have noticed but your mother isn't around any more, and as long as she's away, what I say goes."

That was perhaps a bit harsh, after all she's only ten, but the obligation to wear a helmet is just about the most stupid law that's been passed over the last few years. For me it illustrates the ridiculous, fussily overprotective nature of our present government – as if safety can mean anything on such a knackered planet – hey, sorry, we still don't know how to stop the rising temperatures and the slowing down of the ocean currents, which means that in five or, at most, ten years Homo sapiens will snuff it, so abandon hope, but until it's all over keep wearing your bicycle helmet or you'll be paying a hefty fine.

I know, I know, bicycle helmets existed before the women – with the support of willing idiots such as myself – seized power, but they weren't required by law then. At least for grown-ups. I mean, look at them, all these stylish young and true-young women ministers with at least five piercings in each ear and three in their nose, and their forearms tattooed right up to the elbow, as if they're still so nonconformist they have to go out after finishing at the office and seize the odd cargo ship. And what are they actually doing? Spoiling the bit of fun that's left to us – the feeling of the wind and the sun in our hair – and using the road traffic act to compel us adults to abandon our dignity and stick a brightly coloured bit of plastic on our heads.

I'm not saying our parents were perfect, but at least they weren't tattooed like pirates and, despite everything, were at least a hundred times more relaxed in the way they dealt with children and road traffic. For example, as a joke my father sometimes used to lock us in the car boot – mostly in the summer, when we were coming back from Coppermill Pond and he didn't want us to mess up his Opel Rekord with our sandy feet and wet bathing trunks. On the way home he would stop now and then, tap on the lid of the boot and get us to guess where we were. Moreover it was a matter of course for our parents that when we were going away on holiday the youngest child at the time would travel on the back shelf of the car, and no customs officer or policeman ever objected. Nowadays our children would be taken into care and the case would make the evening news.

Suddenly I hear a stifled cry behind me. When I turn round I see Binya's bike lying in the grass and she's rolling on the ground in a buzzing black cloud. Rape bugs! Unfortunately, as well as her yellow helmet my daughter's also wearing a white blouse, which attracts the undivided attention of the little black bastards. I jump down, tear off my shirt and scoop most of the bugs off her face with it, then stretch the material tight over her lips so that she can breathe without getting a mouthful of bugs. But Binya doesn't realise what I'm trying to do, she pulls the shirt away, flailing her arms around and screaming in the midst of the swarm of insects. I have to use one hand to hold her arms so that I can take off her helmet with the other and unbutton her blouse, and I have to do this holding my breath because I'm stuck in the cloud of insects as well. The revolting creatures are already attacking my torso and swarming up and down my arms. It's good that my hair comes down over my neck, that protects me a bit. Racke stands there with his little child's bikc, keeping his distance from us, howling – with fear or perhaps just because he feels so sorry for us. Finally I've got hold of Binya's helmet and blouse and I stuff both of them, together with a million rape bugs, into my saddle bag and zip it up. And the other bugs gradually leave us in peace and buzz off into a nearby garden. As I said, Binya hasn't exactly got a pretty face, but now it's all swollen and bitten by thousands of mini-mouths with micro-jaws.

"Just look at the poor child!" Grandma Gerda cries, succumbing to hysteria the moment we arrive, even though the swelling on B's face has gone down and it's not half as red as my bare back, that's coming out in blisters from second-degree sunburn.

Binja's got my blue shirt on. She's wearing it as a skirt over her jeans with a bungee cord from my luggage rack as a belt. And she can't feel that bad, for she immediately dashes into the living room to check her email on the compunicator. Racke rummages round in his backpack for his pROJEKTa and resurrects the 'Destroyer' in the hall. I give Gerda the bicycle helmet with the scrunched-up blouse inside it.

Gerda immediately starts moaning, "You didn't say you were coming on bicycles," but then switches off. Our struggle over the children was long and fierce after it had become clear that Christine wasn't going to turn up again that quickly, but naturally I was granted custody.

The old girl isn't much older than me but looks a lot older. I wonder why she's gone in for the grandmother style, happy with the appearance and fitness of a well-preserved fifty-year-old. Nowadays it's only the ninety-years-olds that look fifty. And Gerda was one of the first to go through the rejuvenation programme when it was really dangerous back then – when the probability of getting cancer within the next five years was still eighty per cent. That's left her with her watery eyes that are weeping all the time and the swollen lymph glands in her neck. At least she hasn't got cancer yet. Well, as far as I know. I have a slight suspicion that she's deliberately adopted the grandmother look in order to remind me of my own advanced years behind the youthful façade. It's always bothered her that her daughter married a man twenty years older. She's never become reconciled to it.

"I want to be your friend," the Destroyer rasps, opens and shuts his crocodile jaws, then waddles down the corridor, stopping next to Gerda.

"You've got to reply, Grandma," Racke shouts.

"Great. Thank you very much. I want to be your friend as well," says Grandma Gerda. The Destroyer gives a satisfied grunt.

"Let's make a rumpus," Racke shouts and for a moment the Destroyer, undecided, surveys Grandma Gerda and me but then, fortunately, it remembers that it's loaded the tamer version for under-tens and smashes its hammer on the corridor mirror.

"I have to talk to you," Grandma Gerda says to me. I can see what an effort she has to make to sound friendly.

"Oh," I say, "don't start going on about the points again."

"But I simply can't manage!" Gerda cries. "Just work it out yourself. I have to drive Binya to her riding lessons twice a week and Racke twice to football and once to his piano lesson. And if the hurricanes start again, I'll have to drive them to school as well. I need to fill up at least three times. And Racke said he'd love to have Königsberg meatballs again, but the few stamps I still have are not even enough to give them milk every day."

"I've told you often enough that children don't need milk products at all."

That I have, and if she wants to throw away her CO_2 points on yoghurt produced by cruelty to animals, that's her own lookout.

Now she can't restrain herself any more. "But they're the

children's points and they happen to be living with me, if you remember. It's not fair that you keep the children's allocation for yourself. How am I supposed to feed three people with a single person's allocation?"

"What do you mean by that? That I'm eating the children's meat myself, driving around on their petrol? They get their share all right when they're at my place. Ask them what there was for lunch today. Go on, ask them. I can tell you: meat stew, seventy euros a kilo – and five points, I could have filled my tank for that."

"But the children have only been with you twice this month. I was looking after them the rest of the time. It's just not fair…"

"Well, if it's getting too much for you… I'll be happy to have the kids come and live with me."

She slumps. "Please," she says, "we're getting so terribly short… Racke keeps having to ask the others in the team whether he can get a lift with them, they're starting to complain that I never…"

From the very beginning I intended to give her an allocation. I am human after all. But I always wait until she's come down off her high horse. I've been manipulated by women and their stupid arguments for long enough. I have the right to spend the last few years before the end of the world in peace. Gerda gets Binya's CO_2 allocation; I've hardly siphoned any points off it. I transfer it to her account on my egosmart. I let her watch.

"Thank you," Gerda says, meek and mild again. "Thank you, that's a great help, thank you very much."

So there you are. Things are okay after all.

3

Back home the first thing I do is to go down into the cellar to be with Christine for a while, to have a chat with her and help pass the time. I'm well aware that it can't be very pleasant to spend forty-eight hours by yourself, locked up in a room with no windows, and she takes every opportunity to make that perfectly clear. So I take the tins – the peas, the carrots, the peaches – off the cellar shelves, push the rack to one side, take the screws out of the plywood panel with my 1970s Black & Decker and pull it away from the wall, then tap in the number combination to open the steel door. Voilà, there I am in my little secret comfort zone, my safe haven: eight by four metres, plus the curtained-off bathroom unit – the classic prepper-room proportions. Enough room for an old-fashioned brass double bed, some yellow IKEA chairs round an occasional table with an IKEA kitchen island in the middle of the room. There's a smell of biscuits, freshly baked biscuits, a smell I really love. Christine is standing at the stove in a pink-and-white check apron holding the baking tray in her pink-and-white check oven gloves. Four months ago she went through a phase when she really let herself go, but I made a few things clear and now she's wearing lipstick in a pastel shade that matches her nail varnish and her eyebrows have been plucked to create a curve that gives her eyes a questioning and intelligent look. Under the apron she's wearing a light-blue floral dress and her blond hair falls down onto her shoulders, where it curls up in a beautifully natural way. She gives me a smile. But I know I can't trust her, so first of all I close the steel door and, as Christine puts the tray down on the stove – she's made afghan biscuits, my favourite, little lumps of chocolatey pastry with walnut halves on top – I lean over the keypad, so she can't see the number combination I put in. Then I get her to go close to the wall, where I've fixed three metal rings with snap links into the masonry, one at knee height, one at shoulder height and one above head height, and hook the chain attached to Christine's collar as tightly as possible in the middle one. It sounds awful, I know, the chain and collar, it makes you think of the Inquisition right away or S&M, but I'm not a pervert, just a man with his perfectly normal needs. I'd be happy to do without the mediaeval rattle of chains, but that just isn't possible with a woman like Christine. In the two years she's been living down here she's tried to inflict a serious injury on me eleven times. She unscrewed a chair leg and hit me over the head with it, she tried to pour boiling water over my face, stick a wooden spoon in my back after she'd gnawed it to a point with her incisors and once she even pulled the power cable out of the stove and lured me over near to it by saying the oven wasn't working, could I have a look at it. And in between she keeps putting on a convincing act suggesting she's come round, has finally given up, has reconciled herself to the situation and is prepared to cooperate. She kept it up for weeks, for months even, until I was lulled into a sense of security, almost trusted her and then, at the slightest negligence on my part – pow! – she struck again. Therefore it's perhaps understandable why, at every visit, I first of all attach her to the wall, frisk her for weapons and then give the room a thorough inspection, checking whether there's a loose chair-leg somewhere, cable sticking out of the wall or some other change that arouses my suspicions. After she'd been terrorising me for six months, I made another serious investment and installed the security lock with the secret code. Even though I'm not much of a handyman. But if you really want something, you suddenly discover you have unsuspected abilities. I check the room systematically, concentrating and not saying a word. Christine's not allowed to speak to me while I'm doing that either. Only when I've finished do I allow her the full chain length on which she can move freely in two thirds of the space. Only then do I address her.

"Hi Christine."

And she bows her head and, without looking at me, says, "My Master," as I've taught her and there's no suppressed rage in her voice, at most a touch of irony.

I introduced this form of address about four months after I'd brought her down here. I remember that when I did so I couldn't help feeling somewhat ridiculous myself. But every time she addressed me by my name, it brought up umpteen memories of other situations in which she'd called me Sebastian. "Surely you're not serious about this, Sebastian?" Or when she separated from me – she left me! – and thc matter-of-fact way she demanded the flat for herself, "Surely you're not going to take the flat away from the children, Sebastian? Do you want Binya to have to change schools? Can't you remember how long it took Racke to get used to the kindergarten? Whatever we've done to each other, the children shouldn't have to suffer for it. Can't we at least agree on that, Sebastian?"

Ultimately it was only logical that she grabbed the flat. After all, over the years she was the one who'd decided how our flat was furnished and painted – with her fussy woman's taste that couldn't bear an empty surface but had to stick some stupid wooden bowl on it, then fill that with polished semi-precious stones or the dried-up pods of some African plants. And when I consented, what did she say? Did she thank me? You must be joking. She said that on my salary I'd have had difficulty keeping up with the rent anyway. It was only with hindsight that I realised how far that woman had undermined my self-respect. Just the way she says Sebastian is enough to drive me into the depths of resignation, threatening to turn back into the man she knows from the old days when manipulating me was the easiest of exercises for her.

When I proposed she should call me 'My Master' from then on, Christine bit her lower lip and avoided looking at me.

"What's the matter?" I said. "It's no more than a formality. If someone called our son 'Master Racke' you wouldn't think they regarded him as their master, would you? And that being so it can't be that hard for you to say 'My Master' to your real master. Basically all you'll be doing is to recognise the existing power relations in this room."

"Sounds a bit like *The Arabian Nights*, don't you think?" Christine said.

Oh, that's why I love her, when she can say things like that even though she has a chain round her neck. She's a brave little terrier. There's nothing I can do about the chain but otherwise I do try to make her stay here as pleasant as possible.

Christine takes off her apron and we sit down next to each other on the yellow sofa; I stretch my arm out on the back of the sofa behind her. On the little table in front of us is the bowl with the warm Afghan biscuits, the walnuts on top looking like mouse brains. Beside them is a yellow-striped jug with lemonade, Cathedral Ceramics from Limburg. My mother had the same jug except with pink stripes, but I could only find a yellow one. I used to have it up in my kitchen but at some point I was so put off by the wrong colour that I transferred it to Christine's quarters. And it goes very well with the set of chairs.

We chat, and I tell Christine what the weather's like outside – the way it's been for weeks, she should be glad she's down here underground in the cool – and that Racke got a 'sun with cloud' in *Dancing* and *Gymnastics* and Binya a 'notable' in *Chinese*, and I tell her about the glacier that slid down into the reservoir. We both wonder why no one foresaw it and instigated the necessary evacuation measures in the two villages, and that takes us onto the latest developments in politics, geology and climate change and it's really nice, nicer than it's been for ages.

It's almost like when we came across each other on the Democracy Committee and began to fall in love while we spent whole nights with the others making plans to restructure the state without abandoning the basic principles of democracy. I take a biscuit from the bowl, nibble off the walnut and put the biscuit back. And while Christine gets worked up about the fact that the possible technique of cooling the world down by creating artificial clouds is only being pursued half-heartedly – "it ought to be a top priority, have they *still* not grasped that?" – I let my arm slip down onto her shoulder, take a strand of her hair and twiddle it in my fingers.

"I still think you're beautiful," I say and it's the absolute truth. I give her a third of my daily dose of Ephebo. After all, I can't just let her rot away down here. She's forty-eight but with the Ephs she looks as if she's in her mid-thirties whilst I, with double the dose, can pass for a man in his late thirties. No one would suspect that I'm twenty years older.

It's odd to think that without the drugs Christine would now look as old as her mother. She gives me a smile and we get up together and go over to the bed. Because of the chain all her clothes have to be done up with buttons at the front, like the dress she's wearing. I unbutton it down to her hips and run my hands over her warm skin and the fancy red-and-black panties I got for her by mail order. It feels good, and I try to imagine what it would feel like if I were to give Christine the full Ephebo dose for a couple of months. I pull the dress down over her hips and take my own clothes off.

"Why don't you let the hair on you chest grow again," Christine says. "No one has it shaved today."

"Well, you should know," I say.

We get into bed and I draw her body close to me. She kisses my neck and strokes my chest.

"Nobody's been going round with their chest shaved for the last ten years. I'd like to see what it looks like on you."

"Stupid," I say, "it would look absolutely stupid. An island here and there and a wreath of bristles round each nipple. You wouldn't want to see that."

We make love, the smooth, tender sex of an old couple with young bodies. Afterwards Christine lies in my arm and fondles and plucks at the non-existent hair on my chest. It makes me feel quite sentimental.

"Just like the old days," I say.

But Christine can't let it be, she has to spoil the mood again. With a jerk she sits up and pushes my hand off her thigh, as if I were an importunate pet.

"Just look at me," she says. "It's not like the old days. Nothing is like the old days. I'm tied up with a chain. That's not normal. You must see that what you're doing here is sick."

So off we go again. Christine never manages to pull herself together for more than a few days. We've had this discussion a hundred times already and we're getting better at it all the time. That is, I'm getting better, my arguments more polished every time. Christine basically keeps on saying the same thing, that it's sick, that *I'm* sick.

"In a lot of countries the men lock their women up," I reply patiently, "and it's a hundred per cent socially acceptable. Indeed, it's actually expected. Why should I deny my innate male needs, simply because I'm unlucky enough to live in this tiny window of time in which the government here has been handed over to the women. Just a few years sooner and things would have looked quite different. In most countries things still look different even today. Or again today. Men have been ruling over women for thousands of years. And they would continue to do so for the next thousand years if humanity was going to last that long. What's happening at the moment in Europe and North America, this feminisation of culture and that you can have your say in everything, is a short-term historical abnormality. A slip-up in the history of humanity. Islam will sweep away these pathetic, tolerant, limp-wristed democracies that haven't got the balls to make decisions. And if the Muslims don't do it, then the Chinese will. At least they would, if they had the time and the whole planet weren't going down the drain. Societies that are ruled by women are condemned to collapse."

She lets me finish, as I've taught her, something that would have been unthinkable earlier on. She would constantly be butting in, couldn't let anything go without contradicting it. But now I can enlarge on the subject as much as I like, she lets me have all the time in the world, waiting for minutes, if necessary, for me to finish before she replies.

"There's no country in the world where women are put in chains," Christine says. "Even in Saudi Arabia they're free to go out in the streets."

"Yes, but only because there's nowhere they could run to.

They have no option but to go back home. If I could rely on you coming back to me, I'd let you go shopping as well. But as long as that's not possible, you should just be glad that I'm doing that work for you."

To which she says, "No one can keep their wife on a chain, that doesn't exist in any culture, that's a crime everywhere. That is sick!"

"I doubt that," I say calmly, "but even if it is regarded as a crime in a few cultures – it's still far from being sick."

"Oh yes it is! Sick, sick, sick!"

She squeezes two importunate tears out of her eyes.

"Nonsense," I say, and despite the act she's putting on, I keep my calm and reply politely and dispassionately. "Just remember the white-slave ring that was busted after you thought you'd finally got rid of the nasty, nasty business of prostitution. They kept their girls in chains all day, but as far as I can remember none of the guys was seen as psychologically disturbed and committed to a lunatic asylum. They all received prison sentences. And don't try to tell me the men kept the girls in chains just because of the money – they got all sorts of fun out of it. Why did it never occur to the judges to classify them as mentally ill? Given that in your opinion the idea of putting a woman in chains can only come from a sick mind. I'll tell you: because every one of the judges could comprehend the fun it gave them. Because they also secretly dream of having that kind of power. You see, for a man it's something wonderful to utterly dominate a woman. And, above all, it's something completely normal, a healthy male need."

"It is not, as you well know, Sebastian. And, anyway, it was a female judge who pronounced sentence. And you're not seriously going to maintain…"

"Shut your gob," I say. "You should get out of the habit

of always wanting to have the last word. And don't call me Sebastian!"

I'm not demanding blind obedience. As you can see, I let her get away with quite a lot of bits of impertinence – but my name is absolutely taboo.

"Oh, forgive me, Master," she replies, holding up her hands, waggling her fingers in a stupid way and giving 'Master' an affected pronunciation. "I quite forgot – if I use the forbidden name you might turn back into the poor soul you are in reality and won't be able to put on the act of the great guy who's a woman-tamer."

I keep my cool and survey her. There she is sitting next to me, locked up, chained, utterly at my mercy. She's in deep shit, right up to her neck, but she still thinks she can stir things up. I could get really furious now. I could do anything I liked to her. But I'm quite calm. Without a word I get out of bed and grab her. She shrinks back, automatically putting her hands over her face, but I have no intention of hitting her. I simply take hold of the chain right by her neck and drag her over to the wall, to the snap links. She tries to resist, to kick me, to hit me with her fists. I'm just as naked as she is and so more vulnerable than usual, but her attempts are pathetically weak. I just have to give a vigorous tug on the chain and she immediately loses her balance and stumbles along beside me like a good girl. I pull the chain through the middle link until there's just a metre of free play left so that Christine can't sit down or go anywhere but just has to stay standing by the wall. It does me good to see her like that, her overbearing I'm-going-to-tell-you-what's-wrong-with-you arrogance has taken a bad knock. She sobs, sobs the whole time as I go back to the bed, put my clothes back on, tie my shoes, go over to the kitchen island, pull out the drawer and rummage round for a cable tie.

"Don't do that," she sobs as I tie her hands behind her back. With no shoes on there's just a miserable five foot six hanging from the chain. How small she is! She stands there, slumped, shoulders drooping and lips trembling. But she should have thought of that beforehand. I turn down the heating and leave without a word.

4

When I wake up, I'm lying on the corduroy sofa in the living room, fully dressed and with the TV on. A black cartoon creature is being thrown straight up in the air off a seesaw. A high child's voice – perhaps there are several voices or just the one, it's hard to tell – is singing a song, something about a sombrero.

"...in his sombrero... in his sombrero," the voice sings and now I recognise the cartoon figure. It's Calimero, the TV chicken. Can anyone remember it? A cartoon series from the 1970s with a black chicken called Calimero who, as a symbol of its incomplete development and excessive need of protection, still goes round with a stupid bit of eggshell on its head. Just the way our caring government would like to see its poor subjects: all cyclists with a Calimero shell on their fragile skulls, then no one can get hurt any more. Only... now Calimero looks somehow different – his eyes! The designers have given him those awful manga eyes so that he goes round gawping as if he's on drugs. The red digital display on the bottom of the screen shows 7:12. I look at my wristwatch – yes, I still have one – and indeed, it's already gone seven. I must have fallen asleep while watching television last night. Seven in the morning, that's still too early to get ready for the office. Most of the others don't arrive until after ten. Then a hot flush comes over me as I remember: seven in the morning, that means that Christine has been standing in the cellar for seven hours, waiting for me, with her hands tied behind her back. I didn't mean that to happen. I intended to go back two hours later to lengthen the chain, perhaps not let it out to its full length, but at least enough so she could sit down. I don't want to torture her. I just want to show her what I could do. Bring her defiance down a peg or two. Respect – that's what it's all about. But to be honest, I simply forgot about her. Every time I close the cellar door behind me, replace the rack and put the tins back on the shelves, the room down there – and Christine's existence as well – immediately becomes unreal, as if it was all just a fantasy I had. It was even somehow unreal at the very beginning, in the first two weeks after I'd locked her up. And that despite the fact that I was thinking about Christine all the time, euphoric at the thought of her stuck down there, in an environment where I made the rules. Yet even back then this second, secret world was so unreal for me that I had to go down several times a day, clear out the shelves, unscrew the plywood panel and open the soundproof door, in order to convince myself that the place really existed. Every time I went in and saw Christine on the chain I felt a rush of joy. It was real! It was *really* real!

Unfortunately you get used to everything. There are studies that have shown that even the joy at winning the lottery only lasts for three months. Afterwards people are just as depressed as they were before.

Last night I watched a Formula 1 race on television. Pullman was leading Lambert, who was sticking to his non-existent bumper all the time but just couldn't overtake. First he tried on the right, then the left, then the right again, on a bend, on the straight, with the centrifugal forces tugging at his helmet – and then I must have fallen asleep.

And now it's seven. I have a horribly guilty conscience.

To tell the truth, I'm afraid to go down and face her. Almost as afraid as the first time I had to go down to her. In theory it sounds very easy – to abandon your former role and invert a power relationship simply by behaving as a completely different and very dominant person. But in practice it meant facing my wife who, after twenty years of practice, was highly trained in nagging away at me and manipulating me emotionally in the most perfidious manner. Who above all was particularly good at making me feel guilty. And since I had just drugged and abducted her, locked her in and chained her up, the odd reproach naturally made itself felt. It took two whole days before I had picked up enough courage, and my hands were so sweaty the screwdriver kept slipping while I was removing the plywood panel. No explanations, no arguments, no excuses was my plan. It had to be made clear to her right from the start that from now on I was to be her lord and master. When I opened the door and saw her sitting there on the side of the bed with the chain round her neck, so small and slight, I immediately regretted what I'd done. She was wearing the short shirt I'd put on her for tactical reasons. To make her aware of her own vulnerability. Christine was staring at me, eyes wide, the white bedcover over her knees. To be honest, at that moment I wished I could undo everything. Go back to the point where we were having a meal together in the restaurant, just before I tipped the stuff into her glass.

Fortunately she made it easy for me. "Listen," she said in a poorly put on pretence of composure, "you can still get out of this. Whatever you had in mind to do, no one can prove anything. You just wanted to give me a bit of a fright, or something like that. German courts are completely impotent, they never convict anyone. As long as you haven't killed me they can't prove anything against you. At most it'd be a one year suspended sentence… but the case would probably be dismissed anyway. Yes, definitely. If you release me now, we can go out into the street together, we'll be free. We'll have a good laugh about it. We can carry on living the way we used to. But if you do something now…" here her voice broke and her face crumpled against her will, like a child about to whimper, but she didn't cry, she still didn't cry but went on, her voice becoming gradually steadier, "…if you do something to me now, you won't be able to get out of it any more. Your whole life will change. You'll have to go through with it and if you're caught, you'll be locked up for years, your whole life will be ruined, it's not worth it…"

If there's one thing she can do, then it's talking, arguing, offering solutions. You have to give her that. She wasn't so stupid as to promise not to go to the police. We both knew that the first thing she would do would be to go straight to the nearest police station and report me. So she tried to persuade me that there was still a way out, used the poor children as emotional blackmail: "Whatever it is that makes you imagine you need to take revenge on me… just think what you'll be doing to the children."

As she went on and on, I gradually recovered my self-assurance. I grabbed a chair, sat down by the bed facing her and watched her as she reeled off the arguments she'd worked out during the last two days, her fingers tugging at the bedclothes. No reproaches crossed her lips. Not a single 'How could you, Sebastian?' She'd already realised that the rules of the game were quite different down there. I didn't need to tell her. I just had to sit there.

"But Chrissi," I eventually said with a smile, "Chrissi, dear, what is it you're afraid of? Surely you don't think I'm going to do anything to you?"

My friendly tone of voice gave her hope. Her fingers let go of the bedcover. She took hold of the iron chain, lifted it up and tried to smile as well.

“Well what’s all this…?” She was trying to adopt the same chatty tone as I’d used but her voice failed her. All that came was a gurgling sound. Then she sobbed, completely lost her composure, the snot was running down from her nose. She was twitching and shivering. I waited until she’d calmed down. “Feel better now?” I asked.

“Why?” she snapped.

I had to smile again. Of course I didn’t give her the real answer. If you want to control a person completely it’s important initially to leave them in the dark as to why what is happening is happening. Instead I replied, “I’ve been wondering myself whether it wasn’t a mistake. I could have picked a prettier woman or a true-young one. But you made it so easy for me. That secret meeting so that your new guy didn’t know. Somehow I must still be crazy about you.”

I leant forward and stretched out my hand. I was just going to touch her – a tender, propitiatory gesture. It couldn’t be misunderstood. But Christine screamed and shrank back as if I’d burnt her. Totally over the top. The old ploy of making me feel guilty. In fact it made me furious.

“Oh my God!” I said in exactly the same theatrical way, “I’m a man and I’m oppressing women with my desires.”

After that I was away. I stood up and grasped her head, pressing the balls of my thumbs behind her ears. Then I pulled Christine’s face so close to mine that our noses were almost touching.

“To deny your manliness is to castrate it,” I said very calmly and masterfully. I could see her fear, all the white in her eyes. She didn’t even try to resist and I could feel – perhaps for the first time – how strong I was. I don't have a particularly powerful physique, six foot tall and rather lanky, but in comparison to her – and practically all other women – I'm strong, immensely strong. Physical superiority just happens to be a fact. I realised how easy it was to control Christine and before things could get difficult again, I quickly let go of her, turned on my heel and left. By the door I took the fuse out of the fuse box and left her in the dark. I did that for the next two weeks.

In order to avoid getting involved in any argument, I decide to behave as if I'd deliberately left Christine waiting for seven hours. I fling the door open, as far as that's possible with a security door that weighs a ton, and go in with a cheerful expression on my face and whistling softly to myself. Christine's in a pitiful state. She's kneeling on the floor – the chain just about allows her to kneel – in a puddle of urine. Naked and pathetic like a bird that's just hatched. I feel really sorry for her but I mustn't show any weakness now, so I draw myself up to my full height before her and ask whether she thinks she deserves a longer chain again.

"Please," Christine whispers, "please release me. I'll do anything you want."

Her whispering's almost inaudible. She runs her dry tongue over her dry, chapped lips and you imagine you can almost hear them rustling. She looks as if she's been hanging there for a week already and was about to die of thirst. She's still got the knack of making others feel guilty. I have to remind myself that she's been chained like this for just seven hours. That's certainly unpleasant and I am sorry that she's kneeling in her own piss, but it's all the tea she keeps guzzling that's to blame for that. Any normal person can surely go for a few hours without peeing. And the chain was long enough to allow her to stand up and kneel down alternately, so that will have kept the muscle pain within bounds.

Since she's more or less made the offer, I say, okay, I'll give her six foot more if she'll give me a blow job. I'd have let her have the full chain length right away if she hadn't put on such a show, but she insists on playing the poor victim. Well, that's her affair. I lengthen the chain by not quite two metres, just enough to allow her to kneel down comfortably in front of me and do the job. Her hands are still tied behind her back. Then I go back to the security door, that I left open after I'd made my entrance, place my left hand so that it hides the key pad and demonstratively enter the code with my right.

"I would like to remind you that you can never get out of here without me," I say and turn round to face her, "so just think well about what you do."

Christine simply nods without raising her head. Squatting down on her heels, she has difficulty keeping her balance.

By now I can understand what was going on inside the bosses of agribusiness and the oil industry back then, why they so adamantly insisted on pursuing a catastrophic course that has sent us all heading for disaster. It wasn't about squeezing a dollar or two more out of us, and it wasn't stupidity or ignorance either – it was about the pleasure that goes with exploiting weakness. They knew very well what they were setting off with their CO_2 emissions, their effluents and clearing the rainforests. It must have felt intoxicating to be doing something so absolutely evil, something of such horrendous magnitude that had never before existed. And no one stops you because no one realises what's happening, or they don't believe those who do. The guys will have been slapping their thighs with pleasure as they watched the demonstrations of helpless furious environmental campaigners, or when despairing scientists, on programmes that were shown just before midnight, were trying to explain to humanity and their stupid politicians just how urgent the situation was, that it wouldn't be long before the planet was uninhabitable – all interrupted by advertising slots in which the bosses' billion-dollar industry assured the viewers that meat, milk, plastic and petrol formed the essential basis of a healthy, happy life. They'd have been jerking off watching the TV – they weren't just in cahoots with the government, they were the government.

I stand in front of Christine, pull down the zip of my jeans, grab her head round the jawbone and lift it up so that I can look her in the eye once more, just to check whether there are any signs of malicious intent. I'm practically putting myself at her mercy. And that after all the times she's tried to murder me. Crazy really. But she's physically too shattered to be dangerous. She just wants to get it over with so she can lie down and stretch out on the floor. Or whatever. I pull her head back and forward rhythmically, thrusting in and out myself because she's all in, and on her knees.

"Try harder," I say, "otherwise we still won't be finished tomorrow."

You never feel your own power so much as in those moments when you're misusing it. Only when you do something really nasty, something almost everyone would condemn and you still do it and get away with it – that alone is real power. The bosses of the industrial corporations, for example, were respected, even admired members of the society whose destruction they were bringing about. Still doing so even today in some cases. They're still sitting in their air-conditioned offices, rubbing their hands as they watch the children getting fatter and fatter and the environment ever more polluted, the weather going crazy, the glaciers melting and the life-support systems of the planet collapsing one after the other.

Now I don't want to exaggerate. Of course my behaviour towards Christine can't really be compared to the viciousness of the bosses of the big corporations. After all, I'm not destroying the basis of life for the whole of humanity, nor am I doing anything really bad to Christine. I'm not demanding anything of her that she didn't often do willingly for me in the past, nothing by which I'll destroy her. Moreover, she herself offered to do it. However, emphasising the involuntary aspect, making Christine feel her helplessness, does increase the enjoyment. It's very powerful and, yes, a bit nasty, perhaps I'll try something of that kind a bit more often in future.

I've just finished and I'm wiping my prick dry on her hair, when my egosmart suddenly rings. Christine freezes, we both freeze. But I recover more quickly, jump away from her and stagger back until I'm out of her reach, the reach of the chain that is. Again it rings. I take the egosmart out of my trousers pocket and switch it off with trembling fingers. I forgot to take it out before I came down to Christine. A stupid bit of carelessness like that could be fatal for me. If the ego had rung just one minute earlier… Oh my God! She could have bitten my prick right off. She wouldn't give a damn about that! And while I was writhing on the floor, bleeding, she'd have torn open the pocket of my jeans with her teeth, taken out my egosmart and keyed in the emergency number with her nose. And that would have been that.

A cool puff of air from the air conditioning wafts over my penis that's still hanging out. I stow it away and pull up the zip. I look at Christine. She's kneeling, hands behind her back, head bowed so that her hair is falling down over her face. She looks helpless and submissive, and pretty sexy, but she can't fool me like that. I know what's going on inside that little head of hers; she's regretting having missed an opportunity. How incredibly careless of me! I hate to think what… And it puts us back several months as well. Once again Christine will be nourishing hopes of escaping at some point or other. Dealing with her will be more difficult again.

"My hands." The whisper comes from behind the curtain of her hair. "My hands are really hurting, and my shoulders…"

Here we go again. But I'm not stupid. First of all I go straight out of the room with my egosmart, close the security door and replace the plywood panel. I even refill the shelf, checking my every movement three or four times. Just to make sure I don't make some stupid mistake again. Unfortunately Christine will have to wait a little longer until she's released. Her chain's long enough now for her to lie down on the floor, if she keeps close to the wall. In an hour I'll take her some water and a blanket, and then I'll cut her hands free – perhaps I'll even allow her the full length of the chain. But first of all I have to calm down and think everything through in detail. I don't trust her! I simply don't trust her. When I imagine what might have happened just now – Oh my God!

The call is from Lanschick. Biafra Lanschick of all people was the one who almost caused the disaster. I call back from the living room.

"Did I tell you that you have to bring a clean bill of health?" Lanschick says, "because of the araucana flu."

"Man," I say, "did you have to ring me at eight in the morning to tell me that? The reunion's two months away. By then we might have been given the all-clear."

"Niebel's insisting on it. If you haven't got your bill of health, you won't get into the pub. And it has to be at most five days old."

"Who knows what the new health scare will be by then."

Lanschick thinks for a moment. "The best thing would be to have yourself checked for all the current epidemics, definitely for ebola and araucana. Or I'll ask Niebel a fortnight beforehand and then email everyone to tell them what has to be on the certificate. By the way, I still haven't got your email address. Can't you just give it me, then I won't have to ring you up."

I tell him again that I've cancelled my email address – he obviously didn't take it seriously last time. His response is the same again: a silly smile and a suggestion that I need my head examined.

"And I need some CO_2 points from you as well. You have to transfer them to my account beforehand. There's going to be a meat buffet. A huge amount of meat, just like it used to be. Niebel has his own butcher's. A whole pig, what d'you think of that? At least four points then, but of course you can give more voluntarily, no limits there."

"Four points? Is that for the women too?"

I imagine the whole pig, with its curly tail, heart and liver, laid out on a table and the women's reaction to that. They're almost all vegetarian.

"I'm only asking for three from the girls. Niebel's going to make salads and that kind of stuff as well. The girls can have the salads."

"Don't call me on my mobile again," I say. "Use my landline number, I'm going to cancel my mobile as well shortly."

"Oh boy, I'm really looking forward to seeing what the girls look like this time," Lanschick says. "Will they look like they used to back then or somehow different, know what I mean?"

"Yes," I say, "I feel the same way too. Who're the ones who've accepted already?"

"More or less all of them. Actually there's only Maybrit Möller and Kerstin Ahlrichs I'm still waiting to get replies from."

"And Kathrin Kessler and Elisabeth Westphal?" I ask in as neutral a voice as possible, "will they be there too?"

"She's dead," Lanschick says. "Cancer."

I feel sick. The floor sways under my feet. For a moment I feel like one of those polar bear animations on the Outer Alster. Perhaps I should explain that for anyone who's never been to Hamburg and hasn't seen the Outer-Alster hologram: every hour on the hour the hologram of a polar bear on an ice floe is projected onto the surface of the water from the Harvestehuder Bank. The bear and its floe then spend the rest of the hour drifting right across the Outer Alster; the bear fools around, does a few step-dance moves, handstands, that kind of thing, while all the time the ice is melting under its paws. Just before the next full hour, when the bear is opposite the Atlantic Hotel, it pulls an enormous alarm clock out of an imaginary trouser pocket and holds it up, howling and stamping its feet – the clock is always at five to twelve. Then the crummy bit of ice breaks under its feet, the bear falls into the Alster and lots of water splashes up. No hologram that but – the highlight of the show – real water squirted up into the air by an underwater pump that's been anchored below, so that when there's a strong wind – and that's quite often nowadays – the people walking and cycling along the bank are on the receiving end. Once that's finished the polar bear hologram appears by the Harvestehuder Bank again, with a large, complete ice floe, and the whole thing starts all over again.

That's the way I feel, as if I were jumping about on an ice floe that's melting all the time. I'm losing everything that's important to me, everything's slipping away from me, nothing's left for me, nothing.

"Elli?" I just manage to squeeze the question out. "What did Elli die of?"

"Not Elli – Kathrin Kessler."

I try not to let my relief be audible. "And Elisabeth Westphal? Is she coming to the reunion?"

"Well, you don't seem particularly affected by Kathrin's death. It really hit me when her brother emailed me about it."

"I hardly knew her."

"She was the one with the fantastic boobs."

"But Elisabeth Westphal's coming – or isn't she?"

"I can't say for sure, but probably yes. You seem to be very interested in her?"

"So-so," I say. "I'd just be interested to see what she looks like now."

"Yes," Lanschick says, "it's going to be really fascinating this time."

5

It was obvious that Wellingstedt was going to get hit as well at some time or other. Though we haven't had any superstorms so far, that was just a matter of luck, unfair favouritism on the part of Fate, but ultimately it was merely a postponement of course. Until now, in June. Now, two days before the class reunion of all days, a purple alert has been announced for the whole of Hamburg. There's no school, offices, shops, factories and businesses have closed and sent their employees home, the airport and railway stations aren't operating and anyone who hasn't got home yet has to find their way to the nearest public storm shelter on their egosmart. Officially at least. No one does, of course.

I ought to have secured the house hours ago, but I wasted too much time messing about with an Internet auction. What was on offer was a 1965 white Opel Rekord Coupé in perfect condition – the car my father drove. My father loved sporty-looking cars and regularly forgot when he bought a new one that he had a family of five and their luggage to get into it. Which was why my little brother and, later on, my little sister always had to lie on the rear shelf when we were going away on holiday. I bid up to 7888.89 north euros and then the Opel went for 8065.70. For a short while I was annoyed with myself, on the other hand an old Opel like that is such a gas-guzzler that I'd have had to go vegetarian to manage with my CO_2 points. Then I wouldn't be able to give Gerda any points at all and there'd be no end to her nagging. I could of course have parked the old Opel in the garage and only used it for Sunday outings and kept my little hydrogen runabout for everyday driving. But then that would have had to stay outside and, with the kind of weather we're getting nowadays, that's just not possible.

At that point in my reflections I remember the imminent hurricane. I shuggle the weather site: the hurricane is to arrive in one hour and twenty-three minutes. The Hamburg alert has been upgraded to blue, blue means wind speeds of over one hudred and fifty kilometres per hour. Lanschick calls to confirm that the reunion the day after tomorrow is definitely still on. A whole pig that's already been slaughtered, he says, you can't cancel that. And he's already checked in at the hotel. While we're talking, the northern districts of Hamburg are upgraded to black. I've no idea what a black alert means but it's certainly time I went up to the loft and from there out onto the roof.

When I push up the skylight the warm wind immediately tears it out of my hand. With a crash it hits the tiles above me. The glass has cracked, but at least it's still all in the frame. Like an evil spirit the heated air whooshes past me, howling, whips round – if not through – me, goes wailing across the loft, tearing up the lids of the cardboard boxes with my old toys, books and school exercise books and making them beat a tattoo. Then it's suddenly calm again and I cautiously put my head out and feel my way up onto the tiles. It's as hot as hell. And sultry. It's still calm out on the roof, but higher up tattered banks of cloud in all shades of grey are scurrying across the sky, briefly tearing apart to let a beam of sunlight through, then immediately closing up again and making everything dark. On my hands and feet I crawl the three metres to the ridge. The warm wind is whipping over me in waves, tearing at my feet and at the same time pressing my shoulders down onto the roof, then letting my feet go and tugging at my arms. A batch of dry leaves flutters over my face. I really ought to have got up here sooner. It's not exactly safe now. When I've got to the top I don't try to stand up but drag myself along towards the chimney on the seat of my pants. There's a rumbling from the darkening clouds behind me. The huge conifers are twisting and shaking in my neighbours' gardens. In the street down below leaves, bits of plastic and yellow, genetically improved pollen are swirling round in circles. A round, dried-up bush rolls out of the drive opposite, hops across the roadway, jumps over a low stone wall and spins round irresolutely in the Pickards' garden. Not a soul out in the street, not a child in the gardens, not even a dog. It's the end of the world.

I finally reach the chimney and after I've spent a minute clutching on to it and got my courage back, I slowly and carefully go down the rear side of the roof on the metal steps of the chimney sweep's ladder and give a tug on the wire ropes that are lashed down over every fourth row of tiles and the solar panels. Unfortunately I couldn't stop them installing the solar panels but I've just managed to put off the compulsory heat insulation for two more years simply by claiming I was about to pull the whole house down and replace it with a soulless, low-energy Swedish-designed house. The wire ropes are sitting tight, as tight as could be. Despite that I give each of the turnbuckles another turn with the heavy Allen key the roof-security firm left me. And all the while the wind's tugging at me, tugging from the right and from below, then suddenly stopping, only to start tugging from the left straightaway. The rumbling behind the black clouds is coming at shorter and shorter intervals, and there's another noise coming from the other side of the roof, where the road is, a disturbing drone.

When I climb back up to the chimney there's a tousled budgerigar there, a blue one with its feathers all stuck together. It's cowering against the masonry and watching me with increasing concern. Unfortunately there's nothing I can do, I have to go past just where it's sitting. It hops a bit to one side and no sooner has it done that than it's blown off the roof like a crumb off a plate. It hurtles through the air horizontally for a bit, then it's plunging down, goes into a spin, pulls out of it and tries a few wing-beats before it's caught in the next gust and forced into some shrubs. The swirl of yellow dust in the street is twice the size by now. It's spinning round and round at incredible speed and as well as gravel, scraps of paper and rubbish, it's sucked up the rolling bush. Right through the middle of all that the old hybrid four-by-four of Herr Priesack, the chewing-gum manufacturer, comes gliding past like a white barque. He's the only man in Wellingstedt who's still out in the streets. Ah, our entrepreneurs, always highly motivated – the world may be coming to an end all around but you can forget all that while there's still another little deal to be finalised, another little profit to be made. The rolling bush gets stuck under the spoiler of his car and is dragged along into his drive that's three houses farther on and flanked by two enormous cypresses. The cypresses are being battered by winds from opposite directions and look as if they're tussling with each other. There's a flash of lightning, disturbingly close, two seconds later a crash of thunder. It seems that it's still far enough away then. The chewing-gum manufacturer's having difficulty getting out of his four-by-four. The door swings back, jamming his leg. With his jacket flapping out behind him, he limps towards his white marble monstrosity of a Tuscan villa. Then he suddenly lowers his head and starts to run. I have a closer look: indeed, it's pouring down over the Tuscan villa while I'm sitting by the chimney not fifty yards away and completely dry. Then all at once the temperature around me drops by several degrees, the hair on the back of my head stands on end and then the rain's there. Drops the size of tadpoles patter down unrelentingly on my head, plastering my hair to my temples and running down inside my collar. In less than a minute my shirt is sticking tight to my body. I crawl on my hands and knees back along the ridge. Water's running down my forehead, trickling off my eyebrows and dripping off my nose. The gale-force wind blows a wet strand of hair up my nose just as I'm breathing in, sending the hair up into my brain; at least that's what it feels like and there's an awful itch in my sinuses. But I can't do anything about it, I need both hands to cling onto the slimy ridge. How long would Christine last if something were to happen to me? She's got running water in the cellar and provisions for just two weeks – if she rations herself strictly. A brown plastic lounger goes sailing down the street.

Having put on some dry things – my old, faded Superman T-shirt and some tracksuit trousers – I'm rubbing my hair dry with a towel and looking forward to going down to see Christine for a chat and some mutually desired and enjoyable sex with her, when the doorbell rings. Oh no! Please, not now! But the rain's splattering on the window like gravel, assuming it's not gravel that's flying through the air out there, and the thunderstorm is getting louder by the minute, the whole house is booming, rumbling and rattling. Not to ask someone in during weather like this would be a failure to render assistance in an emergency. So I open the door and, together with a torrent of water, a little branch, a quarter pound of wet sand

and a yellow budgerigar, the gale spits a fat, bearded man in a black, ankle-length, latex raincoat into the hall.

"Woe unto thee, thou great city of Babylon, in this hour shalt thou be judged," he bellows, wringing out his revolting tangle of a beard. Then he notices the dead budgie on the black linoleum tiles and prods it with the toe of one of his biker boots.

"Don't squash it," I say, picking the bird up, "I'll freeze it and send it on to the Conservation Association."

"Still the old Greenie," my brother says.

The fat man is my crackpot, religious brother Uwe. Crackpot he always was, religious he's been for the last eight years or so. Uwe belongs to the 'Disciples of St. John of the Trumpets of the Seven Last Plagues', one of those splinter religions that have sprung up like mushrooms over the last few years. They're hardly distinguishable from each other, all equally lacking in a sense of humour and all potentially violent. However, the Disciples of St. John have significantly greater financial resources than most sects, they have their own TV channel with a 24/7 stream of uplifting programmes, and support various hospices where anyone can enjoy free end-of-life care if they're prepared to listen to their drivel all day and be baptised.

Their hospices are all full to overflowing – even though everyone I know, man or woman, claims not to exceed the recommended maximum daily amount of a one-third dose of Ephebo, most of them are clearly taking a half or even a full dose, which means that there is at least a twenty-five per cent probability they'll get cancer in the next five years. The probability of getting it during the next ten years is sixty per cent. Prognoses beyond that have not been published. That's the reason why, every time we receive the nice green pills, we have to sign a declaration that if we should develop cancer we will make no claims for treatment on the state health service and content ourselves with minimal care in a twelve-bed hospice ward. The Disciples of St. John of the Trumpets of the Seven Last Plagues have quickly moved in to fill this gap in provision. There are communal dormitories in their hospices, as in the nineteenth century, but at least you can expect a decent supply of painkillers and the nurses sit with the patients and dispense a certain amount of sympathy. They also distribute a brightly coloured pamphlet, *The Book of Irrefutable Knowledge* containing the aims of the Disciples, namely the complete remodelling of society according to the bizarre ideas of their leader, Sir Randolph. You only have to hear Sir Randolph speak a few words to realise that he comes from Bavaria and our future laws were dictated to him personally from Heaven, which is why my brother rolls his eyes ecstatically whenever he quotes from *The Book of Irrefutable Knowledge*. Which he does frequently and at great length. I'm not particularly looking forward to this visit.

"What are you doing here?" I ask in as friendly a tone as I can manage while putting the budgie down on the shoe-cupboard. "I thought you didn't want to be tainted by my unbelief any more."

In the good old tradition of sects, Sir Randolph forbids his followers to have contact with the unconverted members of their family so that they won't catch the bug of reason off them. However, Uwe has risen to the fourth highest rank, therefore belongs to the elect circle of Randolphians and can now do as he likes. But of course they're still not happy when he visits me.

Undeterred, my brother takes off his latex coat and hangs the dripping monstrosity over the filigree metal banisters separating the hall from the gorge of the cellar stairs. Underneath it he's wearing a black shirt and black jeans and a black leather belt with a massive buckle in the shape of the crucified Christ with the lower end of the cross raised slightly on the bulge of his trousers.

I have my own theory as to why the followers of the New Religions often look like members of street gangs. It's the same reason as why the groups of youths are looking more and more like religious fanatics, pray before their big street battles, go round in sweatshirts with monks' hoods and think up ever more grimly ascetic rituals. (For the first four weeks anyone who wants to join the gang actually called the Monks has to wear a vest under his clothes knitted out of glass wool that rubs on his elbows until the bones are sticking out and turns his chest and back into two huge, weeping sores.) They're both aiming at the same target group: maladjusted, chrono-young male dropouts from the education system who hope to regain an importance that is withheld from them in this society where women make the decisions.

"I'm on my way home from my fellow Randolphians in Sasel," Uwe says, smugly stroking the black material of his jeans stretched over his belly. "We're going to establish a new hospice there. You were the nearest refuge for me. The storm wasn't supposed to come until tomorrow. At least that's what it said on the Internet."

"On yours, perhaps, but there it also says that the earth's a flat disc."

"If I'd known you were going to insult my religion again, I'd have taken the risk of going straight home," Uwe replies, standing on his dignity. "But unfortunately it's too late for that now. I can't expose myself to the danger any longer."

His presence could be a problem, for at some point or other

the storm might reach such proportions that we're forced to go to the cellar. I don't want Uwe down there at all. He's probably too self-centred to notice the changes, but you shouldn't tempt Fate.

"Nonsense," I say hopefully, "you can do it. If you get in your car right away, you can be back with the wife and kids before the storms really breaks."

Uwe's only had four girlfriends in his whole life, and just one of them stayed with him for more than a year. He only got married six years ago, to the daughter of one of the sect's bosses, true-young, not yet thirty. They've already managed to have four children and a fifth is on the way – the two of them think that there can't be too many of such splendid specimens as themselves in the world. All the kids – I once ran into the whole unbearable lot of them in the supermarket – are frighteningly chubby but perfectly healthy. Which surprises me, for I assume that Uwe takes Ephebos as well, even though that's frowned on by the Disciples of St. John, as it is by most of the sects. He claims he doesn't, but he's sixty-five and looks fifty at most. His beard conceals half of his face, of course, but it ought to be much greyer and his forehead is too smooth, even for such a stupid and complacent man. It's not natural. But if he does take Ephs it would be a minor miracle that none of the children have any deformities.

Uwe takes an egosmart on a watch-chain out of his waistcoat pocket and taps in a number. A border of green and purple lights keeps flashing on and off round his egosmart.

"Hi," he bellows, "that you Babro? Can you hear me? I'm at my brother's place… What? I can't understand, the sound's all broken up here. Are the children in? What? Can you still hear me? Hi, give me a wave if you can hear me… Hello? Yes, I can hear you again now… What? Are you still there?"

You wouldn't think it was possible. It's 2031, but the telephone connections are worse than in the Lassie films of the early twentieth century when Timmy's dad would keep cranking a handle and shouting, "Hello? Hello? Is anybody there?"

Uwe shuts down his egosmart and puts it back in his waistcoat pocket.

I make one last effort to get rid of him. "Where's your trust in God? Surely one of the elect of the Revelation of St John the Divine, a true Randolphian, isn't afraid of a bit of a storm?"

At that moment there's a quite furious wailing in the timbers, an ice-cold draught whistles in under the front door and an invisible gigantic hand plucks a metallic chord on the wire ropes fixed over the roof.

"And the second angel sounded his trumpet and a great mountain burning with fire was cast into the sea," Uwe cries, his eyes turned up to the ceiling in ecstasy. My brother can't wait for the world to come to an end when low-life unbelievers like me will roast in the white-hot fires of hell until their flesh liquefies and drips off their body, while great guys such as himself are allocated a seat right next to Jesus Christ's armchair and can spend the whole day licking ice cream.

"I have to use your toilet," he says, stomping off to the bathroom in his biker boots and closing the door behind him. Some time passes. I hear the lavatory flush and then the sound of the shower. My ignorant brother probably won't notice that I've restored the bathroom to what it was between 1958 and about 1975: large grey tiles, flesh-colour wash basin, flesh-colour lavatory, flesh-colour corner bath with a black-and-white striped shower curtain and a relatively neutral mirror from the sixties. I just couldn't remember the mirror – what it looked like back then. Just a mirror. How many children notice a detail like that anyway. And the icing on the cake is a banknote towel hanging over the side of the bath, an oversized fifty DM note in terry towelling – the old fifty DM note, of course, with the thin-lipped, sinister-looking guy wearing a fluffy fur collar and dark cap pulled well down over his forehead.

The bathroom door is flung open.

"Just the way it was! It looks just the way it was!" Uwe bellows. He's stark naked. I'm uncomfortable seeing him like that, even though he is my brother. He's holding the precious fifty-DM towel that I spent years searching for on ebay and is uninhibitedly drying his strikingly large testicles while he's talking to me. The way he's always been, shameless and repulsive.

"When did you do that?"

"Last year. I had the whole house made the way it was back then. The hall there too. You didn't notice that did you"

"Oh, yes, yes! Now I see it."

My brother galumphs into the hall, his big, red testicles dangling below the taut bulge of his tummy like a turkey's wattles. He puts his head back and turns round, as if he were standing in a cathedral – and the ceiling's the only part of the hall where there's nothing to see.

"Have you got those light blue face cloths with spots that we used to have?"

"The hall wallpaper was the most difficult item to procure," I say – it's red paper from the 1950s, with fine white and grey lines suggesting sailing ships – "to be precise, I didn't actually procure it. I was about to get it made from old photos when one of the tilers suggested it would be worth just having a look under the last wallpaper. And it really was there. Of course I had a hell of a job getting it off without tearing the paper underneath."

"Do you remember, when we were kids, how we had to

queue up outside the bathroom because Papa spent far too long in there?" Uwe says. Then he goes and fetches the hairdryer from the bathroom and starts to blow-dry his backside. I try to keep my eyes averted.

"Do you recognise the lino?" I ask, pointing at the tiles with streaks of black. "Did you know that in the whole of Europe there are just three factories, belonging to two different firms, that still manufacture lino."

"Five people," my brother shouts over the noise of the hairdryer, one hand ruffling the black hair on his backside, "who all wanted to use that one tiny bathroom at the same time. Actually it was totally irresponsible of our parents to have so many children – all of us in this tiny little house. Don't you agree?"

He's always going on about this, that our parents didn't have enough money or didn't give us, especially him, enough money. Uwe, the guy who always got a raw deal. Behind that was the fact that my parents clearly preferred me to him – there is, unfortunately, no other way about it. They even preferred my sister to him. They simply ignored him, as far as that was possible with such a fat child. But you have to bear in mind that Uwe was a mendacious, permanently aggrieved hypochondriac from very early on. The kind of child it would have been extremely difficult for any parents to love.

"Nonsense," I say, turning away in disgust. "Mama always woke us at ten-minute intervals. Tell me – do you have to blow-dry the hair on your arse in front of me? It's a bit much. What's the point of it anyway?"

"I have to get it completely dry," Uwe says. "I've had a fungal infection since our house was inundated. And if I'm just a tiny bit damp down there, it breaks out again. Hey, you've even installed the hip bath again. Just imagine, all three of us used to sit in it together. And Papa would use the water again afterwards."

He switches the hair-dryer off and galumphs back into the bathroom. While he's sitting on the side of the bath putting his biker boots back on, there's a loud rumbling noise on the roof; something heavy seems to have landed on it, certainly something bigger than a wheelbarrow, perhaps even one of the conifers, for it scrapes over the whole surface of the roof before it goes.

"Shouldn't we go down to the cellar?" my brother asks.

"No, what's the point? God will look after you."

"God sent the cellar for me," Uwe replies without hesitation.

"How about something to eat?" I ask in an attempt to distract him.

"To eat? What is there? Now if you've got some meat… Or are you still a vegetarian?"

I entice him into the kitchen with the prospect of a chop. It's the only room I left the way it was when I took over the house. Actually my intention was to restore every single room in the house to its state in the fifties and sixties, to find furniture and material that corresponded to the ones it had been furnished with back then and to fill every room with exactly the same kind of bowls and vases, book-club books and plastic toy figures from cornflakes packets as it had back then – right down to the tiny miniature gramophone in my sister's printing set. But then I decided to make an exception with the kitchen because it was still in its wonderful original 1976 state: blue work surface, blue-brown-and-white curtains and orange tiles, still impregnated with the presence of the fifteen-year-old boy that I once was. A version of my own self that I sorely miss but that I come to resemble more and more when I'm buttering my bread for breakfast in the kitchen. Moreover it would have been sacrilege to destroy a genuine seventies kitchen in order to replace it with a copy of a sixties kitchen, however well it was done. The only change I made was to break a hole in the wall to restore the hatch through into the living room. And I replaced the refrigerator, which wasn't a seventies model anyway but a modern, energy-efficient appliance, with an even more economical one with the door-trim of an AEG fridge from the sixties.

"I think it's good you don't take such a narrow-minded view of these things any more," my brother says with a greedy look at the greasy paper in the fridge. Of course he thinks it's good. Everyone I know who still eats meat is delighted that I'm doing so again. They feel confirmed in their base greed. I put the chop, that cost me enough points to fill my tank a quarter full, on a board and hand Uwe the little wooden hammer so that he can give it a good thumping. Meanwhile I pour the oil in the frying pan.

"Yeah, great," I say. "We wouldn't be able to enjoy the fresh breeze out there, if we hadn't always been good boys and eaten our meat and licked the plate clean…"

"Now, now…" my brother says as he gives the chop one last blow with the hammer before handing it to me. Once in the hot fat the side of the chop away from the bone immediately curls up, the pink flesh turns greyish and the fat spurts up as high as the extractor hood.

"What I don't understand," I say as I press the curled-up side of the chop back down with a wooden spoon, "is why, in all your rules and regulations, you Disciples of St John don't devote a single line to animals. I mean, you're not even allowed to shake hands with women, but killing and eating animals is completely okay. For God's sake, you've got over three hundred thousand adherents on whom you could exercise real influence, and what do you tell them? How many buttons they should have on their shirts and that they should pester the poor women who run our ministries with demands to reintroduce the law against blasphemy.

"It is perfectly acceptable to kill animals," my brother says with the expression of amused serenity he always adopts when he's left his brain in the cloakroom and just parrots his sect leader's pearls of wisdom, "Sir Randolph made that perfectly clear at the last synod. Human beings are aware of their future, animals aren't. Thus animals don't suffer a loss when you kill them. And eating them is permitted."

"That's nonsense," I say. "What if I'd found a bundle of banknotes or a cheque book somewhere here in the house? According to your philosophy I wouldn't need to hand over any of it to you or our sister. Since you don't know the cheque book exists, you can't suffer any loss and I can keep it all for myself with a clear conscience."

"You've found a cheque book?" my brother exclaims, jumping up from his chair. "Of course you have to share it with me!"

"And with Sybille," I say. "Don't forget you've got a sister in China as well."

"How much was in it?"

"Now you just calm down. I didn't find a cheque book at all. It was just an example…"

"I always thought Mama must have slipped you something before she died so that you got more than me. Otherwise you wouldn't have been able to buy the house. How much was it?"

"I didn't get anything…"

"Oh, I've known for ages. Just tell me how much, I won't lodge a complaint."

"Nothing, for God's sake! There's no cheque book and

Mama didn't slip me anything."

At last he seems to believe me. I pull out the table top from under the cutlery drawer and put a plate on it. "Do you want peas or beans with it?"

"Only if they're fresh from the market. Not if you bought them in the supermarket."

"It's just prejudice to think that fresh fruit and vegetables taste better," I say. "If you're honest, tinned peas are much better than fresh or frozen ones. When we were children we were given stuff out of tins almost exclusively and we always enjoyed it."

"That's not the point," my brother says. "The point is the barcode on them. If you have a close look at the barcodes on supermarket products you'll see that there are three extended double rows on them – the sign of the beast."

"The sign of the beast?"

"The double rows stand for the six, three times the six – the sign of the beast. And thus it has been foretold that in the last days of the apocalypse all goods will bear the number 666. So of course I don't eat that stuff."

"But then you can't buy anything any more."

"Oh yes I can. It's only with food that I check."

I bite back my response, it would only trigger off a tsunami of quotations from *The Book of Irrefutable Knowledge*. What a nightmare it will be if these lunatics should actually get some seats in parliament. Which is not *that* unlikely. There are enough eschatological nutcases who'd vote for them. Fortunately, however, Sir Randolph and five of the leading members of his sect failed miserably in the selection process (a colleague told me that – though unfortunately he wouldn't tell me on what grounds – Sir Randolph and his gang were refused the right to stand as candidates, but I can well imagine what they were: megalomania, lack of a sense of reality, avarice, perhaps even paedophilia). Naturally it's only a question of time before they find a Disciple in their lower ranks, who's not quite so far round the bend as the rest of them and if he passes the test and gets elected, then God help us! These guys will see to it that we have to go through hell down here on earth. Everyone will have to be baptised again, anyone who has the wrong number of buttons on their shirt will be given a public flogging. At least they want to reintroduce polygamy, which they claim was recommended in the Old Testament. I could acquire a taste for that.

"You're not eating anything yourself?" my brother asks, placing his arm protectively round his plate. "Won't you at least sit down with me and say grace?"

I drag over the other kitchen chair. Uwe folds his podgy fingers and closes his eyes. Even his eyelids are fleshy.

"Heavenly father," I begin the prayer, as we used to back in kindergarten, "thank you very much that my brother can guzzle a chop and see to it that in future things should be better for us than for the nations at whose expense we are living, above all better than for those who do not believe in you, for they are nothing but vermin. Amen."

"Don't imagine I can't see what you're trying to do," he says as he saws off a piece of the chop. You can't provoke me. Yes, I do believe in a Lord God who looks after our immortal souls. And I believe with such certainty and devotion as you will never be capable of."

The chop isn't quite cooked right through. Some red juice trickles onto the plate. Uwe dips his finger in it, drawing a trail to the edge of the plate. He starts rambling on about the red tides and the second angel with a trumpet who was seeing to it that the third part of the sea became blood. For all those who aren't quite in the picture about how the end of the world will come according to the Revelation of St John the Divine: seven angels will blow seven trumpets one after the other, at each of which terrible things will happen to warn the unchristian sinners that the end of the world is nigh – amongst other things a third of the water of the seas will turn to blood. According to the Disciples of St. John of the Trumpets of the Seven Last Plagues we have reached that point because a red carpet of algae has spread out along a third of the Mediterranean coast. It's poisonous and immediately kills any fish that even just come close to the dark clouds. No bathing whatsoever allowed. In the Gulf of Mexico and off Dubai as well the spread of the dead zones has reached record levels this year.

"Did you read about those tourists," I ask, "the ones that went riding on the beach and had to go into hospital because they'd ridden over algae that had been washed up on the shore?"

"That is no surprise to those of us who know our Bible," Uwe replies. "Once all seven trumpets have sounded, another seven angels will come and this time they will pour out bowls of the wrath of God and the second angel will pour out his bowl upon the sea and then not just a third but all the water will be as the blood of a dead man and every living thing in the sea will die. And then soon all men."

He hooks his left index finger over the bridge of his nose and digs his thumb meditatively first up his left then his right nostril.

My brother is not entirely wrong with his prophesies – even though the red tides are not of supernatural origin but just the result of global warming and of the phosphate and nitrogen fertilisers that have been washed down from the fields and via the rivers into the Mediterranean. But once the phytoplankton, the first link in the food chain, die, once all the microscopically small diatoms and green algae and other micro-organisms that are busy producing oxygen have suffocated under an algal bloom, then all the fish and crabs and whatever else there is scraping a living down there will die, and the algal bloom doesn't even have to be poisonous for that. Anything that doesn't starve to death will suffocate. And since phytoplankton are not only the basis of marine life but also produce most of the oxygen, then eventually all the terrestrial animals will die and with them we human beings. Thus the red tides are in fact harbingers of our end. It's a joke, really, that these nutcases, that insist on holding out their tedious pamphlets to you at Central Station and telling you the end of the world is nigh, should be right after all.

"There's not a single case in which science has proved the Scriptures wrong," my brother says.

It looks as if it's going to be a very, very long afternoon here. I imagine how nice and cosy it would be down there with Christine now. Of course she's still pissed off because I left her waiting for hours recently. But she can't afford to bear grudges for too long. After all, she has no one but me to comfort her, even if it is to comfort her for something I've done myself. Anyway, we're pretty well attuned to each other. Just another old married couple.

Again there's howling and banging in the timbers. It's doing it all the time but this time the whole house shakes, as if it were just a toy house, a doll's house with a giant baby jiggling the roof, trying to pull it off.

"God will hold his protecting hand over your home as long as I am with you," Uwe says, without even a hint of irony, "yet once again I have to suggest we go down to the cellar. God has guided my steps to a house with a cellar."

"Do you still have insurance?" my brother asks as we go down the stairs.

"Forty per cent if the roof gets blown off," I say, "but only because I had tension cables fixed; otherwise it would have been just thirty-three per cent. For damage to the foundations, or in fact any water damage at all, there's nothing."

"What? How do you get that much? We now just get twelve per cent, though for all damage, except from water, of course."

I open the cellar door. Now we'll see whether the insulation I put in round Christine's dungeon is any good.

"I only get forty per cent because I took over Papa's insurance when I inherited the house. I don't think any of the newly built houses in the street are insured any longer."

We sit on the floor. Directly opposite the rack with tinned food. I make an effort not to look at it.

"We should have included that when you paid us off," my brother says. "After all, taking over the insurance is better than cash in hand now that the insurance companies are wriggling out of their obligations everywhere."

"Oh do stop it," I say. "You're not getting one pfennig more out of me. Anyway, we've got other things to worry about. Perhaps this is the end of the world you're so much looking forward to."

"The end of the world will not come before the Holy Ghost has put His seal on the forehead of the hundred and forty-four thousand elect," my brother says. "Tell me, didn't Papa's workroom use to be over there?"

I break out in a cold sweat. I pretend I didn't hear his question.

"That's a relief," I say, with feigned irritation, "and there was me worrying that Hamburg was about to be devastated by a megastorm, as has already happened to eighty per cent of all

German towns."

"If you want, you can hold my hand and we'll pray together," my brother says. "As long as I'm here nothing can happen to you. Over there, where those shelves are, surely that was Papa's…"

"Well, if God has His hand on the control knob and I've got such a great guy as you sitting next to me – then nothing at all can happen to me," I cry with put-on fury. If I manage to start an argument, perhaps I can divert his attention from the shelves. "Those eighty dead in Essen last year, they must all have been sinners who deserved nothing better. All their own fault, eh? If they'd prayed a bit more they wouldn't have had roof tiles and trees falling on their heads. Is that what you're saying?"

Sadly my brother shakes his head. "You poor unbeliever, its your anger that's speaking. But if you don't restrain yourself and go on blaspheming, you will burn in hell for all time."

Aha! At last he's taken the bait. I really let myself go.

"And you think that's okay, do you?" I say. "For you that's a great result, eh? And I, who've spent my whole life working my balls off to preserve God's creation, who've even gone as far as the pack ice to stop the whales being slaughtered… I should burn in hell, just because I'm not one of you lot?"

"It's still not too late to accept baptism."

"And you, you miserable wretch, who even at school pinched everything that wasn't nailed down, you'll get to heaven simply because you're in the right club, eh?"

Before my brother got religion and rose to the fourth grade of his charmless sect, he spent six years studying philosophy, after which he established and subsequently gave up several firms. The last one was a company that provided toilet facilities for department stores and motorway services, which in practice meant supplying dispensers for soap and paper towels and employing toilet attendants. He paid those African and Greek women four euros an hour (old currency) and pocketed all of their tips. All those fifty cent and one euro coins that were put in their saucers. And why not? After all, his firm supplied the saucers. Even when the new women's government pushed through a legal minimum wage of fifteen euros an hour, he went on paying four euros. And he couldn't give a damn when the court forbade him to take the tips. When his flat was searched they found fourteen sacks full of coins in the kitchen. Just like Dagobert Duck. The police could hardly lift them. Since he already had a suspended sentence, he was sent to prison for a year and that was where he shared a cell with a Disciple of St. John. I gently remind him of all this.

"Our Lord is a forgiving God," Uwe says, blushing all the way round to his ears, but basically still smugly complacent.

"Yes," I bellow, "but only when you repent and change your ways. But not when you're still the same hypocritical arsehole you've always been. Someone like you can only pray that God doesn't exist! Because I hardly know anyone who deserves to go to hell more than you!"

"There's no need for you to work yourself up into a phoney rage," my brother says, pushing himself up off the floor and going over to the shelf with the tins. "I know what you're trying to divert my attention away from. It was a ploy you used to use when we were younger. Whenever you started an argument for no reason at all, it was because you wanted to stop me noticing that you'd broken another of my model cars. "Here, just here," – he pushes the tins to one side and taps the wall with his knuckles – "just here was Papa's workroom."

"So what?" I reply coolly, while I can hear the blood throbbing in my cars. "I had to fill it in to give the house better foundations, more stability. It was a requirement for the insurance."

"Don't try to put one over on me," my brother says, "it sounds hollow here, completely hollow. You really are an incredibly poor liar."

He pushes the tins farther away, leans right up over the shelf, puts his ear to the plywood panel and thumps it with his fist. It almost gives me a heart attack. Can Christine hear him? Will she try to attract attention? And will Uwe hear her? Or will the steel door and insulation be enough?

I pick up a tin of beans. Probably not heavy enough to smash my brother's skull. If the worst comes to the worst, I'll have to think up an excuse to go out to the garage and get the sledgehammer.

"Oh, I know what you've done," he gloats, "I know."

I grasp the tin tighter.

"You've set up one of these prepper rooms for yourself, like they have in the States. Come on, admit it. You think that when the end of the world comes you'll be able to crawl underground and hide from your Creator. You think God won't find you there and you can escape His judgment. Oh, how pathetic!"

I breathe a sigh of relief and put the tin of beans back on the shelf.

"Wrong," I say, "if there's anyone I want to hide from here, then it's not your Lord God, but the marauding hordes who'll smash my skull for a tin of beans."

"And you said nothing of this to me, your own brother? You're not going to offer me and my family a place in your survival room?"

"What would be the point? You told me yourself that you're one of the hundred and forty-four thousand elect. Why then would you need a storm cellar?"

"Well, perhaps I might like to appear before my Lord at the Last Judgment alive and unscathed. Is that so difficult to understand? Now let me see what it's like."

We spend the rest of the afternoon with me refusing to show my brother the supposed prepper room and him demanding to be shown it at five minute intervals. Finally I unscrew the plywood panel and at least show him the steel door and promise to take him in if there really is a crisis and if he promises in return – it's in his interest as well – not to tell anyone about it.

"Woe betide you," my brother says, "if you don't keep your promise."

"Of course I'll keep it," I say. "You're my brother. I would have told you, but only later on, for reasons of security."

With a sullen grunt Uwe sits back down on the floor. He doesn't trust me. And why should he? He knows just as well as I do that – at least in the long term – no one will have to worry about the consequences of their lies and misdeeds. Even if there is no all-forgiving God, I can say and do as I like. We can all do as we like, without having to worry about the consequences. That's the good thing about it, if there's no future.

6

I've taken a portable TV (still with an aerial!) down to Christine in the cellar so that she can see the damage in Hamburg with her own eyes. There might even be a few pictures of Wellingstedt. There was a film unit out in the street here. It's all pretty spectacular the way the massive conifers are lying all over the road with the men from Technical Emergency Services crawling over them like little rodents with little rodent chainsaws. The two pugnacious cypresses from Herr Priesack's drive are lying beside each other as if they'd continued to tussle, after they'd fallen down, until eventually they rolled apart, completely exhausted. The large birch tree in my garden got torn up as well. It's stuck in the roof across the road and the Möllers are really pissed off. Ever since I moved in they've been going on at me to have it chopped down – it's much too big, too dangerous, the next storm… Well, it's down all right now. My own house hasn't come off too badly: two solar panels ripped off, a few roof tiles dislodged and the broken glass in the skylight. It really is a pity about the birch tree, though. It was there beside the drive even before I was born. Wellingstedt's going to look terribly bare and different once all the tree trunks have been cleared away. On the other hand it'll look more like the Wellingstedt of my childhood again, when the plots had just been built on and the gardens planted. I decide to buy a birch sapling once this mess has all been cleared away. Even if I knew the world was going to end tomorrow, I'd buy a young birch tree today.

I'm channel-hopping – by hand, this wonderful television set has no remote control – but the storm over Hamburg, never mind Wellingstedt, isn't mentioned at all. Well, I assumed it wouldn't be the first news item, not even the first report on natural disasters. But not to mention it at all, that's a bit much. The hurricane did actually miss Hamburg and the wind speeds were significantly lower than expected, but there must have been people injured or killed, and material damage costing millions. Here in Wellingstedt alone I've counted eight houses whose roofs have gone. They can't just pretend it never happened. Instead they're going on about Hanover, Cologne and some burning peatland in Russia, and about the 1.2 million people fleeing the floods in Bangladesh who can only be kept under control at the Indian wall by force of arms. The people in Hanover are really in a bad way. They caught the superstorm that was predicted for Hamburg. Some streets look the way they did after the Second World War, an impression that is only emphasised by the fact that we're watching on a black-and-white TV. And Cologne is completely flooded. The damage goes into billions. The mobile flood defences round the old town were erected in time, but it's not just the Rhine pressing against them, in the last three days two hundred litres of water per square metre have fallen and you can go round the streets in an inflatable boat; in the few streets that haven't been turned into rivers yet water is spurting up out of the drains. One shot shows Bishop van Elst standing outside the cathedral, that's like an island with water washing round on all sides. Then views of the wine villages that the Rhine floods have already swept through. The locals in wellingtons, putting their ghastly three-piece suites and wall units, swollen with the damp, out by the roadside.

"It's a mystery to me," Christine says, "why people never manage to put their furniture and things up in the loft, or at least up on the first floor. The upper floors weren't affected at all and the flood was announced days in advance. That surely left them enough time."

"Excessive optimism," I say, "a genetically determined attitude that things won't be that bad after all. Was probably useful during the Stone Age – good for stomach ulcers. Catastrophic today, of course."

A member of the regional parliament appears on the TV promising swift financial help. Can he say that? Just like that? Then a close-up of a granny crying, a true-old granny in a flowered housecoat. The camera guys probably couldn't believe their luck when they came across this pitiful granny's face, furrowed all over with wrinkles, that's never had even a whiff of Ephebo. Granny live: "What's going to happen now? We'll buy new things, renovate others and in two or three years the next flood will come. If no one's going to help us, then I don't know what I'll do." There follows a close-up of a bitter, sweaty man in dungarees, standing in his wellingtons in his flooded garden holding a banknote stretched out in both hands.

"We're left completely on our own here. The hundred euros emergency aid is just about enough to refill the fridge."

"Interesting." I say to Christine, "The first thing that occurs to these guys is to fill the fridge again. That's exactly what they'll do with the hundred northern euros – buy some nice CO_2 – intensive steaks to fill their bellies so that global warming will progress that little bit quicker, making the next flood even worse. And then they'll start moaning again why they don't get more aid for even more steaks."

The number of an account for donations for the flood victims is shown. And right below it another account number for the victims of the storm damage in Hanover.

"Are there still charity gala performances?" Christine asks, "Or those calls for donations on the Internet? Do you think there are still people who donate to others?"

"What kind of idiot would do that?" I say. "It's enough that our hard-earned taxes are going to these guys. They knew the facts. They had the information. They knew exactly what damage they were causing. And now they're going on as if an unpredictable disaster had suddenly struck them – as if the floods had nothing to do with their sausage-guzzling, with all their dashing around in cars and their little weekend trip by air to Barcelona."

I talk myself into a fury and Christine listens, wide-eyed, laughing at the right moments – she's actually hanging on my lips. And that after we've been married for twelve years.

"Well then," I say, laughing myself, even though it's a bitter laugh, "should we deny ourselves those lovely plastic bags, our flashy car, meat every day, breakfast, lunch and dinner – just to save the world? They should have eaten just a third of that meat or, better still, none at all, to avoid floods like that. They haven't even got the idea of having just one meatless day a week. And listen to the way they go on, claiming that the allocation of meat and heating oil by CO_2 points is an infringement of their human rights. Like kids throwing themselves to the floor and screaming at the supermarket checkout because they can't have their light-blue Smurf lolly. And don't try to tell me they didn't know the damage they were causing. They knew very well and couldn't care less. They simply assumed the catastrophic effects of climate change would come after their death. It would only affect their great-grandchildren! They thought the floods would only hit the Indians and Pakistanis. Bugger the Indians and Pakistanis!

The only thing that wasn't clear to them was that they'd cop the lot themselves. They weren't just despicable, they were stupid as well. And now they're moaning away and feeling hard done by and want, first and foremost, to have a full fridge again. And I should make a donation towards that?"

Christine shifts uneasily forward in her chair. "Please don't take this as criticism," she says, "after all, it's entirely your own decision, but you've been eating meat again during the last two years. That's why I can't quite understand how you…"

She falls silent and stares at the floor. Recently Christine has become very cautious. Sometimes I miss her tart repartee, on the other hand it's okay for a woman to be a bit afraid of her husband.

"That's true," I say calmly, "but I only started when the point of no return had already been passed. If I have to perish along with all the idiots who got us into this mess, I might as well enjoy myself as much as them. In fact I intend to be even worse than the most inconsiderate bastards."

"Is that the reason?" Christine asks, staring into space.

"One of several," I reply.

"I'd so love to get out," she says softly, and suddenly the tears are pouring out of her eyes. And they don't stop. "I'd love to walk round Hamburg now and see what damage the storm has done."

"You know that's not possible," I say gently. "Be sensible."

She sniffs and wipes the tears off her face with the back of her hand. "If at least I could see the pictures on a smart."

"I haven't got my old laptop any more," I lie, "and even if I did have one, bringing it down here would be too dangerous – I look away for one second and you'll have sent an SOS. It's just not possible. You have to be reasonable."

She nods and stares into space again. I've noticed her

behaving like that recently. Either she's learnt something and is putting on a much more convincing act than before or she's really given up now. I just have to make sure it doesn't turn into a full-blown depression.

Once I'm back up in the house again, I sit down at the compunicator and print out a few Hamburg articles and pictures for Christine. As I trawl I come across a minor sensation. Because of the terrible devastation everywhere in the city the *Hamburger Abendblatt* has decided to publish a special edition – and that in printed form. Oh, the good old *Hamburger Abendblatt*. To read a proper newspaper again at last! That will cheer Christine up. I slip into my red-and-black lumberjack jacket, jump into the car and drive over to Poppenbüttel. I have to go round three shops in the Alsertal Shopping Centre before I finally find the printed version of the *Hamburger Abendblatt* in the supermarket in the basement. There aren't any daily papers at all in the kiosks any more, but there are at least eight magazines for meat-eaters: BEEF-EATER, MAN'S RIGHT, CARNE and so on, but also some hardcore mags like DIE-VEGAN-DIE and THE BIG BUTCHER, which are less concerned with recipes than with the act of killing and cutting up. There are pages with photo-series of cows rolling their eyes as they bleed to death and vegan girls with piercings crying buckets but at the end falling for the brawny heavy-metal guy who's chopped up the carcass with a chainsaw.

The *Hamburger Abendblatt* is hardly half as thick as it used to be, otherwise it looks just the same: a green banner headline across the top, the name in Gothic script and so on. And the editors haven't restricted themselves to the storm disaster, but revived the whole paper, with the gossip column in the middle and the poor joke on page three. And below the joke there's the photo of a dog from an animal shelter again, a melancholy chow that's looking for a home. I'm so pleased I buy five copies, one for me, one for Christine, one for Christine's mother and the other two… well, you never know. And then, as a further treat for Christine, I buy *Brigitte*, a magazine for women. So far I haven't let her have any magazines or a television, and no more than one book a month (or two very slim volumes), to stop her feeling too much longing for the world outside. After all, she can get an interpretation of current events directly from me.

With the pile of physical media under my arm, I join the queue at the checkout and, of course, as usual it takes ages for the people in front of me to put their items through the scanner. At the moment it's a guy in his late twenties, a student to go by his dress, who's struggling with it. At first sight you'd take him for a real, chrono-twenty-year-old – chequered animal-mood jacket, stylish android steel-rimmed glasses and no bulges in his neck – but the way he's fussing about at the scanner gives him away: he must be ninety at least, from the generation that used to delegate the shopping entirely to their wives. Hold it straight man, hold it straight. And don't slap the barcode down on the glass, put your sliced bread on the tray underneath. He tries to be nonchalant, but the hair on his animal-mood jacket is bristling with nervous tension. I wonder how anyone can be so stupid. No wonder the planet's beyond saving. Next is a fat guy in a denim jacket. His greasy red hair is tied in a ponytail that hangs down over the embroidery on the back of his jacket. 'Moto Racing' is embroidered on it, 'Honour' and, in large letters in the middle, 'Fat Rats'. He can't manage either, of course. At the pack of sliced salami the beeper goes off, because our motorcyclist has clearly exceeded his CO_2 allocation. But he refuses to accept that, keeps slamming the pack of sausage down on the tray, setting off the bleeper five times. I'm wondering whether to go over and explain the problem to him but at the last moment I see who it is I'd be dealing with: Ingo Dresen! I spent my whole childhood keeping out of the way of Ingo Dresen, just as my father spent his childhood trying to avoid Ingo Dresen's father. Criminals and bullies for generations. My first meeting with Ingo Dresen was on the Kaiserberg, a little hill that goes down to the Alster. In those days we used to go sledging on the Kaiserberg; the thrill was less in the not-very-steep slope than in the fact that you had to swing off to the side at the right moment if you didn't want to end up in the icy river.

I was five and was making a snowman with my friend Wilfried when Ingo turned up, rubbed snow all over our faces and knocked out one of my eyeteeth with the runner of my sledge. He was eight. When I started school the next year, the way there was always a nerve-racking affair because it went past Ingo Dresen's house and if Ingo caught you he would hang on to your satchel until you fell down on your back, then he would sit on your chest and rub his knees over your arms until you were crying and admitted you were a scaredy-cat or would drink pee or were in love with Sylvia Clubfoot (actually she was called Sylvia Klumbert) or whatever Ingo Dresen happened to want you to say. A dangerous arsehole. I went rigid with terror when he was put in my class after having had to repeat a year several times. The whole class went rigid with terror. We were already at secondary school by then, in the second year. He was chucked out the next year, thank God. He was always bunking off and when he was there he spent most of the time bringing his death list up to date. On his death list were people he was going to kill one day when he had the time. I was one of those on it. One third of all the pupils were on his death list and all the teachers, apart from our social studies teacher, Herr Ritterle. Probably because Ritterle was always saying. “There’s more in you, Ingo. You’ve a good mind. You just have to make the effort.” Then Ingo handed in an essay in which he explained why he admired Adolf Hitler. What it came down to was that Adolf Hitler was the only politician who wasn’t a sissy. Ritterle said he must have overrated Ingo, he had to take back what he’d said about intelligence. After that Ritterle was on the death list as well.

Ingo Dresen’s got pretty fat. When he was young he was a tall, lanky guy with no backside. But he’s still got the nasty, reprobate look about him, despite his double chin and jowls. Ingo’s bio-age is mid-forties. He presumably takes the mid-thirties dose but, given his lifestyle, the Ephebo just doesn’t have a chance to take full effect. Even when he was fourteen Ingo looked totally dissipated.

I slowly slip out of the checkout queue so that I can unobtrusively stroll back between the supermarket shelves. At that moment Ingo Dresen turns round and fixes his eyes on me, as if he’d known all the time that I was behind him. For the first time I regret my youthful looks. They make me that much easier to recognise.

“Basti, you old bastard,” Ingo Dresen bellows over the confectionery shelves, “come over here, you can put your stuff through here with mine.”

I make an effort to produce a delighted smile as I go forward, my back slashed by all the other customers looking daggers at me. But no one dares to start an argument with a guy like Ingo.

“Basti, you old bastard,” Ingo Dresen says again, once I’m beside him, and gives me a look of such nostalgia, you’d have thought we’d been best friends all those years ago. “What are you doing here?"

Sticking the salami with the excess CO_2 in his trouser pocket, he takes my newspapers and slams them down on the scanner. I shrug my shoulders. If you say something different from what Ingo Dresen wants to hear from you, he can quickly turn nasty. Even in reply to such harmless questions as to what you're doing in a supermarket. Better to say nothing.

"Well," he says, "well, well, well. Now there's a thing. Basti the bastard in the supermarket."

From the scanner we go to the checkout. Ingo Dresen holds out the receipt to the cashier. She knows he hasn't rung up the salami, she can't have not noticed, given the number of times he set off the bleeper. But she behaves as if this was nothing. And no private security man turns up to stop him either. They must all be terribly busy just at the moment. His bulldog head held high, he stomps out of the supermarket. I try to keep up with him.

"There you are," I say, "the money for the newspapers," and hold out an orange note to him. With an indignant growl he brushes my hand aside, together with the banknote, but doesn't give me the papers. Instead, without slowing down at all, he has a look at what I've just bought.

"*Brigitte*," he says, "are you a poof?"

I respond to his smug grin with a pained grin.

"Do you still have those eco-groupies, or have you made it with some proper bird? What kind of a tart are you shagging at the moment?"

I shrug my shoulders again. I realise now how careless it was for me, as a single male, to buy a women's magazine. It was bound to lead to questions.

"No offence meant," Ingo Dresen says. "but if you're fed up with your old woman… We're meeting next Wednesday in the clubhouse…"

No offence meant? Since when has Ingo Dresen been using expressions like that? Since when has he been speaking in complete sentences anyway? If I wasn't so afraid of him I'd be quite interested.

He takes a postcard-sized visiting card out of his jeans jacket and hands it to me. On the front it has a black-white-and-red coat of arms with two bloodthirsty but otherwise quite cute rats with double-headed axes in their paws, on the back the address of his clubhouse in Bartgeheide.

"In what used to be the Atahualpa," Ingo says and when I give him a baffled look, he adds, "The place that burnt down back then."

Sometimes I understand why the true-young despise us so. 'Back then' – that can have been ten years ago or fifty. And he looks at me as if I ought to know right away what he's talking about.

"That used to be the 'Bally Hoo'."

I nod. 'Bally Hoo.' The Proll disco where we dropped in for a short while on the way to the 'Auerland'. Late seventies. In my mind's eye I can see the young Ingo Dresen, just a leather waistcoat over his bare chest, on the dance floor of the Bally Hoo swinging an imaginary lasso over his head together with one of his asocial friends – actually a rather poofy dance as it now, with hindsight, seems to me.

"We meet there. Men only, no bitches. Among ourselves for once."

Among ourselves? Ingo Dresen regards himself and me as 'us'? Should I feel flattered or despair?

"We need more good people. You, for instance."

Now I do have to laugh. Fortunately Ingo Dresen joins in. "Of course we do. We need people to represent us and for all the legal stuff. You're still at the Democracy Centre, aren't you?"

How the hell does he know that? How does Ingo Dresen know that I work in the Democracy Centre? That means he'll also know where I live. He'll know everything about me. Oh shit, shit, shit.

"What kind of a club is it?" Actually I'd rather not know. Why on earth am I asking?

"Well, we see things that are happening here with Germany and Europe a bit differently from most people. We still have the old values."

The old values? Extortion? Thumping other people in the face? Or is it just the kind of stuff men talk about at the bar, all sweat and underarm hair – although underarm hair's in again, you just have to ride out the fashions like Ingo Dresen.

"You'll see for yourself if you drop by. Bring your tracksuit. Every session starts with body training – self-control, discipline, rituals."

At last he gives me my newspapers. "I'm counting on you."

Back in the cellar I wait until Christine's enthusiasm for the *Hamburger Abendblatt* has abated a little and then quite casually take *Brigitte* out of my shopping bag and place it on the table.

"By the way, I've got something else for you."

I revel in the expression on her face, eyes wide, mouth gaping. Her first magazine for two years.

"Thank you. Oh thank you, thank you, thank you."

At last I see her smile again.

"I can't see why you women are so attached to this superficial, brightly coloured nonsense."

I gently stroke her head and she goes along with it, though

still slightly cowering and tensed up. Then we both make ourselves comfortable, she with the *Hamburger Abendblatt* on the sofa and me sitting in the armchair. I also leaf through the *Abendblatt* then have a look at the old school exercise books I've brought down from the loft – my set theory book from the fourth year of primary school and a geography workbook from the second year of secondary school. They were in one of the cardboard boxes that had the lid torn off by the storm.

The geography book is an A4 exercise book with a cover of thin black cardboard. A dull black. How restrained, how elegant it looks compared to my children's gaudy exercise books that are teeming with kittens, chubby pandas, the Star Wars crew, supposed top models or the inhabitants of Duckburg. However, Geography at Ohlstedt School also seems to have included education in racism. "The Indian of Peru is quite content with his poor economic situation and with carrying heavy loads. That comes from his phlegmatic disposition." My twelve-year-old self will hardly have thought that up off his own bat. The set theory book from primary school on the other hand has pure poetry on the glued-in notes: *In mathematics a collection of things that are clearly distinguishable is called a set. The individual things making up the set are called the* e l e m e n t s *of the set.*

I instinctively sniff the purple letters, trying to inhale a trace of the odour of the print, that vanished years ago. Underneath is a cloze exercise completed in scrawly pencil: *Opium is an element of the set of drugs. Pistol is not an element of cutlery. Göhte is not an element of the set of hippies. Frau Semel is an element of the set of working wives*. Well what about that! What a little clever clogs with a sense of the out-of-the-way I was. What strikes me is how close ϵ, the symbol for 'is an element of', is to the old euro symbol.

A set can also be represented by a Venn diagram. We draw the elements and draw a line round them. Set of articles of clothing: below that I've drawn – pretty clumsily for a ten-year-old – a pair of very flared trousers and the blue bathing trunks I had at the time (recognisable from the swimming proficiency badge). But a surprising number of women's clothes occurred to me as well, an orange mini skirt and – I find this rather surprising now – a light-blue blouse with puffed sleeves. Was that right? Were blouses with puffed sleeves worn so often in the late sixties that they immediately occurred to a ten-year-old boy as representative elements for the set of articles of clothing?

For *the set of coins valid in the Federal Republic* I gave up relying on my meagre talent for drawing, instead I simply placed the coins under the page and rubbed over them with a soft pencil. Drew a wobbly circle round them and that was that. How familiar the coins still are, I wouldn't hesitate for a moment if I had them in my hand today, even though I've been through two currency changes.

I yawn and glance over at Christine who has stretched out on the sofa and is absorbed in *Brigitte*. I go across and lean down over her. Immediately she closes the magazine.

"What's that you're just reading?"

"Everything. I'm reading everything."

"And just now?"

"Nothing. I was looking at the fashion pictures."

As she says that, she takes out her index finger, that she'd left between the pages as a marker, but it leaves a little bulge where it was placed. I stick my own index finger in, take the magazine off her and open it at that place. It is in fact the fashion section: "The ten most important women in Germany and what their dress style reveals." What is there to be surprised about in that? I glance at the cover. I should have had a closer look when I bought *Brigitte*. The cover picture seems innocuous enough, it is, as ever, the photo of an attractive woman, elegantly but not too strikingly dressed. She's laughing and seems happy with life. But then the article headings: 'How to be fair and still get to the top', 'The new time management' or 'How the crisis makes us strong – self-coaching'. Christine's waiting, head bowed, to see if I'm going to give her the magazine back.

"Just look at all that," I say. "if you were to compare this with a magazine from, let's say the turn of the century – no, we don't need to go back so far – let's say from 2020. What strikes you? I mean the topics they deal with?"

Christine leans forward and reads through the titles, nervously brushing a strand of hair out of her face. "The most beautiful summer dresses," she reads out, "The new time management," and gives me a questioning look.

"Well? And what else? Isn't there something missing? Doesn't it strike you that there's something missing?"

She shrugs her shoulders. Her expression now is more one of irritation than of fear.

"The psychological topics," I say. "In the past there always used to be articles like: 'What is my husband thinking when he's not saying anything?' or 'Why does he feel threatened by emotions.'"

"Perhaps there is something like that in it, only it's not on the cover."

Christine takes the magazine off me and starts to leaf obligingly through the pages at the end.

"Don't bother," I say, leaning my hands on the back of the sofa. "Since you women have grabbed all the well-paid jobs, you're no longer interested in what's happening inside us. You've written us off. I think you don't quite realise what damage you're doing by that."

Christine gives a sardonic smile. "Oh really. And what kind of damage would that be?"

"I know that you women in the ministry of education think you're incredibly committed and positive towards men because you've set up one development programme for boys after the other and give grants for special tuition for male pupils: anti-aggression workshops and financial awards for finishing school. But these boys don't get from you what they really want: importance. They'd do anything at all just to be noticed. That's what you women have never understood: that what's most important to us isn't justice or freedom or wealth, not even sex, but importance – to be important in other people's eyes."

"You were always important to me, always, even when we were separated," Christine says quietly.

"Lies!" I say brusquely. "You were far too occupied with yourself and your great career, Mrs Minister. And you still would be if I hadn't seen to it that you rediscovered your interest in me."

She's about to disagree but I shut her up with a movement of my hand. We both know I'm right. Of course how I happen to be feeling is very relevant to Christine now. It's of vital importance for her to understand me. But only since she's been stuck here in the cellar. In life nothing is as important as the person you're dependent on – especially when it's the only person you're in contact with.

7

When I go through the amber glass door of Gasthof Ehrlich about a third of my former classmates are already there. The most boring third, as I feared. The most important and interesting people – that is those who back then, in 1981, were important and interesting for me – only come towards the end. Or not at all. The punctual bores have spread out in little clusters round the saloon bar, a room with black beams and chairs upholstered in material with the kind of ghastly pattern you find on tour coaches. I'm greeted by restrained hoots, the loudest from the buffet. There my old pals Bernie and Rolf are leaning on a rustic bar beneath a rustic beam and, although the buffet hasn't been opened yet, Bernie's already chewing with bulging cheeks. Nodding, grinning and shaking hands I work my way over to them through a forest of egosmarts held up in the air, pursued by a swarm of smart drones buzzing round my head like fat beetles. At first it's a shock, a real shock, to see them looking so young again, not just Bernie and Rolf, but all of them, the likable and unlikable ones, the swots and the slackers and the class clowns, the poseurs and the bores, the school tarts and the untouchable girls – Maybrit Möller, Kerstin Ahlrichs, Jürgen Kleinschmidt, Silke Gross, Norbert Misselwitz, Kai Gorny. The last reunion was ten years ago and at that point only two from our year had undergone the course of Ephebo that in those days was incredibly expensive. Women, of course. And the first-generation Ephebos were nothing like as effective as the later ones. Last time Maybrit Möller and Yvonne Garzin looked at best as if they were forty. Now Maybrit looks like a twenty-year-old, just the way she did in 1981. Not quite, of course. Back then Maybrit's hair was ferociously backcombed, now it's smoothly permed and dyed dark blue; she's a bit fatter too and there's something about her face that's different, though it's hard to say exactly what. Whatever, I recognise her immediately and, unlike last time, don't have to puzzle over who I'm talking to.

Norbert Lanschick intercepts me with something black and angular under his arm. "Good to see you. Let me have your health certificate. And write something in the register, do it now or you'll forget. Something amusing or whatever."

His jowls wobble as he hands me the open book. I'm sure that by now he's regretting that he's one of the few who look over forty. I leaf through it, looking for something that will spark off an idea. But people only think up rubbish and before I write something stupid or with forced humour, I decide to write formal thanks for all the effort Norbert's put into making this reunion possible and so on and so forth.

Lanschick has indeed arrived with a new wife, red-haired and significantly younger – but I don't think she's chrono-younger, she's probably just more willing to take a risk than his first wife. Before I hand the book back, I quickly leaf through to the letter 'W'. There's her name. Norbert Lanschick has squeezed it into the top right-hand corner in his tiny, meticulous handwriting. Otherwise the page is still empty. Elli didn't come to the reunion ten years ago. As I said, it's often the most interesting people who can't be bothered with class reunions. They probably think attending an event like that might damage their prestige if they haven't got something to show like a fat bank account, a big house, a wife or husband or some trendy job. So they leave the field free to the Norbert Lanschicks of this world. I always thought that was an error. Class reunions aren't about what you've become but about what you used to be. The older you get, the more important it is to meet people who knew you when you were young, I mean true-young. They know who you really are. That's why I've always gone to the class reunions – even in the year when I was already fifty and was starting all over again as a trainee with Foodwatch.

At last I've fought my way through to Bernie and Rolf. Rolf now has a patriarch's beard and a rather conventional suit that is presumably meant to signify that he's got somewhere in life. Bernie's become somewhat podgy and is wearing a sweatshirt with a hood and a leather jacket that looks bloody similar to the one he used to wear fifty years ago. Like myself, both have gone for a moderate form of rejuvenation and have turned up as well-established men in their late thirties. They've taken up a strategically advantageous position right by the buffet, in the middle of which an obscene pyramid of meat dishes has been set up, crowned by a red roasted pig's head that has its teeth, that are so much like a human's, stuck in an orange.

"Greenie, my old eco warrior," Bernie shouts, "Come over here." He grabs me by the shoulders and embraces me. Then Rolf embraces me and Bernie picks up a lined sheet of A4 covered in scrawly old folks' writing off the bar and says there's still time for me to join in – they're betting on which of our classmates will turn up in which state of biological preservation.

"One westo per guess. The stakes will be divided out among those that are right."

Bernie hands me the list, grabs a plate that he's clearly already used several times and piles jellied pork, mozzarella with tomatoes and something fishy on it. I take a closer look. The pieces of fish look like plaice. Unbelievable! I put the sheet of paper back down on the bar.

"No thanks," I says. "Anyway, it's pretty clear with the women already."

More or less all of those who've turned up so far have come as people in their early twenties, have made as much of themselves as possible. If it had been possible they'd probably have reversed puberty and turned themselves back into lanky teenagers. Only two – Isolde Pinzgau and Susanne Stein – have chosen the more moderate version of just turned thirty.

"I'm looking forward to seeing what Kathrin Kessler looks like now, whether she still has those fantastic boobs. They stood out horizontally, as if they were made of plastic, just like something out of a comic," Rolf says.

"I'm going for very young," Bernie says. "Anyone against?"

"Kathrin Kessler's dead," I say.

"Dead?"

"Yes, cancer."

"Yvonne Garzin and Miriam Krüger as well," Rolf says. "I heard it from Yogi. And Kathrin Hoffmann. Only this year. They say she died from multi-resistant germs. They're coming thicker and faster now."

"Just look at them," Bernie says, rubbing his hands, "Just look at all those hot little sprats with their smooth, firm bodies. Last time they were old crones with no waist."

"Five years," Rolf says, surveying the women, the girls, with a malicious grin, "five years I give them, your hot little sprats. Then they'll all die from some strain of cancer and no hospital in the world will take them in."

"Five years at the most," I say. "Who knows how long they've been taking them. And that only if they stop taking all the Ephebos and the senescence-repair whatsit at once."

"And do you think they'll do that?" Rolf asks and answers his question himself. "No, we don't think they will. Who wants to wither away at top speed in front of their innocent little grandchildren?"

"That's all in the future," Bernie says, turning up the collar of his leather jacket, "but at the moment they look really dishy."

Oh God, he actually says 'dishy'. Here at the reunion it does sound touchingly nostalgic. Rolf puts on a disparaging expression and strokes his patriarch's beard. "That's just the paint-job," he says, "the chassis's completely kaput."

"But not yours, eh?"

"Nah, not mine."

As far as the men are concerned, most of them have arrested the slide into old age somewhere between thirty and forty on average – much more sensible as far as health is concerned. Four of them, including Lanschick, have decided that around fifty bio-years is a perfectly satisfactory rejuvenation. Still reasonably physically fit but with the reliability of a man in his prime. At least that's what they assume. Though of course you never know when you see a man who looks fifty whether it's a seventy-year-old who only takes the minimum dose of Ephebo or a fifty-year-old religious fanatic who refuses to take any at all.

Bernie gives me a nudge. "Mummy alert!" he growls from behind his clenched teeth like a ventriloquist and places his hand on his chest, just sticking out his index finger in order to point as unobtrusively as possible at the door where Reinhard Hell and Guido Lehmann are just coming in. They have indeed come as the old folks we'd all be without the aid of the pharmaceutical industry. They're even wearing spectacles, vision-aid spectacles. Actually I only recognise Guido, and that simply because I can still remember the last time I met him. He looks like what we used to call a well-preserved, active grandpa. And if one of the two mummies is Guido Lehmann, then the other must be Reinhard Hell, they used to be very close friends.

"Let it be," I say to Bernie because I somehow feel sorry for the two old men – though I couldn't say why.

"Guido still looks quite acceptable," I say, though it's a lie. "In the old days a guy like that could have been in adverts for children's chocolate or pension funds or stairlifts."

"So what?" Bernie says. "Who wants to be like that? Who wants to play the dear old grandpa?"

"And just look at Helli," Rolf groans, "just like that ancient corpse preserved in a peat bog they found at Schloss Gottorf. Is that musty smell coming from his suit or from the man himself?"

He lifts his nose and sniffs demonstratively.

Reinhard Hell does indeed look worse that Guido, he looks decrepit, even for an untreated seventy-year-old: like a shrivelled chestnut, yellowish skin and unhealthy bluish lips, bald on top and eyebrows like geraniums in a window box. Moreover he's wearing a corduroy jacket with leather patches on the elbows.

"Compared with those two, even Lanschick looks the very picture of health," Bernie says. "Actually, it's a bit much turning up here like that."

"Guido's got religion," I say. My brother told me that. The two are in the same outfit. "It's God's will that we should go mouldy while we're still alive, so the Disciples of St. John think it's okay."

"But what's got into Helli?" Bernie wonders. "Can anyone

tell me why a man should voluntarily look a hundred? Do you realise that we'd all look like that now if there wasn't a remedy for it? Just imagine what a crowd of zombies we'd have here."

He shudders.

Guido and Reinhard are standing by themselves beside a window ledge with brass flower pots from which long, limp leaves are hanging down. Now and then a sympathetic soul goes over to join them. Every time it looks like a former pupil going to greet their old schoolteacher, who is now even older; they exchange a few words and then the former pupils clear off as quickly as possible, perhaps then furtively taking a photo of the mummies. The two ancients simply spoil the mood. Out in the street we've got used to seeing more and more bio-oldies going around, poor sods who simply can't afford the Ephs any more – poor teeth and old, those are the signs of poverty, good teeth and old, those are the religious fanatics, but you'd really rather not see either at a class reunion.

By now almost everyone's there, only Elisabeth Westphal still hasn't arrived yet. I try to get myself to accept that she's presumably not coming, but that makes the whole event turn dreary. And that even though I don't know Elli all that well. She was in a parallel class and even in the final years we didn't do any of the same subjects. Despite that I haven't been able to get her out of my mind through all these years. Over the years, over the decades I've kept on telling myself not to be so silly: how can you miss someone you've hardly ever even spoken to?

When the amber door opens again my heart misses a beat.

"Hey, hey, just look over there," Rolf whispers in my ear, giving my elbow a tug.

But it's only Dr Thomas Bergheim, surgeon, specialist for gastric sleeve resection, coming in. At every class reunion

Bergheim tries to treat us in the same patronising manner as he does his obese patients, who need his surgical skills and are oozing gratitude. But that still can't make us forget that after a party in 1979 he climbed in through Birgit Lammert's window and begged her, "Hey, Birgit, can I do it to you with my mouth? Just with my mouth?" That became a catchphrase for us whenever Thomas walked past, 'Just with my mouth,' – the story went round quicker than a pig can blink. If Thomas should start going on about the advantage of his new method of operating as against the old gastric-band operation, we'll all still be thinking, 'Just with my mouth,' and if he's out of luck one of us will say it out loud. We're all still the same clowns we used to be. Hardly one of us has really changed. That's the frightening thing about a class reunion: it suddenly becomes clear to you that these people who now hold responsible posts, possibly even government offices, are still the same self-important, screwed-up and unreliable guys who used to sit next to you at school. Fidgety boys who dealt drugs are suddenly running hospitals, girls who had posters of horses over their beds are trying to sort out the budget. No wonder, then, that the planet's beyond repair. The very idea of a loser like Thomas Bergheim cutting a hole in your stomach and rummaging round in your entrails is enough to give you the willies.

Bergheim has quite seriously turned himself back into a twenty-year-old. Not only has he been absorbing the full Ephebo dose, giving his complexion the elasticity of naive youth, he's even wearing the latest teenager dress: animal-mood trousers and a matching tiger-print T-shirt. Bernie peers and flutters his eyelids.

"Has something gone wrong with my laser op? Or is Bergheim really wearing trousers with a tail?"

"Everything that's wrong with this world has always been called Thomas Bergheim," Rolf says over his shoulder with an expression of profound disgust.

I'm about to add a comment of my own, but the words stick in my throat, for at that moment Elisabeth Westphal comes in. It's Elli. Oh my God, it is Elli – but not the Elli I saw the last time, fifteen years ago, who was almost an old woman but whom I couldn't speak to because my throat went dry every time when she was close, as dry as if it had been papered over with blotting paper. It's the old Elli, that is the young one, of course: the old young Elli I've been in love with all my life without ever being able to tell her. Elli's long, long legs are in deep-blue drainpipe jeans, she's wearing neoprene cowboy boots and a grey denim shirt, and she looks as if she's just stepped out of a time machine: in 1981 a moment ago, now here with us. Even Elli's hair looks the way it did in those days, but that's no problem for her; she'd always ignored the fashion for frizzy permanent waves and simply wore her hair smooth and long.

Thomas Bergheim immediately makes a beeline for her. He tries his old ploy that worked so well fifty years ago: the wide-eyed, innocent look, maintaining eye contact for far too long. Delighted with himself, he paws Elli's arm and once he even touches her hair; and as he does all this, the five-foot tiger's tail, that comes out of his trousers at his coccyx, lashes his legs in an amazingly true-to-life manner.

"How I hate these shitty tail-trousers," Bernie says. "I don't even like the caps with those little ears; the way the brats sit there on the Underground waggling their ears at each other and telling each other how cute they look, and then the whole troop comes trotting along when one of them has their floppy ears drooping and pats them and comforts them until their ears stand up again and they all applaud. It really makes me want to throw up."

Just at that moment Elli laughs at something Thomas Bergheim has said and immediately I regret not having taken the full Ephebo dose – at least I could have increased it in the short term for the reunion. For the pair of them over there do go together perfectly in bio terms. They're the prettiest young pair imaginable. Elli of course, but also Bergheim with his straight, shining white teeth, his evenly tanned complexion and the stray lock of hair that falls down over his forehead. What does it matter that he's an idiot. And what should a bio-girl like Elli do with one of us men in our late thirties?

Bernie puts his hand on my shoulder. "Do you think no one notices how you're staring at Elli?"

My first impulse is to deny it, but then I think, what the hell, the world's going to end in ten years at the latest, what's the point in trying to keep up appearances.

"Right then," I say, turning up my shirt collar. I have to go over now, straight away or I won't have the guts to do it for the rest of the evening.

Bernie sticks with me. "I'll come too and keep the way clear for you."

He heads straight for Bergheim and starts yakking as I say "Hello" to Elli.

"Well, young man," Bernie says, putting his arm patronisingly round Bergheim's shoulders and turning him away from Elli, "you look really great, if we ignore the tiger trousers. Have you been away, or are you on the self-tanning pills?"

Bergheim shrugs his shoulders irritatedly, a bulging V appears in the smooth skin of his forehead. You can tell how uncomfortable he feels beside a bio-older man, a real man. His tiger tail goes limp and sinks down to the floor.

"Greek islands," he says. He tries to re-establish eye contact with Elli, but she's already turned to me.

"Sebastian," – she still remembers my name! – "nice to see you."

"A bit uncanny as well, isn't it? I mean the way we all look like we used to?"

She smiles but doesn't answer. She probably thinks I don't look like I used to at all, but like an old fart.

"On the Mediterranean?" Bernie blethers on at Bergheim. "I thought all the beaches there were closed because of the plague of algae?"

"It really freaks me out to see you like this," I say to Elisabeth. "In fact to see you here at all."

Is it really me saying this? I blush a bit, but that doesn't matter because Elli blushes as well and looks to one side in embarrassment. We're as shy and awkward as a couple of fourteen-year-olds. You really couldn't convince anyone that we're both almost seventy.

"Oh, all that about algae's just a load of nonsense," Bergheim says. "Jellyfish, the whole place was covered in jellyfish, you could more or less walk on the water. The sea was completely covered in slimy stuff. Off Naxos there were even those six-foot jellyfish."

"Talking about slimy stuff," Bernie says, turning to us and releasing us from our embarrassment, "have you noticed that half of what Niebel calls an assortment of fish consists of jellyfish rubbish: jellyfish salad, jellyfish sushi and jellyfish lasagne. Do I have to eat that, eh? Do I have to fork out four CO_2 points for that?"

"At least it's better than if the whole 'assortment' consisted of fillets of plaice," I say, grateful for the diversion. "I can't understand how people can toss fish that are practically extinct in the frying pan."

"But that's precisely what the attraction is," Bergheim booms. "You particularly enjoy it when you know it's going to die out soon.."

Bernie giggles. Elli looks at me. I remain perfectly calm. Despite that Bergheim turns to me and says waspishly, "Here's our eco-warrior getting all worked up again, telling us it means the whole world's going to fall to pieces because of that."

"Not at all," I say with dignity and without taking my eyes off Elli. "I've no objection to idiots like you, who insist on remaining blind to the dangers of consumerism, coming to a pitiful end. What does bother me is that someone like me, who has reached an evolutionary stage of intelligence at which it would be possible for the species to last for a few more centuries, will have to die along with you blockheads."

Bergheim laughs. "There goes our Greenie again. You really do believe that, don't you? You think the end of the world is just around the corner?"

"That must have got round even to you by now," says Elli, unexpectedly coming to my aid.

"Oh do stop it," Bergheim groans exasperatedly. "Greenie was telling us the world was going to end fifty years ago. Well? Where is it, your absolute cataclysm?"

A strange phenomenon. For decades people have been persuading themselves that it won't be that bad and now, when everything that was predicted is happening, they're neither surprised nor horrified, but simply say it's the way it's always been and settle down comfortably for the catastrophe. When the roof over their heads is blown away or it doesn't rain for six months, they just attribute it to the natural fluctuation range of the weather statistics. Seen it all before.

"To be honest, I think all this pessimism's exaggerated,"

Bernie says, “that’s the way it’s always been: the politicians wait till it’s five to twelve and then at the last minute something’s found that speeds the ocean currents up again.”

“It looks as if you really haven’t understood,” Elli replies. “It’s already too late. Or do you seriously think your children are ever going to see anything of the money they’re paying in for their pensions? They’re handing out CO_2 points as if the climate change could still be stopped. But have you ever asked yourselves why the banks don’t make long-term loans any more?”

Well, well, well. Since when has Elli been so committed to action. As far as I know, she studied business management and then climbed the career ladder at breakneck speed, eventually managing a plush hotel. At least that’s what I was told.

“That’s all rubbish,” Bernie says, “of course you can get a loan. Loans for solar energy units are even supported by the state.”

“Have you ever tried to get one?” Elli mocks.

“Let’s be relaxed about this, guys,” Bergheim says, all composed and supercilious. “Okay, it’s gradually getting warmer, you can’t deny that, but only gradually at the moment. We’ll be long dead by the time all hell’s let loose here. And be honest now, are you really interested in what will be happening here after we’re dead? Of course I don’t want my children to have to suffer under it, no one wants that, but it will probably be the grandchildren who’re going to get it, and they really will get it, but so what, someone’s going to get it eventually.”

Lanschick comes trotting over to us and presses his visitors’ book to Bergheim’s chest with his huge skeletal hands. “Will you write something here? A witticism or something like that? And I need your bill of health.”

“Write that the fillets of plaice were delicious,” I say, “so delicious in fact the you could happily let your grandchildren die for them."

Elli's still going on at Bergheim too. "Do you seriously believe you've still got time, plenty of time – in five years the world as you know it won't exist any more."

Lanschick looks from one to the other in irritation, still holding out the book to Bergheim.

But he has no intention of taking it. Instead he says, "Ooooh, now I am afraid," raising his arms and waving his hands about like an apparition on the ghost train. "We're all going to die! Come on, guys, let's have a general panic."

He looks all round at the 1981 school leavers chomping on tortured pig or near-extinct fish and happily chatting to each other. Behind the bar is Niebel, bio-age around fifty, polishing the glasses in slow motion.

"Perhaps you'll be lucky," Elli says. "Perhaps India and China will agree on who should pay for making clouds out of sea-water and we'll get a few months' reprieve. Perhaps you'll still be alive in ten years' time, but the life you have won't be worth living. You won't particularly enjoy it."

There's an angry glint in her eyes as she looks at Bergheim. Then she turns to me, probably expecting support, but I'm much too spellbound by Elli to be capable of thinking up a clever remark. How I've missed her! I feel like an animal in the zoo that's been kept in solitary confinement and suddenly encounters another member of its own species.

"Shall the earth our own dark grave be?" Bernie declaims with a bleak look up at the blackened beams.

"Why do you have to go on about this every time?" Lanschick says to me, the only one of us who's said nothing; he manages to get exactly the same tone of voice as my mother. "You know it always leads to arguments."

Sticking his visitors' book back under his arm, he stalks off to find another victim.

"You have to see the good sides as well," Bernie says. "After all, our generation has had the best time humanity's ever had in the course of history: no war, lashings of food and alcohol, dope, cars, TV, the Internet, picture-phones, egosmarts – every kind of luxury imaginable. Things were going uphill all the time. Until recently we even had good medical care. And on top of that we're young again. Actually, we ought to be grateful for all that…"

"Au contraire," Rolf breaks in; he's suddenly there with us and he's brought Margitta Kleinwächter. "We're probably just too early for the really best times. When – some time in the future – they've sorted out the carcinogens, you'll be able to live to be really old… really… really… old: a hundred and fifty, two hundred, perhaps even three hundred. But it's hardly likely we'll be here to see that."

"Perhaps God had some reason for us not to get that old."

Margitta – the voice of undemanding, devout womanhood. For all that, she's been taking the full Ephebo fix without bothering about God's intentions.

"There's no point in getting that old any more," I say, "or do you fancy being around when the tornadoes are sweeping over Germany every other day and people are at each others' throats? The official approval of Ephebo is another indication that we won't be taking it for long. Has it never occurred to you to wonder why our usually overcautious lady ministers waved it through almost unanimously – even before England and Poland. And that with the incidence of cancer! They'd never have done that, if we'd had even the slightest hope of a future."

"What rubbish," Bergheim says, "the Ephs are completely

safe now. You just don't have to overdo it."

"Perhaps our ministers' unexpected willingness to take a risk is connected with the fact that the health service was falling to pieces," Rolf interjects. "To make an obese, ageing society twenty, thirty or even fifty years younger at a stroke – that's not something to be sniffed at."

"Exactly," says Bergheim. "Dementia, osteoporosis, type 2 diabetes, rheumatism and Parkinson's disease – all gone! Or as good as. At least not a cost factor any longer. And if you get cancer, the hospital produces your contract right away, the one you signed saying that in return for the Ephebo allocation you release the state health insurance from any obligation to cough up for expensive chemotherapy. A win-win situation you'd think."

"I don't believe all the cases of cancer are triggered off by Ephebo." It's Elli of all people stabbing me in the back. "That was perhaps the case at the beginning, but since then they've changed the composition twice and it shouldn't have occurred at all. But in the same year those new pesticides came on the market."

Bergheim yawns, mouth wide open. "I think I'll go back to the buffet before the others have eaten up all the plaice."

"We'll join you," says good old Bernie, grabbing Rolf and Margitta by the sleeve. "The plaice may have all gone by now anyway, but perhaps there's still a bit of the baby dolphin left. Anyway, I want to ask Niebel if he can give me a doggy bag of jellyfish lasagne to take home."

Elli and I stay back by the door.

"I don't know why I'm getting so worked up about Thomas Bergheim," Elli says.

"But I do," I say. "I've had his concentrated stupidity up to here." I show where with my hand.

"In point of fact I'm actually happy that people are dying out," Elli says. "The things they've done to the poor animals – it takes my breath away when I think of that. And to each other. How self-satisfied and stupid and hypocritical they are. And how ugly."

Bernie, who ought to be out of earshot by now, turns round again. "What d'you mean? Those who take Ephebo don't look that bad at all."

"It'd still be better if they all disappeared," I shout back, "and I hope everything else dies with them as well."

Elli squints up at me, her green eyes narrowing to slits. "I'm absolutely serious about this," she says.

"Me too," I reply. "What an idea to create a world in which the creatures feed themselves by eating each other. What an incredibly shitty idea! The sooner it stops, the better."

Elli looks deep into my eyes. "It's unlikely that everything will die," she says. "Something or other will be left, even if it's just black bacterial slime."

I sustain her look. I used to be unable to do that. Before I put Christine in the cellar I was a rather shy type of man. But now. Now suddenly I can do it. Everything inside me is relaxed. All at once I know as clearly as you can know anything: Elli is everything I want from life. I've no need of anything else.

"Oh no!" I exclaim with feigned horror. "Does that mean everything's going to start over again. Eating and being eaten, all that senseless cruelty, in which the intelligent and nice creatures are pushed around all the time while the near-imbecile and aggressive ones call all the shots…"

"Well," Elli says, "at least there'll probably be peace and quiet for a few hundred thousand years…"

We fall silent, still looking at each other. All around the murmurs and laughter of our former classmates. I have to say something before some idiot comes over to join us again.

"I've been in love with you all my life," I say. "You can have no idea how deeply I've always been in love with you. I wasn't aware of it – because I didn't really know you. But now, now I am aware of it."

8

Around two in the morning apart from me and Elli there are just Bernie, Rolf and Margitta, Thomas Bergheim, Hanno Scholz and Yogi Putfarken sitting at a table, more or less drunk. Lanschick – sober – has just come back from the loo. He yawns and looks at his watch-smart. His wife went back to their hotel three hours ago. Even Niebel disappeared at some point. Replacing him behind the bar is a male temp in a faded grey T-shirt – long-haired and true-young. Lanschick flops into a chair and watches while Bernie and Rolf burn their initials into the table top with the op-laser on Bergheim's medical smart. Until about eleven o'clock they kept themselves reasonably under control, but since then they've been behaving as if they were twelve again. Margitta has put clear distance between herself and Rolf and moved over to Elli, where she's sucking disappointedly at her glass of cola.

Yogi Putfarken, who used to be a punk and lived in a squat, but has now assumed the bronzed complexion and bleached hair of a thirty-year-old surfer, is playing with the awful droplight, pulling it down as far as it will go, then letting it shoot back up, until something in the spiral suspension breaks and the brown-glazed ceramic shade is left hanging about a centimetre above the table top. Hanno Scholz, chubby and pale, is silently brooding over something. He's the other man beside Bergheim who is obviously taking the full Ephebo dose. Hardly understandable really, for Hanno Scholz has no reason to want to look the way he did in 1981. Back then he was one of those nondescript types who didn't really count. Not graceless like Lanschick, just withdrawn, rather vacuous. He had dark, wiry hair, almost like pubic hair, and he was the first one of us who could grow a beard. We called him Jolly-Scholly and for a while it was a standard bit of fun to muss up his hair. Five, ten times during the morning someone would creep up behind him, shout, "Hey, Jolly-Scholly, it's muss-up day today!" and run his hands through his hair until it stood up like a mad professor's. Now he's a physicist at a prestigious American university. I've forgotten which one, but when I saw him at the reunion ten years ago, I didn't have that in mind but the way we used to muss him up and I said "Hey, Jolly-Scholly" and put my hand on his shoulder. With a look of distaste at my hand, that was still touching him, Scholz gave me a cold look and said, "We don't use that appellation any more, do we?"

A voice like brittle plastic. I immediately withdrew my hand and mumbled an apology. It wasn't his job or his bank balance that intimidated me, nor was it the 'doctor' and 'professor'. It was the slightly aggressive sense of self-assurance he gave off, the aura of unshakable self-esteem he suddenly seemed to possess. Scholz didn't just think he was something better than me, he could put it across so convincingly that I immediately started wondering whether he might be right about that. He was the only one of my former classmates who had succeeded in changing himself to his advantage. No matter what old images of him were still going round inside my head, within five seconds Hanno Scholz had managed to change his status from Jolly-Sholly with the mussed-up hair, to the daunting Professor Doctor Scholz, simply through his demeanour towards me. It was through him that I first got the idea that it might be possible to invert the power relationship between Christine and me. I couldn't understand why Scholz should now want to be a chubby youth again. He looks as if he suffers from depression. At least he's lost his intimidating aura. He's even shaved off his beard.

I tell Elli and Margitta about how, during my Greenpeace days, I went on a ship to the Antarctic in order to disrupt the Japanese whalers. I lay it on a bit.

"The polars seas are unrelenting," I say, "the swell is unbearable. After the roaring forties you get the rolling fifties, once I spewed up right onto the keyboard of my laptop."

Yogi Putfarken grabs the lamp that's hanging right down and shines it straight in my face. "Who is this actually," he says, slurring his words and pointing to me. "Can anyone tell me who this guy is?"

I can feel the anger rising up inside me. This arrogant little piss artist is trying to challenge me. The male temporary barman comes, a blue check cloth slung over his muscular shoulder, and puts Yogi's beer down and Yogi lets go of the lamp and sucks the foam off the top of the glass. The lamp swings to and fro over the stained table.

"But once you get there, the Antarctic is incredibly beautiful and peaceful," I say, turning to Elli and Margitta, "the light refracted in the ice, penguins floating past on icebergs. At the same time you know that there are people out there shooting at whales with harpoons, that somewhere those huge floating whale butcheries are cruising round. And you can't help wondering how those guys feel about all that beauty, whether they admire it or can't see it."

"I once went on one of those Hurtigruten cruises," Bergheim remarks, "fantastic, all that blue. You always assume it's white but in reality it's mostly a very bright blue. The most beautiful thing I've ever seen."

I really have a go at him. "You have no right at all to find that beautiful. Go and eat your fillets of plaice instead."

"If you eat fish, you don't have the right to think icebergs are beautiful, is that it?"

"No," I say, "you don't. At least you've finally managed to understand that."

"I can't understand it," Elli says and rambles on a bit, "I never have. People love to see films in which the good guys fight against the bad guys. They get excited as they follow the good guys and when the bad guys get on top for a while they get all worked up and breathe a deep sigh of relief when the good guys come out on top in the end after all. And then these people go and vote for guys who look like the bad guys in the film and behave like the bad guys in the film. And then they're surprised when those guys drag them down with them. You wouldn't believe people could be so stupid."

"As an activist you have to be an optimist," I say, "a professional optimist. Even though you can't ignore the fact that conditions are getting worse and worse all the time, you have to believe that things can be turned around after all. There came a point where I just couldn't do that any longer. For a while I behaved as if I still believed we could, but eventually it was getting me down so much that I got out."

Yogi Putfarken gives the ceramic lampshade a push, sending it swinging over towards me and then back to him. "Hey, who are you? Do I know you? I don't know you at all."

When the lamp comes towards me for the third time I simply grab it and keep hold of it. "Doesn't matter," I say, "you don't have to know everything."

I try to push the spiral suspension back together but when I let go it sinks back down almost to the table top again.

"I don't want to know you." Yogi says, sucking at the top of his beer again. I still have a cable tie in my pocket that I didn't use when I went to see Christine. That allows me to fix the recalcitrant spiral in its original position. The women applaud.

"A practical man," Bernie says, "one with cable ties in his pocket."

It's a strange feeling to have brought something from the cellar up into this world. It makes the cellar real in an obtrusive way. I don't want to have the cable tie with me here. Not at my class reunion. I simply don't want to be reminded of Christine at the moment.

As if a wave from my brain had reached him somehow, Lanschick immediately asks, "Have you heard anything from your wife lately?"

They all stare at me. I look down at the table and slowly shake my head.

"To be honest I don't believe it was those Yellow Monks who kidnapped your wife," Bernie says. The way he slurs his words he must have had quite a few. "With the job she had she must have been completely burnt out. I could imagine she killed herself somewhere or other and her body just hasn't been found yet."

"What? It was the Yellow Monks? And they're still going round free and can even advertise?" Margitta says.

Rolf moves over closer to her again. "It was one of their radical splinter groups that admitted responsibility. But that doesn't mean they really did it. They might just have wanted the publicity."

I lean on my elbows and put my hands together with the fingertips on my nose. "Would anyone object if we changed the subject," I said.

For twenty seconds they all remain quiet. The only sound

is Yogi sucking the foam off the top of his beer. Then Bernie raises his glass to Elli and Margitta: "To the two prettiest women of the class reunion."

Bergheim can't hold back any longer. "No offence meant," he says to Elli and Margitta, "you really look very nice but there's something about you that's somehow... well, you know... the thing is, I'd never go after a bio-young woman. If I did it'd have to be a true-young one. She could even be thirty – as long as it was chrono-thirty."

Elli laughs. "How very broad-minded of you!"

"Yeah, great," says Margitta.

"Now be honest," I say to Bergheim, "you're not saying that you really can tell whether a woman's chrono-young or is taking Ephebos. I mean if she's wearing a roll-neck sweater and you've never met her before."

"Of course I can," Bergheim says with an ugly twist to his lips. "The women who were here this evening all lack a certain something. They all lack that glow of innocence, that delicate lustre in their faces, that wonder at life."

He's spent the whole evening trying in vain to get off with one woman after another. Now Elli and Margitta are going to pay for it.

"I can't understand why you do this to yourselves," he says, turning to them. "Do you actually know all the things that Ephebo contains? It's bloody dangerous. Why can't you just get old with dignity?"

"Get old?" Elli asks. "Are you seriously suggesting that's what we should do? We should be the only ones to get old and ugly?"

"You're taking the full dose yourself," Margitta snarls.

Bergheim continues to stir things up, though he too is starting to slur his words. "It's no use to you anyway. What if a man is taken in by you," he says to Elli, "and fancies starting a family with you again, huh? You can't have children any more – unless you fancy bringing up a hydrocephalic monster. I happen to have seen one of those. It had a real pig's mug. You two are nicely tarted up but that's all."

"What makes you think anyone here wants to start a family?" Elli says, waving her hand like a windscreen wiper in front of her face. "Moreover Ephebo prescribed for women has a contraceptive mixed into it, if you didn't happen to know."

"Yes, but people are taking legal action against that again and they'll probably be forced to withdraw it because there are ethical or whatever doubts about it."

I'm slowly starting to get really pissed off. "Oh, give it a rest," I say to Bergheim. "The only thing that bothers you about bio-young women is that they're no longer the helpless, timid little bimbos who used to succumb to your charm. Your problem is you can't get anywhere with mature women."

"Oh just listen to our little slimy-slimy Greenie," Bergheim says venomously, his tiger's tail furiously whipping the legs of the chair he's sitting on, "sucking up to the women because that's the only way he can score with them."

"Well?" Elli says to him. "Is Bassi right?"

"There you are, the women side with Greenie, of course. That was to be expected. After all, he's one of the men who put you in power. After all, you have him to thank for everything."

"Sorry," Margitta says, "what was that? What have I to thank Sebastian for?"

"Well, everything – that you're earning more money than most men nowadays and that you're still promoted even if you do everything wrong – simply because you're a woman because that means it's really great when you do anything at all..."

"What nonsense you're talking," Margitta says, "you know nothing about my life at all."

Yogi's fallen asleep with his head on the table.

"Since when have I been earning more than any man?" Elli snorts. "Could you please explain that to me? I think you've no idea at all how lousy teachers' salaries have become."

I prick up my ears. All that about the hotel and her great career doesn't seem to be right.

"…and that you women have seized almost all the posts in the government with your grasping cunts," Bergheim goes on.

"I think that's enough of your sexist remarks," Rolf says.

"What d'you mean? For a woman being the target of sexist remarks is the best thing that can happen to her today. That could make Elli our next defence minister."

"Perhaps you ought to stop drinking," Rolf says, sliding the bulbous bottle of red wine to the other end of the table where Bernie's sitting – the only one who's more drunk than Bergheim.

"Not even half the ministries are run by women," Elli says. "And could it be that you haven't heard that at the moment we've got a male chancellor?"

Bernie spills some of the wine he's pouring into his glass and licks up the spillage off the table top. Then he looks up at us. "I think it's a good thing that the women are taking over the whole caboodle. Let them get on with it. Right away, for all I care: the economy, the environment, finance. Then we men can lounge around in peace at last."

"If you women had just a spark of pride inside yourselves you'd have refused to clear up the mess after us," Rolf says.

"But they didn't," Bergheim mocks. "That makes you think."

"There's this male tendency to lounge around," Bernie

goes on undeterred. “Getting up late, drinking wine, sitting in the sun, whittling away at a piece of wood. That’s what corresponds to a man’s true inner nature. Let the women see to all the rest.”

“That’s nonsense, Bernie,” I say. “What on earth are you talking about?”

“Well,” Bernie says, “just look at typical men’s hobbies: stamp collecting, for example, or fishing. In reality they’re both excuses to sit around doing nothing. That’s what we men are made for, you see.”

“You really are talking rubbish,” Bergheim says, “I don’t know a single man who collects stamps.”

“Has it never struck you that at kiosks there are always men standing around with a bottle of beer in their hand, otherwise doing nothing? It’s genetic. You never see women there. Always just men.”

Hanno Scholz wakes from his depressive stupor, stares at Bernie, completely nonplussed, and opens his mouth for the first time. “Yes, that’s right, at home they’re always standing under the roof outside the supermarket, where they have the trolleys.”

“Yes, true,” Bergheim says, “but they’re alcoholics.”

“Yes, but that’s still just an excuse,” Bernie says. “In reality they’ve become alcoholics so that they have a reason to hang around, which fits in with their nature. Otherwise they could just as well be alcoholics at home.”

Elli puts her hand on Bernie’s left shoulder. “Well, if you say so…”

Bernie nestles his cheek so close up against her hand that I feel a twinge of jealousy.

“Elli understands me.”

She laughs and tousles his hair with her other hand.

Suddenly I can imagine a future with Elli. She's bold and purposeful and I can visualise myself going through the woods with her, picking berries, digging up roots and holding up petrol stations. However things turn out, with Elli any kind of future is worth living.

"Oh yes," Yogi says, suddenly coming alive again, "today they're running their hands through your hair and in the morning they're ditching you without batting an eyelid.

"That's the way things are," Bergheim says, "nowadays they're cruel. They have all these rights and freedoms but they can't deal with them. They don't realise how they can ruin a man with all that."

"Oh, Thomas," Margitta says, "all that simply because you've probably just had a bit of bad luck."

"Not me," Bergheim says darkly, "but my friend. He was completely bloody destroyed by a woman."

"Is that what feminism is," Yogi moans, "to let yourself be bawled out by a woman?"

Rolf starts up again. "We men have become toys. Suddenly women can have lots of men, so we've just become pieces in a game of chess."

I have to smile. All this moaning and groaning because women have escaped from our control – what a load of wimps! I look over at Elli and she smiles back.

"I'm going to order a round of coffee now," she says, "before one of you bursts into tears."

9

Elli places her wrist with her watch smart on the lock and the door of her hotel room opens with a sumptuous slurping noise, as if it were being drawn into the room by an invisible lackey. The room itself is less sumptuous, however, it's more in the style of a teenager's room: light veneer, small double bed, tiny desk, a cheap framed print of some lock on the Alster and a compunicator screen. Elli goes first, holding my hand and pulling me in behind her. She heads straight for the minibar and takes out a little bottle of wine with a screw top.

The screen flickers and turns on, "Good evening, Frau Westphal," says the face of an elfin, almost human being with a cloud of purple, almost realistic butterflies fluttering round it. "Nice to see you again. Have you brought someone with you? Don't forget to pay the double-room surcharge tomorrow. I will go now, I wish you a good night. You will find our special films on channel three."

Elli giggles. I take off my jacket and hang it over the shining green eye in the egg-shaped bulge on the top edge of the compunicator. That's my first article of clothing removed.

"That's not a camera," Elli says, "it's probably a sensor."

She turns the two water glasses on the desk right way up, pours the wine and hands me a glass. We drink standing up and looking at each other.

"Since when have you been a teacher?" I ask. I say that to show that I want to take my time with her. And I am actually interested. I want to know everything about her.

"To be precise, I'm just a teaching assistant. I'm not qualified as a teacher."

I put my glass down on the desk and take off her jacket. It almost goes wrong because Elli still has her glass in her hand. She laughs, puts the glass in her mouth and holds it tight with her teeth while I pull her denim jacket off over her arms. I turn her to face me. Elli has her glass in her hand again.

"I studied Business Administration, then Hotel Management, I even managed a hotel once. Until at some point I asked myself if that was what I really wanted my mission in life to be: to see to it that rich, pampered people had every wish fulfilled before they could even express them."

She undoes the buttons on my shirt, one after the other, pulls it up out of my trousers and softly and slowly runs her hand over my vest.

"After that I was in animal welfare, for over twenty years. I ended up in a place for rescue animals, but there came a point when I simply wasn't up to it physically any longer. That was before Ephebo."

I kiss her, draw her to me and feel her warmth, the wine-sweetness of her mouth. Our tongues wrap round each other and I let my hands wander under her denim shirt and up and down her warm, perfect back. Can a teenager's dream be fulfilled fifty years later? Can time simply be switched to reverse, as on a cassette recorder?

I undo Elli's belt, put my hand down her trousers and do what I would never have dared to do back then. I do it with masterful charm, not with the quivering lust of a twenty-year-old, and we're looking into each other's eyes all the time.

"Show me your young body," I say, undoing the buttons on her black jeans and pulling them down, together with her panties, in a single, smooth movement to her ankles. Black panties, but very plain, cotton. The movement means that now I'm kneeling before her and the position corresponds exactly to what I'm feeling. Reverently I take hold first of her right, then her left foot and free them from jeans, undies and the black-and-grey hooped socks. Very innocent. And since my face is on a level with her shaven pussy – in that she's just as old-fashioned as me – I press my lips to Elli's little youthful slit. Until now I've never slept with a bio-twenty-year-old. Christine was always very health-conscious and never took more Ephebo than was needed to keep her body in the early thirties. Moreover she's followed the new fashion for slovenliness and let her hair grow everywhere. Elli, on the other hand, feels so delicate and virginal that I briefly wonder whether the firm swell of her pussy is solely due to Ephebo or whether a plastic surgeon has had a hand in it. Her body twitches as I touch her, as if from an electric shock. The wine glass falls on the floor. She must have been holding on to the table with one hand. I put my arms round her legs, grasp a thigh in each hand and press my tongue into the elasticity of her slit. I lick her, tongue, head and neck combining, in and out, up and down, penetrating as deep as possible. Elli groans and trembles. She's put her free hand on my head and is clinging on tight to my hair. I work on her, faster and faster, and now Elli's groaning is uncontrolled and she's trying to push my head away, to get her little crack safe from me. But I grasp her bottom in my right hand and draw her firmly to me – no escape for Elli. When I stick my finger in, her legs give way and she slides towards me on my finger until I can't hold her any longer and we both fall on the floor.

"You okay?" I ask. "Did you hurt yourself?"

She shakes her head, her eyes glazed over. Suddenly I'm

overcome by fear of failure. It's too good. It's too much. She's too beautiful. It's not possible and I don't deserve it because I'm thoroughly bad. Fortunately my glass is still on the table. I fish around for it, toss the wine back, then pull down my zip, take off my jeans, underpants, socks and the shirt Elli unbuttoned and pull my vest up over my head. I tell myself that the girl of my dreams is lying there, already sweaty and gagging for it. I remind myself that I'm not an awkward twenty-year-old idiot any longer. When Elli takes off her grey denim shirt, I've got a hard-on again. I bend over her and undo her bra, an old-fashioned article made from something like neoprene, full of tiny holes and rivets, a real armour breastplate in yellow and black but pretty sexy despite that. Oh bugger – Elli's had her boobs done! Why on earth!? Round and perfect, they defy gravity and simply can't be genuine. I'd have preferred it if she'd kept her own probably much smaller breasts. But they look good all the same of course. And then I don't let the fact that she's shaved down there bother me, even though she definitely wouldn't have been in 1981. I pull Elli onto my lap and penetrate her. It's great the way that everything works with Ephebo. I wonder what it's like if you take the full dose? I'd probably have to jerk off three times a day. Chrono-young guys are far too stupid to fully appreciate the sexual capacity they possess. Only when you're seventy and have lost and then unexpectedly regained part of it, do you realise what a gift it is. To be good-looking when you were already ugly, to be young again when you'd already experienced old age, makes you wise and humble. Perhaps it even makes you a better person.

I caress Elli's neck with my tongue and move gently inside her, we're both moving, we're making love face to face. Plunging deep into each other's eyes. However much I value dominating Christine, it's a dreadfully lonely business. I take

Elli's false breasts in my hands and squeeze them cautiously until I can feel the implants. At the same time I move inside her, thrust into her until she comes with a scream and I come myself, silently, and we both fall back onto the carpet, gasping for breath and immediately turn to look at each other. How I love her! How I love her! I could make love to her again right away. Best of all from behind. But I won't do that. At least not after the first time. No, definitely not. Not with Elli. That's what I have Christine for.

"You look so serious," Elli says. "Is everything okay?"

"Of course. Better than okay."

"Were you thinking of your wife?"

"Of my wife? No, certainly not. What makes you think that?'

She looks at me calmly and lovingly. The very way she looks make me a better person.

"When your wife disappeared… it can't have been easy."

"No," I say, "it was bad. I'll tell you about it sometime later. But just now I really wasn't thinking of my wife at all."

"What of then?"

"In the old days at school…" I say, "…I always had the feeling you couldn't stand me. You always looked away when we met. You thought I was stupid, didn't you?"

"I didn't think you were stupid. I was even impressed by your talks and the way you collected signatures for your campaigns. But somehow it was difficult to size you up. At school you always intimidated me, you were so clever. I think I was a bit afraid of you. You always looked so mean."

"Looked mean – what, me? I was hopelessly in love with you. I didn't even dare to look at you, never mind meanly."

She snuggles up in my arm. "But you had all those girlfriends, you didn't seem particularly shy to me."

"They were all just those eco-groupies," I say, combing the hair at her temples with my fingers. "They weren't like you. I was with the campaign for nuclear disarmament and you… you were gorgeous and superficial, you were one of the preppies. I would never have dared to approach you. Instead I tried to despise you but that didn't work. I would have given anything just to be allowed to touch you."

"Well, well, so I was gorgeous and superficial. That's a great compliment," Elli says, stroking my nipple with the tip of her nose. For a while we lie on the carpet, not saying anything, but then Elli starts to feel cold and we stand up and get into the teenage bed, burrowing down under the duvet. I feel for the knob of the radio but instead the compunicator turns its random TV function on. Sharks are swimming towards us, one of them cleaves the blue sea and shoots out of the screen right into the hotel room. Over the bottom of the bed it makes a swift turn in the air and zooms back into the screen.

"Sorry," I say, "I wanted to switch on some music."

"Just leave it on," Elli says. "It's probably no bad thing if we find something to take our minds off what's happened. It's just too intense. My feelings are so strong, I'm worn out just now. Hold me tight for a bit."

Her wish is my command. So we lie there, Elli in my arms, and watch TV. However it's not the nature film we assumed it was but an episode of the *Jackass* series in which five severely handicapped guys – a man in a wheelchair, one with just one arm, one of restricted growth and a pair of Siamese twins attached at the hips – regularly get into stupid situations where they can easily be injured. This time they've sailed out to sea in a chartered boat and are luring sharks by pouring fish blood into the sea and then chucking half chickens in. The boat's very quickly surrounded by sharks, not particularly big ones, perhaps six to ten feet long, but big enough to give you a heart attack if you were to encounter one while swimming. The midget has tied his barbecued chicken to a cord and keeps pulling it up at the last moment when a shark snaps at it, so that the shark shoots up out of the water, at which the midget whacks it on the nose with a fly-swatter. The Siamese twins join him. They've got banderillas like Spanish bullfighters, though with suction cups instead of barbs, and they try to stick them to the backs of the sharks, taking turns because of course only one can lean forward at a time while the other has to lean back to maintain their balance. Naturally the suction cups don't stick to the wet fish. While all this is going on, the one-armed man is helping the wheelchair user to get into a diving suit, strap himself in his wheelchair and attach the oxygen cylinders to the arms. Then they all get together to push him overboard and split their sides laughing when he and the wheelchair immediately sink to the bottom like a stone. The underwater camera shows the wheelchair eventually getting stuck on a coral reef. Now the sharks have surrounded the quadriplegic who's trying to keep them off with a walking stick.

"That's odd," says Elli. "Did he have the walking stick when they chucked him in?"

"I'd have noticed," I say, twisting one of her locks round my forefinger. In the meantime the one-armed man, equipped with only a pair of diving goggles, has jumped overboard straight onto the back of one of the bigger sharks. With his one arm he holds on tight to its dorsal fin, digs his heels into its sides and shouts, "Yippee" until he's dragged under water, where he continues to kick up a racket, though we can't understand a word. The shark's disturbed, it's really distraught, it doesn't quite know what the situation is and when the one-armed man lets go, it beats a hasty retreat. In the meantime a hammerhead shark has sunk its teeth into the back of the wheelchair and is shaking the chair and the man strapped in it to and fro. But hardly has the shark paused for a minute than the guy reaches back over his shoulder and sticks two little German flags, the kind you'd put on a cheese sample, right up its nose, which is too much for the hammerhead and off it swims. And it's good, so good, to be lying here with Elli in my arms watching this rubbish.

10

When I get to the prepper room – that's what I call this part of the cellar for myself now, and it will have that function one of these days – Christine makes a scene. She says I've deliberately not come to see her for five days in order to "do her head in." That's the way she puts it.

"Why do you treat me like this? I haven't done anything. What have I done? Haven't I done everything you said?"

She's panting hysterically as I clip the carabiner hook to the neck-ring and frisk her for weapons.

It's clear to me what significance regularity and reliability have in the life of a prisoner. I have an above average capacity for empathy, even if Christine refuses to believe it. It has happened a few times before that I've left her by herself for two or three days, but there's always been a good reason for it. I've only done it when all other strategies for getting Christine to cooperate had failed. Over the last few days I simply didn't feel like going down to see her. First of all Elli and I spent the Sunday in the hotel as well and in the days that followed we were telephoning all the time, I went over to see her twice and next Monday she's going to have a tour of the Democracy Centre with her class. I'm head over heels in love. That's why I simply didn't feel like seeing Christine.

"What makes you think that everything has to revolve around you all the time?" I say irritatedly. "Perhaps I now and then have more important things to do than to sit around down here with you and listen to your prattling. You haven't much in the way of news anyway. And didn't you tell me not long ago, in your refreshingly open way, that you feel like screaming when I just touch you? So you should be glad when I'm not here."

"You've got another woman, haven't you? Why are you wearing your best shirt? There must be a reason. Come on, admit it – you've got another woman."

"Rubbish," I say. I've no desire at all to talk to her about Elli. "And even if I did, it's no business of yours."

"At least tell me the next time you're going to forget me for a few days. I don't know what's happened. I keep thinking you must have had an accident in the car and I'm going to starve to death down here by myself."

Christine's almost in tears now.

"That won't happen," I say. "That's why I deposited that statement with the lawyer."

So far she's always behaved as if she believed the story of the sealed envelope that is to save her life if the worst comes to the worst. Not today.

"You lying arsehole." She spits on the floor at my feet. "You really are a poor sod."

She says it in the tone of cold contempt she used the first time I hit her. This time I stay calm.

"There's something you've got quite wrong there," I say serenely. "You can't feel contempt for me. You can hate me and loathe me, but you can only feel contempt for people who are below you. It's simply impossible for you to despise someone when you're at their mercy, when your very survival depends on their goodwill."

"If you're not wrong about that," Christine says.

"Do you remember that newspaper questionnaire?" I reply – Oh, the good old *Frankfurter Allgemeine Zeitung* with its good old questionnaires in which philistine politicians always answered the questions about their favourite books and painters as if they were avid readers and spent hours every Sunday going round museums – "Do you remember how they all dutifully replied to the question, 'For which historical figure do you feel most contempt?' with 'Adolf Hitler'? It annoyed me even back then. I'm not saying you have to like the man, but contempt is simply the wrong word for someone who was powerful and dangerous."

"Do you think you're powerful and dangerous? Is that what you're saying? Perhaps I feel contempt for you because you feel you need to lock me up here so that you can feel powerful and dangerous," she replies waspishly.

"That's rubbish too," I say patiently. I'm feeling far too euphoric to let myself be provoked. "You could just as well feel sorry for a millionaire because he feels he needs to be a millionaire ."

"If he feels he needs it, then you can feel sorry for him for that," my wife insists.

"Whether I need it or not is not the question at issue. It's a simple fact that the basic difference between the sexes is that men are physically stronger. And once you no longer enjoy the protection of a society that's biased in favour of women, but we both face each other the way we happen to be made, then it's quite clear who's the boss round here."

"You don't even dare to risk that," Christine snaps. "You don't even have the guts to take me on unless I'm shackled to a chain. And you had to drug me before you could chain me up. Wow, what an achievement, really! Actually, do you know that poison's considered a typical woman's weapon?"

She stands there looking at me, arms folded. There's a glint in her eyes. Suddenly I desire her again. Who knows how long

I'm going to have her for?

"Okay then," I say, "you want a fight? Then let's see."

I go to the steel door, tap in the code, open the door wide, take the key for the steel collar off the hook and go back to Christine with it. She's staring at me open-mouthed.

"Keep still," I say.

She obediently leans her head to one side. I can see her arms trembling. She thinks she's tricked me and that now is her chance. I'm not aiming to hurt her but I do have to teach her a lesson. So that she'll finally understand. I gently undo the collar and carefully place the metal thing on the coffee table. Christine's standing in front of me, head bowed and rubbing her neck. I can almost see what's going on inside her head and clench my fists in anticipation. Throughout our married life she's insisted on baring her innermost thoughts and feelings to me, forced me to share her banal emotions, and now I know her inside and out, and I'm always one step ahead of her. She knows practically nothing about me.

She leaps at me with a hoarse cry. She's aiming for my neck, trying to bite my Adam's apple. Not a bad idea. But the impact of her body on mine is touchingly weak. I hit her on the chin with my fist, knocking her head to one side. Now at the latest she must realise that on the day when I supposedly lost control and hit her, I was actually very much in control of myself, in fact was very careful in the way I hit her. Now she knows the difference. She staggers, making a gurgling noise but, to my surprise, stays on her feet and tries to make a run for the open door, I kick her on the back of the knee. She falls down and I kneel with one leg on her back and pull her arms behind her. We're both panting, but neither of us shouts or even says anything at all. Christine tries to dig her fingernails in my hands and arms and since by now I'm fed up with all this, I let go of her wrists, grasp her head and hit it hard on the floor – twice, once with her forehead and once with her face. Now she is screaming. The second time there are smears of blood on the vinyl. Christine doesn't resist any more, not even when I drag her over to the chain. She just sits there, sobbing, while I put the collar back on, turn the key and take it out. I stroke her head comfortingly, then slowly stand up and walk calmly over to the security door, lock it, tap in the code again and hang the key for the steel collar on its hook.

"Sit down on the bed," I say and she gets up and sits down on the bed, like a puppet with no will of its own. I get a facecloth out of the cupboard and hold it under the sink tap. With the moist cloth I carefully wipe the blood off her nose and her burst lower lip.

"Open your mouth."

When I pull up her top lip with both thumbs, I see that her left front tooth is quite crooked. Half of the eyetooth beside it has broken off. I push the front tooth back into the right position. Christine moans softly.

"Get undressed," I say.

Is there anything more beautiful to see than a woman getting undressed? As Christine, head bowed, unbuttons her dress, I can feel my heart pumping the blood with regular powerful beats through my youthful, completely non-sclerotic and clot-free arteries, taking the joy of living and ruling with it to every single part of my body. There's no equality between men and women, there's just the victors and the vanquished.

Christine is sitting naked beside me on the side of the bed, eyes down, her trembling hands squeezed between her knees.

"Lie down on your stomach," I say.

She starts crying again. "No, please. I think I've got concussion."

Her voice is so soft I can hardly understand what she's saying.

"Lie down on you stomach."

I'm enjoying being cruel. This time Christine obeys without a word. I lie down heavily on top of her, fish around for a pillow to put under her hips, then fuck her, deliberately being rough, while she cries. Women are always asking you to show consideration – because they've got a headache, or because they feel the cold more or are slower or weaker. Even during an emergency at sea. Let me get into the lifeboat first, I'm a valuable woman. Why should the less well-equipped specimen of a species be given preferential treatment? Why should I show consideration for the fact that a person is physically weaker than me? That's just their evolutionary bad luck. Fate has allotted them their place – under my heel. Everything women do they can only do with the permission of us men. And if they can now make themselves at home in the government, the ambitious little minxes, then it's solely because no one's bothered to stop them. The fact that we've been treating women as people of equal value over recent decades is not a matter of course, it's just a quirk of our civilisation. Civilisation is not based on kindness or a sense of justice. A civilisation promotes the things that makes it stronger, that are of use to it. And allowing women to have a say in society only made sense while we still hoped that with their social skills, their sense of responsibility and all that sort of stuff, the women would get us out of this mess we're in. Since global warming has progressed in the worst way imaginable and we know that things are beyond remedy, there's no longer any reason to let women share power. Justice? Justice is something only the weak profit from. It would be really stupid of the strong to allow that. And the strong – in the coming years that's going to be the unscrupulous, crafty and aggressive guys, the ones who simply push their way to the front of the queue in the pharmacies to grab the last remaining Ephebos from under the noses of the others. And if I may venture a prediction: it won't be those wearing bicycle helmets who survive longest.

After I've had sex with Christine, I lie beside her for a while, my body pressed against her back. I stroke and comfort her. She stiffens in my arms.

I kiss Christine behind her ear. "You silly cow," I say. "Just now you need comforting, so accept it. You've got no choice, just me."

She stiffens even more. I stick my hand between her legs from behind and move it slowly to and fro until Christine starts to cry again. I carry on, increasing the pressure.

"You have to know how to lose," I say, still close to her ear. "You underestimated me but now you know better."

I penetrate her once more, but this time very gently and cautiously.

"Just be glad I still want you. Perhaps the day will come when I'm simply fed up with you. I bet you can't imagine that, eh?"

This time it's almost a quarter of an hour before I come and my mind keeps going back to Elli, with the result that I'm much more passionate and tender to Christine than she actually deserves. It becomes clear to me that I must give up the prepper room. No, not must – I want to give it up. The prepper room and Christine. For Elli. I want to start afresh. What is developing between us is something pure and sacred, something that must not be defiled.

11

Elli arrives at the information unit of the Democracy Centre with a group of twenty pupils. She's wearing black jeans again, biker boots with metal studs, almost like my brother's, and a parka with such an improbable green gloss it makes me think of the wing sheath of some tropical insect – one of those rare, particularly large and beautiful insects that are condemned to extinction. Though by now we all are of course. Johannes, the deputy director of the information service, takes her coat. He's a lanky, wimpish guy, with melancholy St Bernard eyes and a walrus moustache that's just come back into fashion. Johannes, however, has been wearing his for the last thirty years. When the Democracy Centre was set up he was briefly head of the information unit until it turned out that the forty per cent quota hadn't been reached in the distribution of managerial positions. He could have transferred to the management of the election committee, but even though he'd been jettisoned like that, he preferred to stay in the sphere where he'd suffered his humiliating loss of power.

Elli gives me a long, deliberately neutral look. With her thick android spectacles she looks incredibly sexy. Like the fantasy of a woman bookseller from the last century – you long to take off her glasses, undo her ponytail and, pressing her against shelves of genuine dusty books, rip off her high-necked blouse. A herd of grumpy-looking teenagers trot behind her into the lecture room. Although Elli told me she taught at a secondary school, I somehow always imagined she'd turn up with much younger kids. Funny little dwarfs, at most Binya's age, who hang on her lips, tug at her sleeve and squawk, "Frau Westphal, Frau Westphal," all the time.

But what we have lounging around on the terraced seating are arrogant young women with sharp little mouths, who keep checking their emails and dream of getting a million ebucks for their fashion blog. And petulant young men with garish woolly hats and the sparse beginnings of a patriarchal beard; they immediately scan my neck for swollen lymph glands. Although there are at most minimal protrusions to be seen, there's a contemptuous knowing twitch round their lips. For them I'm an old man, nothing but an old man pretending to be young. The fact that I take such a low dose of Ephebos that I look at most twice their age does nothing to appease them. It makes me an old man twice over. The true-young hate us bio-young because we're like them – only better: the same taut skin, the same fit and resilient body, but more gumption, more knowledge and, thanks to the so-called 'black pedagogy' of the last century, a greater sense of duty and of commitment. Since the arrival of Ephebo they're just awkward and financially less well-off versions of their extravagantly youthful parents. Why should a firm take on a chrono-young maladjusted idiot when they can have someone of the same age only educated, disciplined and experienced? Consequently our government, fanatics for justice as they are, immediately introduced another quota – at least fifty per cent of employees younger than chrono-thirty for new appointments and at least eighty per cent for jobs requiring qualifications – but it's not coming into effect until next year. Until then the younger generation will just have to keep on washing glasses.

I walk slowly over to Elli, shake her hand and welcome

her with businesslike politeness, the way the press adviser of the Democracy Committee would greet the person in charge of a group of visitors. Only when we release our hands do I let my little finger run over the back of her hand. She shows no reaction.

Anja's going to give the talk. Anja's thirty already, but at least chrono-thirty and therefore more favourably regarded by the pupils, even though she's dumpy and has acne. She's wearing a white animal-mood cap with black Dalmatian spots and the little ears are pointing at the audience in such an exaggerated way that would never occur to a genuine floppy-eared Dalmatian. Immediately two of the girls from Elli's class take out their ear-caps and put them on, showing Anja with their tiger's or sheep's ears that they are listening attentively. Anja gives a pleased smile and leans her podgy arms on the lectern.

She gets down to the topic straight away: "There are people who say that our Controlled Democracy is not what you can call real democracy."

Personally I think it's wrong to start straight out with the criticism if you want to get pupils to appreciate our new system of government, but then that's part of our new system: to allow mistakes, tolerate different approaches, to let incompetents mess things up.

"Because they claim it is part of a democracy that everyone has the right to present themselves as a candidate for election," she goes on. "Naturally freedom is an important aspect of a democracy – freedom, rule by majority, opposition, they are all doubtless important. But what a democracy needs above all are rules. Free speech? Certainly, but limits have to be imposed if it turns into hate speech or insults minorities. And the exercise of political power is restricted by the rule of law for good reason. Elected governments must abide by fundamental, civic and human rights – however large the majority was with which they won the election…"

The schoolkids sprawl on the benches, staring at the displays on their egosmarts without even pretending they're paying attention to Anja. Even the tiger and the sheep let their ears droop with boredom. Listen? Not them! Anything that demands just a minimum of concentration is repugnant to them. Acquiring knowledge, understanding correlations is something that went out with telling stories round the camp fire and making notes with a ballpoint. Why gather knowledge when all it takes is a quick question to their egosmart's voice recognition system to access much more detailed, more precise versions of that knowledge. What counts today is to have mastered the technique of getting to the knowledge. Knowledge itself is accessible at all times, for everyone. Therefore it's worthless.

So there they sit with their atrophied matchstick arms, their giant swiping thumbs and their inane half-open mouths, and think themselves so superior because they can deal with the Internet better than the generations before them having been plugged into it when they were still hardly more than babies.

Anja, used to her lecture being completely ignored, carries on regardless, giving the same talk, word for word, that she gave the last time, the time before that and goodness knows how many other times.

"I hope this background makes it clear that restrictions placed on the right to stand for election do not undermine our democracy but, rather, strengthen it. With that we have defused the greatest weak point – and by that I of course mean the greatest weak point besides the institutional shortcomings… the institutional shortcomings in dealing with long-term ecological dangers… which was, of course, the greatest problem with democracy…"

"Democracy wasn't a problem at all as long as women didn't have the vote." The voice comes from the back row. Well, well, one of them at least was listening. A typical back-row brat: short mohican strip on a poorly shaved head, military camouflage gear, a necklace of stones, bones and bits of plastic. Cautious laughter from a few boys and Anja loses the thread for a moment. I touch Elli's knee with mine, she keeps her eyes fixed on the lectern where Anja is fiddling with her printouts, leafing through them, blushing until she's found the right place.

"It is, of course, in the nature of things that it is the greediest and most undemocratic individuals who look for power," she goes on, "therefore it is not enough for people who want to become candidates to have to satisfy no other requirements than having the right address and a certain age. We have every reason to expect more from our future representatives, for example that their social skills, their sense of justice and responsibility should not be too far below the national average. If we restrict the right to stand for election to competent citizens alone…"

"Ecofascism," a skinny boy in a woolly hat shouts. His cap looks like a deerstalker, only it's been crocheted and has a pattern of yellow, green and white lozenges. His chin is fluffed with the downy beginnings of a patriarchal beard. His mates look up from their displays and laugh agreement. Anja is unperturbed. As I said, she's been giving this talk for four years and the points of criticism are always the same.

"It is possible that you are unaware that there were grounds for exclusion even before the democracy reform, for example compulsory confinement in a mental hospital. I think everyone can understand why people who have been diagnosed with severe psychological disabilities should not become politicians determining the fate of this country. Why then should people in whom such disabilities are present but have simply not yet been diagnosed, be allowed to contest the election? Does it not stand to reason that anyone who wants to exercise power in this country should first of all undergo a check on their mental health? What has it got to do with ecofascism if we ensure that those who in future determine the course of our state are not being recruited from that group of ambitious, not very caring people with criminal tendencies, who automatically seek power, but from various representative groups of the population?"

"Because they're all far too stupid and don't even want to do it."

The guy with the lozenge-pattern cap looks round for applause and once more gets snickers of approval from his mates. No respect for the argumentation, the brats. They just imagine they know everything better.

"Well if you don't like this system of selection which, moreover, is not unlike the one by which lay assessors have always been selected for courts, you always have the option of proposing people you think more competent. I assume you will have made full use of that possibility, given your active participation in our discussion here."

"As if there would be any point to that," says one of the thin-lipped girls. "As if you'd put forward anyone I proposed as a candidate."

There are four inflamed bumps on her forehead, where she's had something inserted under the skin. Probably semi-precious stones. I've seen that in Racke's elementary school teacher. Once the inflammation has died down, the skin is slit open and you can see the glitter. What on earth will these kids have done to themselves next?

"You're all welcome to download the brochure explaining our election system once we've finished," Anja says. "And if you don't believe me, you can read it there: fifty per cent of our election candidates come from suggestions made by the general public."

That, however, is not quite true or, to put it crudely, a downright lie. In the Democracy Committee we very quickly realised that it was a mistake to allow the general public simply to make direct proposals. But once that idea had been brought in, we could hardly rescind it. It gives people the feeling they're directly involved and seems tremendously democratic. But of course the proposals we get are mostly nonsense. Or people have been paid to propose someone. We accept all offers, recommendations and unreasonable suggestions and put them in a huge pile; then the interns make a preselection until there are just ten per cent left that are then reviewed by the voluntary workers, so that ultimately of the hundred thousand suggestions there are only thirty or forty left whom we actually invite and put through the test. And perhaps ten will get through that. We rely mainly on the ideas of the Nobel Committee and the major research institutes. What we are looking for are sufficiently competent and intelligent citizens with a certain authority and a clear mind; for a few candidates, for example when it's a question of electing the federal president, we also take charisma into account.

"Is it not a problem that the procedure by which you check candidates has been developed by someone or other? Does that not mean that they have a disproportionate influence on who will be federal chancellor? And what kind of people are they who are allowed to determine which test procedure is used?

Who has authorised them?"

A little eager beaver. A colourless face and undyed hair, nose piercing and ladybird tattoo on her bare lower arm. In my day she would have been wearing a pleated skirt and spectacles. The other girls look up briefly from their displays, glance at each other and roll their eyes. How uncool to show interest in this talk where attendance is compulsory.

"As I said: ecofascism," the boy with the lozenge-pattern cap says and at once the girls look more interested and a few of the other boys give an appreciative laugh. Anja clears her throat.

"When you say ecofascism you probably mean epistocracy? I can reassure you: it is exclusively the right to be a candidate for election that is reserved to competent citizens today. The right to vote has not been affected. Moreover the competence our candidates have to show they possess is not a matter of education but of character. The diagnostic instruments for that were developed some time ago in the economy and have been constantly improved since then; the PCL-R-R checklist is standard for the diagnosis of psychopathy and CCL is the established assessment tool for the early identification of people with unfavourable personality characteristics and low integrity."

Well done, Anja. Hit them with a few technical words and lippy challengers will go back to shuggling and griddling.

"Aha!" the lozenge-cap exclaims. "And what kind of bad personality characteristics will they be? Ambition? Is even ambition too much? And being young? Is that allowed, being young? Chrono-young?"

"A little ambition or greed are fine, but if these characteristics define your whole being, then you're out. The same goes for aggression, a noticeable propensity to take risks, a pronounced tendency to wheeling and dealing and underdeveloped social behaviour. There's no limit on youth and excessive self-assurance, so don't be shy, ask your friends, perhaps they'll propose you." She gets a few laughs.

"The aim is not to ascertain the presence of certain desired characteristics or to find the ideal chancellor or minister. What we do want is to exploit the diversity of society to the full and that is only possible if we also have the kind of people in government posts who do not regard political power as a prize to be won but as a burden to be borne. Only then will that part of society which, by its very nature, is capable of directing the whole, be in charge and the other part will be happy to trust and submit to it."

"And as far as competence requiring knowledge and training is concerned," I interject before lozenge-cap can get his 'ecofascism' in again, "our government has a board of advisers to support them."

"As well as that," Anja continues, "the government is controlled by our laws. The sole aim is to exclude behaviours that are damaging to society and to exclude from government posts the type of person that in the past has brought disaster and destruction down on humanity."

"How are you going to figure that out?"

"Oh, we'll figure it out, don't you worry."

"Ecofascism!"

Anja blushes and stares at her sheets of paper. I quickly step in.

"Your concern for the rule of law is very commendable," I say to the boy in the crocheted deerstalker, "but if there's anything we're living to regret, then it's not that we have restricted the supposedly precious freedom of democracy but that we naively believed in the self-regulation of politics and the economy. Admittedly it was only a small number of people whose character led them to destroy the environment in which we all live for short-term financial gain or who messed about with the complex life-support systems of this planet out of stupidity or carelessness. But this handful of unscrupulous operators was enough to bring about serious climatic change that might perhaps already have reached tipping point and which might well rob you, ladies and gentlemen, of your future. The democratic movement, which you find so ridiculous or call ecofascism, is an attempt to stop this process in time, if possible, and save your life. Not all environmental problems can be solved by the market, sometimes it takes a stronger state. You will hardly believe this, but only a few years ago there were, even in Germany, industrialists who, instead of using their resources for practical projects for the good of mankind, preferred to invest them in lobbying instead."

Now they're looking at me, somewhat sceptically but at least they've taken their eyes off their displays.

"If you believe a hunger for power and unregulated markets are actually such a wonderful thing, then you perhaps ought to ask yourself why, after the takeover of power by the 'Controlled Democracy' movement, so many top executives emigrated to the Islamic Confederation."

"But if someone sees what's behind your questions, surely they could lie to you. You can't do anything about that."

The ladybird tattoo.

Anja takes over. "Individuals displaying behaviours that are harmful to society are filtered out by means of an instrument that operationalises the diagnostic criteria in the form of a semi-structured interview."

Now they're all shuggling away like mad again. The children of the educated middle classes have always been quite easy to dominate with the power of complicated phraseology.

"We are on the lookout for superficial charm, the absence of nervousness, we test for the presence of feelings of remorse and guilt, the probability of suicide and so on and so forth. I'm sure that by now word about what we are testing for and how we do it will have got round. But we are constantly modifying our approach. And many deficiencies, for example the inability to learn from experience, cannot be concealed, even by people with a talent for acting."

"But that's totally unfair. It's not a man's fault if he can't do that. It could make him a good politician."

"Yes, exactly…"

General chatter. Anja looks for help in her dossier.

Some time later I'm sitting in the Democracy Centre café with Elli. The schoolkids are already on their way home. Elli's eating a salad with polka-dot champignons that look like little round fly agaric mushrooms; for myself I've ordered a creative drink and a lupin beastie-burger.

"Something wrong?" Elli asks. "You look totally pissed off."

"No. But recently I've come to understand Islamic Root better and better. It must be nice to live in a society in which you're allowed to mete out punishment immediately to anyone who talks crap. On the spot, out in the street, a clip round the ear, left and right. That must be profoundly satisfying."

Elle raises her eyebrows but can't help smiling. "You mustn't be too hard on them. What's in store for them is too big and too bad. So they're in denial about it, and that's when they get stroppy."

"They're too soft," I say, "they've been spoilt. At least in the old days young people knew they were stupid, but this lot of slowcoaches even think they're superior. They think they're the new version of humanity with their implants and earplugs and their three thousand Facebook friends."

Oh I know, nothing makes you look older than complaining about the youth of today, but the inferiority of this generation is so evident that I'm surprised they can't see it themselves.

"It's not called Facebook now," Elli says.

"If these prats think I'm going to smile and give up my job for them, they've got another thing coming. We belong to the generation with a high birthrate, thank God, and as long as our democracy continues to function more or less, we'll always be the ones who call the tune. And if we decide to have a good time at their cost, they'll just have to put up with it."

"I hope you don't mean that seriously?"

"I'm just saying what the situation is, not that it's fair. Anyway, we've been working our guts out and paying for all the others for long enough – first the pensions for the generation that reduced Europe to rubble and now the unemployment benefit for the chrono-young who, so we're told, will see to it that we get cared for in our old age. And then we have to listen to lectures from them telling us how nauseating we are with the youth we've acquired through chemicals and that we're taking their jobs when we refuse to retire. As if you could call the pittance we're offered a pension."

"Can't you understand the anger of the true-young? What's left to them if they haven't got their youth to gloat over? It's not that bad for the girls, they'll get by one way or the other, but the boys really are in a bad way. They're totally at a loss. The ministry of education is making us give them one development programme after another: de-escalation training, emotional-competence training… next week it's 'Pride and Politeness'. Now even saying 'Good morning' when they go for a job interview is beyond them."

"Have you ever asked yourself what would happen if your development programmes were successful and these grubby little dropouts got somewhere with your help? What would these guys do if they were in the government? Their first official act would be to throw the women, who'd supported them and helped them get the post, out of the ministries and send them back into the kitchen – assuming they didn't decide to make them wear veils first. I have to admit I'm moved by the way you've staunchly stood by us men, no matter how much we betray your interests. But I'm not sure whether I think that's very sensible."

"It's very straightforward. Education is the task I've been given. I take it seriously and it concerns everyone in the class including the boys, even those who swap Islamist collector cards under their desks."

"But it must be clear to you that you're giving this support to precisely the guys who, if the situation were reversed, would be saying, 'If you're not up to it you've no business being at the high school.' They'd rather take it as a reason to exclude girls from advanced secondary education entirely. Just the way it used to be."

"But if we provide a good place in society for them it will no longer be necessary for them to exclude women from anything."

"Perhaps we men denied you access to the universities precisely because we knew what would happen: hardly have you been allowed to study there than you're swotting away until you leave all the lads behind you and rob them of their last vestiges of self-confidence. Had we been sure you wouldn't make it, we wouldn't have needed to ban you from going to university at all. Things would have sorted themselves out."

True, I'm laying it on a bit thick but that's a sure-fire way of winning over a woman with feminist leanings – and which woman isn't like that today? Self-incrimination à la Mao.

"But that's just what you did yourself," Elli says. "With your work for the Feminist Democracy Committee you campaigned for more women in politics. I very much admire the way you put the general good above your own interests and have been happy with a place in the second rank. Not many would have been capable of that."

"Hmm," I say, "to be honest back then it wasn't so clear to me that the new form of government might be contrary to my own interests. For me it wasn't a matter of women and men. We were simply a bunch of people who were concerned about the environment and wanted to see the food and resources of this world fairly distributed."

"What are you trying to say? Surely you're not saying you regret it?"

"No. Well… I still think the idea's okay, but at the time it just wasn't clear to me what feminist democracy does to a man. I didn't realise that the end result would be to be forced to give up my masculinity bit by bit. This eternal jabber. I had the choice of either exposing myself to it constantly or simply giving way, and more and more I simply gave way. Eventually there wasn't much left of the man I used to be. That's why I've gone over to working from home as much as possible."

Elli looks at me, slightly confused and concerned. I'm already starting to worry that I've revealed too much of myself. But then she strokes my face, leaving her hand on my cheek, and I go all soft and gentle inside.

"I can't go on with it any longer," I say, "I can't go on fighting any longer."

'What would you like to do, then?"

“Oh, I don’t want to do anything any more. I’ve done too much already. Before the world comes to an end I want to feel what it’s like when someone holds me dear again.”

“Don’t worry,” Elli says. “I’ll see to that. I’ll hold you dear.”

12

When I open my eyes there's a bright orange poppy in bloom a few inches in front of my face. My father forced me to have that wallpaper years ago: "Orange. That's a cheerful colour." For myself I'd wanted to paint my room dark brown, the ceiling as well. When I reconstructed the room four years ago I briefly wondered whether, for a change, I shouldn't do it the way I'd wanted back then – in a 'shoe-box from inside' style – as a belated act of rebellion. But I'm a purist after all and I decided on historical precision again.

There's a pattern of shadows drifting down over the poppy wall paper; it spreads, tears apart then comes back together again. When I roll over onto the other side I see that the rain's running down the windowpanes in long streaks. For a moment it's the way it always is when I wake up: I feel bleary, a bit grumpy, disappointed with life but, all things considered, not entirely discontented. Then it occurs to me that life is great because I'm together with Elli now. That's why I'm now lying in the old bed I had as a teenager – because Elli dropped by briefly. I usually sleep in my parents' old bedroom where the bed is much wider, but it would have felt strange to have sex with Elli in it. Elli! It's as if Fate wanted to apologise to me: I'm really sorry that your life's been rubbish so far, Sebastian, a steep, stony path through the bone-dry valley of loss and constant pressure only for it to turn out in the end that all your efforts have been in vain. But even you are not going to come away completely empty-handed. Actually a second chance isn't in the scenario, but you know what, for you, just for you I'm going to make an exception. Don't mess it up this time.

If there is any possibility at all of being happy, then it's having the dreams and longings of your youth fulfilled. I can start a new life with Elli, become a different, better person – no, not different but the good, idealistic man full of hope that I used to be. Elli left in the middle of the night – because of a cat with dementia that's waiting for her at home. I could strangle the beast. What I'd most like to do would be to ring her up straightaway, but that might make me seem desperate. If she misses me, she can give me a buzz or a quent. It's a good thing I haven't deregistered my egosmart. I just have to get through the long Sunday somehow or other.

I take a long, hot shower until I'm wreathed in misty clouds and steaming myself and the softened rubber curtain is sticking to my backside. Then I give my teeth a thorough clean, taking my time over it so that I can feel every stroke of the brush on my gums. I take a two-thirds dose of Ephebo and put a shrink-wrapped double row of tablets for Christine on the rim of the wash basin. I have to start giving her some Ephebos again – you can tell from the way she looks that I've made her stop for a week. I didn't realise it happens so quickly. But you can already see the effect on me of having taken the full dose for the last seven days. Early thirties, now I look as if I'm in my early thirties – or at worst in my mid-thirties. In order to express the euphoria I feel, I put on my favourite shirt. The favourite shirt isn't really navy blue any longer, it's rather greyish and scrumpled. The edges of the cuffs are worn and the narrow collar went out of fashion ages ago. I'll have to buy some new things, shirts and, above all, underpants, almost all my old ones have holes in them. That will help me pass the time until the evening. Perhaps I'll buy myself a new pair of jeans as well. I briefly think about buying myself a pair of animal-mood trousers but they would look ridiculous on a bio-mid-thirties man. Even my face looks a bit scrumpled, dammit. Despite the full dose of Ephs I've been taking over the last few days. What will I look like now if I go back to two-thirds. After a brief hesitation I go back into the bathroom and take one of the tablets I'd put aside for Christine. One more day on a lower dose won't kill her and no one sees her apart from me anyway.

It's pouring down outside. I pull the hood of my waxed jacket up over my head and run to my little hydrogen runabout. Shallow streams are meandering across the garden. The ground is completely dried out but baked so hard it scarcely absorbs any water. The streams are a dirty yellow from all the dust and pollen. That's another level of drought: so much dust that even the rainwater doesn't look fresh. But we humans don't deserve anything better. People knew what was coming but they just called it 'a natural climate cycle' and decided not to do anything.

When I get to the Ford I'm already drenched through. Once I'm in it, the windows immediately mist over. I wipe the water off my face, switch on the fan and select driver mode. I'm not so decrepit that I have to let my car drive me to the Alstertal Shopping Centre. The windscreen wipers sweep the curtain of water aside but another immediately covers the screen. At snail's pace I turn into the Redderkamp that's flooded ankle-deep. The brown sludge is pouring towards me and a miniature whirlpool has started in the drain. I can't help it, but the end of the world is fun. At least it still is at this point. And here in Wellingstedt. It will be different, of course, if you live in Bangladesh.

As every Sunday the shopping centre is jam-packed. I snap up the last parking space from under the nose of a dilatory Poppenbüttel housewife in her small stupid egg-shaped electric car. I can remember how at school we were given the task of drawing the car of the future and we all without exception drew these egg-shaped, drag-free crates you see everywhere nowadays. That was fifty-eight years ago. Why has it taken the engineers fifty-eight years to develop a car shape that occurred to every twelve-year-old during a double art lesson? There's one of these eggs in almost every parking space. I wonder what all these people are looking for here, given that there are hardly any shops in the centre that cater for your everyday needs any more. The only supermarket has been banished to the basement and the greengrocer makes splendid pyramids of waxed oranges and has polished cherries in wooden designer boxes, but he's so expensive you buy the cherries by the piece. Hardware store and cobbler's? – no way. Instead you're surrounded by the most with-it clothes shops and others full of the most stupid trash where you can buy the fetishes of an upmarket life either incredibly cheaply – 'Well-I-Never' – or absurdly expensively – 'Alstertal Interiors': tin or wooden lamps of every shape and size, paper napkins, owls, pigs, old-fashioned clothes hooks, candlesticks with rhinestones implanted by the hands of Asian children.

Whole families, dressed up as if they were going to the theatre, are strolling round, doing what in previous times used to be a tedious task – shopping – as recreation. Buy, buy, buy as long as the planet has some last resources left that can be turned into tasteless crap decorations or a technical gimmick no one needs. Any squirrel that buries its nuts in the autumn so that it'll have something to eat through the winter is making better provision than humanity. On the other hand it is, of course, very interesting to get an idea of the degree of degeneration that we've reached by now. At the baker's the size of the cakes has reached new dimensions: you need both hands to eat one of these rum truffles. As if there weren't enough obese children already. And normal-size Viennese whirls, that is Viennese whirls that were normal ten or twenty years ago, are now sold as 'minis': three minis for one westo. Amazingly the two bookshops are both still there, though the window displays are more or less interchangeable. Nothing but crime novels: women's crime novels, environmental crime novels, fish crime novels – and books about cancer: 'Swan Song – How Ephebo Destroyed my Life'. Dreadful, who wants to read that kind of thing? And that right next to the Alster Pharmacy that is advertising that very medicine in block letters: YOU CAN'T ROLL BACK THE YEARS? OH YES YOU CAN! WITH EPHEBO!

Given the meaning this slogan has acquired for me, I'm overcome with a wave of profound gratitude for the pharmaceutical industry and their scientists who, after thousands and thousands of probably cruel experiments on animals, sussed out the ageing process. What clever clogs we human beings are!

In the shop window there's a diorama of the fountain of youth. The back of the display consists of a two-dimensional plywood landscape with rocks and hills, castles and towers, with trees and a group in Renaissance dress feasting. In front of them a square basin has been let into the floor with two steps going into it all round and a fountain in the middle. The old women are carted along on wheelbarrows, litters and the backs of horses; they're all about the size of a Barbie doll, dressed in the style of a century that is long gone – that is when they aren't already naked – and are astonishingly lifelike. Every single wrinkle, every potbelly and every sagging bosom has been created in loving detail. In the basin itself bio-thirty-somethings are splashing about and on the right-hand side young girls are climbing out of the water. I'm not the only man with his nose pressed against the glass.

"Hey, you old voyeur."

God help me, it's Ingo Dresen. Unmistakably Ingo Dresen. His greasy red biker's mane and fat, brutal face in which his innate nastiness is manifest. Moreover he's wearing that denim jacket again. I make every effort not to look too horrified.

"Ingo… oh hi…"

"What nonsense it is actually advertising Eph here. They're making a killing anyway."

I wish they wouldn't hand out any Ephebo at all to people like Ingo Dresen. Without the stuff he'd be over seventy by now, a grandpa, and with all his boozing probably in a care home, incontinent, with dementia or even already dead. Already dead would be best. Even as a care-home case Ingo Dresen would still be frightening. But here he is, standing in front of me, fit as a fiddle. Awful.

"I've seen worse," I say. "It could be the Old Bridge in Mostar in ruins to remind you of fallen arches. The pharmacy probably simply had the display done out of gratitude."

"The best window display I ever saw was somewhere on the Gänsemarkt," Ingo says. "Pod-something – looking after your feet. And in the window display there were these thick brown toenails, real big ones. Did you happen to see it? It must have been back in the eighties."

I did in fact see it. There was a sign: "Ingrowing toenails we have removed" and beside it the horror – corkscrew-like objects as thick as your finger. But you couldn't help looking at them every time you passed.

"Nah," I say, "never saw it."

"Well it was there," Ingo insists, "on the Gänsemarkt. That's where we hold our rallies."

I just nod and mutter, "Uh-huh." I certainly don't want to know what kind of rallies these are.

"Why haven't you come to our meetings?" Suddenly his tone is harsh and tetchy. "I was counting on you. Why did you say you'd come if you're not going to. You have to show more respect, man."

"I've met someone," I say. It just slipped out. It's the strain of facing Ingo Dresen. Actually I don't want to tell people about Elli, and certainly not Ingo Dresen.

"I've met this woman and it's made me forget just about everything."

I hate myself for saying that. I hate myself for trying to placate Ingo Dresen with an inane smile. But at least it works. Cowardice is shameful but it's healthy.

"We've joined up with MASCULO now," Ingo growls. "We'll get nowhere if we all muddle along on our own. There's something big in the making – action on a broad front, you understand?"

I nod and mumble my agreement. "Oh yes, on a broad front, say no more."

"What d'you mean, say no more? You've no idea. What's coming is going to be bigger than Islamic Root."

I shrug my shoulders and smile inanely again. I just have to avoid saying the wrong thing. I've already heard of MASCULO but always assumed it was an association for frustrated male victims of divorce. I'd no idea people like Ingo Dresen were involved.

"I'll tell you about it," Ingo says patronisingly. "We'll go in there, you'll buy me a drink and I'll tell you about it."

He points to the Starbucks with the coffee lounge in the middle of the concourse. His sleeve slips back, revealing a tattoo: leaves, flowers and creepers with their stalks coming out of the eyeholes of a skull, a lot of green. Ingo sees me looking and pushes his sleeve up farther, revealing a whole pullover of tattoos, a jungle with Jane and Tarzan and Cheetah in it. The he puts his arm round my shoulders and steers me over to Starbucks. What on earth does he want? I don't know who he takes me for. A former friend? I was never his friend. Unless he feels he's on friendly terms with those he used to tyrannise and beat up, that is.

We get coffee and a glass of wine for Ingo. They don't sell beer. Even the wine they're not supposed to serve until after 5.00pm. "See what things have come to," Ingo Dresen says, shaking his head. "In the old days we had sex, drugs and rock 'n' roll and now they won't even let you smoke in a pub."

He lights up. No one complains and we head for a group of chairs in white leather. Even though the place is crammed and there are people there already, within a few minutes we have plenty of empty space round us. The effect of Ingo Dresen is like a drop of vinegar in a bowl of oil. I would quite enjoy the situation – being part of a focal point spreading fear and terror all round is somehow flattering – if I weren't so afraid of Ingo Dresen myself.

"Everything's forbidden nowadays," he moans, "and then quotas for women and keeping an upper limit on lottery prizes in order to increase the lesser prizes instead. It makes me sick. Are you going to put up with all that?"

"Well," I say, "what can we do?"

"Shall I tell you something," Ingo Dresen says. "Men are accepting things they think they deserve."

"Aha..."

"Society?" Ingo Dresen says. "Society, what's that when it's at home? A few people who've come to an agreement about what's allowed and what isn't. And not a hundred miles away the arrangements look quite different."

On the opposite side three men are sitting round a bistro table, owners of small businesses or local politicians, that kind of thing, guys who like no one apart from themselves and who want to make their contribution to the end of the world. A business lunch. The prospect of a stay in some stuffy health spa. A risk assessment cancelled and the – let's say – methane leak in Hummelsbüttel is okay for the next two years.

"If you don't have the bottle to defend yourself, you don't deserve to survive as a civilisation," Ingo goes on. "I don't believe in words, I believe in force. Islamic Root – I can't stand those muftis but at least they know what they want. They don't bother with kid's stuff, they go and blow up the Cheops Pyramids and Europe starts squealing."

"That was really shitty," I say. "Those pyramids had stood for thousands of years and now they're gone."

"Yes, that's why," Ingo Dresen says, "and now there'll be something new. And the way the stupid culture vultures all over the world were whining and moaning about an old gold mask!"

I'm desperately looking for a plausible excuse so I can finally get away.

"We can learn discipline from Islamic Root. Rituals, prayers and so on. The re-establishment of traditional morality. Rules! That kind of thing strengthens the cohesion of a group."

Ingo's opinion is that it's because of the femi-nazis, the feminist mob, that men aren't seen as men any more. And he apparently sees me as a real man, at least that's what he says, though with the best will in the world I can't believe he really means it. A real man who deserves better. Deserves better? Better than what? Ingo Dresen reminds me of the inner potential I still possess. Since when has he been talking like that?

"You're not the money you have in some bank account or other," he says, "and you're not the sissyish car you drive and certainly not the bloody job that squeezes you dry. You are you! You only have to rediscover your own strength and rage! Did you know that by now almost ten per cent of shares are in women's hands?"

Where's all this leading? Could it be that the Fat Rats have turned into another religious sect? Have they found a faith for people who are keen on violence and are looking for a religious superstructure to go with it?

"You have the power to control your own life," Ingo urges me, "and to make history change its course. You mustn't wait until you get a fatal disease to finally do what you've always wanted to do."

I nod nervously, envying the people walking past at a safe distance of at least ten feet. Hundreds of people, all of whom can clear off while I, of all people, have to sit here with Ingo Dresen.

"We have to develop a consciousness for our own history and our own values. What's happening here is a radical feminist attack on our values – and that when our history is a history of men, not the 'herstory' the femi-nazis keep going on about. Wc built all this. We – you understand? And we're not going to let it be taken away from us unresisting."

It's not very clear to me what he's driving at, but by and large what he seems to be saying is that men are the more important sex and women actually superfluous. With a vitriolic stare he follows the legs of a bio-thirty-year-old woman in a tulip skirt walking past surprisingly close to our table before continuing his rant.

"The growing strength of feminism has set off the decline of the nation. The cunts are pulling out all the stops. Have you had a look at GQ or Men's Beauty? What kind of a world is it in which magazines expect men to be beautiful? That's psychological warfare against men, I tell you. And if they can't screw you up with that, they report you for sexual harassment. There's not a man in the country who still believes in justice."

I can understand Ingo's anger. It's typical that a brutal, criminal tub of lard like him, who takes up and discards women at will, should feel unhappy and humiliated in this thoroughly feminised society. But does he have to go on about it like this? When I listen to him I'm almost embarrassed at my own convictions. I don't want to agree with Ingo Dresen even on the odd minor point.

"Feminism has destroyed the defensive strength of the Christian-European stronghold from within. Since the women's libbers have been able to decide for themselves whether they want to have children or not Europe has become an open gate for the Muslim population offensive."

I'm being worked on, there's no doubt that his aim is to recruit me for something. How can one give someone like Ingo Dresen a polite refusal?

"We've got great plans and you can be part of them. We need people like you. You're still at the Democracy Centre, aren't you? A broad-front strategy, you understand? We're warriors but we've even got people in the government. That's why I know that Olaf Scholz is going to resign this year. Supposedly for reasons of age – but since when do people resign for reasons of age? In reality he's just going to free up the position for a woman, of course. They want to get their claws on the office of chancellor again and then we'll be surrounded by femi-nazis and men will just be treated like doormats."

"Oh come on," I say.

The man should be on the psychiatrist's couch. It's bad when such an aggressive disposition falls prey to conspiracy theories. And I've no desire for revolution anyway. I'm quite happy with things the way they are. I don't want to get worked up any more. Not about femi-nazis nor about the catastrophe with the climate. I don't even want to get worked up about the mini Vienna whirls. I think we should go on as we have been. Go on just as we have been and then go out in a blaze of glory. We've had a good time. And the next five years will be the best of all for me. And then that will be it. Lived happy, died in peace.

"So what next?" I ask out of politeness.

"What d'you mean… next?"

"How will things go on – after the revolution or whatever you have in mind?"

Ingo Dresen fishes round and pulls a chain with a gold crucifix out of his shirt and hairy chest and kisses the Christ on the cross. "National Catholicism. But first of all the big towns will have to be uprooted and the men return to their natural way of life: chopping wood, paddling a canoe, sleeping in a hut and crapping out in the woods. Does Torau mean anything to you?"

"Torau?"

"Torau! He lived like that and wrote a book about it. You must read it. And then when we come back to the towns there'll be values again, decency. No mingling with other ethnic groups and religions, and the banks have to be taken back out of the hands of the women and the Jews. We'll re-establish patriarchal structures and make male superiority the basis of the law. For example the father will automatically be given custody of the children. We will set limits for acceptable and unacceptable behaviour, and the women will know where their place is again."

He's gone quite red in the face. With his fat paunch he looks like a lump of plasticine. He gives me another of the postcard-size visiting cards. This time it shows a sheep with its throat cut. 'Protecting animals is protecting our homeland' is written underneath. 'Against the cruel slaughtering of non-stunned animals in the grounds of the former Hamburg abattoir.'

"Right," he says, "now I'm desperate for a pee. So long, old man. If you miss the meeting again I'll really take it amiss, so pull yourself together."

He stomps off, much to my relief.

13

"I don't believe it," Elli says. "Did you open them specially for me? But the nuts won't be edible any more. How old is that?"

She's talking about the original box of TV Snax that's at least forty years old. I've put it on the coffee table to evoke the television mood of a bygone age.

"Don't worry," I say, "I bought the nuts just now from Aldi and Zasko."

"Oh, that's great, that really is great. Are they vegan? If those are the ones from Zasko, then they will be vegan."

I've invited Elli round for an evening's television because from what she said she hardly watches any at all. I'm doing a bit of proselytising, trying to get her to appreciate the charm of the hopelessly out-of-date medium.

"With its systematic presentation of six different nut specialities in six golden compartments," I say in a lecturing tone, "TV Snax represents the well-structured order and quality of the television of those days, if not the well-structured order and quality of the whole of society in those days."

Elli is about to shove a chocolate-covered almond behind her broad, white teeth – that are unfortunately rather short from her grinding them in her sleep – but I give her a light slap on the fingers. "Only once the programme's started."

Obediently Elli replaces the almond, sits down beside me on the sofa and leans on my shoulder.

"You seriously want to watch television with me now, yes?"

I nod and programme the remote control to ignore stations 22 to 288. The remote and the screen are some of the few things in my house that don't obviously come from the last century. On account of the compunicator functions, if nothing else. At least I've chosen a retro model for the remote – it even has buttons to press. In theory you can even use it like an old remote control.

"We could have sex instead or download the latest Birdy Russell film," Elli says. "We could see any film – whichever we want. We could do whatever we like… Why do you want to watch television of all things?"

"That's the good thing about the TV schedule: you don't select what you want to see yourself but happily consume what is on offer, zap through a manageable selection and don't moan about what you feel like viewing at the moment not being available. If you always watch things you've selected yourself, with time your horizon becomes more and more limited. That's why your pupils are so desperately ignorant. In theory the whole of human knowledge is available to them but in practice they have no idea what they should be looking for because they always click on the things they already know."

"Shuggle," Elli said, "they say shuggle now."

"Whatever. You need information you haven't ordered yourself."

"And if there's only rubbish on now?"

"The important thing isn't just what's on the TV but who's sitting watching. I've had some of my very best ideas while watching the very worst programmes."

I shuggle the remote control onto Elli's smart watch, switch on the receiver and compunicator screen.

"Those were the days when the television simply went on when you pressed a single button," I can't resist saying.

"Oh yes, and when there was only one currency," says Elli, trying to wind me up as she wriggles her right leg in between my back and the sofa.

"Off we go then," I say, grabbing her right foot behind my back and pulling it out the other side. I keep hold of it.

"What shall we have? The news?"

"If you like. Anything – we'll watch and see what it does to us."

With Elli I could even watch the world disintegrating and enjoy it. Unfortunately what she gets is the O-TV nature-film channel. I've nothing against animal films, but Oligarcho TV is that Russian channel that makes second-class documentaries and peps them up with strippers. The kind of thing you prefer to watch on your own.

"Okay," I say, "you can switch that off if you like."

"No," Elli says, pouting in a very sweet display of defiance, "no, I'm going to watch this and see what it does to me. May I have a nut now?"

"Of course. As many as you like."

I put my arm round her shoulder and we watch the Oligarcho camera team laying out a dead kangaroo as bait.

And there's the first stripper emerging from the bushes.

"Hey, Candy, d'you think you could do a strip for us while we're waiting for the Tasmanian devils?"

"But of course, Joe. I've been waiting two hours to show what I've got."

Candy starts wriggling out of her mesh shirt, waggling her breasts at the camera all the time. I clear my throat. Elli laughs.

"Well? What do I learn from that?"

"Switch over to something else," I say, taking a handful of nuts.

Elli pretends she's completely spellbound by the striptease

show. By now Candy has her shirt off and is pressing her huge breasts with their ugly long nipples against the camera lens. At the same time there are news items running uninterruptedly across the top and bottom of the screen, sport above, share prices below, interrupted by adverts for water purification powder and chrono-young part-time workers – The Future Team. Elli looks at me and grins.

"I'll tell you what you're learning from that," I say, giving her foot a squeeze. "In all that you can see the principle that has led to the decline of civilisation. Why everything's going to the dogs."

"What am I learning it from," Elli says, "from the stripper or the Tasmanian devils?"

"From the way quite ordinary animal films have changed over the years. When I was a boy it was enough to flush out a few moth-eaten lions and leopards, to show how they hunt and fight and bring up their cubs to get us glued to the screen. But at some point or other that wasn't enough. There had to be more and more, just as with the constant increase in economic growth. The sharks and lions and crocodiles had to be tearing their prey apart on camera or having sex or getting drunk on fermenting fruits. Then there came the point where it wasn't enough just to show the crowned crane doing its courtship dance, no, it had to take place against the backdrop of an unnaturally bloodshot sunset with two hundred thousand wild geese flying past. Then eventually that wasn't enough any more and the birds flying past had to be forced into a heart-shaped formation by an image-editing programme and now it has to be presented by some idiot B-list celebrity or Candy has to take her bikini off before the Tasmanian devils appear."

Although Elli likes to pull my leg a bit for the way I cling to the past, she is still suitably impressed. She looks at me with that expression of true admiration you very rarely see in women nowadays.

She told me recently that her father had shown no interest in her whatsoever, had completely ignored her. That could well be the reason she's so receptive to male instruction. She sees it as attention being paid to her and is correspondingly grateful. Nowadays, however, when the girls get every kind of encouragement and recognition and are praised for any crap they produce, when even the worst at sport get a certificate of merit and the career women are handing out the best jobs to each other, female admiration for male knowledge is naturally becoming a thing of the past. By now the insufferable little hussies are bursting with self-confidence. I can even see it in Binya Bathsheba. Grandma Gerda's given her that 'Tough Teens' gridlet, the sole aim of which is to get girls to like themselves – whether they have any reason to or not. I shall have to start doing something about that if Binya's to grow up to be a pleasant young woman, capable of admiration. As a single parent I'm in a position to see to that myself. Pay little attention to her, now and then drop a disparaging remark about her appearance or her weight… Rejection is the magic word. So that one day she'll… One day? What do I mean by one day? Love obviously affects your brain. Since I've been together with Elli I keep finding myself thinking that things might not be quite as bad as the climatologists predict. Or that we at least have a bit more than the five years they've calculated before everything goes to wrack and ruin here. It's simply too wonderful with her for me to contemplate giving it up. Has science not been wrong often enough before? Suddenly I can understand all the idiots with their undying hope that things might turn out all right despite everything, that technology might still drag us out of the mess, that something might be invented that will make the ocean currents start flowing again at the eleventh hour. To make a correct assessment of a hopeless situation you mustn't be too happy. You clearly need to be properly depressed for that.

Candy has put her khaki hot pants and mesh shirt back on and the Tasmanian devils have reduced the kangaroo to a skeleton in no time at all. Now Candy's in a jeep with her friend Natasha heading for a marsh with some terrapins. And of course they get stuck in the mud and Natasha has to get out and push, then Natasha takes over the wheel and Candy pushes. Because it's so hot, they both strip to the waist and because they're wearing high heels they keep falling in the mud. Elli laughs so much she's almost falling off the sofa.

"Whee! TV's really great!"

"You see what I mean? The animals aren't the interesting thing about animal programmes any more. The true-young lack curiosity. If you can choose between an infinite number of films on offer, then you'll always select the ones with the strongest effect and in the long run that will always be sex and violence. Even TV has adapted to that. What you can see here isn't proper television but basically a copy of the Internet."

"The Internet!" Elli says, wiping away the tears of laughter. "I like the quaint, old-fashioned way you talk, you're not desperately trying to sound young."

I haven't told her that I've increased my dose of Ephebo. She doesn't seem to have noticed either my physical change nor my new clothes. Mortifying, actually.

"My young years were the days of cassette recorders, televisions and pocket calculators. And if you ask me, they could well have left it at that."

"Oh, come on now," Elli says, "you don't need to pretend

you're that old." But at least she's reasonable enough to switch channels. An advert for equipment for prepper rooms and non-perishable crispbread, then the news: Twenty-four refugees shot on the Hungarian wall, at least six hundred drowned in the English Channel, the formal opening of the Pleistocene Park in eastern Siberia, where fifty mammoths bred from old DNA are to stamp the permafrost to keep it firm and slow down the release of methane into the atmosphere; the female trade and industry minister announces Frugality Week.

"I don't want to live in these times," I say, "I'd like to live in the past. In the distant past. I hate the present."

"That sticks out a mile," Elli says, "but you can't bring back the past, not even with a rotary-dial telephone."

"The telephone's my litmus test," I reply. "I'm firmly convinced that in life one should have enough free time that it's possible to work with a dial telephone. If that's not possible, if you haven't got the half minute it takes to dial a number, then there's something terribly wrong with life."

Elli blithely zaps through the channels. Donald Duck, still in his sailor suit but now with manga eyes, is running after Daisy, wielding a cudgel; pathologists are snipping the nails of a corpse and collecting them in a little bag; a smoothly polished loving couple are kissing in front of a Black Forest waterfall; then another waterfall, a different waterfall with a naked man in the lotus position meditating beside it: "Insecure? Despairing? In fear of what the future will bring? It's still not too late. Experience moments of contemplation and spirituality in the five-star Yellow Monks Resort. Look forward now to your reward after death."

Eventually we get hooked on that talk show with the incredibly stupid but really pretty and, above all, chrono-young presenter. She's got one of those science fiction hairstyles, hair down to her chin and white with thick strands of black. Three of her guests I've never seen before but that actor's there, of course, the one they're all mad about, an unsavoury individual, bio-thirty with long, matted hair and a manic look in his eyes. He's best known for bawling people out. During the last shoot he almost strangled the director. But the culture journalists are delighted with him and take his outbursts as an infallible sign that they're dealing with a genius. You really wonder what goes on inside their tiny android-bespectacled, arts-section heads. They probably imagine he's a free spirit, unconcerned about what other people think, with the guts to do things they'd never dare.

The other character I recognise is Johannes Bartenboom, one of the various vice presidents of the German Farmers' Union. One glance at his ugly mug is enough: arrogance, blind assurance, aggression and almost no lips at all. Even though he's treated himself to a bio-rejuvenation (he must be well over eighty but passes for forty) the distortions of a malevolent, self-interested and domineering nature have left their mark on his face. Actually nowadays you only see guys such as him in the films of the fifties of the last century, and that is in those that are now only allowed to be shown after a cautionary statement before the opening credits: 'The opinions expressed in this film do not reflect the opinions of the supplier and should be seen as a product of their times, which were times full of prejudice against people belonging to other ethnic groups, the opposite sex or different income brackets.'

Bartenboom is just explaining that the turn-around in agriculture has once again failed, in particular because, in his opinion, it's merely a campaign to stir up discontent and to allow female politicians to take up a stance. In his opinion it is the lack of trust in agriculture that causes the greatest damage.

For years now the man has been plying the consumer with disinformation.

"Can you give me a single realistic alternative to genetically modified rape?" he snarls at the presenter. "Your vague criticism of modernisation completely ignores reality."

"That man would chop up the last nightingale and the last marsh orchid and feed them to his pigs if there were one or two westos more in it for him," Elli says.

With the stupidity of youth the presenter makes one more attempt, "But surely you can't deny that the recent floods had something to do with climate change caused by the emission of CO_2 for which modern agriculture is partly responsible."

Of course he can. Bartenboom is a beast of prey who can lie to your face without moving a muscle and has no sense of guilt or remorse. Because of the way he constantly fixes his eyes on those of his opponents, he has retained an unnaturally smooth, wrinkle-free zone around his icy blue eyes.

"My dear child, are you clear about the damage you can cause with that kind of scaremongering? You don't have to accept everything the Greens want to talk you into believing. The floods are the result of straightened watercourses and surfaces sealed with asphalt."

The camera focuses on the unsavoury actor who's clearing dried bits of spittle out of the corners of his lips with his tongue.

"Agriculture," Bartenboom declaims, "sees to it that we have unsealed surfaces, also areas where the water can escape to during floods. I think you're too worried, it's the in-thing nowadays constantly to create crises by talking them up. But if you look at the past few years you will see that here in western Europe we've profited enormously from global warming. Most people like the longer and warmer summers, and last year many German farmers profited from an additional harvest period – and with them the consumers."

He's just warming up. He goes on to declare that all environmental problems could be solved through market forces or new technologies, and suggests there is no need to worry because with the ruthless exploitation of nature everything has still turned out well, which was doubtless proof that everything would continue to turn out well. And that after a bitterly cold, never-ending winter, a spring that made all non-genetically manipulated plants wither and the deluges of the last few weeks that have ruined the harvest of at least one third of the farmers he's supposed to represent. Bartenboom maintains that the CO_2 emissions of agriculture cannot be further reduced because then the Chinese would take over the market. Therefore we had to wait until the Chinese started reducing their CO_2 emissions, then we could start by taking over their market and see how things went after that. That's not the way he puts it, of course, but that's what he means.

Meanwhile the camera catches the unsavoury actor picking his nose, giving the result of his excavations a good look, then eating the bogey. Shame is a concept that doesn't exist in his universe.

"As the voice of farming families we are proud of our history on the basis of Christian manly values and we will not stand for any green cranks or self-sufficiency jobsworths…"

"He knows very well that our death sentence was signed long ago. And now he's getting all worked up about people trying to stop him speeding it up," Elli says and – regrettably, I think – changes channels.

Well, it is her TV day. I don't interfere. Two-for-You is showing a repeat of *Methusalix*, a mixture of quizzes and sports competitions in which chrono-young compete against bio-young people and Team Bio more or less always wins.

Because they simply know how to go about these things or because the participants have been specially chosen for that result.

"Where is the last elk population still living in the wild," the eternally forty-year-old Günter Jauch asks, "A in Norway, B in Sweden, C in Canada or D in Russia."

Elli switches channels before I can check whether my answer (A) is correct. Strangely enough, there's a programme about elks on the next channel. But now the elks are shuffling across the screen, scooping up vegetation out of a lake with their antlers while a man's voice explains why they're dying out. "The warmer climate prevents the formation of reserves of fat, weakens their immune system through stress and increases their vulnerability to parasites. If the next winter is wet and ground ice covers the plants they forage for, the last three hundred specimens could become extinct at one blow." The voice is that of a confidence-inspiring man in a suit who is now standing in a smart restaurant. Distinguished guests are chatting over their meals. "A good cut of elk is like a good wine," the pleasant man in the suit says. "A pleasure, a sign of refinement and an investment. Order a kilo or two – or a hundred kilos – today while it's still available. Talk to your adviser at Hamburg-Mannheimer."

"The people that do that," I say, "the people who are still buying elk meat, will be the ones who will be the first to embrace cannibalism afterwards. They'll still be insisting that they have a right to meat, even when all the other animals have long since been eaten up."

"When did you actually become a vegetarian?" Elli asks.

She naturally thinks I'm still a vegetarian because I told her about my time with Greenpeace and Foodwatch and in her eyes working for that kind of organisation presupposes firm, sacrosanct principles. And in fact I was vegetarian for thirty years, eleven of them even vegan. Then I gave it up from one day to the next. Everyone else was stuffing themselves with meat like the Tasmanian devils and it was fairly clear that my abstention wasn't going to save a single pig, never mind the world. Eventually I was even eating more meat than anyone else, as much as I could get for my points. I didn't eat it just because I liked it but also because I thought it was a good thing that mankind in its stupidity would die out in the near future and I couldn't wait to see it drown in the coming flood. My only fear is that Elli won't be very sympathetic to that idea.

"I was already over thirty," I say, trying to avoid going any further into the subject.

"What I always find worst of all," Elli says, "is vegetarians who suddenly start eating meat again. After all, they know exactly how awful conditions in the fattening units are, that's why they became vegetarians in the first place, then suddenly they think, 'I don't care, I want to eat meat despite that.' Then they'll tell you something about their blood group, their blood group is such that they have to eat meat. Revolting, lying bastards…"

I break in quickly. "Do you know who I ran into recently in the Alster Centre? Ingo Dresen! Do you still remember Ingo Dresen?"

Of course Elli remembers Ingo Dresen. No one who went to the same school as him will ever forget that name.

"Not only from school. I had dealings with him when I was working at the animal-rights farm in Bargteheide. That must have been around 2020."

For years Elli ran an animal-rights farm just outside Hamburg and stuck it out there right to the end while the others left one after the other because neo-Nazis had taken over the village and were threatening the animal-rights activists.

"Eventually Tom tipped me off about that animal-welfare biker gang from Hamburg. They were delighted to have a genuine challenge for once. Until then they'd only been called out when someone was refusing to hand over the dog they neglected and kept in a cage. They would turn up, twelve hulking great guys on motorbikes, and simply ask politely. They never had any problem taking the dog away without further ado – they had a special sidecar fitted to one of the bikes for the dog."

"Don't tell me it was Ingo Dresen's Fat Rats."

"You can imagine my expression when he suddenly turned up there at the farm. But they were a resounding success. They told the Nazis where to get off and from then on we were left in peace. They always called us 'our veggies', as if we were their mascots or something like that."

Ingo Dresen preventing cruelty to animals! It's a funny old world.

Right then, from tomorrow I'll just have to be a vegan again.

14

I haven't the least desire to go down to the prepper room, I really have to force myself, but someone has to fill the fridge. Since Christine's stopped taking Ephebos she's been ageing at devastating speed. Much more quickly than I'd expected. You can almost watch the wrinkles appear. Since I only go to see her every two or three weeks now, it's a shock for me every time. Like in a horror film when the vampire's had a stake plunged into its heart and then – the picture of youth a moment ago – rapidly turns into an old man, then into a mummy, then to dust. Only Christine doesn't do me the favour of pulverising. On the contrary. She begs me to come and see her more often and goes into a hysterical fit of tears when I'm about to leave. Even begging me to make love to her, begging for Ephebos.

I should have put an end to the whole business ages ago, but somehow I've become attached to this little room that's outside time. In there I never have to prove myself, I'm never rejected and I enjoy all the privileges that are due to me by virtue of my gender. Okay, there has been some backchat, even physical attacks, but they all ended with me victorious and Christine getting what she deserved.

So once again I clear away the tins of peas and carrots, the meatballs and peaches and switch on the Black & Decker. But when I open the security door Christine is nowhere to be seen. The floor is covered in grey polystyrene granules and there's a gaping hole in the ceiling. A chair is standing underneath the hole. The shock is so great, I can hardly stop myself vomiting. There's the chain, the neck-ring has been opened. A bent spoon is lying beside it. She's actually managed to unlock it. It was a solid neck-ring with a padlock, not a dressing-up piece for bedroom games. My whole body feels as if I'm about to dissolve, I can hardly stand up. When was the last time I was here? It must have been at least two weeks ago. It's all over. Christine could have escaped days ago without me realising. Perhaps she's simply too confused to go to the police and is out there wandering through the woods somewhere. The important thing is not to make any mistakes now. First of all I close the security door and key in the code. Then I cautiously go over to the hole in the ceiling, get up on the chair and peer into the darkness. After thirty seconds, the time it takes my eyes to get accustomed to the darkness, I think I can see something doubled up over there in the corner, something blacker than the blackness all around. But it could just be wishful thinking.

"Come on out," I say, "come out at once or I'm coming in."

I won't do that of course. Who knows what's waiting for me in there. Even where I am I have to be prepared to be pounced on at any moment. With my hands I can feel torn sheets of polystyrene and a loose plank. To increase the soundproofing I put in a second ceiling on flexible suspension. These are parts of it. Then I feel something soft and yucky with something nasty inside it. When I take it out into the light it turns out to be a polystyrene mouse's nest with specks of shit and three neatly mummified baby mice. A little work of art, the Egyptians couldn't have done better. I put it back and poke around in the darkness with the loose plank, hit the rafters to the right and left, plunge it into the polystyrene as if it were a living body. No cries, not a sound. But if Christine had managed to work her way upwards, I would surely have noticed, and there can hardly have been enough time for her to dig her way out through the outside wall. At least I hope there hasn't. A sudden thought makes me jump down from the chair and check the bathroom. Then under the bed. Then I go and stand under the hole again and shout up. "You don't want me to come in there, that's for sure. Just see to it that you get your fat arse back down here."

'Please, God,' I pray, 'see to it that Christine's still there and I'll find a neat and tidy solution.'

Quiet animal whimpering comes from the space between the two ceilings. I'm immensely relieved.

"Get a move on. Do I have to wait all night?"

There's rustling and creaking. Then two dirty legs and a rucked-up skirt appear and, in a cloud of dust, wood chips and polystyrene confetti, Christine's lower half slips out of the hole. Her feet are feeling for the chair but can't find it and I have to grasp Christine by her scrawny hips and draw her to me so that she doesn't fall down.

"You bitch," I yell, though more out of relief than genuine rage, "do you realise how bloody expensive that ceiling insulation was, you stupid bitch?"

Not to mention the work I put into it. I set Christine down in front of me. Her hair is covered in spider-webs, her expressionless face smeared with dirt, her formerly yellow dress totally crumpled. Again a quiet, hardly human whimper comes from her throat, her face is completely lacking in expression. Oh my God, now she looks as if she's over forty, almost as old as her mother, that is. Distinctly older than me, at any rate, now I can pass for someone in his mid-twenties and my skin has regained that youthful, rubbery tautness. And I see that there are a lot more men taking the full Ephebo dose than

I thought. Now that I'm doing it myself and paying attention to it, I see bio-twenty-year-olds everywhere and more of them with every day. To be old is worse than cancer, a sign of poverty and scruffiness. Anyone who simply grows older without doing anything about it has lost control of their life. I feel a certain disgust at the sight of Christine – there's one of those loose folds on her neck and then the wrinkly skin at her elbows.

"What are you doing, going round like this?" I say. "Just look at yourself – you're filthy. Do you imagine I find that attractive?"

In a hoarse whisper Christine says something that's presumably meant to be an apology.

"Go and have a shower, woman," I say. "I really can't stand the sight of you."

She trots off to the bathroom, as if operated by remote control. While I'm filling the fridge with soya yoghurt and margarine, I can hear her crying under the shower. I also fill the kitchen island: as well as crackers and noodles, there are Danish oat biscuits, fresh full-fibre rolls, mangos and polangas – all things she particularly likes and that I bought specially for her while she was destroying the ceiling behind my back in order to trick me. I pick up the neck-ring to see if the key still works. The padlock sticks but with a certain amount of force I can still get it locked and open again. I wait for Christine to come out of the bathroom.

She's naked now and her body's still not that bad.

"You needn't get dressed. I'm going to fasten you here again."

"Are you going to leave already?"

"Of course," I say. "I have to go to the DIY store, to clear up the mess you've made here."

"Don't leave me alone. Just one hour. Please."

"You've annoyed me, you bloody bitch. Why should I do you a favour now? If I want, I can leave you here to rot, so stop making me angry."

"Stay with me," she wails, "I'll do anything you want."

"Anything?" I ask, locking the neck-ring and putting the key in my trouser pocket.

"Anything," she wails, throwing herself on the floor and clutching my shoes. The chain makes a decorative squiggle down her back.

Now I've got her where I always wanted her. But it doesn't mean anything any more. Pity actually. If only I'd had the idea of taking her Ephs away before. Then I'd have been able to get much farther sooner. As long as she still looked young and attractive, she still had one last bit of power over me. It's much easier to dominate someone you don't desire.

She's still clutching my feet. Her snot's soaking my socks.

"Please don't leave me alone here. Please! Or at least tell me when you're coming back. I can't stand it any longer. Give me a time… so that I can have something to look forward to."

The last time she persuaded me to leave my watch with her – an antique, of course, without smart functions. Actually she wanted a television. If the news and programmes were still dominated by male opinion, as they used to be, I would probably have agreed. Why shouldn't she watch TV, since I was hardly there at all anyway and didn't want anything from her any longer. But just in time I remembered that nowadays even on TV it was mostly woman-talk. And that could have a disastrous effect on Christine. She'd have been back on top of the world in no time at all. I gave her my wristwatch as a compromise.

"Right then," I say, "you want a fixed time – you can have

one: in two hours I'll be back from the DIY store. You'll be waiting for me, naked of course, in the base posture."

It's ages since I demanded the base posture from her. I tried to introduce it right at the beginning of her incarceration, when she was still defiant. To break her more quickly. But it almost went wrong. I was afraid she might go mad, so I quickly gave it up.

Hardly has the expression 'base posture' passed my lips than I get an erection. In that respect I have the body of a twenty-year-old again.

Christine's hands let go of my feet. She keeps her eyes on the floor. "Yes, Master," she says hoarsely through the strands of hair and it's not just desperation, there's also genuine gratitude in her voice. How compliant she can be if she only wants to. Suddenly I couldn't care less how slack the skin on her neck is.

"Right then," I say, pulling her up to me amicably by the hair so that I can see her face, "I want you now. In the base posture."

There's a slightly insane look on her face, uncanny, but all the time the tears are running down her cheeks, which reassures me. I let go of her, she turns round, kneels down in front of me, leans forward and stretches out until her forearms are lying flat on the floor and puts her head between her arms. Everything as assiduously as if her life depended on it. And now I think about it, there's something in that of course.

"Open your thighs more," I say. "Get your bottom up higher." I don't say arse, I say bottom. After all she was once my wife.

For a while I look at her and touch her, lying there in front of me offering herself. The flesh on the inside of her thighs is soft, almost limp already. Should it happen in the next few years that the Ephebos suddenly run out because nothing can be produced or delivered any longer, it won't be pleasant to see. All at once there'll be zombies going round everywhere, people who age by forty, fifty or more years within a few months, mummies you can watch putrefying.

I grasp the flesh of her thighs and roll it with a sense of melancholy between my fingers, pluck at it. Make Christine feel what's become of her. Then I unzip my trousers and use her the way I like. I like it in her arse and hard. She doesn't resist, even tries to suppress her whimpering, so as not to arouse my displeasure. She doesn't have to make the effort for long, I come almost immediately.

Afterwards I get her to massage my feet while I lie on the sofa, light a cigarette and blow the smoke in her face. It's hard to believe this is the same woman who beforehand used to cut me short and chipped away at my personality until it was a ridiculous, submissive nothing. Then something suddenly makes me think of Elli. Yesterday I was in bed with Elli and now this here. Immediately I feel awful. I ask myself why I'm actually doing this? Why do I come down to the prepper room at all any more? If Elli and I are in love, then that's something clean and pure. Not just because of the natural beauty of our youthful bodies, but above all because of what we feel for each other. How can I even desire someone like Christine? I can't understand how this old witch keeps managing to bring me round.

Christine is assiduously kneading my feet, she's really making an effort, you have to give her that. She rolls each toe separately between her thumb and index finger, pulls it and stretches it, then takes my whole foot in both hands and wrings it out like a wet towel. I sigh in spite of myself.

"Master…," she says, stroking the arch of my foot with her thumb, "may I ask you something?"

This is what it's like every time. She never does anything just for me. A sudden spurt of anger makes me kick out at her and I hit her on the head, which wasn't my intention. I simply can't stand this old woman any longer, her constant begging. And now she's crying again, crying and clutching my ankles and swearing that she'll mend her ways, that she'll do everything I say.

"Just bring me the biscuits," I say and she immediately jumps up and runs off to fetch the biscuits. I have to get rid of her somehow or other. On the other hand I can't really kill her, even though her attempt to break out gave me a good reason to. Otherwise she does everything I want. If I were to order her to go down on her hands and knees so that I could use her as a footstool, she'd even do that. I imagine what that would be like and then I imagine what it would be like if I were wearing boots with spurs instead of trainers and at once it's back again, the joy of life.

15

"Wake up, arsehole!"

The darkness tears apart and in the gap Christine's standing with a bucket in her hand. She's still naked and her face is distorted with hatred. I'm lying on the floor with water running down me; the darkness closes up again and then it gradually gets lighter around me, though I can't make anything out. I have a terrible headache. I try to get up but then I realise that my hands are tied behind my back and my legs bound at the ankles. A nightmare, it's a nightmare. Christine grabs my shoulder and shakes me. The headache becomes unbearable and I start retching.

"Yes, have a good puke," Christine says, "but first of all tell me the code for the door."

I still can't quite find my bearings, never mind think, but it slowly becomes apparent that there's something wrong. Something terribly wrong. I feel sick again and close my eyes.

She slaps my head with her hand, on a place that hurts incredibly. As if she were hitting right into my head.

"Stay awake," Christine's voice says, "Stay awake Sebastian. Sebastian!"

Sebastian, that's that crazy saint, that icon of the queers, who stands there tied to a stake, riddled with arrows. She shouldn't call me Sebastian. I must have fallen asleep. In the prepper room. That's never happened before. And now she's got me.

"Wake up, you stupid bastard, wake up, dammit!"

Each time she hits me on the same spot and each time there's an explosion of fireworks on the insides of my eyelids. Okay, I think, okay. That's enough. Why can't she just leave it at that. I keep my eyes closed, pretending I'm still asleep. My head hurts so much I must be seriously injured. I didn't fall asleep. Of course I didn't fall asleep. Christine hit me on the head with something. I just want to drift off for a while so that the headache will go away.

There's a rustling. She's getting dressed. Then the sound of metal on metal. I try to open my eyes just a little but now my eyelids are swollen and I can't blink or Christine would notice. Anyway, I can imagine what she's doing – she's trying to open the neck-ring with the teaspoon. The word teaspoon appears in my mind's eye in capital letters and with despair I notice the way the word 'open' seems to contain an echo of 'spoon' and to me that sounds like proof that Christine will succeed in freeing herself: spoon – open, just the long 'o' sounds. Then I realise that she must have long since taken the key out of my trouser pocket. My hands hurt. It feels as if they were about to burst. And I feel sick.

Christine bends over me. She has her clothes on now. A different dress. The beige one with the neck-warmer collar. A granny dress. One of my mis-purchases. But given the fusty way Christine looks now it's a perfect match. She's rummaging round in my pockets, turning them inside out. She finds a vitamin tablet which she pops straight in her mouth and swallows, without a sip of water. She probably thinks it's an Ephebo.

"Ah, you've woken up at last, have you? Just tell me where the key is. You might as well as I'm going to find it anyway."

She sticks her hands in my trouser pockets. The side ones,

the back ones. My trousers are wet. I seem to have peed in them. Or no, that was the water, of course.

"Either you tell me where the key is now or I'll hurt you until you do."

"My hands," I say. "The cable tie's much too tight. My hands are going to go completely dead."

She doesn't answer, instead she continues to rummage round in my pockets. I don't understand why she can't find the key. Perhaps it slipped out. Or there was a hole in the lining.

"You won't find the key," I say, "I've swallowed it."

Christine straightens up and gives me a good kick in the ribs. She's wearing her long black patent-leather boots. A sharp pain and my lungs empty instantaneously. I'm gasping for breath, making a croaking noise.

"Don't give me that nonsense. You put it away just now."

"No," I pant triumphantly, "swallowed it. I swallowed it when you thought I'd fainted. And now you can release me or we'll both starve to death down here."

Christine draws her leg back and kicks me in the ribs two, three times, it hurts dreadfully but it's not as bad as the first time. The first time she must have hit a particularly sensitive spot. She leans over, grabs me by the collar and holds up the bent spoon in front of my face.

"Tell me where it is or I'll tear out your eyes with this."

This is the true face of my wife. In public she is known – or, rather, was known – as a loving mother and an altruistic minister who was committed to trying to save the world. To me she played at being the poor, broken victim who would do anything to please me. The truth, however, is that she's full of hatred and contempt for others. The truth is that she's a person who enjoys inflicting pain. I should have done away with her. I should have killed her long ago. But I felt sorry for her. Stupid idiot that I was, I even pitied the bitch.

"I've swallowed it! We can't do anything about it."

She tries to kick me in the balls but I get them out of the way in time. Which means she kicks me in the stomach. Again I'm gasping for breath. I just about manage to suppress a scream. Christine hoicks over one of the kitchen chairs and sits down on it. Right next to me. I'm still struggling for air. She crosses her legs and jiggles her foot up and down.

"Then we'll just have to wait until it comes out at the other end," she says, suddenly gets up and kicks me hard on the kneecap, as if she were trying to crack a nut. Now I do scream. Out loud and uncontrolled.

"The code for the door," she says, climbing up on the chair and looking down at me. She underestimates me, she's always underestimated me. That's her biggest mistake.

"You're never going to get out of here," I tell her, grinding my teeth. "This cellar is my world and you can't get out without me. Here I'm the one who decides the way things are and you have a chain round your neck."

Christine jumps up off her chair. I just have time to tense my stomach muscles but I still can't help giving a piercing scream. I'm sure a muscle or something must have been torn.

"The number code," Christine says. "Don't make me get really angry."

"If after all this you intend to present yourself to the world as a poor victim that only just managed to free herself from the claws of a nasty pervert, you shouldn't knock me about too much," I reply. She kicks me in the face, hitting that sensitive spot between my upper lip and my nose, even though I've long been ready to give her the numbers. Blood pours out of my nose, dark blood splashing on the floor.

"Forty-seven eleven," I mumble, "four, seven, one, one."

Of course that isn't the right code but she can't check it as long as she has the neck-ring on.

"That's just like you," she says.

Christine sits down on the kitchen chair, picks up the bent teaspoon again and tries to fit it into the lock.

"I'd have let you out soon anyway," I mumble, trying to wipe the blood from my nose off on the sofa cover.

Christine lowers the teaspoon. "Shut your gob," she shouts, her face totally distorted, "you just shut your gob."

"I've fallen in love, you see. I don't want all this here any more."

"You're to shut your gob or I'll kill you."

I shrug my shoulders and look the other way. Only now do I see that all over the room there are smears of blood. Not just here by the kitchen island. There's a huge patch on the bed as well and streaks on two places on the floor. There must have been a real struggle. And Christine doesn't have so much as a scratch. I was probably dragging myself across the floor while she was whacking me all the time. I'd like to feel the wound on my head but that's not easy with my hands tied behind my back. They're almost completely numb by now. Black presumably. As unobtrusively as possible I check whether I'm capable of standing up and try to assess how quickly I could move, tied up as I am. Less than four metres and I'd be beyond the reach of the chain Christine's attached to. Just four metres, and I'm starting to feel less dizzy as well. The most difficult part will be standing up. My knee's had it. Now it's nothing but a bundle of dull pain the size of a medicine ball. The best thing will be not to try and stand up at all but to crawl, to worm my way across the floor to the door like a snake. I have to stop Christine getting the neck-ring open. Once she's done that I've had it.

"Actually it's a kind of reconciliation that we're going to die here together," I say. "Perhaps it's not meant to be, my new love. Perhaps we belong together for good now. I think we would actually have made a good couple. We could have been happy if you'd been able to respect my masculinity. I know that for the women in your ministry masculinity is nothing but a problem and you think you have to deal with it, but in reality masculinity is a value, something really good."

I've straightened up somewhat, tucked up my legs and pressed the sole of the foot on my uninjured leg against the sofa, to improve my start in the snake dash to the door, but as long as Christine's sitting right beside me I'll never make it. I'm sitting on something hard. Of course – the key. It's in its usual place in my back trousers pocket. In that little pocket inside the pocket. Christine was so stupid she simply passed over it. Stupidity has its consequences. In slow motion I manoeuvre my bound hands into the pocket and pull out the key with two fingers. Christine watches me suspiciously as I twist and strain.

"If you could come to terms with my masculinity, the two of us might still have a chance," I say to divert her attention by making her angry.

Christine jumps up and kicks me in the side. The key slips out of my fingers and slides across the floor. Although I'm doubled up with pain I manage to use my bound legs like a golf club and putt the key fairly precisely in the direction of the bathroom.

Christine stares at the little metal object, uncomprehending, then she looks at me. I stare at it as well and pull my legs up as if I'm going to wriggle my way after it. Christine falls for it and rushes over to the bathroom while I push off from the sofa leg and crawl and worm my way in the opposite direction.

As I said, she's always underestimated me. That's her biggest mistake. I concentrate on working my way forward, don't waste energy looking back. I've no idea whether she's noticed what I'm doing by now, whether she's after me or not, until I hear her footsteps right behind me. But I'm already almost beyond the limit of the chain and take a swipe at her with my feet, hitting her on the head – I hope it was her head and I hope it was a place that's particularly painful. Then her hands slip off my legs – there's no more chain. I've made it, I've made it, I'm out of her reach. She howls with rage, with disappointment, being forced to realise that I've been too good for her again, that she simply has no chance against me. We stare at each other, full of hatred. Then realisation comes for both of us at the same moment. It's not over yet. There's still the key. The key! Christine rushes back while I throw myself against the wall, brace myself against it with my shoulder and manage at least to get up onto my knees. My left knee is a pulpy cushion of pain that is hurling flashes of fire against the back of my eyeballs. That's as far as I can manage at the moment. When I try to stand up both my thighs are seized with terrible cramp. It's awful – as if my pulverised knee were spreading. Oh God, I'll never make it. I can hear Christine scraping and scratching with the key on the neck-ring, unable to find the hole. She's just as panic-stricken as I am. Perhaps I still have a chance. Pushing my forehead against the wall and my cramped legs on the floor, I shove myself up through the pain and my pulped knee. I'm just a bundle of pain as I force my way, soaked in sweat, up by the door until I'm facing the keypad of the security lock. A quick look back at Christine. She's staring at me, deathly pale, but the key's already in the padlock. It's impossible for me to enter four digits before she's freed herself. As calmly as I can, I get my nose close to the first digit: seven, press the tip of my nose against the button. I hope it really is the seven, for once I get close up I can't see it. Christine's wrestling with the key, it's stuck – praise be to Allah – it's stuck, it's stuck! The second digit, four; get my nose right on it, just don't miss. Christine's making a weird groaning noise, tearing and twisting at the jammed lock that she broke herself with the teaspoon. It's her own fault, she's brought it on herself. Third digit: seven, And then the zero. Christine freezes. There's a deathly hush. Nothing happens. Oh God, nothing. I must have made a mistake. So I have to go through the whole thing again while Christine is wildly poking around with the key in the padlock. Seven-four-seven-zero. The lock rattles like a mechanical toy from the nineteenth century, clicks back and the heavy door swings open. I take the door-handle in my mouth and pull it open wider. Despite the chain Christine runs over towards me and, attempting the impossible, jumps at me before I get out of the door. Naturally she's pulled back a yard away from me and thrown to the floor. She lies there, wheezing and gurgling, clutching at her throat with both hands. Her fingers feel for the padlock, the key, but there's nothing there, the key has slipped out and landed at my feet. I can't pick it up now, but Christine can't reach it. Fate is clearly on my side, just the way it ought to be. Christine's whining and whimpering like a little baby. I refrain from taunting her. If she ever had a chance of getting out of there, that was it – and she wasted it. I can imagine how she feels. Without a word I stagger and shuffle out through the door. With a complicated contortion of my feet I manage to pull it back closed behind me. I can hardly use my hands, they don't seem to belong to me any more.

Only now, as the security door clicks shut, am I overcome with exhaustion and relief. I sink to the floor and lay my face on the concrete, still feeling the pain in my knee, my wrists and my ribs. It was almost all over. I was close to never seeing Elli again. She wouldn't have wanted to see me again. But I've got away and I feel so grateful I don't know what to do with myself. Suddenly my brother's ecstatic faith seems vaguely plausible to me… no, come on, that's not it at all, I still can't understand my idiot of a brother. But no matter what the nature of the universe is, whether there's a creative authority or not, I'm grateful, grateful, grateful and life is wonderful.

16

I'm going to immure her. In the space above the false ceiling. I've just discussed that with her and she accepted it with amazing composure.

Whilst I'm preparing the planks, tools and mortar, Christine is baking a stock of afghan biscuits for me. My favourites. I have to stop to watch her. She's wearing the blue check dress with the light blue apron and they go perfectly with the yellow jug on the kitchen island. She's put on pale pink lipstick and if you don't look too closely, she still looks great. Before Ephebo people would probably have said she's an attractive woman in her late thirties. During the last few days I felt sorry for her and let her have some Ephebos, but they don't work so quickly that a clear difference can be seen after a week. The other way round the changes are visible much sooner. Christine's hair is still all mussed up from the sex we had. Furious sex. As if it was the last time.

She's given up all her little quirks and we talk quite calmly and normally. During the first few days after her latest attempt to take me by surprise I chained her up in the bathroom, just to be on the safe side; with a new lock, of course, and two and a half metres of chain. Anything that looked remotely likely to be used to pick the lock I put well out of her way. After that it was enough just to check up on her once a day. The rest of the time I spent in bed to get over my concussion. But even at that point we were very cautious and polite to each other.

I simply behaved as if nothing had happened. She was meek and grateful, so I felt I could lengthen the chain back to four metres and attach it to the kitchen island. I called in sick at the Democracy Centre. Bicycle accident. To Elli I said something about a business trip. Since we've only been together for a few weeks, she doesn't know that I never go on business trips and suspected nothing. That meant I could be with Christine every day, allowing her neither the time nor the opportunity to get up to mischief, until I'd made all my preparations. At some point or other we then started sleeping together again.

The hole in my head still looks pretty bad. The doctor on call, who happened to be the chrono-forty-year old son of my mummy classmate Reinhard Hell, didn't believe my story of a bicycle accident but asked no further questions.

"Going to the police is sometimes not the worst decision to take," he said in a cryptic sort of way. Perhaps he thought I was the victim of some kind of extortion racket. It's hard to believe anyway that my head wound came from a simple china mug and the kicks from a delicate little woman. My infrapatellar fat pad is gunged up with the synovial bursa and my kneecap is criss-crossed with hairline cracks, like the craquelure on an old painting. Arthritis pre-programmed, the orthopaedic specialist says. As if any knee on the planet had enough time to develop arthritis.

Christine looks up from the baking sheet on which she's spread out the dark brown balls of pastry.

"What are you looking at me like that for?"

"Nothing. Nothing at all," I say. "I'm just thinking how nice that is: a woman at her baking."

She smiles and bends over the biscuits again.

"It didn't have to come to this, you know." I say. "Our relationship had already developed quite a bit. Eventually the point would have come when I could do everything with you and then I'd have let you go outside."

"You don't have to kill me," Christine says very calmly as she puts the half walnuts in place, carefully pressing them down on the balls of pastry.

"Oh yes I do," I say, "and you know that yourself. Don't make it harder for us than it already is anyway. After you almost succeeded you'll keep on trying to put one over on me. You simply have no respect for me, and in the long run that's dangerous."

"I do have respect for you. You are my Master. And if you want to kill me, you will kill me. How could I not respect you?" she says softly and without looking at me.

"How stupid do you actually take me for?" I reply. "Do you really think I'd fall for that?"

She looks up again, her expression frantic with despair. So it's not going to be quite as easy as I thought.

"Just give me a few books and magazines and only come to see me when you feel like it. I'll treat you with respect and deference and do everything you want. You don't have to kill me."

"Deference? You haven't got the least idea what that means, deference."

She puts the baking tray in the oven. When she pops up behind the kitchen island again I can see the thoughts going round and round inside her head, how she's making an effort to do everything right and to win me over at the eleventh hour.

"Deference," she says, lowering her eyes, "is what the woman feels for the man who has the power and to whom she gladly submits. You are my Master. I will never rebel against you again."

I laugh. My nice, youthful laugh that she used to love so

much and now sounds even more youthful.

"Above all deference means that a woman defers to her husband's assessment of a situation. And I'm telling you that unfortunately killing you is unavoidable."

"I bow to your every decision but I'm sure you're clever enough to find a better solution."

I have to laugh again. "Are you trying to manipulate me?"

Immediately she's prickly again, all her gentleness disappears in a flash. "I'm trying to avoid my execution."

"When do the biscuits have to come out?"

She gives me an annoyed look. "In fifteen to twenty minutes."

"Then drink it now."

I push the yellow jug, in which the sleeping pills have been dissolved, to her across the kitchen island.

Her hands are trembling as she takes hold of it. "Is there no hope at all for me?"

"There's no hope for anyone or anything on this planet."

"Then you drink it." She pushes the jug back across so hard that it almost falls over the edge. I just manage to catch it.

"If you want to get rid of me you're going to have to get your hands dirty yourself. I'm not going to make it that easy for you."

"Above all you should make it easy for yourself," I say, "but if you prefer I can beat you to death or cut your throat."

I push the jug back to her. Then I stand up to get a glass from the kitchen cupboard. I'm quite sure she won't attack me while I've got my back turned. I'm absolutely sure. When I turn round Christine is sitting down staring at the jug. I give her the glass.

"Why didn't you just order a woman from the catalogue, if that's what you must have – someone to dominate? I'm sure that would have worked without you having to set up a torture chamber and make yourself into a criminal. Islamic Root will deliver suitably conditioned women. And then you wouldn't have had to kill her now, you could have simply got a divorce. Or you could have gone to Syria and simply said, 'I repudiate you, I repudiate you, I repudiate you' – and you'd be rid of her."

Christine clearly wants to gain a little time. She's welcome to. I'm not in a hurry.

"But I didn't want a slave-girl from the Islamic State. Nor did I want a submissive Asian or east European woman. That doesn't fit in with my socialisation. I wanted the company of an intelligent, educated and amusing woman, who has grown up under the same conditions as myself. Surely that must be possible without having to be completely at the mercy of women."

"What do you mean, at the mercy of? If a woman doesn't have a chain round her neck, you're at her mercy, is that it?"

She's trying to argue, her tone is unpleasant and nagging, but I can see the naked fear in her eyes and the bead of sweat on her upper lip, so I'm forbearing.

"I wanted to have a woman who is completely aware of her powerlessness," I say gently, "and who despite that cannot help arguing with me, mocking my political opinions, constantly finding fault with me. And who, at the end of the day, still has to do exactly what I tell her to. I wanted you, do you understand? You in this specific situation."

"That's the nastiest thing I've ever heard."

That's Christine getting on her high horse again. At least ten things instantly occur to me that are distinctly worse, for example what my brother did to his lavatory attendants, or that guy from Poppenbüttel who set up the tsunami aid project and siphoned off money to fill in the holes in his shipping company's accounts and used the aid-ships to Thailand in order to smuggle tanks to Myanmar. True, that was some time ago, but it's clearly worse.

"Being good all the time is a soul-destroying way of spending your life, and anyway, we men aren't made for that," I say and point to the jug.

Making Christine die is rather sad, but surprisingly, it's also exciting. She's not dying by chance nor has God any say in the matter either, she's dying simply because that's what I want. I'm the one who makes all the decisions here.

"You lousy little toerag, you shitbag."

"Now then, where's all that deference you assured me of in such touching terms just now? Perhaps all this here is just a test? If you'd remained respectful and deferential right to the very end, I might perhaps have let you continue to live."

"Fuck you, fuck you, you lousy little toerag, you cowardly little turd."

And so it goes on, with the swearwords repeated and every second one prefaced by the adjective 'little'. There comes a point when I've had enough. I go over to her, grab the chain and knock her down with one punch. When she's lying on her back I grab the jug, sit on her chest, put my knees on her upper arms and pour the solution of water and sleeping pills into her mouth. She spits it back at me and presses her lips together. I gradually get furious. I put the jug on one side and sock her on the jaw again.

"You damn bitch!" I bellow. "You've never respected me. You've never even believed in me."

She doesn't resist any longer. I pick up the jug again in one hand and keep her nose closed with the other. She swallows. I repeat the dose and she swallows but has to cough and part of the liquid seeps out of her nose. I wait until she's stopped coughing, then slowly pour in some more and now she swallows it like a good girl. That way two thirds of the suicide drink end up in her stomach. Half would probably be enough.

I put the jug down and Christine starts coughing again, coughing and retching, but Dormiol-Sedata is popular in the assisted-suicide centres because it has a pleasant taste and is well tolerated, and it stays down in her stomach. I get off her arms and help her up. Christine starts to cry.

"Don't, please don't. Please, please, please."

Her crying turns into uncontrolled sobbing. She falls to her knees before me.

"Stand up."

I grasp the chain and pull her up with it, even though she tries to cling on to my legs. Then I take the first cable tie out of my pocket and tie her hands, but this time at the front and just tight enough so she can't slip her hands out. Not so tight that it hurts. Only then do I unlock the neck-ring and lead Christine over to the step ladder I've put up under the hole in the ceiling.

"After you."

She stumbles at the second step, falls and brings the ladder down with her. I know that can't be the tablets taking effect yet. It's just one more of Christine's histrionic performances. But since it's going to be her last, I let it go, put up the ladder again without a word and guide her up the steps until her upper half is in the space above the false ceiling.

She sits herself on the side of the hole so that I just have to take her legs and lift them up. Then I climb up into the space myself and bind Christine's feet with the second cable tie. She looks at the plastic bag and adhesive tape I've put down beside her.

"Slide across," I say. "To that rafter over there."

I switch on the torch I hung up there the previous day and then help Christine to slide across so that she doesn't get any splinters, even though my knee hurts so much that I actually need help myself. Under the rafter there's a duvet and a pillow. I couldn't get a mattress through the hole. There's a rope hanging from the rafter and I put the noose round Christine's neck. If she should move in her sleep, the noose will automatically tighten.

"Please stay with me until I've fallen asleep."

"Of course," I say. "I just have to slip down to switch off the oven."

When I come back up she has stretched out on the duvet. I stuff the pillow under her head, stroke her hair. She holds her bound hands out to me and I take one, stroke the hand that still has my old watch round its wrist and wait with Christine for the sedatives to take effect. We don't talk any more. Everything has been said. Shortly before she falls asleep she withdraws her hand and turns her back on me. The noose is already tightening a little. I wait another ten minutes, to be sure she is really asleep; looking at the shadows and remnants of polystyrene in Christine's burial chamber I discover a mummified peacock butterfly. When I pick it up, it crumbles to dust. When can it have been immured here? Perhaps even eighty years ago, when my father built the house so that it would be bequeathed from generation to generation? Life is a bridge, cross it and do not build a house. I take the plastic bag, one of the last ones made for the supermarkets, and put it over her head, making an airtight seal round her neck with adhesive tape, without waking her up. The plastic is drawn into her mouth, her lips appear briefly through a Lidl advert for vegan sausages, then the bag is blown up again. I hope Christine will dry out here just as cleanly as the baby mice and the butterfly, that she will just disintegrate. It's dry enough here and the initial body fluids will be soaked up by the duvet. If she still starts to stink, then I'm going to have a problem again.

I take back my wristwatch and then creep on my hands and my one uninjured knee back to the hole and immediately set about closing it up and plastering it over. I feel slightly melancholy. After all this is where an important period of my life has come to its end. Its final end. I try to take my mind off it by thinking of Elli. The day after tomorrow she's going to meet my children for the first time. Only now that Christine's dead do I realise how much my wife stood between us until now. But a new age is dawning. A better age. It just happens to be a law of nature that you can't have any fun or enjoyment in life without someone having to pay for it. And the less you let that bother you and the more ruthless you are about doing others down, the better your life is.

17

I put the salad bowl down on the dinner table, the old original Formica table from my original childhood with the two pull-out leaves, that haven't been pulled out for ages, because there's mostly enough space anyway. Racke and Binya-Bathsheba are already sitting down but Elli's still in the kitchen. She hands me the vegan dhal casserole through the hatch, takes off her apron and comes to join us in the living room. She looks really great, her long hair hanging smoothly down over her back and she's wearing a short black-and-white striped skirt made of loba.

"I'm not eating that," Racke screams.

"Oh," Elli says. "You don't like lentils? Should I get you some bread and paprika spread.

"No, I want meat," Racke screams. He's in a bad mood. It bothers him that I've changed my appearance once again. He thinks the blue marks and grazes on my face come from some pill or other. Just like my rejuvenation which disturbed him immensely. As well as that Racke wants the new version of pROJEKTa that will give his robot crocodile a chainsaw. Naturally there's absolutely no question of that. CrocoChain2 saws up living beings, sending red hologram-drops spurting out in all directions.

"Normally we always eat meat," Binya explains in superior tones. I could throttle the brats.

"True, unfortunately," I say in a casual tone to Elli, as I sit down at the long side opposite Racke and spoon out a large helping of dhal onto my plate. "Well, I don't mean always, of course… but sometimes we do actually eat meat. Until five years ago I was a hundred per cent vegan but since it's become clear that there's no hope any more… I mean, you and me, people like you and me that is, who've made an effort throughout our lives not to damage anyone and to live in an environmentally conscious way and have accepted all the restrictions without complaint in order to save what might still be saved… And despite all that we're now going to perish miserably along with all the fat, flesh-guzzling people simply because they can't hold back, but carry on gorging themselves and consuming and burning petrol… Have you never asked yourself why you should be the only one not helping yourself to the great apocalypse buffet?"

Jesus! What crap I'm talking. Elli brushes a bit of coriander leaf off the sleeve of her white, fair trade cotton blouse, then turns to me. Her look is gentle and disappointed and distanced.

"Because of the animals that have to be killed for it," she says calmly. "Because of the boundless contempt it shows to kill someone in order to eat them."

What I'd most like to say to Elli is that since the class reunion I've only eaten meat twice and that I won't eat any more in future. That eating meat was just part of my disappointment, of the feeling that everything had become pointless anyway but above all part of my hatred of everything and everyone. And that she's cured me of that hatred. That since we met it's no longer a matter of indifference to me if someone dies so that I can enjoy my food for ten minutes. But I feel it's pathetic to have to justify myself in front of the children. I'm not going to justify myself. I simply nod.

"So what!" Racke shouts. "Bloody animals! Dead animals

dripping with blood. Hunks of meat dripping with blood. Yummy! Yummy, yummy, yummy!"

"You hold your tongue," I say sharply, "or you can eat the rest of your meal on the toilet. There's not going to be any more meat here."

"Not ever?" Binya cries, outraged.

"Didn't you read your essay to me not long ago? The one about the aims of society." I ask. "Well – and what are the aims of a civilised society?"

"Equality, justice, fairness..." she falters, she can't remember the rest.

"And," I say, "does it go with a just society for it to say to an individual, 'All that doesn't count for you because you've got a lot more hair than us. We don't need to be fair to you, we're just going to eat you up.' Do you think that's okay?"

Binya stares down at her plate and starts ruminating, actually going through the arguments and forgetting her own interests. She's easy to deal with. Not so Racke.

"I want some meat," he cries, jumping up from his chair, running round the table and planting himself in front of Elli. "If I don't get any meat, I'll put a dead pig in your bed. A dead pig covered in blood! I'll chop off its head and there'll be blood everywhere. And I'll smear it all over your bed until there's blood everywhere."

Elli stares, aghast, at the look of hatred on Racke's face. She stretches out her hand to him.

"Don't touch me!" Racke screams, doubling up and retching, as if the idea of her touching him was nauseating. That's enough. I get up. My knee feels as if there's a hedgehog inside it. But as I hobble round Elli to grab him he slips out of my hands and runs off until the table's between us again. Binya laughs as he runs past her.

"I'll slit the pig open, take out all the entrails and put them in your bed, for the two of you," Racke shouts and laughs. Elli gives me a baffled look.

"You'll stay there," I say in threatening tones to Racke, "you stay there at once or you'll get your arse tanned for the first time in your life."

But as I go after him – my knee a furnace of pain – he runs back round to the other side of the table and he and Binya laugh at me again. In front of Elli. They're making me look like an idiot in front of Elli. I can feel myself going red in the face with fury.

"Meat," Racke shouts, "meat, meat, meat!"

"Don't get worked up about it, Bassi…" Elli says.

With one kick I overturn the table, my plate with the red dhal flies through the air, crockery smashes, lentils splatter on the floor. Now Racke's not laughing any more. He's looking at me, wide-eyed as I stride over the table towards him with one step. All the pain that might restrain me has gone. I grab Racke by the collar and shake him. He starts howling.

"I don't want to see you again," I bellow at him. "I don't want to see you here ever again!"

Now Racke's howling his head off. I keep on shaking him.

"Bassi," Elli says in a strained voice, "Leave him be, Bassi."

"Let go of him, Papa. You're hurting Racke. He's still just a little boy," Binya shouts.

"And I don't want to see you any more, either," I bellow at her as I drop Racke on the floor. He lies there, a twitching, howling bundle. "I don't want to see the pair of you any more. You can stay with Grandma Gerda."

Now Binya's howling too. The howling bundle that is Racke pushes himself up on his elbow. "And if Mama comes home," he whines, "what if Mama comes back?"

"That's just your hard luck," I bellow, "it's not going to happen in your lifetime."

Elli goes over to Racke and squats down beside him. She helps him up onto his legs and wipes his face on her sleeve.

"I'll take the children home," she says without looking at me. "I think it's better if we all cool off a bit. Then perhaps we can discuss this sensibly."

She talks and acts in a quite relaxed way, but I can see that in reality she's shocked at me. That she's questioning the idea of being together with me. Even after her death Christine is still managing to ruin my life, even if it's just through her obnoxious little brats. I'm close to bursting into tears. I love Elli so much. She's my life, my all, she's something I never thought would happen to me again. And these ugly, spoilt little beasts might well have ruined everything before it's really got going.

Elli goes out into the hall with them, helps Racke put on his yellow anorak with the humming spiral patches. I'm panicking. What if she doesn't want to see me again now? If she simply parks the car outside the door and disappears for good. Doesn't get in touch again? Doesn't answer the phone?

"I'm sorry," I say. "I don't know what got into me."

"We'll talk about it later," Elli says. "I'll take the kids back first."

It's over. Elli thinks I'm the kind of person you have to keep the children safe from. What should I do?

"I'm sorry, Racke," I say, although inwardly I'm still gnashing my teeth. I'm not really sorry at all, in fact I'd love to lay into him with a stick. "I didn't want to frighten you. It's just that I love Elli so much. I can't bear it when someone hurts Elli. No one should insult Elli the way you did – not even my own son."

Racke has pulled the hood of his anorak right down over his face – he looks like a miniature version of one of the fanatical yellow monks. He's snivelling and sniffing back the snot. I hold out my hand to him and squat down, despite the raging pain that's started in my knee again, so that I can look him in the face – man to man – even though I'd be much more interested to see how Elli responds to my apology. Racke takes hold of my hand – probably simply out of fear of what might happen if he didn't.

"Right then," Elli says, putting on a cheerful tone, "now you're going to show me where your grandmother lives, yes? Or should we stop off somewhere for an ice cream on the way?"

Neither Racke nor Binya reply. They mutely go out of the front door with Elli. I don't shout 'Bye' to them. I know they won't answer.

"Press nine on the satnav," I say to Elli.

I stand in the door and wave farewell as they leave. Only Elli waves back and that probably because she doesn't want to show me up in front of the children. I won't find out whether we're still together until she gets back. I'm afraid, terribly afraid that she might leave me. I don't want to live without her. It was only through meeting her that I found out how miserable and wretched my life until then had been. I don't want to be so alone again. I don't want to be so nasty again. I'll admit everything she reproaches me with. If she wants me to have therapy, then I'll even go through that. Whatever she demands, I'll do. And if she leaves me despite that, I'll shoot myself.

I hobble down into the cellar, clear the tins of peas, carrots and peaches off the shelf. Elli will take at least an hour, probably two. That's time enough for me to take at least one of the rings with a snap hook out of the wall and plaster over the hole; if I'm very quick maybe I can even bury the chain in the garden. Or perhaps not, I'll just get rid of one of the rings. I mustn't take any risks. I get the workshop radio out of the garage and switch on a bit of music to distract me from the thought of Christine's body lying there above me, gradually starting to decompose. I'm not sure, but I think I might even possibly be able to detect a sweetish smell. It's probably just the stale air. The ventilation's switched off now. It's an oldie that's being played at the moment, they were probably playing oldies all the time but I don't perceive them as oldies because I've hardly been interested at all in what's new in music for the last twenty years. I wonder what it would have been like in a hundred years time, if the world weren't going to end now, but decade after decade a bigger and bigger stock of popular music had accumulated. The day might come when no one could tell whether they were listening to something brand new or as old as the hills. And how would a poor, overstretched radio presenter decide what was worth clicking on again? Since I've been together with Elli, I keep finding myself thinking as if we still had a future. But what's playing at the moment is clearly a song from my days, 'Saddle up and Ride your Pony', a song I used to despise when I was young but which, in the state I'm in at the moment, my fear of losing Elli, is surprisingly enough of a comfort and seems strangely beautiful and significant to me. Saddle up and ride your pony, sit around and you'll be lonely, saddle up and let the dust fly… It does me good to take the ring out of the wall, to smooth over the wall, to smooth over old wounds, to remove evidence and with it the horror at what I once did in another life. I'll tell Elli I'm in an exceptional situation at the moment, that I feel torn between her and the children. That I have feelings of guilt towards the children. But also towards her. And that for some reason I was impelled to do the opposite of what I really wanted – to take the kids in my arms and calm them down. Elli will understand. She'll forgive me.

And those bloody brats are never going to set foot in here again. If I see them at all then from now on it will be at Gerda's place. They won't get any more CO_2 points either.

I haven't time to let the filler dry before painting it over. Perhaps it'll stay on anyway. Most of all I'd like to fill the room in. However, doing that might just arouse suspicion. Once I've got the rings by the kitchen island and in the bathroom out of the wall and taken the chain out and buried it, this will look like a perfectly normal prepper room, apart from the fact that it's distinctly better furnished than usual. And apart from the little bloodstains on the sofa, of course – I just couldn't get them out. Thousands of people have a prepper room. It's the time for it. And it's perfectly normal for a person to try to keep the existence of such a room secret. After all, in five or six years there'll be a run on secure places. You don't arouse suspicion by possessing one but by filling it in.

"So this is where you are. I've been looking for you everywhere. Didn't you hear me calling?"

The voice hits me like an electric shock. It can't be Elli, for Elli's on her way to Grandmother Gerda with the kids, isn't she? Past Reinhard's bakery, where you can get his excellent but incredibly expensive marzipan cake, past the concrete monstrosity of the shopping centre, past the Jolli filling station, that takes at least twenty minutes. And by the time the kids have got out and Elli's introduced herself to Gerda and found some excuse to explain why they've come back so early, that's at least another twenty minutes. And it's as good as certain that Gerda will invite her in and press a coffee on her. Even if they don't have coffee the journey back will take another twenty minutes.

It is Elli. She's in the cellar, staring at the open fifty-centimetres-thick security door and then comes in to join me, slowly and looking amazed. I can feel the blood rushing to my face. No, not that! Just don't blush, I must act casual, simply act casual. This is my prepper room that I happen not to have told her about yet.

"So now you've discovered my survival bunker," I say calmly, and I can tell that the rush of blood is subsiding. "I suppose I'll have to offer you a place here when the world comes to an end."

She looks round, amazed at the clean little cell. Dammit, where's the chain? It's somewhere on the floor. By the fridge? I go up close to Elli to restrict her field of vision.

"Has something happened? Where are the kids? Surely you haven't been to Gerda's yet?"

Elli stops looking round and turns to me. That's better. Look me in the eye, my dear, and then you won't see anything that might frighten you.

"An absolute disaster," she says. "They're still sitting in the car outside. Just before Reinhard's Binya somehow got the idea that I'd murdered your wife and now I was trying to kidnap her and Racke and dispose of them. At least that's what she said to me and Racke immediately started to scream and was so beside himself that I was afraid he'd jump out of the car at full speed. So I switched on the child locks and turned round. They say you have to drive them. And they're so afraid of me they even refused to come back in the house with me."

"Oh God," I say, "I'm sorry, I really am sorry. You probably imagined your first meeting with the kids would be rather different. I'm terribly sorry that I flew off the handle like that earlier on. I'm afraid we're all a bit overwrought after the business with Christine."

"Go to them now," Elli says, "I'm worried that they might get up to something if they're left alone too long. They're completely distraught. And be nice to them. Patient. And above all tell them that they can still come and see you."

"Okay," I say, and try to take Elli's arm to lead her out with me. "What about going in the car together?"

With a smooth sidestep she avoids my arm and starts looking round again. "I don't think that's such a good idea. We've got to take that more slowly. You talk to your children first and I'll pass the time examining the place where we can spend the end of the world fucking."

She smiles, she's forgiven me. She doesn't think I'm the type that can fly off the handle at the least excuse. Things are back to normal between us again. I just have to get her out of this room. Calmly and casually, so as not to arouse her suspicions. But Elli's strolling along the wall and the room's so bloody small, and where's that chain, where is it – there, by the fridge. And just at that moment Elli looks at me, sees my gaze fix on something and, of course, she looks in the same direction and sees the chain, four metres of strong iron links and the big padded ring attached to it. It used to be round Christine's neck and now it's lying there wide open, like a hungry mouth. Elli looks at me again, surprised and slightly alarmed. But she still hasn't quite understood.

"That thing there?" I say. "That's just for emergencies. Who knows how many of us there will be stuck down here. And if someone gets stir-crazy… to protect the others."

"Well, that really is looking ahead," Elli says with a laugh, but she's gone deathly pale, there's panic in her eyes and she's looking for the way out.

I go over to her slowly, hands raised and fingers splayed, soothing, the way you try to catch a wild animal that's been hit by your car.

"But just think about it," I say. "If things really get bad we might have to spend months down here. We might even have to move in here permanently if there are hordes of cannibals prowling round Wellingstedt."

I laugh. Elli laughs. But her eyes are saying: Oh God, oh please, please help me God, see that I get out of this cellar and don't fall into the hands of this psychopath.

I could cry. Cry. It's over. It's all over. I can't lock Elli in here. Not Elli, my Elli! What there is between us is something pure and good. With her I'd have become a different person.

"I'm worried about the children," she says. "We ought to go up and check on them right away."

"Okay," I say and let her lead the way. She's trying to keep herself under control, not to run because she knows she has no chance of getting away from me. I'm right behind her. As she walks on ahead of me, bravely erect, her knees suddenly give way and I have to catch her and hold her in my arms.

"Oh Elli," I say.

I can see the abyss, deep and black, in her eyes. I help her up on her feet again and she goes out of the door. I can sense the relief she feels when she's out of the room. The hope that she might still escape me springing up inside her. Oh Elli, my poor, dear Elli. When she gets to the steps she loses her nerve and sets off at a run, taking three at once. She could have done it if she hadn't been so stupid as to run. If she'd stayed calm I presumably wouldn't have been able to bring myself to harm her. I might have even stood by and watched her go to the telephone and call the police to have me arrested and taken away, simply because I love her so much. But her headless flight triggers off the hunting instinct in me, my rage boils over again, my rage at being taken in and betrayed by everyone, even by Elli. Adrenaline floods through me, neutralising all sense of pain. I throw myself at her like a goalkeeper, grab her legs and pull her off her feet so that she falls with a scream on the hard steps, hitting her head on the green stone slabs. Blood pours out from under her hair. She struggles in desperation, kicks at me and tries to get back on her feet, emitting piercing screams all the time. Suddenly I'm struck by fear, perhaps she's left the front door open because the kids are still in the car and I'm supposed to go straight to them. So I have to stop Elli screaming. There's no other way. I have to overcome her resistance – as quickly as possible. I hit her on the back of her head, just with my hand, with the flat of my hand, lie on top of her and pull up her right arm behind her back as far as it goes. She's still screaming, but more quietly now, it's more a wail of despair. In vain she tries to scratch me with her other, free arm. With my free hand I press her head against the edge of the stone step. Not too hard, but it's enough. She stops screaming, stops resisting. She's just crying as I stand her back up on her feet, twist her other arm round behind her back and frogmarch her down into the shelter. She gives a loud sob as I lay her on the floor there, place my uninjured knee on the point between her shoulder blades and lean on it with my whole weight as I put on the neck-ring. The little lock engages. I take the tiny key out. Elli's not resisting any longer, she just lies on the floor, whimpering quietly, her eyes closed, her fringe floating in a sludgy pool that looks like oil. I take a cable tie out of the kitchen drawer and tie her hands behind her back. Then I frisk her for her phone. It's in the inside pocket of her jacket, together with the car key. I switch the phone off and stuff it in my pocket, the car key as well, then stroke Elli's head to calm her down. I hook the end of the chain in the ring by the kitchen island.

"It's not what you think," I say. "You've no need to be afraid. I'll take the kids away now, then I'll come back as quickly as possible and we'll discuss everything. I can explain it. I can explain everything. Don't be afraid."

But she is afraid. She's rolled herself up like a hedgehog. Like an embryo. Like a hedgehog embryo. She's still whimpering with fear. I can't bring myself to look at her as I close the steel door.

18

In the garage I put her phone in one of the plastic dog-waste bags my parents got for Rusty, their Saint Bernhard, and which until now had contained a greasy sprocket for a bike that no longer exists. I smash it with the hammer, then I go back up the steps, ready for anything. Fortunately the front door is closed. When I open it I see that the kids are still sitting quietly in the back of the car. Still and silent with their little white faces. I go over to them.

"Okay," I say, "you two stay where you are. I'm just going to go and put a jacket on, I'll be back in a minute."

I go to the bathroom, turn on the tap and hardly is the water running than the tears are running out of my eyes. Whole streams. I'm really shaking. I lean on the basin with both hands and roar like an animal with a fatal wound. It's unfair. It's so unfair. I have to pull myself together, the children are waiting outside. I try to calm down, slowly count to a hundred but when I get to twenty-two I start shaking again and yowl like something having its skin ripped off. Happiness – I could have had it. It was within my grasp. These last five or six, perhaps even eight years left to us before civilisation in Europe collapses, they could have been the best of my life. I had the chance of starting afresh with the woman I've been in love with for decades. We would have been young together, just twenty, at least in our looks and physical capacity, but not as stupid as you are at twenty and therefore I would have managed to do everything right this time.

I slosh water over my face with my hand, but I can't stop crying and wailing. For Elli, for us, for myself.

If Racke hadn't put on that act… I imagine him lying in a pool of mud and hitting him with a club, again and again until he's not yelling any more and his little head, smashed to pieces, sinks into the brown sludge.

I dry my face and comb my hair. My face is pretty puffy but it'll be dark enough in the car so that Binya and Racke won't notice. And by the time we get to Gerda's I hope I'll look normal again – or I won't get out of the car. I quickly slip on my red-and-black lumberjack jacket. Binya and Racke, who are usually squabbling all the time, are sitting huddled up together and stare at me apprehensively as I open the driver's door.

"Okay," I say as I reverse out into the street, "so you're afraid of a really nice person like Elli, who wouldn't kill even a fish because of her convictions, who refuses to put a scrap of any animal at all in her mouth just because it tastes nice… unlike the pair of you… so you're afraid of being in a car with Elli – but you're not afraid of me, are you? Have I got that right?"

There's an uneasy silence in the car. (The engineers didn't think of that when they made the new hydrogen engines so quiet that silences, that will keep on cropping up, especially on lengthy journeys, are immediately noticeable and uncomfortable. That's why Mercedes are planning to put a fake diesel-engine noise on the market next year.) Binya and Racke don't dare answer me and that's the most sensible thing they could do. I don't know whether I could restrain myself if one of them uttered a single word. Hatred is swilling round in my body, hatred that turns the blood in my veins into black syrup. I want to make these brats pay for having got Elli in this situation. They've destroyed her life and mine, and they should get some idea of what they've done.

"What were you thinking of, insulting Elli like that?" I say to Racke. "Did you imagine that if it comes to the crunch I'd come down against Elli and for you? Do you think I like you better than Elli? Why should I? What's so special about you that makes you a match for someone like Elli?"

Racke starts to sob quietly and I feel a bit better. Yes, yes, I know, here children enjoy absolute protection and understanding, even if they've just destroyed your life. Why, actually? Is it to their credit that they go about their intrigues in a way that's clumsy, stupid and easy to see through? Does that make their nasty intentions any less nasty?

"Cry away, cry-baby," I tell him. "Do you imagine I feel sorry for you? Do you think I love you? Do you realise how tedious you are? How boring it is for me to have to spend a whole Sunday with you?"

Now Racke starts wailing out loud.

"Shut your gob!" I bellow. "Just you shut your gob, you useless piece of crap."

Now Racke and Binya are both wailing in muted tones. The greenish beam of the headlights of my hydrogen car bathes the road and rape-infested footpaths in eerie and oppressive pseudo-colours, greenish yellow and grey-green, the shadows blacker than black. When I look in the rear-view mirror, I see that Binya has stuffed the end of her scarf in Racke's mouth and the other end in her own. I must see to it that the kids calm down somewhat before we get to Gerda's.

"Take your scarf out of your mouth," I say to Binya, "and out of your brother's mouth as well. Or do you want him to suffocate?"

Their whimpering gets a little louder.

"Look," I say to Binya, "don't you try to tell me you seriously believed Elli was going to do something to you. You're too old for that. It was a nasty trick of yours to make Racke panic. I'll tell you – both of you – something now: we're not going to see each other for the next eight weeks. Have you got that? You can't come and see me any longer. In eight weeks' time I might perhaps come and visit you at Grandma Gerda's. But only if Elli forgives you. Otherwise I'll never come again. And you can explain that to Grandma Gerda. And tell her she's not to phone me for points any more. Tell her she's to give you vegan food. If she does call me, then you won't be allowed to live with her any more. Tell her that."

They haven't stopped sobbing. I let them out at Gerda's and just wait until the door opens. Then I drive off. If I break off contact with Binya and Racke, they can't notice that Elli's not there any more.

On the way back I turn off at Bäckerbrücke to the Poppenbüttel sluice, park the car in a woman's car park, hobble with the little plastic bag containing the bits of Elli's smashed-up picture-phone over to the sluice and shake everything out into the raging white water. I wished I'd had a look to see who Elli had phoned today and yesterday before I hit it with the hammer, then I'd have some idea who might be a danger. But perhaps she didn't make any calls at all. Perhaps we have a lot more time than I think.

19

Elli's standing behind the kitchen island. Her eyes are puffy; above them is a red-purple-and-green rainbow where I pressed her forehead against the edge of the step. The blood has dried and is caked over a few strands of her fringe. I close the door, put down the jute bag and enter the code, holding my other hand over it. Then I take out a pair of scissors and a padlock, go over to Elli, cut through the cable tie that's holding her trembling hands behind her back and replace the snap-hook attaching the chain to the kitchen island with the padlock, remove the little key and slip it into my pocket.

"Come and sit down," I say, picking up the jute bag, "I've got some plasters."

Not only plasters, I've also brought a face-cloth and gauze and some gel for bruises. I want to play the paramedic for a while, but Elli won't go along with it.

"Please," she sobs, "please let me out of here. Please."

She's completely hysterical. It's impossible to have a rational conversation with her. I have to give that to Christine: the first time she was facing me in the prepper room she showed much greater composure. Elli's nothing but a panic-stricken bundle of nerves.

"And do stop sobbing," I bellow. "There's no reason for it."

Now, of course, her sobbing gets even louder. Today's the day of tears. I sit down beside her, take her chin in my hand and carefully rub the encrusted blood off her temple with the damp face-cloth. The cut is in her hair.

"Listen," I say when her sobs gradually get quieter, "it wasn't my intention to lock you in down here. It wasn't planned. You'd never have learnt that this room exists. But now that it's happened we have to think what we do about it."

"I won't say anything," Elli sobs in my face. "I swear I won't say anything. Please let me out. Please. I definitely won't say anything."

The tears are dripping down her face. There's nothing between us any more. As if we'd never been in love.

"Oh, come on, Elli, don't talk nonsense. Of course you'll report me to the police once you're out of here. You'd have to be insane not to do so."

"No, word of honour! I swear I won't say anything. Not a word."

I'm slowly getting rather impatient. Elli simply lacks the class Christine showed back then when she was in the same situation. But that means it will probably be easier to deal with her. From the start I won't let her make any kind of scene, I'll demand absolute obedience right from the word go.

"Now pull yourself together, Elli, right? I love you, I've always loved you and I won't do anything you don't want. And I will let you out of here, okay? But not right away. I can't do that because you'll go to the police at once. Now don't start arguing again, of course you'll go to the police. And that means I must first of all prepare my escape properly, get money from the bank, find a place where I can go to ground and so on. Surely you can understand that, can't you? And then I'll let you out or ring someone who'll let you out."

Slowly something of this trickles into her little, panic-stricken brain.

"You'll let me out? Really?"

"Yes," I say. "But first of all I must arrange my escape and before that I also want to explain to you what this room is. It's not what you think, it's something else."

That's a story I worked out on the way back from Gerda's.

"Right then, listen. This is the old coal cellar from the days when the house was heated by coal. There came a time when my father converted it into a workroom and I decided to turn it into a survival bunker. Then two and a half years ago my ex-wife and I were arguing about the children. She wanted to take the kids away from me and somehow or other I lost my rag and hit her and then she screamed that I'd never see them again. I snapped and locked her in the cellar to give myself time to flee abroad with the kids. But she made such a racket I was afraid she'd get out before I'd checked in with the kids – that's why I got the chain and tied her up. I would have rung someone up to get her out as soon as I was safely away with the kids. But when I took some food in shortly before we were to leave, I found her dead on the floor. Perhaps a heart attack or a stroke – even today I don't know for sure. Perhaps she even did it herself deliberately. I wouldn't have put it past her. She'd always done her utmost to make life difficult for me. Anyway, there she was, dead all of a sudden, and I buried her in the garden at night and I haven't opened the bunker door since then – until today. I wanted to sort everything out before we two made a new beginning. I didn't want any stuff left over from the past lying around. That's why I thought I'd have a quick clear out. And if you hadn't come back sooner than expected, we'd have been happy together and this room would never have been mentioned."

Elli looks at me as if she believes the story, but she doesn't, of course. I wouldn't buy the story myself. Everything here – the worn sofa, the burnt fat in the oven, the shiny places on the chain where Christine always picked it up when she went round the room – suggests a longish stay. While I was taking the kids to Gerda, Elli will certainly have had a look in the fitted cupboards and found Christine's clothes and cosmetics. Actually it's quite good that I haven't thrown them away. I won't need to buy new stuff for Elli. Apart from a toothbrush.

"When are you going to let me out?" she asks. "Why don't you let me out right away? I won't give you away."

"Oh really, Elli," I say, "I'm not that stupid. I am going to let you out. In a week or perhaps ten days. Depends on how long it takes me to make all the arrangements." I lean towards her to stroke her cheek and she flinches. Okay, I did hit her. But after all it was only on the back of her head. With the flat of my hand. I didn't beat her up. I didn't hit her any harder than, bearing her physique in mind, she could have hit me. I think that's always the limit: never hit anyone harder than they could hit you.

Suddenly I'm overcome with tears.

"I'm sure you'll be able to survive the few days," I say in a strained voice. "Can't you see what's the bad thing about all this – that everything between us is over. That's much worse. I love you, Elli. I love you much more than I've ever loved anyone. And I'd never harm you. Never! It's for your sake that I'm going to let myself be pursued by the police. And of course they'll get me at some point or other and I'll spend the last few years left to humanity in prison. And why will I do that? So that you can be happy. That's how much I love you, Elli. I love you more than I love myself. And you can't understand that, then tremble and cry as if I were the lowest of the low."

As I get to the end I start shouting again. But at least it's made me stop weeping.

"Sorry," Elli says almost inaudibly. "I'm sorry."

"That's all right," I say. "Would you like me to stay with you tonight? Or would you rather get yourself sorted out first?"

She doesn't reply, simply stares into space. All right, then. It's her own fault if she has to spend her first night in the prepper room by herself. She's just making things even more difficult for herself. She's voluntarily submitting to a procedure that is employed all over the world to make prisoners tractable: to follow up a sudden, unexpected abduction with immediate isolation. It's in every brainwashing handbook. I'd just have to take her clothes off to accentuate the feeling of vulnerability. But I could never do something like that to her. Just leaving her alone here hurts. I would have loved to have lain beside her during this terrible night, to have taken her in my arms and soothed her. Breaking her is the last thing I want. At least she'll probably be relieved to see me tomorrow.

20

"I've thought things over," Elli says the next morning, scratching nervously with her little finger under the neck-iron. "Now that I've had the night to sleep on it, I can think clearly again. You don't have to go off and hide. Things between us aren't over. No matter what happened to your wife, the two of us belong together."

If I needed any proof that I've lost Elli, that's it. She's spent the night wondering how she can manipulate me. From now on I won't be able to believe a thing she says, everything will simply be part of a strategy.

"Please, Elli," I say, "can't you just wait these one or two weeks. Even if you don't trust me, just think about it. The moment someone reports you as missing someone or other will mention my name. At the class reunion everyone saw that things clicked between us. And then it won't be long before someone remembers that my ex-wife also went missing. And then they'll have me. Two women I was involved with reported missing, I couldn't get away with that. And this time I hardly expect the Yellow Monks will pop up to take responsibility for your disappearance. Even if I intended to keep you here for ever, I wouldn't have a chance of getting away with it.

"But I mean it seriously," Elli says. She looks terribly crumpled: crumpled loba dress, crumpled blouse, crumpled hair and dark rings under her eyes. The poor woman's probably spent the night tossing and turning on the mattress. At least the purple streak on her forehead has faded a little.

"I love you as well," she says. "I love you so much that I can forgive you everything. I can do that. Why don't you think I'm capable of that? And why should I go so far as to lie to you? When everyone's seen us together and you can't keep me here anyway."

She's right about that, of course. But my instinct tells me that she's lying.

"Everything could be the way it was before. You've nothing to fear from me. But if someone has to come and fetch me out of this cellar, then it'll all be common knowledge. Please – don't make us lose the time we could still spend together. I can't bear the thought of having to live without you again. I don't want that, do you understand? What have you got to lose?"

What have I got to lose? My freedom. Though the temptation is pretty strong. What if she does love me that much and I'm missing out on the chance simply because I'm so distrustful?

"Then prove it and sleep with me," I say. "Now."

"What!?"

Her jaw literally drops.

"Well if you really do still love me as much as you claim, you ought to be really dying to sleep with me."

"It's perhaps not quite the right situation to… Okay, I'll sleep with you."

She grabs me by the collar, as if I'm the one who can be pulled around at will, and drags me over to the bed with the rumpled pillows and screwed-up blanket that give you an idea of what she must have been feeling last night. There she gives me a friendly shove on the chest and I obediently fall backwards onto the mattress where I've had it off with Christine hundreds of times. With her knees and hands either side of me she creeps over me on all fours, sits on my loins and starts to fiddle with my zip. She's one of those women who like to be on top, she really likes it. Christine once claimed women had no interest in that at all. That women being on top while having sex was the only thing about emancipation that men had accepted without objection, lazy bastards that we were. And now, she added, we were constantly urging women to do that, imagining we were being incredibly emancipated, while the women were just doing it to please us – as usual. It's disastrous that most of our information about what women think comes from our own wives, which can be extremely subjective.

Elli unbuttons her blouse, casually slipping the chain at her neck over onto her back. I wonder what she'd have done if she'd been wearing a pullover or a sweatshirt or something else she couldn't undo? She lifts up her little bottom to help me take off her panties, and when they get stuck over her knees and I exaggerate how I have to pull them down with both hands, growling like a dog, she even laughs. When I penetrate her, she briefly flinches but then she's all over me, her lips clamped over mine. If Elli's just putting on an act, she's doing it very well. I stroke her fantastic false breasts and feel her nipples harden – well, that can hardly be something she's putting on – then run my hands down to her slim waist, drawing her to me. Elli cries out.

"Too far," she pants, "too far in."

She slips down off me and doubles up. I lay her on her back and play with her breasts a bit, brushing the back of my hand over them and things like that, then I carefully penetrate her again. She groans, pushes against me and throws her head back – just like a porno star. That's enough! I'm not buying that. It's awful making love to her and knowing she doesn't really want to. But I'm beyond that now. Even if I were to go inactive or someone threw a bucket of cold water over me, I can't hold back my ejaculation. Elli comes at the same time. She's lying underneath me, giving herself up to the moment, arms outstretched, fingers digging into the mattress. I can feel the sweat on her skin, the twitching inside her, and I see the patches of red on her breast. It's genuine, unequivocally genuine. I roll off, lie beside her and she nuzzles her face up to my neck, breathing right next to my ear. I kiss her, kiss her on the forehead and over the place where the ring goes round her neck.

"Okay then," I say, "okay, I guess I've got to believe you. But give me until tomorrow before I let you out. I want at least to withdraw some money and think about a hiding place. In case things should come to the worst. So that I can disappear quickly in an emergency. You must grant me that little bit of distrust."

"That's okay," she says. "I'm just delighted that you believe me at last. But in that case you must go to my place and feed Murri."

I love Elli too much to point out to her that it's nonsense in her situation to use 'must' to me. Instead I say, "Cats are tough. They can stand a day without food. If necessary she'll catch herself a mouse."

"Murri can't. She's got dementia. The food's on top of the kitchen cupboard. Dry food and tins. She needs both – because she never knows what she wants."

Elli gets up and, half-naked, only wearing her loba skirt (and the neck-ring, of course) goes over to the chair her anorak's on and fishes her house key out of the pocket. I do up my zip and lie back on the pillows.

That's when I suddenly notice it: there's a hole in the

ceiling. A hole right where I plastered over the way into the space over the false ceiling. It's a pretty small hole, just the size of a five-mark coin and Elli's stuffed toilet paper in it so that it's not that obvious, but you can see the scratches round it. Probably made by a spoon. There's nothing else here. She must have noticed the fresh plaster and of course when the chain's attached to the kitchen island it's long enough for her to work on the ceiling there.

I can't say how devastated I feel. There's no truthfulness, no love between people. I was a simpleton, a hopeless fool, even to have considered trusting Elli.

She's scrambling back up onto the bed beside me, cuddling up to me again. She drops her keys on my chest and kisses me on the shoulder, on my shirt, sucking at the cloth until it's soaked and I can feel her kisses as if she were kissing the skin. I should thump her. Right in the face. But I don't, of course. Fool in love that I am, I swallow my bitter disappointment and behave as if nothing had happened. I even stroke Elli's hair before I pick up the keys and get up so that the goddam cat can get its revolting, stinking food. Actually I ought to find some excuse for shortening the chain length drastically so that Elli can't do more serious damage to the ceiling. Fortunately the chain isn't long enough for her to get up in between the two ceilings and find Christine's body. Though the torch is still hanging from the beam by the entrance. If she should find that and shine it all round… I'm so furious and disappointed I think the shock would serve her right. If she should come across the corpse it will be clear to her what a mistake it was to try to escape and that things between us are at an absolute end. She's going to bitterly regret having abused my trust like that, but by then it will already be too late and I don't need to feel any obligation towards her any more. An abrupt trauma right at the start will also speed up her readiness to submit. That's the third step in professional brainwashing: give the victim a shock to make them submissive. Not that that was what I intended but Elli herself has seen to it that that's going to happen.

I take the little key for the neck-ring padlock from its hook by the door, sit down beside Elli again and take the chain right off.

"This," I say, "is presumably not necessary any longer."

I give her a kiss on the neck, quite the trusting lover, and so that she'll have enough time to scrabble her way in through the false ceiling, I add, "I'll probably be away overnight – to give me time to prepare everything."

"Thank you," she says, giving me an ostensibly uninhibited kiss on the cheek. "Give Murri my best wishes."

If Elli can no longer be the love of my life, then perhaps she can be something else. Even if she doesn't love me any more, she'll be at my disposal for the next week or two. She'll be a less worn-out, prettier and much more lovable substitute for Christine, with fresh, unforeseeable reactions. I couldn't hurt her at all and in two weeks at the most I'm going to set her free. But she still belongs to me, even though it's in a different way from what I imagined.

21

Elli's still living in Bargteheide, even if no longer on the animal-rights farm but in a block of flats. I've only been to her place once, when I had the pleasure of making the acquaintance of the dementia-stricken Murri. Afterwards I argued that we should meet at my place for preference. At least going to feed the cat gives me the opportunity to get Elli's car-share Egg out of my front garden. I should have done that right away. Yesterday. Even though no one will miss her yet.

On the way to Bargteheide I work out a plan of how best to deal with Elli in order to get as much as possible out of my last days with her. I just want to have a great time with her, even if she doesn't love me any more. I'll treat her well but we have to be clear about the allocation of roles. She's not going to be constantly giving me commissions. Feed the cat and that's it. Discipline's important, establishing clear rules from the very beginning and insisting they be observed. It's better for prisoners as well if there are clear guidelines they can adhere to. Above all I have to think about preparing my getaway. Abroad? I probably won't be able to avoid going abroad. Oh God – and I'm enjoying life so much here.

I park the car-share Egg in a fairly central position, close to the old pond, so that it will find a new user pretty soon. Elli could have parked it there to do some shopping and then gone on foot to her flat that's only four streets away.

It's horribly hot again. There's a shimmering heat-haze

over the cobbled street and in the pond eight nursery-school kids and their paedophile teacher are splashing about round the fountain that comes spurting out of the palms of three life-size female figures – just one presumably wouldn't have been enough.

Elli's flat is in a brand-new cul-de-sac that has been driven right through a generously laid-out housing complex in order to squeeze in two more blocks. Hanging around by the entrance are two male bio-twenty-year-olds in animal-mood trousers, a leopard and a giraffe, with cheap, totally uncool dinkie boards under their arms. Early twenties isn't enough for them. They want to look sixteen again but they're far too portly for that. Completely lacking in dignity.

The stairwell still smells as antiseptic as the last time. There are still no smears of dirt on the walls and not even one bit of fluff on the doormats. Just one cactus has made it onto a window ledge, otherwise it looks just the way it did when it was ready for the final building inspection. Elli lives on the fifth floor, of course. E. Westphal. The name plate on the door makes me quite melancholy. This is where Elli is going to take up her old life again and I won't play any part in it. Behind the door a brazenly insistent miaowing immediately starts up. We can't have that. The little beast will draw the attention of the whole building. I'll have to take it with me. And I can't stand cats. In my view they're lousy bootlickers and poseurs, the psychopaths among the animals.

I open the door and immediately the red devil's prowling round my legs, rubbing against my calves and purring for all it's worth. By now it has been established that purring isn't a sign of affection or contentment but a hypnotic low frequency by which they put other creatures in a state of trance so that they can use them as living cushions. The nice thing about

Elli's flat is that it isn't particularly feminine in its furnishings but more neutral. White walls and in the little hall there's even a genuine seventies wardrobe: wooden octagons arranged in a honeycomb pattern on a black-painted metal frame. Almost impossible to find today and, if you do, horrendously expensive. It isn't like the wardrobe my parents used to have, but if things had turned out differently I'd have still tried to talk Elli into letting me have it. Apart from the wardrobe, there's just a Greenpeace calendar on the wall. A bottle-nose dolphin. It could be really nice here if it didn't stink of cat's piss and cat food. Oh God, what a stench! With the cat under my feet I stagger into a miniature version of a country-house kitchen – a particularly plain and tasteful version, of course – and take one of the tins of cat food off the top of the cupboard. The tin doesn't have the usual picture of some other cat with a stupid grin on its face but, quite seriously, one of the animal that's the source of the food, in this case a donkey. Well, with that at least you know what you're doing. When Elli, her halo resplendent, berated me for my boundless contempt for life because I still ate animals, there was no mention of the fact that she fed meat to her cat. The little monster's going crazy, purring like a helicopter and throwing itself alternately at the dirty empty bowl on the floor and at my legs in order to rub them. I can't find the cutlery drawer but there's a knife in the sink.

"Yes, yes," I say, shovelling the tinned donkey with the knife into the bowl. That's at least what I meant to do but the cat hurled itself on the oily lump with such a lack of control that only a third landed in its bowl. A further third was spread over the cat itself, while the last third ended up on the floor. And the smell! Now the stench in here is even worse.

Whilst Murri is furiously wolfing everything down, I grab

the jute bag hanging on the radiator and fill it with the remaining tins and half a sack of dry food. Then I look round for a pet carrier but can't find one. I can't really ask Elli if she has one. She'd have realised that I have no intention of releasing her tomorrow but am making preparations for a longer stay. What I do find instead of the cage is a further reason for the infernal stench in the flat: the cat has shat on the floor several times. The cat litter box in the hall on the other hand is untouched. I tear off a few sheets of lavatory paper, gather up the black turds and dispose of them in the human toilet. Revolting beast. I tilt the window and lock it in that position – I can't open it fully because the demented cat might jump out from the fifth floor. Then I pack Elli's toothbrush in a striped toilet bag which, according to the label, was woven by a Nepalese women's project, add some skin cream and cosmetics and her tin of Ephebo – from the black rubber pimples on it, I first of all took it for a sex-toy. While I'm still rummaging round among the cool little woman's things in her bathroom cabinet, I suddenly hear someone outside trying to turn a key in the lock. Which doesn't work because Elli's key is in it on the inside.

I freeze.

Someone rings the bell. Then a woman's voice, "Elli? Is that you, Elli?"

In slow motion I put the toilet bag down on the washing machine. Then, fortunately, I realise there's no point in pretending the flat's empty. If the key's in the lock on the inside, then logically there must be someone in there. And, anyway – why shouldn't Elli's boyfriend get a few things from her flat for her?

I open the front door. A pretty girl, as young as the two guys hanging round outside would like to be but which even Ephebo can't manage, is standing there.

"May I ask who you are?" I say in a slightly sharp tone. Immediately she becomes a little ill at ease.

"Sorry, I'm Grit, one of Elli's friends. I'm supposed to feed the cat."

"Oh," I reply, raising my eyebrows, "you too?"

"I thought she was at your place and I should feed Murri and clear up the shit."

"I've done that already," I say. "I'm Bassi." I shake Grit's pretty, slim and slightly rough hand.

"Elli and I know each other from Fur & Rights," she says. "We did the campaign with tins of human flesh together. I designed the labels then the two of us put them on the tins of stewing meat in the supermarket."

I laugh – my nice, engaging boyish laugh. Happy animal rights campaigners, the generations getting together peaceably to fight for the common cause. In the past that was always one of my motives for joining in with animal-rights organisations – the high proportion of young girls in them.

I suddenly get a great idea. "Tell me," I say, "could you perhaps feed the cat for another week? You see Elli and I want to…"

"No, I can't, I'm afraid. As Elli knows, I have to go to prison in four days' time."

"You have to go to prison? She didn't tell me that."

"Only for a month. Of course the judge would have liked to get out of it by giving me a fine or a few hours of community work, but I insisted on going to prison. And now I have to arrange for someone to water my flowers and so on."

"What did you do?"

"Liberated a piglet. Not for the first time, of course, so they couldn't let me out on probation again. I'm looking forward to prison. They're obliged to give me a vegan diet. Vegan bedclothes, vegan mattress, they're really going to have to get their act together. I sent them a list."

"Good idea," I say. "The best would be to incite other prisoners to follow your example, then they'll start wondering whether they shouldn't change all the prison furnishings to vegan."

"So what are you going to do with the cat now?"

"I'll just have to take her with me. Tell me, have you any idea if there's a pet carrier here?"

"I've got a whole boot full of transport cages. You can take your choice."

And there I am going out of the flat and down the antiseptic stairs with Grit. She leads the way and she has just the same sweet little bottom as Elli. Only hers is somehow that bit more authentic. However, since she drives a car she must be at least seventeen.

"Are you sure you want to take the cat? That's really nice of you, not every man would do that."

The undignified bio-almost-teenagers are still hanging round outside and they stare at Grit as she goes past. They're the sort of old farts who try to infiltrate a school class and then grope the true-young girls, the sixteen-and-seventeen-year-olds.

Grit heads for a mottled green Mercedes van. The latest and biggest hydrogen model, the H-560. Not exactly what I would have imagined as the car of an animal-rights activist. She opens the tailgate and I can take one from a pile of transport cages.

"Elli will bring it back in a week at the latest," I promise. I'm slowly starting to feel safe and impregnable in my role. The trick is simply to behave normally. To relax and to believe what you're saying as you say it.

"Can I give you a lift anywhere?"

For a moment I'm tempted, but there's no point in pushing my luck. "Thanks, but I've come by car."

Car my arse! I'll have to make my way back home by public transport, carrying the cat and its food, bowls and litter. At least that's one of the few things our lady ministers have sorted out: the free bus and tram network that runs smoothly.

Grit gives me a farewell hug – after all, anyone taking a demented, incontinent cat home with them has to be a good person.

22

I'm woken up by the cat's yowling. It's just six. The door to my teenager's bedroom is closed, and it's sitting outside, yowling. Hoping it will give up, I stare at the poppy wallpaper. Orange is a cheerful colour. The cat's yowling turns into a kind of bleating, not bleating like a goat but a sound that could come from a bird, a magpie perhaps. I'm not going to give in. If I let the cat get away with it, it'll be trying it on every day.

By now Elli will probably have found Christine's body. If she failed to see the torch hanging from the beam, she'll have blindly felt her way on all fours round the space, until she suddenly came across something cold, also soft and unyielding. She will have shrunk back and then cautiously stretched out two fingers then her whole hand and felt it again. And when she realises what's lying there in front of her, she'll feel sheer horror crawling up the back of her neck. Perhaps she screamed, staggered back on her hands and feet, screaming, hit her head on a beam, knocked the chair over as she climbed down and ricked her ankle. Then she'll have crept back into her bed and pulled the blanket up over her head. She's probably crying now. Having lain there awake all night, aware that there's a corpse putrefying on the ceiling above her. She'll hate me. Of course. But she's already done that before, when she coldly made love to me, even though she hated me and that didn't even prevent her from coming. I could have made it even worse. I could have taken out the fuse, then she'd have spent the whole night in the dark with the dead body.

The cat starts scratching at the door like crazy. It'll ruin it if I don't do something to stop it. Unfortunately the door doesn't open outwards, otherwise I could smash the creature on the head. So I get up, at least then I can bawl at the cat. Completely unimpressed, it follows me into the kitchen. As far as I can see, it at least hasn't shat anywhere. As a reward I put a double portion of tinned kangaroo into its bowl. The red beast looks at the bowl, then it looks up at me as if I'm not quite right in the head and starts wailing again – on a high, long-drawn-out, querulous note. Audible dementia. There isn't another bowl so I tip a load of dry food on a saucer. There's a repeat performance: saucer on the floor, a quick sniff, then the questioning look as if I'm not quite right in the head, renewed wailing.

"Eat that or go away and die for all I care."

I refuse to let myself be tyrannised by the fleabag. A second sniff, then Murri picks up a lump in its sharp teeth. It's Elli who's going to have to look after it from this afternoon on, thank God. I wonder what's she's doing at the moment? I don't want to release her too soon, but by now I'm too wide awake to go back to bed. First of all I make myself a decent breakfast, scrambled eggs on toast and muesli, then clear up the mess in the living room that's still there from yesterday: pick up the table I knocked over, wipe the dhal casserole off the carpet and the walls. Then I have a quick session at the compunicator, looking on ebay for a saucepan like the one my mother used to use: a whopping great pan, light blue with a border of dark-blue apples. To find a saucepan from the 1970s you don't just have to enter 'saucepan' and '1970s' but '1960s', '1950s' and '1980s' as well. Most of the sellers on ebay haven't the least idea of the difference between a 1970s saucepan and one from the 1960s. After I've spent long enough on a fruitless search, it occurs to me that a saucepan like that's hardly something I can take with me when I disappear. At least by now it's half past eight and that seems to me a suitable time to see what mood Elli's in. I grab the toolbox, the pot with the filler and the two planks I sawed to size yesterday to fit the hole in the ceiling, and make my way to the cellar, take the tins off the shelf, the peas and carrots, the meatballs and the peaches, push the shelves to one side, unscrew the plywood sheet with the Black & Decker, take it off the wall and tap in the code to open the steel door. Voilà!

Elli's sitting on the bed. She's still wearing her loba skirt and the blouse, she didn't even think it necessary to get changed. It takes me a moment before I realise what the situation is. Elli must have gone mad, crazy with fear or whatever. She's taken Christine's body out of the false ceiling and laid it out on her bed; she's sitting beside it, trying to pour some water in between her dead lips.

I walk over slowly with the toolbox and the planks under my arm. Elli jumps up.

"Quick! You have to call an ambulance."

I'm thunderstruck. "Elli," I say, closing the door and tapping in the code. "Elli, please calm down, Elli. She's dead. Can't you see she's dead? What have you done?"

"She isn't dead."

Elli comes over and stretches her hand out to me. I grasp her tiny, crazed hand and let her pull me over to the bed.

"You must call an ambulance."

With a sense of disgust I bend over Christine's stiff body, over the hollow at the bottom of her neck, and then I see it – a movement, swallowing. Oh my God! I just make it to the bathroom, into the shower, before I'm sick, writhing and retching until my forehead's covered in sweat. I stay there doubled up for a moment, staring apathetically at the scrambled egg and muesli, until I'm capable of turning the shower on and swilling my sick down the plughole. There must be a curse on me. No one has that much bad luck. I put my head under the cold water, push back my wet hair and, more or less calm and collected, go back to Elli – or should I say to Elli and Christine? I look down at my wife. Her breathing is hardly perceptible.

"If she isn't dead, then she's as good as dead. Even an ambulance isn't going to change that."

"You bastard!" Elli cries. "That would just suit you, wouldn't it."

Now I'm quite calm again. "Elli," I say, "poor, dear Elli. I'm sorry you had to see this, I would have liked to keep you out of it. But if you look closely you can see yourself: she's going to die today."

"Nonsense. I was talking to her just now."

Things are getting worse and worse. I'm already starting to retch again. I look at Christine, more closely this time. She doesn't look all that dead, her breathing is hardly perceptible but otherwise she looks quite alive, only rather flabby and worn-out – the way people between forty and fifty used to look. She must have been through another phase of ageing in the last few days.

"What did she say?"

Elli gives me a black look. "She said, 'Sebastian. My husband Sebastian did this to me.' That's what she said. Would you now please call an ambulance."

It's time I went on the offensive. "What makes you think you have the right to give me orders?" I reply harshly. "I will not call an ambulance. On the contrary, I'll finish the job off."

I take a step towards the bed but Elli throws herself in my way.

"Over my dead body."

I simply push her aside. "So what? Then I'll just kill you as well. Do you imagine my situation will be any the worse if I kill you? I'll get life for this anyway. Even if I only get eight years, that will still be a life sentence, as you very well know."

Elli clutches my arm. She's crying now. "Don't do it. You don't need to kill her. If you're going to let me out, you can let her out at the same time. You're going to flee the country anyway."

It's terrible to see Elli crying. But it would be even more terrible if Christine were actually to wake up and incite Elli against me. I put my arm round Elli, press her to me.

"You wouldn't be doing either her or yourself a favour," I say. "Christine was really done for. She wanted to die. I offered to let her out shortly. I was willing to hand myself in and reveal everything so I could start afresh again with you. And then she killed herself, or at least tried to. She begrudged me my new happiness. You've no idea what kind of person my wife is."

Elli pushes me away. I can see her struggling with herself, how she has to control herself to stop herself from launching into abuse of me. Admittedly my last excuse wasn't particularly convincing. I have to go up into the false ceiling to get some idea of what Elli found there. She takes a deep breath.

"If you love me, even just a tiny little bit, then you won't kill your wife. If what I think of you is of the least bit of importance to you…"

"I'll think about it," I say. "But only if you're sensible now and don't make a racket."

"Okay," Elli says, "I'll stay quite calm."

I pick up the chain with the neck-ring. "Come here."

Elli hesitates for a moment then comes and stands with her back to me. I put the ring round her neck. When I try to lock it I see that the key isn't there.

"Where's the key?"

Elli lowers her head and points to Christine. "In her sleeve."

I take the neck-ring off again. "Get it."

Elli gets the key that was indeed in Christine's sleeve. I put the neck-ring on again, turn the key and slip it in my pocket. Then I think again and go to the security door to put the key down out of Elli's reach.

"What is going to happen is this," I say. "As long as you do everything I tell you to, I'll let Christine stay alive. If you resist me or try to fool me just once, then that's it. As far as I'm concerned you can nurse her here, but don't delude yourself. She's going to die anyway."

"But you were going to let me out today? You said that you..."

"Surely you don't mean that seriously, Elli? You think you can go behind my back and demolish the ceiling and after that I'll take you up with me and trust you not to go and denounce me to the police? Well, really."

I put the chair under the hole and place the toolbox and the new planks in the ceiling space. Elli is standing by the kitchen island like a watchdog on a chain, watching me with an unfathomable expression on her face as I pull myself up. The torch is still hanging on the beam. I take it down and switch it on, shining it on the floor as I crawl across. The blanket, the crumpled pillow, the plastic bag with the strip of tape, a dried up pool of vomit – either Christine wasn't asleep at all when I left her or she must have woken up immediately afterwards. Perhaps because she needed to be sick. I pick up the plastic bag. It's been torn open at the place where it was over her face, the picture of the vegan sausage is in tatters. There's no vomit stuck to the bag. Why didn't I stay here until Christine was dead? Why didn't I wait half an hour? Well, I didn't actually want to see it of course. Anyway, she was as good as dead: sedatives, plastic bag, noose… What else could I have done? It's just a case of bad luck. I crawl back, let myself down onto the chair and set about replacing the broken pieces of wood. Unfortunately Elli has done more damage than Christine did before, the new ones are too short by quite a bit. So it's back to the DIY store.

Elli's sitting on the bed again, helping Christine to sit up and giving her a drop of water to drink. All that in the pose of Mary with Jesus who's just been taken down from the cross.

"I hope it's clear to you," I say as I cut through Christine's bonds with a pair of pliers, "that I don't have to do all that. I don't have to write a letter just so that you'd be found. I could just take off and wait to see if anyone's on to me. Whether anyone at all is looking for you. I could have arranged everything to look as if we'd gone abroad together. Perhaps I'll get away with it this time as well. So if I do do that, if I tell someone where you can be found, it's purely out of the goodness of my heart. There's nothing in it for me. That's why I expect the same cooperation from you. I don't want any argument, any disputes or questions during the few days until I've arranged my escape. We have perhaps another seven or eight days together and we should take advantage of them, don't you think?"

I don't look at her as I say that, I just pack the tools back in the box, but the soft clink of the chain tells me that Elli is nodding.

23

I found the planks ages ago and put them in the trolley, but I'm still hanging about among the display shelves because I saw the black-draped figure of my brother at the checkout together with his heavily pregnant, chrono-young wife and their ugly brood. I don't want to have to talk to them now, I've got enough on my plate as it is.

Two women! Two! That's the very worst thing that could happen. My dominance over Christine was so complete simply because she was entirely shut off from the outside world. Why else do we make women into housewives and move out into the suburbs with them? I'm still hoping Christine will just die, but if she doesn't, I won't get much out of my last week in the prepper room. Nor from Elli.

One more week. I hate to think that I'm going to have to give all that up. I don't want to go away. After all, I've got a super job here. And where can I go? To Greece? To Syria? China?

I make a detour round the garden section to have a look at the latest eccentric box-tree sculptures and the rainwater tubs shaped like dinosaurs or safes.

Christine would actually have deserved to die. She's destroyed my life. On the other hand I have got pretty far with her – perhaps I can deal with both of them. And the life I intended to have with Elli is down the drain anyway. As a prisoner she's been more of a pain in the arse so far.

There's nothing new in rainwater tubs. The range is very

reduced anyway. Instead there are massive ten thousand litre tanks everywhere in the section that home gardeners can have installed underground in the garden. And there's a twenty thousand litre above-ground tank in the form of a little mountain. It's not badly done actually, it reminds me a bit of the artificial rocks in Hagenbeck Zoo. And then I see something that gives me an idea of how I might be able to solve part of my problems with Elli and Christine. It's an assembled construction kit for a raised bed but in size and shape it's very much like a crate – a crate in which you could lock one person while you're occupied with another. Sold out unfortunately, new stock not coming until next week. And then I come across something else, something I've long been searching for and which wasn't even to be found on the Internet. My heart leaps up: there it is again, the black garden hose with one thin and one thicker yellow stripe that used to writhe around on the lawn of my childhood like a dangerous snake. Sold by the yard, twenty-one north euros per yard – a crazy price, but normally I'd have taken half the roll straightaway. Unfortunately I'm no longer in the market for garden equipment, it would be just as absurd as looking for hostas to go round the pond. And even if the world were to end tomorrow, I'd plant another hosta today. Suddenly the putative five-year period until the world comes to an end is like a huge span of time beyond imagining. An eternity in which whole flowerbeds of hostas could be planted out. The problem is that my old life is only going to last for a few days, that in a short time I'll be an exile.

"So there you are," my crackpot sanctimonious brother says. "Babro saw you when you turned away deliberately so as not to meet us."

He's beaming, his face is shining. Blessed are the poor in spirit.

"Hi," I say in such a friendly voice my brother is quite surprised. The thing is, it's just occurred to me that this could well be the last time I see him. It would have been fine by me if I hadn't run into him at all, but since he's here, in his black jump boots, with a kind of Batman cape over his shoulders and the crucified Christ on his belt buckle, sweating, grinning, I feel quite conciliatory. I have a quick look at his trolley. There's a piece of furniture in it the function of which isn't clear to me. It looks like a stool with steel legs and a thick, square block of wood as a seat. He has three carpet knives as well.

I had no intention of asking him about it – after all I don't want a quarrel – but my brother takes my glance as a pretext to go on at length about his latest project. The stool is a chopping block in authentic old-fashioned design. The Disciples of St. John of the Trumpets of the Seven Last Plagues are going to mount a religious sacrificial feast and slaughter animals in public, appropriately on the site of the old abattoir in Feldstrasse.

"Why do you have to do that, for God's sake. I thought you were Christians – at least in the broadest sense. You've never had sacrifices. Why don't you leave that to the Muslims?"

My brother rebukes me. "You should not take the name of the Lord in vain. Of course we're Christians. Jews, Muslims and Christians all look upon Abraham as the founding father of their faith."

"Oh, great," I say. "So if it's slaughtering your own son at God's command, you're all in agreement for once."

"It was a test of obedience. What we are celebrating is that God sent an angel to stop Abraham and get him to slaughter a ram instead."

"I still think it would be better not to go ahead with it," I say politely, "it's not going to make you very popular.

Civilised people don't like it when animals have their throats cut in public."

I'm making an effort. No one can say I'm not making an effort. I could also ask what Isaac thought about his father being willing to cut his throat at a nod from the Lord. Did that put some kind of strain on the relationship between father and son? But I hold back. Because this is the last time we'll see each other.

My brother gives me a friendly smile. "But they're only animals," he says mildly. "You don't have to get worked up about it."

That's what you always get from the religious crowd – they're only animals or unbelievers, so it's not a crime, it's not the obscenity it clearly is, but pleasing unto God.

"Why don't you give each other presents of little marzipan or chocolate rams instead," I say. "Or some kind of pastries?"

"It's more important to obey the rules of God than those of men," my brother says loftily. "A religion that tries to suit everyone turns sacred rituals into a show pandering to the lowest taste."

I don't believe a word of it. If the Plague Trumpets want to go in for killing lambs in a big way, in violation of all laws about the prevention of cruelty to animals, hygiene regulations and ethical norms, then it's not the will of the Lord they're concerned with but establishing themselves as a religion with a claim to political power. That's why religious leaders never make concessions but, against all reason and humanity, get their followers to cut a bit off little boys' penises or slit open animals. Every breach of the law that the state sees itself as compelled to tolerate is a victory over the state. We don't care what it says in your statutes, that is our God's will. Religions are totalitarian systems and peoples' longing for religion is peoples' longing for totalitarian systems.

Uwe hands me a flyer. "On Saturday evening. I'd be delighted if you could be present at the sacred act – provided of course that you can keep your blasphemous tongue in check."

I have another look at his purchases. "Surely you're not going to slaughter them yourself? With a carpet knife?"

"At the sacrificial feast I will use a ritual knife, of course. However, they won't be delivered until the day after tomorrow and I thought there would be no harm in me getting some practice in beforehand. So that it looks good later."

"Oh great," I say and clear my throat. "I have to go now. I want to drop in on Gerda."

Which of course I don't want to do. But if I go on talking to my brother for much longer there'll come a point when I can't control myself any more and I'll simply thump him. I'm just glad I haven't got Elli with me. It would really have driven her wild.

"Take a flyer for Gerda as well. Take a few, you can put them out, in a pub or in the Democracy Centre."

"Of course," I say, stuffing the leaflets in my jacket pocket. "They'll be delighted in the Democracy Centre."

In the car park I drop the flyers in the rubbish bin of a hot-dog stall. Strangely enough, whenever I hear about cruelty to animals I get this incredible urge to eat meat. These, however, are vegan hot dogs. But there's a butcher's not far from here. A proper little family business with a laughing pig with an apron round its belly and a knife in its hand by the door. And I haven't had meat stew for ages. However depressing it was to come into contact with my brother and his holy bullshit again, at least he's given me an idea: I'll put Elli's willingness to obey to the test. I'll get her to make a stew for me. That will nip any resistance in the bud. Unfortunately I haven't the time to familiarise her with the realities of her new life step by step.

However, I'm going to need all the CO_2 points in my account for my air ticket. I'll probably even have to buy a few more. If I want to eat meat, then I'll have to go and see Gerda and beg a few points off her. She hasn't been in touch since I deposited Racke and Binya at her place. I've no idea what the kids will have told her. I had assumed she'd ring that evening, but perhaps she wants to break off contact with me completely, thinking she's found a pretext for taking them away from me. Of course she doesn't know that I'll have disappeared by next week.

Suddenly I have a longing to see Racke and Binya, Racke especially, and it's so strong it hurts. No one can forbid me to see my children. And while I'm there I can try to beg a few points off Gerda.

It's Racke himself who opens the door.

"Daddy! Daddy!"

He jumps at me, jumps up into my arms so that I have to drop the two fluffy toys I nipped in to a filling station to buy. Racke clasps me tightly round the neck and, oddly enough, he hardly weighs anything at all, he's floating in my arms. I go hot all over as I remember that our last journey in the car together wasn't particularly nice, that I bellowed at them and once even treated them unfairly. I'll probably never see him again, the brave little lad, and he doesn't feel any resentment towards me, no resentment at all. Binya Bathsheba, who has come running up, doesn't say anything but clings to my arm as if she wanted to keep hold of me for ever. Suddenly I have to cry. At their unconditional love that I don't deserve and that they don't know that today will be the last time. Gerda joins us. She's wearing a grandmother's black dress that makes her look like a Greek widow, and an apron with 'The Boss Cooks Here' written on it.

"What's the matter with you lot? Why are you all standing here in the doorway?" she asks in a surprisingly friendly voice, picks up the two fluffy dogs with the infinitely long ears and closes the front door.

"Daddy's crying," Binya says.

"Yes, so he is," says Gerda. "Even daddies sometimes cry. But now let's all go to the living room."

Racke kicks his legs to get out of my arms. "I'll show you the guinea pigs," he roars and runs off ahead.

"Everything okay?" Gerda asks, and from the way she asks and then takes my arm I can tell that the kids haven't said anything about what happened in the car. Otherwise she would definitely be behaving differently now.

"Yes, everything's okay," I say, as I can feel the tears coming again, this time because of the undeserved loyalty of my children and the motherly attitude of Gerda towards me – and because of her apron with the silly message on it which, for some inexplicable reason, also makes me want to cry.

In the living room a compound has been set up that covers almost a quarter of the floor space and contains three light-blue guinea-pig houses, a red guinea-pig church and various pipes, pieces of wood, bowls for water and food with fruit and seeds, and a miniature fodder rack. Sitting among them are the tedious little fellows – apparently four of them – beady-eyed and nibbling at carrots. The floor of the compound consists of several oilcloth tablecloths. The Destroyer, Racke's hologram crocodile, is standing by the TV, like a little lost boy. Shangri-La, the unicorn in rainbow colours, is stretched out on the sofa.

"These are rescue guinea pigs," Racke shouts, holding a

tousled animal with a lot of black in its fur up to me. "Rescue guinea pigs! They had to be rescued because they were in need, you see, in need!"

"Yes, yes, in need," I say, holding the guinea pig and stroking it and still fighting down the tears.

"This one here's called Snowflake," Binya says, bringing me an almost white animal, and I take that one as well so that I have one in each hand. I sit down on the sofa beside the unicorn so that the guinea pigs won't have that far to fall should I drop them.

"Snowflake was in need as well," Racke shouts.

"When need knocks at the door, love opens it," Shangri-La lisps.

Gerda sits down on the other side of the unicorn and explains that the guinea pigs come from an animal sanctuary called 'Guinea Pigs in Need'. They were brought round yesterday, after Gerda had been thoroughly checked as to whether she was worthy of taking the rodents with their matted fur.

Racke pushes the unicorn aside – it's really fantastic the way the hologram shrinks back from his hands, I wish I'd had something like that when I was a child – and sits down beside me, puts his little arm behind me and strokes my back.

"Have you got even younger?" Gerda asks a little pointedly. The lymphatic glands on her neck are bulging more than ever. In fact she looks pretty ill. Her lower lids have turned outwards, like a bloodhound's, and are oozing and dripping like nobody's business.

I shake my head.

"No? Well that's probably not possible any more."

I nod. I'm even grateful to Gerda for getting the conversation back into the familiar bitching tone and, above all I'm grateful to her for looking after the children. I'd like to give her a treat, say something nice to her, most of all I'd like to tell her that Christine's got in touch and will be coming home soon. But that would set off too much of a fuss and, anyway, it's still completely uncertain whether she'll survive. Better not raise false hopes.

"What about these?" Gerda holds up the floppy-eared dogs from the filling station and Racke takes the one with the checked ears and Binya the one with the spotted ears.

"They can wrap the ears round their necks like a scarf," I explain.

Racke puts his floppy-eared dog on the back of the sofa, behind Shangri-La. Binya takes hers to the children's room and comes back with an exercise book to show me her last piece of homework, that the teacher marked as 'outstanding'. I think that will correspond to a ten out of ten, though you can never be sure nowadays when the assessments all have to be in the form of some commendatory adjective. I give the guinea pigs back to Racke. Binya sits down on the other side of me. Now there are five of us, including the unicorn, on the sofa. The top mark was awarded for an essay as part of the 'Voluntary Work Course on Disaster Management'. In it Binya proposes shooting soot and ashes up into the atmosphere to prevent any further temperature rise in the atmosphere. Not a bad idea. I'm rather proud of my daughter and I tell her that, even though I had intended not to do so any more. But I'm moved by the way she's already working at how to fix everything we've ruined. And I'm glad the school is getting the kids to believe we could somehow get the better of the inevitable collapse by developing new technologies that will bring the problems caused by the old technologies under control in no time at all. Even the women who teach them probably believe it themselves. Our European women governments are still determined to save whatever can be saved and if not prevent, then at least do their utmost to delay the end of the world. Every week there's a new self-sufficiency law – new taxation, further import restrictions, compulsory frugality – and all that to get at most six extra months for humanity. They prefer to waste away in misery rather than to go out in all our glory with all flags flying. Women just aren't capable of true greatness. That's always been the case.

"Let's make a rumpus," the crocodile beside the TV suggests hopefully.

"No," Racke snaps. The two guinea pigs are scrabbling up and down his arms and he has to keep twisting and turning them so they don't fall off. Racke looks over at the Destroyer again and adds, in a more amiable voice, "It's not really suitable just now."

He straightens out one arm and places his hand on my thigh so that the white guinea pig can use it as a bridge to run across to me. Racke's fingernails are light blue and covered in tiny silver pimples.

"Tell me, what's that – have you put nail varnish on them?" I ask as I receive the white animal.

Racke nods without taking his eyes off the other guinea pig.

Gerda grins. "Racke's crazy about nail varnish with rhinestone glitter. There's two other boys in the class who do it as well. Don't they, Racke? Olli and Pedro, eh?"

Racke nods again.

I'm really sorry that from now on I can't protect him from the feminist mob any longer. Who is going to help him to feel himself as a man one day without at the same time recruiting him for an extremist organisation?

"Tell me, have you dropped by for any particular reason

today?" Gerda asks.

"Er… yes," I say as I give the white guinea pig a tap on the nose to stop it crawling round. "It's about the CO_2 points. I wanted to tell you that from next month onwards Binya and Racke's points will be automatically credited to your account."

"Oh, Sebastian, do you really mean that?"

She's stunned. Then she suddenly turns to me with a concerned look in her bloodhound eyes. "Has something happened? Are you still okay?"

"Yes, I'm fine. I just thought it was about time. You're looking after the kids really well. Moreover I'm going to go vegetarian again anyway."

"Thank you. That is nice. Really nice. You'll be making our lives so much easier. You don't know what it means to us."

"Sure," I say. "However, I would like to ask a favour of you in return."

"Nothing comes from nothing," says Shangri-La, fluttering her eyelashes.

"Precisely," I say to Gerda. "Could you perhaps lend me a couple of points for this month. I have to fill the car and I haven't any left. You'll get them back in two weeks at the latest."

"I'll have to have a look," Gerda says, "we've hardly any left either."

She turns to the children. "Come over here you two."

Binya presses her homework book into my hand and Racke does the same with the second guinea pig. Now I've got one in each hand. And the exercise book. I'm starting to feel like a juggler.

"Who's going to give me a finger?" Gerda asks. She presses her egosmart and a little lancet pops out.

"Who will it be then?"

"Me, me, me," Racke shouts. Gerda pricks Racke's finger, at which a broad smile spreads across his face. I ask her whether she's acquired a medical smart.

"All values in balance. Keep it up. Eat a lot of fruit and vegetables in the next few days and a handful of nuts," Gerda's smart says in an emphatically male voice.

"A diet smart," Gerda replies. "Everything's in the green range. You can have our last points. I'll pop them across to you."

There are seven. Seven points' worth of meat.

24

When I come into the prepper room with my toolbox and the shopping bag, Elli and Christine are sitting on the yellow sofa drinking tea. I'm prepared for anything and therefore only slightly shocked. Then the two of them look up, as if they've only just noticed me. Christine has rings under her eyes but otherwise she appears to be fully fit. She's wearing a pink dressing gown. The similarity to her mother, now that both have almost the same bio-age, is disconcerting. Elli has finally changed. She's wearing one of Christine's floral print dresses that's a bit too tight at the waist for her and it's obvious she has no bra on underneath. I've never seen her in a dress before. It suits her, it makes her look like a young girl, especially with the clumpy biker boots she has on. But it's also a little strange because I know that Elli would never have put on a dress like that of her own accord.

"So there he is," Elli says, putting down her cup and standing up. Christine keeps her eyes fixed on her teacup and continues to sip at it. It's absurd. Are they going to behave as if nothing's happened, as if Christine wasn't supposed to be dead nor Elli full of fear and panicking. And there's something else that's not quite right but I can't tell what it is and that's what I find most unnerving. I drop the planks on the floor with a clatter, put down the toolbox and lift the paper bag with my purchases up onto the work surface.

"What's all this, then? A tea party?"

I put the meat and the two bottles of wine in the fridge. I've bought the wine for Elli and myself. No one could have imagined that Christine would have come round so quickly.

"I've just been telling Christine how I was almost run over while I was rescuing toads because someone deliberately wanted to run over the toad beside me," Elli says and comes over to me.

Christine's shivering and staring guiltily at the table. They have actually got some biscuits on it. Some kind of wafer curls. Devil only knows where they found them. And of course they'll have been talking about me all the time. Whilst I was out buying planks to repair the destruction they caused, they've been sitting here drinking tea and talking about me.

Now I finally notice what's not right. It's not Elli who's wearing the neck-ring but Christine.

"Tell me," I bellow, "are you trying to take the piss out of me. Is that your idea of a joke? Do you think this is all a game? I want to know at once why it's Christine who's chained up now."

"Of course," says Elli, standing to attention like a cadet of the previous century. "As you can see Christine feels better now and…"

She falls silent.

"Yes," says Christine. Her voice is terribly hoarse and there's that look of slight madness in her eyes, "…and the first thing I did was to go to the door to fetch the key and free Elli. I wanted us to lie in wait for you. I wanted the two of us to attack you together when you came in. But your new vegan girlfriend…"

"I don't want anyone else to be injured," Elli says and now she's my Elli again, just the way she was when I got to know her at the class reunion. There's no despondency or fear in her voice any more. "There's no reason for anyone of us not to get through this."

"Except that the arsehole doesn't deserve to," Christine says.

"You keep your gob shut while Elli's talking," I say, "otherwise I'll shut it for you."

"How? Are you going to kill me again?"

Her voice has the same mocking tone as it used to. I go over to her. I'm only going to grab her by the hair but before I can, Elli screams in a shrill voice, "Don't!"

Christine slumps down and promptly starts to wail, "Please don't, please… I'm sorry, sorry, sorry." Elli stares at me, horrified, her hand still over her open mouth. It's clear – once more I'm the nasty, brutal bastard. The pair of them are in agreement on that.

"We can all get out of here safe and sound," Elli says hastily. "Bassi will prepare his escape and we'll get out because Bassi has no choice but to flee the country and let us out. Moreover he promised me that and I trust him."

Christine looks up at me from the sofa. When she catches my eye, she quickly looks down again.

"So at the moment we're more or less all in the same boat. That's why it's best if we cooperate," Elli says.

"We're not all in the same boat," I say, "and there's no question of cooperating here. You will obey. And first of all I damn well want an answer to why Christine has the neck-ring on."

"The neck-ring is the proof that we could have attacked you but decided not to of our own free will. It's the proof that you can trust us."

"Not true," Christine says. "I told your feeble-minded girlfriend that if necessary I'd attack you on my own so then she chained me up to stop me, thus throwing away the only chance we would have had."

"Your wife is definitely a problem," Elli says. "I trust you and I expect you not to disappoint me in that."

I don't trust either of them. Who knows what plan they worked out while I was away. Perhaps they're putting on an act all the time, playing at good woman, bad woman for me and giving each other their cues in order to take me in.

"You will obey me in everything I say and then you'll get out of here, that's the deal," I reply.

Christine would be too weak to attack me. She was already too weak before she spent three days in a coma. It seems that she was even too weak to resist Elli. Even together Elli and Christine would be ridiculously weak compared with me. How did women ever get the idea that they could have a say in any kind of society?

"That is the deal." Elli says in confirmation. Chain clanking, Christine shuffles over to the fridge and takes out one of the bottles of wine I bought for Elli and myself. I'm about to say something but then I see the anxious look on Elli's face and desist. It's easy to see what Christine's tactics are. She wants to provoke me and make me hit her to show me up as a lousy guy in front of Elli. I simply ignore her as she goes to the IKEA kitchen island, takes a glass off the cupboard and then rummages round in the drawer.

"If it's a corkscrew you're looking for, we don't have one here any more," I say. "The bottles all have screw tops."

And to Elli I say, "I want you to cook something for me, a stew. Here are the onions, the meat's in the fridge and there must be some olive oil around as well. Any problems with that?"

"No, it's no problem. I'll make you some stew. Have you

perhaps got a sweet pepper or some mushrooms as well?"

I don't know what's wrong with women. Why do they have to dump all kinds of vegetable matter in a perfect meat stew, peppers and mushrooms and other slimy things, imagining they don't contain any calories? Christine always used to do that too.

"No vegetables, just meat and onions, pepper and salt."

"Just the way my mother used to make it," Christine says. She's slumped on the sofa in the slovenly posture of a habitual drinker, knocks back the glass and refills it immediately. Her dressing gown has fallen open. Underneath she's wearing a black slip with lace trimming that just about covers her thighs. Like an old whore. I ignore her.

"Shut up," Elli says to Christine. "I'm making the stew just the way Bassi wants it – and I don't need any comments from you."

"You know," I say to Elli, "I'm just demanding this of you so that I can be sure you really will accept everything I demand unquestioningly."

"What's the problem? I'm locked up here in a cellar with no idea whether I'll ever get out again. Do you think I'm shocked at the idea of cooking meat for you? Of course I'll make some stew for you."

"Then that's okay."

Elli drops the hunks of meat in the pan and the fat spurts up. She wrinkles her nose in disgust.

"Anyway, it's not particularly consistent if you feed your cat meat," I say.

"Oh, Murri. How is she?"

"Fine. I brought her back with me and she already feels at home. Either she's yowling because the kitchen door's closed and she can't get to her bowls, or she's yowling because the door's open. She yowls for food, for more food, for different food, tinned food, no, she'd rather have dry food, but in a different bowl. Actually she's yowling all the time. And shitting all over the place. I'll bring her down here afterwards."

"You brought her back here? But there's not enough room for Murri down here. She won't feel comfortable down here. You'll have to keep her up there."

"What do you mean not enough room? There's thirty-two square metres here. There were five of us in my family and we had ninety square metres. And it was all right, we even got along very well."

"But I'm allergic to cat hair," Christine says, without looking up from her glass. That's true, she always has been, I'd forgotten that.

"Okay then, she can stay up there for the few days."

For a moment there's silence. Just the rustling of the pack as Elli takes the onions out and the sizzling of the hunks of meat. A wonderful smell.

"You know what I think about meat," Elli says, "because you're of the same opinion. It's dirty and unjustifiable. But if you were to demand it, I'd make you a hotpot of children's hands."

"Don't give him ideas," Christine says. I go over to the sofa and take the wine bottle away from her, but it's already empty.

"Is there a knife anywhere here?" Elli asks. "Otherwise I don't know how I'm going to cut up these onions."

So I have to go back up out of the cellar. To fetch a knife. Enter the code, open the security door, close the security door, enter the code again.

The dementia-stricken feline's standing at the top of the stairs, yowling. When it yowls it looks particularly repulsive. It's eyes turn into very narrow slits and its mouth is so wide open it's practically dividing its head in two. I wonder what can make a sensible person acquire something like a cat, the most disagreeable of all animals. The wretched beasts despise, manipulate and exploit you. They're ungrateful, devious, cruel and incapable of the least sympathy for any other creature. Not even for another cat. Moreover they keep on popping up everywhere – like unwanted Internet adverts. And Murri's shat in the hall again. Just one metre away from her cat litter. I pick up the cat shit using a cat shit shovel and chuck it down the toilet, pull the chain.

There's a ring at the door. Actually I've made it an iron rule never to open the front door if the shelves aren't over the prepper-room door and filled with tins. But I've just flushed the lavatory with the toilet door open. If I don't go to the door that will seem suspicious. Especially if it's the police already wanting to ask me about Elli. So what? I'm suspicious anyway, I'm not letting anyone in.

The cat prowls round my legs, then it squats down right in front of me and at the end of its arched back, under its erect tail, a black turd starts to emerge, heading for the lino. I aim a kick at the beast but it ducks and gives me a sly look. Again the doorbell rings and I tear the door open. A postman. A real postman. He has a registered letter for me. I take the envelope and sign for it. What a wonderfully old-fashioned procedure, even if I have to sign on a display. The letter's from the Post-Office Bank. They're offering me money if I stop filling out forms for money transfers and do my transactions on the Internet in future. No way. Not for us. We – the last eight thousand users of German money-transfer forms – haven't spent years fighting in the courts for that. Then the Post Office started demanding more and more money for their forms and eventually they tried to refuse to hand any more out. Just so that their last three employees can lose their job and my account finally be cleared out by Nigerian hackers. Fortunately I had foreseen that and built up a stock over the years. And I'm not the only one. That's the one good thing about the Internet, that you can link up with other Internet-haters. And now the Post Office is legally condemned to accept all the forms that are still in circulation. It could go on for years.

I remove the cat shit, wash my hands, get the little black knife I use for peeling potatoes out of the cutlery drawer, go back down into the cellar, enter the code, open the security door, close it and enter the code again.

Elli's taken the pan off the stove and is sitting beside Christine on the sofa. Hardly was I out of the room than they started talking about me. What else would they be talking about? You can't have two prisoners together, especially when they're women. It's like with budgies – they only learn to speak when they're kept alone. As soon as there's another in the cage, they establish a relationship that gives them a counterweight to the linguistic norms dictated by human beings.

"Oh, the knife," Elli says and gets up, taking her glass to the stove. Only now do I see that the two of them have taken the second bottle out of the fridge.

"Who told you that you could have the wine."

I give her the knife.

"I didn't realise we had to ask before we could have anything. Should I do that next time?" Elli asks innocently.

"No," I say and all at once I feel unutterably tired. I'd love to lie down in bed with Elli beside me. I just want to lie down and feel her presence. Have a glass of wine. That's the way I imagined it. Christine can go to the devil.

"By the way, the drain in the shower's blocked," Elli says.

"How did you manage that? With Christine the drain was

never blocked in two and a half years and you've only been here two days."

Elli doesn't reply. I sit down on the sofa beside Christine and drink the last drop of wine in her glass. She's sitting stiffly beside me and turning her head away. Elli switches on the hotplate, puts the pan back on it and starts to peel and chop the onions. For a while everything's quiet. Just the sound of the knife. And the sizzle when Elli shovels the chopped onions into the hot fat.

"May I ask something?" she says.

"Go ahead."

"Well it's about all this here," – she sweeps her arm round with the knife in her hand, indicating the prepper room – "but I had to promise you I wouldn't ask any questions about it."

"Doesn't matter," I say, "Just ask."

The smell of fried meat, familiar and reproachful, wafts over me,

"Why?"

"Why have I done this?"

"Yes."

"Because he's an arsehole," Christine says in a drunken slur.

"Shh," Elli says impatiently.

"Well, why else?" Christine says.

"Great people sometimes do things that ordinary people find difficult to comprehend," Elli says, more to me than to Christine, "and I'd simply like to understand."

Once more I realise how much I love Elli. With someone like her I would have been able to escape from myself. She brings out what's good in me. I try to imagine what my life would have been like if I'd never made the prepper room, if I'd simply swallowed all the humiliations and then at some point had come across Elli. Would we then have got together? Could we have been happy now? Probably not. Back then Christine had undermined my self-confidence. If you lose your self-confidence, things get difficult. You don't get to know new women. I had no choice but to see to it that Christine lost her self-confidence in order to get my own back.

"You always assume that men and women want the same," I say.

"Who is 'you'?"

"You lot. All of you, all women and especially our good lady ministers, of course. You always assume that men and women have a common interest in changing the relationship between the sexes. But that isn't the case. The sexes have entirely different views on that."

"But you've always fought for that. I've been reading your blog and your contributions to the quent. Solidarity, equal rights, respect. Those are the things you supported. And you meant it back then."

"I was just saying that, dammit, because we have to. Because it goes down well with you women. If I'd told the truth, my career would have gone down the drain. And I probably wouldn't have been able to bed a single woman. At least not one with some brains. But it's a lie, don't you see, a lie. We don't want relationships based on equal rights. No man wants that. That there was more or less peace between the sexes in those days was because women identified with their men and gave their interests precedence over their own. But now you've all got your oh-so-important jobs and think you have to save the world, and we're left to shift for ourselves. If you really want to know what men want, then watch porn. The purpose of porn is to fulfil men's wishes, and if what we wanted was solidarity, respect and relationships, then porn would be full of those things. But they aren't. So what does that tell you?"

"Aha," Elli says quite calmly but stirring the stew with unnecessary force, "so love is just a load of women's nonsense. What do you want with your stew? Have you brought some potatoes or pasta?"

"Pasta. There must still be some pasta in the cupboard."

Elli opens the wall cupboard.

"At the bottom," Christine burbles, "it's right at the bottom."

"Of course I love you," I say to Elli, "but that doesn't mean I want a relationship based on equal rights. Anyway, that doesn't exist. One of the two has to be in charge. And I'm not the kind of guy who wants to subordinate himself."

"Except in bed," Christine burbles, "there he really does like to lie underneath."

"You shut up," Elli says. I take the key for the padlock attaching the chain to the kitchen island out of my shirt pocket and unlock it. With the chain over my arm I go across to Christine and take her by the elbow. Of course she cringes and starts whining, as if I were hurting her, but all I'm doing is taking the shuffling, slovenly figure into the bathroom in order to chain her up there – on a significantly shorter chain. Then I close the door behind me and go back to Elli.

"I've never loved anyone the way I love you," I say. "And whatever you say and do, you can rest assured that you'll get out of here. Even if you don't make an effort and keep on bugging me. Now turn the stove off."

Elli pushes the pan off the hot plate and switches it off.

"You don't need to do any pasta," I say, "I'll give the meat to Murri afterwards."

I take her head in my hands and kiss her on the mouth. My tongue slips in unimpeded between her lips but she's hardly kissing me back at all. I stroke the hair off her forehead and kiss Elli's eyelids. She's crying.

"I loved you so much," Elli says, "I was really madly in love with you. I so admired you for your courage, your sense of justice and all the sacrifices you'd made. You were the most important person in the world for me. But now I'm just afraid of you. I don't even believe you're going to let us out."

I take Elli over to the bed and start to unbutton her dress. She lies down without having to be told and I bend over her and kiss her naked breasts. She doesn't move but she's stopped crying. I push up her dress, expecting to see one of Christine's sophisticated pairs of panties but Elli has decided to wear nothing underneath. Short bristles, hardly visible, are pushing up out of the skin round her mount of Venus – politically correct: 'pubic mound' – and scrape the palm of my hand. I'll have to shave Elli tomorrow. I push two fingers in between her labia – politically correct: 'genital lips' – open them up and contemplate Elli's private parts. 'Private parts' is probably not politically correct either. I move my fingers to and fro inside them, circling round the little button and stroking the edges of her labia. She doesn't move, just lies there like a sacrificial lamb staring past me. Undeterred I continue to work on her until I can feel moisture.

"That turns you on, doesn't it, eh?" I say. "I know that turns you on. You like being at the mercy of a man, don't you?"

She lifts up her pelvis and puts her hands under her back in an attempt to turn away, but I hold her tight by the hips, pull her arms out again and lie down between her legs to continue with my mouth. Elli tries to push me away. She kicks out at me, wriggles silently and eventually belabours me with her fists. I rise up and grab her wrists, press her back down on the mattress with her hands, stinking of onions, over her head, and simply keep her struggling body still with my own body weight. She gives up, lies under me, breathing heavily. I let go of her wrists and kiss her on the lips, running my tongue over her teeth. At the same time I undo the zip on my trousers, take out my prick and penetrate Elli carefully but firmly. It's quite easy. I fuck her slowly and gently, only when she tries to put her arms under her back again, do I grasp her wrists and keep her hands fixed by the pillow.

"You are mine," I say. "You belong to me and I'll do what I want with you."

I kiss her again, deeper and more roughly this time, and although there's no response, I can feel Elli shuddering underneath me. I sit up, undo the last button of her dress and pull it off over her arms. Then I turn her over. Elli keeps her eyes closed as I do so, refuses to look at me. I twist the hair on the back of her head into a ponytail and pull her head up. I run my other hand down her back then stroke her bottom and suddenly I come across something sharp, a foreign body. I feel for it and I can hardly believe it: Elli has smuggled the little knife for peeling potatoes into the bed. In the crack of her bottom. Now I understand why she kept trying to put her arms under her back. I have to laugh. I pull it out and hold it against Elli's neck. Then I let go of her hair and grope her between her legs, moving my fingers faster this time and heading straight to the target. She's struggling in my arms and I have to be careful not to cut her. I nibble her shoulder a bit, then throw the knife away and grab one of her breasts instead, tweak, press and knead her nipple until Elli comes with a scream. While she's still twitching in my arms, I grab her by the breast and mount of Venus again and take her from behind, giving her a really good fucking, all the while squeezing her breast, pressing her nipple as hard as I can and not stopping even when she cries,

"Don't", "Stop it", and "Please – you're hurting me", and her moans are no longer those of passion but only of pain and fear. When I come, I give her a hard bite on the shoulder and she screams out loud as I ejaculate and slowly withdraw my teeth from her flesh. We lie there, panting and sweaty, her back against my chest, her little bottom on my sticky cock. She lies there quite calmly and I hold her tight, hold her in my arms and, as uncontrollable quivers run through her body, I press her even closer to me and kiss her on the neck.

"It's still on," I say. "No matter what you do, I'll see to it that you get out of here."

Perhaps what Elli said was true, perhaps I was the most important person in her life. What is certain is that I am now. I'm the only one she has, her only chance of getting out of here, I give her information and pain.

A sneeze makes me swing my head round. Christine is standing in the door to the bathroom wiping off the snot on her dressing-gown sleeve. No, I'm not the only person Elli has, there's still that old woman, that pain in the arse, the person who, with her deviant views, will comment on and ridicule everything I say to Elli.

"Has anyone got a handkerchief?"

"Christ!" I say, letting go of Elli. "Why don't you just use toilet paper?"

Christine disappears back in the bathroom, rolls off some toilet paper with a clatter and blows her nose very loudly. Then she stands in the doorway again and stares at us. Elli has made use of the moment to sit up and is putting her dress on. I do up my trousers zip and stand up, giving Elli the key for the lock on the chain.

"Attach Christine to the kitchen island again," I say. Elli nods. She's crying, but I can't talk to her as long as Christine's standing there in the doorway, arms folded. So I just grab the knife and the pan of stew, go to the security door and enter the code. For the first time I notice all this getting on my nerves: enter the code, open the door, close it, enter the code again, screw on the sheet of plywood, place the shelves in front of it and put the tins back on. Until now it's always been a kind of meditative activity for me, but today it just gets on my wick.

In the living room the bloody cat's torn a plant, the flame violet, out of the walled peat-bed. I suspect it shat in the hole but I don't feel the least desire to go and check. I leave things as they are, sit down on the sofa with the stew, that's still lukewarm, and play back the answerphone on the compunicator screen while sticking hunks of meat in my mouth with the knife.

Two calls. The first is from Margitta Kleinwächter asking if I have the number of Rolf's smart. She's really dolled herself up for the call, she's wearing something loose and red and is holding a glass of champagne. Moreover she's downloaded one of those awful South-Seas-beach backgrounds so she's strolling along the seashore in a flutter of red. How come she's got my number but not Rolf's? Delete.

The second call is a woman's voice, while the screen only shows flags with the Hamburg coat of arms.

Would I please come to police headquarters to make a statement. If that's all right with me? Or would I prefer for an officer to see me in my home, that would be possible. So the time has come. I had hoped it would take a few days more. Preoccupied, I push away the cat that's rubbing against my legs. I click on 'return call' and arrange with the call-centre girl an appointment at police headquarters for next Wednesday. Then I shuggle my travel manager and buy an air ticket for tomorrow afternoon.

25

I'm running, running with the regular long strides of a man who has a goal in view. Running that looks like walking, and deep down inside I'm vibrant with the awareness of the start of something completely new. In my hand I'm holding loosely, almost nonchalantly, a stamped addressed envelope, the contents of which will seal the end of my life so far. If I remember rightly, my friend, the German Bundespost, always empties the postbox on the Gänsemarkt on Fridays, in six days' time, that is. But that's not the only reason why I've driven into the town centre again. I want to buy a guidebook and some maps, proper maps that I can fold and keep in my jacket pocket, and that will inform me without making stupid noises. My nasty little egosmart with all its nasty little apps and gridlets I'll dump in the airport toilet.

The closer I come to the Gänsemarkt, the more crowded the streets are. I can hardly get through. Okay, it's double-shopping day, but strangely enough it's mostly men, loads of men pouring out of all the side streets, and they don't look as if they're just popping into town to buy new T-shirts. Some of them could be hooligans – potbellies, terrible haircuts, aggression written all over their ugly mugs. Hooligans in the early morning, bellowing to each other, stinking of chips and spilling the contents of their bottles of beer over people. Others look like delivery men, there are fifty at least, no, more like eighty, a whole band of them and they're all wearing the same clothes: navy-blue trousers and navy-blue jackets with the word 'proud' embroidered on the back. An arrow pointing up to the right from the 'o' of 'proud' turns it into the male symbol. Slowly it begins to dawn on me what I've got caught up in – a MASCULO demonstration. I have a closer look round. Indeed, there's not a woman to be seen anywhere. According to an online survey published in Bildzeitung yesterday, the average participant in a demonstration of the anti-women's-lib group MASCULO is middle-class and both well-educated and in employment – which doesn't quite correspond to my personal impression. You can well imagine how the survey results were arrived at: nine out of ten times the guy with the questionnaire got the response, "Piss off or I'll thump you one." And the tenth interviewee said, "Yes, delighted, I'm a high school teacher and I've joined simply because I'm generally unhappy with the government's current policies." The delivery men are the group that comes closest to the middle-class theory. Probably men smarting over their divorce or being overlooked for promotion and others who think they've had a raw deal and are therefore devoting their lives to the struggle against the flagrantly preferential treatment given to women. I wish I had your problems, lads.

I push my way through, go down off the pavement into the street, but it's even more crowded there, even more men, men in suits, bikers in their leathers and the crazy monks, their yellow hoods pulled well down over their faces. All heading for the Gänsemarkt. A platform has been set up there and two guys in hooped T-shirts are messing around and plugging in old-fashioned cables. The postbox must be over there, in the middle of the surging crowd. I burrow my way through them, clasping the letter firmly to my chest, wade through beer cans, paper cups and scraps of food, get elbowed in the side, step on someone's jump boots and get clouted on the back of my head for my pains. All round me expressionless faces. It's humiliating, all this instantaneous violence meted out in passing – as if they were brushing a fly off their face. The crowd is piling up, comes to a halt and someone grabs my shoulders from behind and shoves me forward, some brutal moron is using me as a ram to clear the way. I'm on the receiving end of foul language, curses and jabs, but when I finally manage to turn round, the hands have gone and I find myself facing some mean-looking guys, huge, with tattoos up their arms and all over their necks. Not the kind you want to pick a quarrel with. I ought to turn back. If necessary I can post the letter at Central Station. What does it matter if it arrives at police headquarters one or two or even four days sooner – I'll already be in Paraguay anyway.

But it's practically impossible to get out of the crowd. People are streaming towards the platform from all sides and to make matters worse a lorry has driven onto the square. "Down with state feminism," a banner on the back demands. Guys in camouflage suits are standing on the loading platform waving navy-blue flags. In between them is a post with three old-fashioned loudspeakers – it looks like one of those pot plants you get given at Christmas with three great big flowers growing out of the stalk, all at the same height.

"...that's why we need professionals in there again..." comes the barely comprehensible tinny blare from the loudspeakers, "men who know what they're doing instead of women off some list to satisfy the quota requirements... women undermine the economy..."

By now almost without trying I've been swept along until I'm close to the letter box. There it is, next to an advertising column, yellow, solid, confidence-inspiring, tangible and substantial. Police in full riot gear – bulletproof vest, helmet and baton – have lined up in front of it, as if they were there to defend it. Their visors are open and a policewoman – it is indeed a policewoman, blonde with a snub nose and freckles, but apart from that a hefty wench, at least 5′10″ and at least thirteen stone – fixes her eyes on me. She's probably volunteered for this operation, simply begged to be part of it and to have the chance to give a MASCULO demonstrator one over the nut with her baton. I hesitate, stop, look back and forth between the postbox and the policewoman. Again someone nudges me in the back and I stagger forwards until I'm right in front of it. In front of the postbox. And in front of the policewoman. I only need to stretch out my arm, between her and the policeman beside her, and put the now rather crumpled letter in the box. Then I could plough my way through to the nearest station, take a train to Central and from there to the airport. As planned. Instead I'm stuck here with a guilty look on my face. It's always been like that: hardly have I seen a policeman than I start behaving in a suspicious manner. What will the bird in uniform do if I try to post the letter now? Tear it out of my hand, open it on the spot, read it and handcuff me? It's quite obvious she has other things to think about at the moment but I still can't bring myself to post the letter right in front of her – if it's read too soon, it'll send me to prison for years. I just can't. I clutch the brown envelope tight again and wriggle back into the crowd, trying to make myself as slim as possible and slip through the bodies like a piece of soap to get at least as far as the propaganda lorry. An ear-splitting screech of feedback makes me look up. There's a little guy in a silver astronaut suit on the platform now, his head with its flaming red hair is in a kind of goldfish bowl. He taps his egosmart – again there's the remarkably convincing screech of feedback.

The astronaut grins, his red quiff brushing against the inside of his helmet. He taps once more and the guitar solo of 'We Will Rock You' blares out across the Gänsemarkt. Now he has our complete attention but instead of exploiting it, he steps aside. A bald, bullnecked man in a suit climbs up onto the platform, ponderous, menacing – a skinhead trying to look like a politician. Banners are held up behind him: MOTIVATION BY FEAR and STOP MOANING AND FIGHT.

The skinhead politician comes forward with stiff-legged steps and, to the laughter and hoots of his audience, calmly rolls up the sleeves of his suit jacket to reveal black-white-and-red tattoos with plenty of swastikas. Then he leans heavily on the lectern. The muscles stand out under his veneer of tattoos.

"Men!" he says, just that, then pauses. The crowd hesitates for a moment, baffled, then individual laughs can be heard that slowly trickle into the men's consciousness until there's an outburst of cheers.

"Men."

Even louder cheers. The baldie doesn't seem to be a man of many words but that could well be why his audience loves him so much.

"Men, the femi-sluts have not only got their claws on your jobs but also on your pride. Am I right?"

He clearly is, at least to judge by the roars.

"They've taken away the pride in our masculinity to which every man has a right. And now they want to finish us off totally. But we're not going to put up with that. Count us out, ladies."

Hoots and cheers.

"When we go over to the Congress Centre now, we will keep in order. Keep in order, is that clear? Order – I want every one of you to behave himself. They have their slogans and we have ours. And we will rule."

"They have their opinion, we have ours."

Cheers and hoots.

"And we will rule."

Cheers and hoots.

"They've got pussies and we've got cocks."

He's about to add something, perhaps that we will rule, but the raucous cheers and hoots refuse to die down. The little white astronaut, his head in his goldfish bowl, clambers back up onto the platform. He dances like Rumpelstiltskin round the baldie, who must be about twice his biomass, all the time hacking away at his egosmart. From the three loud speakers on the propaganda lorry comes a very strange version of Herbert Grönemeyer's hit 'When is a man a man?' In fact it just consists of that one line, only interrupted by Brian May's guitar solo from 'We Will Rock You'. It doesn't fit the number of syllables but they all join in despite that, a thousand jump boots, dress shoes and trainers thump the ground, a thousand pairs of hands clap: stamp-stamp-clap, stamp-stamp-clap, guitar solo by Brian May, stamp-stamp-clap, a thousand – of course mathematically speaking it was only five hundred – throats bawl "When is a man a man?" stamp-stamp-clap. The skinhead politician raises his right arm – no, not in the Nazi salute, before it comes to that he forms a fist with his index finger sticking up and roars, his voice cracking, "To the Congress Centre!"

The men set off, still stamping and clapping. The rhythm creates a mass, the different men's groups forget their differences and turn into a stamping machine, into a single, unstoppable force with just one aim in mind: to get their own back on women. It works so well it looks as if they've been practising for days. Stamp-stamp-clap, stamp-stamp-clap,

'When is a man a man?' I've no chance at all of escaping the maelstrom. By now, however, I'm pretty curious about what kind of event it is that the MASCULO marchers want to disrupt in the Hamburg Congress Centre and – well, of course – how far they're willing to go. The crumpled letter's in the inside pocket of my coat.

There's a huge police presence by now, a double row of them either side of Dammtorstrasse and they still haven't lowered their visors, even though the first beer bottles are being thrown. It's difficult to be precise, but there can't be more than five or six hundred of us in the demonstration. And for that the number of police is absurd. There's probably one for each of us. Any passer-by, especially female, have been kept well out of the way. The street is ours, ours alone, and the windows of the jeweller's shops are covered with brown nylon mats. The door of one of the shops opens and a woman in a trench-coat peers out, her face hidden behind the turned-up collar. She's immediately bombarded with beer bottles and verbal abuse: crab-cunt, shit-slut, piss-mattress… I would never have thought this horde of skinheads, in which I'm being jostled, pushed and kicked along, capable of such linguistic creativity. The shit-slut hastily withdraws, which is reason enough for the skinheads to break out into jubilant cries of Sieg Heil.

I make another attempt to work myself sideways out of this particularly unpleasant and violence-prone faction. I try to join the navy-blue delivery men who are marching a bit to the left and instead of "When is a man a man" are chanting "Scholz out, women out" or "Chuck the bitches out of politics." I've almost got there when a wedge of bikers in denim jackets pushes its way in between me and the navy-blues. And it's too late, far too late, when I read what's written on their jackets; panicking, I change direction and try to get away from the doggedly driving wedge and infiltrate the group of the beery right-wing extremists again. But it seems that the good Lord loves me and therefore must chasten and scourge me – as my crackpot brother would undoubtedly put it.

"Basti!" a voice behind me shouts – Oh God, spare me this! – "Basti, you cretin!"

I squeeze my eyes shut and throw myself as hard as I can into the group of Neo-Nazis, but I bounce back off their fat bellies like a rubber ball, straight into the arms of Ingo Dresen.

He grasps me – I know without having to look that it must be his arm that's like a yoke round my shoulders, pushing me against other people's backs, shoulders and bottoms.

"You here too? Good man!"

There it is again, that bloated face with nastiness engraved in every wrinkle.

"Ingo," I say, making an effort to sound pleased, and look round for someone, something, anything, anyone who could rescue me.

"You're coming with us," Ingo says and accordingly I'm now walking with the Fat Rats, Ingo's arm round my shoulder. There are indeed incredibly fat members of his gang, but they're not your usual obese men, no manic-depressives beneath those layers of fat but healthy twenty-stone guys in denim jackets. Despite the low temperature all they're wearing underneath them are T-shirts with bare, tattooed arms. Muscular arms. No flab. Of course they sweat, and puff and pant quite a lot, the stamp-stamp-clap is quite an effort for them, but their bodies are less a burden than a means of lending weight to their destructive mania.

"Where are we heading?" I ask, breathless as I stagger along beside Ingo Dresen, the character who destroyed my snowman, emptied out the contents of my satchel and knocked out a milk tooth with the runner of my sledge.

"Clever sod," is Ingo's cryptic reply and we're already turning off left before Dammtor Station. The street forks and the throng stamps off to the right, to the former high-rise Hotel Plaza. Only the Fat Rats, at least the majority of the Fat Rats, around thirty of these massive guys plus me, swing off to the left. In contrast to my efforts earlier on, the Fat Rats have no problem at all making their way out of the procession. They simply lumber off and the throng divides in front of them, like the sea before Moses. The road to the left curves between metre-high concrete walls down into the underground car park. Floating on the wall to the right are purple halogen letters: "More women at the top – We demand the fifty per cent quota – Room 2."

So it's the career women the masses up there want to tell what's what, and they're now marching to a different text: "We are many, we are strong! Power to men!" But why are the majority of the Fat Rats and myself not with them? What are we doing in the underground car park?

"On a broad front, baby, this is what's called broad-front tactics," Ingo says, grinning at me, and I've still no idea what's going on. Four policemen in bulletproof vests are guarding the lower entrance to the HCC. You can see they're scared and have no idea what to do, they clutch their science-fiction rifles more tightly to themselves but it's clear they won't dare to try and stop the Fat Rats getting in; at least they don't move. But now I see the motorbikes. Ingo's gang of rockers have no intention of bursting into the HCC and smashing everything to smithereens. They've just parked their Harley-Davidsons with their gleaming chrome down here.

"Don't ask. Secret," Ingo says, only to explain two seconds later. "Now we're going to give those niggers in the Volkspark a good thrashing. Broad-front tactics, you understand? The pigs can't be everywhere at once."

I don't understand how the Africans, who're living under HGV tarpaulins in the Volkspark, can have attracted the hatred of the Fat Rats. True, the Fat Rats are the scum of the earth, resentful and violent, and even they are presumably disturbed by humanity's lack of future prospects – but why do they see their foremost task in beating up these poor fellows who've already been abused enough by Fate? Do they actually begrudge them the fact that they survived the crossing of the Mediterranean on some death-trap of a rust-bucket boat and managed to cross the border at the eleventh or twelfth attempt? Do the Fat Rats themselves want to earn 3.50 euros per hour, on zero-hour contracts, washing up in an Asian restaurant or drawing turkeys in a slaughterhouse? Do they begrudge them the holes in the ground the refugees have dug for themselves in the Volkspark and where they'll get the araucana flu this winter, if not something worse?

"Someone has to clear that up. The park isn't a ghetto, it's there for everyone, for children, pensioners and dogs," Ingo says. "German children."

End of discussion. I have to get on the pillion behind him. He revs up a few times then the Harley-Davidson rattles off at low speed, accelerates, and as we emerge into the daylight on the other side of the car park the vibration is so strong that my teeth are chattering. For a moment I forget where we're heading and almost enjoy the ride, especially as none of us has a helmet on. It's warm, my hair is streaming out and the bright yellow rape lining Stresemanstrasse – the third flowering – gives off an intoxicating scent. Then I concentrate again on the question of when, where and above all how I can get away from the Fat Rats without being beaten up by Ingo Dresen.

The Fat Rats park their bikes on a woodland footpath close to the St. Francis of Assisi Stadium. The trees are almost bare already, the leaves have simply withered this year and fallen in the summer. One of the Fat Rats climbs into the rampant yellow undergrowth and reappears with a large jute sack that he empties out: baseball bats, steel pipes with rubber tubes wrapped round them and double-headed axes. Axes! My God! Like the Viking berserkers. First of all, though, the Fats Rats take time to have a pee. Every one of them just undoes the fly of his biker trousers where he happens to be standing and holds his little prick in his hand. In reality they're probably not that small at all but they look that way because of their huge bellies. I quickly do the same, unsheathe my tool and piss over the foliage. Just don't attract notice as an outsider. Ingo picks up a double-headed axe, obviously Ingo will take the worst possible weapon. The others also arm themselves. Someone hands me a baseball bat. They're going to creep up unseen on all sides "and then close the sack so none of them can escape".

"We go there, raze everything to the ground and get back here in an hour at the latest. Not one minute later."

They all take out their egosmarts and check the time. Ingo Dresen's egosmart is in a metal case with 'Fat Rats' engraved on it in fancy letters. His hand is placed on my shoulder again and the pressure is unpleasantly cold.

"After this we're going to Feldstrasse and we'll beat up the heretics. Broad-front tactics – you understand?"

He grins, proud that the Fat Rats can wreak havoc three times in one day. Oh my God, I'd completely forgotten – today's the day the Disciples of St. John celebrate their sacrificial feast, the cruelty-to-animals event at which my brother and the other Plague Trumpets are going to cut the throats of a lot of baby sheep. The animal-loving Fat Rats can't allow that to happen, of course. I have to warn my brother. Even if he's a self-righteous moron, he's still my brother.

The Fats Rats crowd together in a closed circle, raise their baseball bats, steel pipes and double-headed axes and jiggle them against each other. In order not to attract attention I join the huddle and tap the other weapons with my baseball bat.

"We are the good guys," we cry in muted voices and then we set off at a ponderous trot, the top speed a Fat Rat can achieve on foot. Once we're in the woods we spread out – broad-front tactics, of course – and at last Ingo disappears from my side. I slip behind the nearest clump of bushes, take out my mobile and call the police.

"Elmsbüttel station. Police Sergeant Quast speaking."

I explain briefly and precisely what's happening and insist speed is essential. An irritated groan at the other end of the line. Then (aside): "In the Volkspark as well now."

He wants to know where exactly.

"Where? Well where the camp is, of course. That's where they're heading now – at a run. And if you don't come over immediately people are going to get killed."

He wants my name and tells me to stay on the spot. Not likely! I'm not crazy enough to give evidence against Ingo Dresen. Herr Quast insists.

"I'm going to the sacrificial feast in Feldstrasse now," I say. "That's where they'll be heading afterwards. I can wait there."

I end the call and tap on my brother's name. Uwe doesn't reply. He's probably switched off his egosmart so that it won't disturb the dignity of his sacred act. When I look up again, Ingo Dresen is standing in front of me. I've no idea whether he heard anything of the conversation. If he did, then it's farewell vile world.

"What are you doing here? Who were you talking to then?"

"No one," I say, "I was just switching it off so that it doesn't ring at the wrong moment."

"I don't trust you. Don't tell me you're chickening out."

"What d'you mean, chickening out?" I reply with the courage of desperation. "I'm not joining in here. What you're doing here is a load of crap. There no reason to kill the refugees. They're refugees, man. Have you any idea what they've probably been through? You simply don't do something like that."

"You simply don't do something like that," Ingo Dresen mimics. "How old will you have to be before you stop asking permission? Before you do what you want and not what Mummy allows? Everything's allowed as long as you don't let yourself get caught. While you're standing here shitting yourself, some of my lads are storming the Bundestag. They're risking their necks while you can't even bring yourself to rough up a few Niggers in order to sidetrack the fuzz." Ingo's pretensions to a putsch strike me as so stupid that I can't help sniggering. But perhaps I'm just nervous.

"Are you a man or a Mickey Mouse?" Ingo Dresen says in a voice full of disgust and contempt. "Give me back that baseball bat."

He says that quite calmly. As if I didn't deserve the honour of wielding one of the Fat Rats' baseball bats and fighting alongside them. I shrug my shoulders, and hand over the club as casually as I can. Ingo drops his axe and takes the bat, his right hand grabbing the handle, his left hand coming up underneath it to grasp me by the neck. And before I know it, he's hitting me in the face with the bottom end. Just a quick jab. A flash of white. The flash comes first, only then does the pain come. I scream like a girl. Blood's pouring out of my nostrils.

"Fuck off," Ingo Dresen says, still calmly. He's holding the baseball bat so that he can bash me on the nose with it again. "You just fuck off. Piss off or I'll do you in."

I prefer to clear off. Strangely enough, I'm limping as I do so. I've no idea why. Perhaps to placate Ingo Dresen. Limping and holding my nose with both hands, I get away. Only slowly at first, as if I still had a scrap of dignity left, and then faster and faster. I let go of my nose, stop limping and finally really take off, my arms pumping hard, running on and on. There's so much adrenaline flowing that I don't feel the effort at all. It feels as if I could keep on running at this breakneck speed all the way to the Pferdemarkt, to the sacrificial feast of the Trumpet Plagues. The summer foliage – some still green, some in October rust colours – rustles and crackles under my feet. Blood is splashing down over my upper lip, my nose is full of it and I snort it out in a spray as I run.

In spite of the real sprint I'm doing, I suddenly hear a bicycle bell behind me, one of those ding-dong-I'm-coming-back-from-the-market-with-flowers-in-my-basket bells. I swing round and the woman on her black sit-up-and-beg bicycle just manages to brake. She doesn't look bad, long black hair and a figure-hugging jacket, also black, big breasts and so on. She's about to give me an earful but I'm already dragging her off the saddle. My face covered in blood probably looks so menacing that she falls silent. I push her into a thicket of rape and jump on her bike. Then I pedal off as fast as I can. Without looking round.

26

It's hardly half an hour later and I'm in Feldstrasse. By now the sky has opened up and the sun is blazing down. The weather's great, really fantastic – or it would be if it wasn't like this every day. It's simply too much. And it will hardly be any better in Paraguay. I prop the bike up against the bike stand outside the fresh-food supermarket that used to be Woolworth's. Some lethargic Egyptians are sitting in the shade moving wooden counters around on a board. Beside them is a true-old Turk who, despite the heat, is wearing a green woollen jacket and a brown bobble hat as he sharpens a knife on a rotating grindstone.

The grounds of the former abattoir are covered in white tents, one little tent after another, thirty or forty of them, if not more. Those on the right are arranged in lanes, as if there were a flea market going on. Right by the entrance is a chubby couple – she in a dress with a large floral pattern, he in a black suit with a black shirt – and they keep petting their personal sacrificial animal. It's a particularly large, beautiful lamb they've bought, a white ram with black patches round its eyes – like a Zorro mask. The woman's taking pictures with her egosmart and the man is posing beside the terrified lamb, holding the rope in one hand and keeping the lamb's head up with the other so that the sacrifice looks good in the picture. Clearly it's not just the Randolphians in their heavy-metal costumes who are taking advantage of the opportunity to do some slaughtering in public but also perfectly ordinary members of the sect. Nice people all of them, who don't think of themselves as being cruel to animals but simply join in everything their religion prescribes and otherwise go about their own private business.

There's something of a public holiday about the whole affair: music, shouting, the baaing of terrified lambs tied to the nearest railings by a rope round their neck or leg, little girls who, in their gauzy pink dresses, look like something you could win at a funfair, shaven-headed bio-young men clumsily dragging the sheep and goats along to the slaughter tents by one leg, their wool or their horns, true-old Turks sucking sweets as they look on, explaining how everything could be done better. Everyone's in a happy mood, no one is bothered by the terrified animals. Just one little boy is crying unconsolably in his father's arms.

"Bassi! Hey Bassi! Is Elli here too?"

Grit. She's wearing sack-like green animal-rights overalls with "No, I won't eat my brother" written on the back and is carrying a pile of leaflets.

"Hey," I say, "what are you doing here? Surely you're not going to start a fight with the Disciples of St. John of the Trumpets of the Seven Last Plagues?"

Now she sees my broken nose that's swollen up.

"Oh my God! Who did that? Did it happen here? You should go to the police."

"No, no," I say, "somewhere else. It was those pals of yours, the Fat Rats."

"The Rats? What have you got to do with the Fat Rats? We've not been working with them for ages now."

"Ingo Dresen to be more precise."

"Is he here?"

Grit looks as horrified as anyone hearing the name Ingo Dresen.

"Not yet, but the whole gang of them are likely to turn up within the next half hour. Have the police not come yet? I rang them up."

Grit shakes her head. "So far I've only seen two – and they didn't look as if they were prepared for the Fat Rats. Perhaps it won't be a bad thing if they do come. That's not to say they'll be violent. Perhaps they'll just round up the sheep."

"You can forget that," I say. "Ingo Dresen imagines he's taking part in a historic event and the others won't be here because of the lambs, they want to have a good punch-up. They enjoy it."

"But where's Elli? Isn't Elli with you?"

"Somewhere over there." I make a vague gesture in the direction of the crowd. "We lost each other earlier on."

Grit takes out her egosmart and immediately starts tapping away. I remain calm. Grit can get as suspicious as she likes. In seven hours I'll be on the plane.

"That's odd. I keep getting the response: this number no longer exists."

"To be honest, we had an argument and she's pretty cheesed off with me. She's probably switched off her mobile because of that. If you want to see her, then come along with me. She's sure to be in the Randolphians slaughter-tent."

I've no idea why I said that. It just came to me somehow. Grit trots along beside me. As we go I take one of her leaflets so that I won't have to explain what Elli and I are supposed to have quarrelled about: "Dear Disciples of St. John of the Trumpets of the Seven Last Plagues, in the big tent on Sternstrasse, opposite the former HELA factory, you can have your sacrificial animals slaughtered by trained specialists free of charge. Please take advantage of this offer."

"I don't understand," I say. "Now you're helping those

maniacs to kill animals. How come?"

"We're doing what we can. Anything's better than having computer scientists, insurance agents and hairdressers, who've never slaughtered anything in their lives, trying to kill terrified animals with half-blunt knives. Naturally we filed an application to have the sacrificial feast banned, but when it's about religion we're banging our heads against a brick wall with the authorities."

I can believe that. Our charming female government has problems when it comes to putting their foot down. Regulate things: yes. Compulsory helmets: yes. But really forbid something? Oh no, they're far too understanding for that. Protect animals: yes – but if it's a religious lot that wants to torment animals or children in order to placate some transcendental being, then it's great. Anything so as not to be suspected of intolerance, racism or Anti-Semitism. And didn't the Nazis use religious slaughter as a way of stirring up hatred of the Jewish population? The rabbis, imams and bishops of St John sit there on their fat backsides on the chat shows, smiling from one enlightened ear to the other and saying, "We've been doing that for thousands of years and will continue to do so for ever and ever and you can't do anything about it, for there's too many of us and there are no laws against large numbers. If you forbid our cruel rituals, there'll be a revolt, or the people will emigrate on a grand scale, or they'll keep doing it in secret and at one blow you'll have turned thousands of decent, ordinary citizens into criminals. So would you therefore be so good as to change your laws?" Democracy is a fair-weather form of government. It can't stand being put to the test.

A ten-year-old boy holding up the back legs of a dirty grey billy goat and forcing it along like a wheelbarrow swerves into one of the slaughter tents right in front of us. The poor animal is bleating pathetically and trying to kick its legs. The boy's a scrawny little lad with ears that stick out and a green-and-orange striped T-shirt, and he's bursting with pride at playing a role in such an important and prestigious event as the sacrifice of an animal and at being allowed to impose his will on one with such dangerous horns. He's laughing and looking for admiration from his friend, the little fat boy who's been waiting inside the tent and who joins in with a nervous laugh, because it's part of being young to laugh when others are afraid.

I give Grit a look.

One of the bio-young skinheads takes the animal, forces it to the ground and kneels on its shoulder while another grabs three of its legs just above its hooves and ties them tightly together with thin black plastic cord. The billy goat has a broad woolly forehead and terror in its light-blue eyes. Tied up, it's dragged to the side of the tent, where several trussed-up sheep are lying on their sides. Their eyes are open wide, their big bodies heaving, their fleeces rising and falling. The billy goat lifts up its head and cries out. It's not bleating now, it's crying out. Incredibly loudly. Like a person falling into an abyss: Aaaaaaaaaaaahhh!!!!! The cry of fear echoes right round the slaughterhouse. Aaaaaaaahhh!!!!

Presumably it's the sound of the vowel 'A' that makes its cry seem so human. What makes it so unbearable is the knowledge that the billy goat has every reason to cry out like that. Whatever it's imagining at the moment, the reality is going to be worse.

The ten-year-old boy with the sticking-out ears bends down over it and copies it with a mocking Baaaahhhhhhh right in its face. His fat friend, not wanting to be left out, also goes over to the animal and the next time the goat lifts up its head to cry out he gives it a slap on the face. I'm itching to pay him back in his own kind. Grit tries to pull me back but I shake her off.

"Just listen, you two," I say to the pair of them. "This billy goat's going to have to pay with its life so that snotty-nosed brats like you can be spared. Are you clear about that?"

"What are you on about, granddad? We're not doing anything wrong," the fat boy squawks, blinking nervously as he speaks. "It's going to be sacrificed."

I'm not going to let myself be spoken to like that. "Wrong," I say. "If anyone's going to be sacrificed here, it's you two. Once they run out of sheep and billy goats here, they'll be coming for you. Your God also accepts little boys, you see. Actually he much prefers little boys to sheep."

"Bassi! That's enough." Grit tugs insistently at my sleeve. "They're only children."

Giving me a wry look, the boys wander off to the other side of the tent, from which a red tide of blood and water is flowing towards us all the time.

"So what," I say. "Above all they're arseholes. Or do you think they'll be nicer when they get older?"

Two bio-young skinheads, identical at first sight in grey overalls and black rubber boots, give me a belligerent look, but they're fully occupied dragging one of the sacrificial animals, a sheep, by its fleece across to the table, where a priest in a brown uniform is waiting, a brand-new knife on the chopping block in front of him.

"Just bugger off if you don't like it here," one of the men in grey overalls says. His ears are very pointed which, together with his shaven head, makes him look like some extraterrestrial species. Now I'm determined to stay there, of course. If I'm going to warn my brother and the other members of the sect, I haven't really got time to lose, but all at once I'm not sure any more whether I want to do that.

The priest, a skinny guy with a thin patriarchal beard, raises his arms up high, knife in one hand, and closes his eyes with an expression on his face as if he's just receiving a message from above. Then he opens his eyes, kneels down behind the ram and bends its head backwards, while one of the grey overalls undoes the black cord binding the ram's legs. The priest of St John carries out the cut with a remarkably steady hand and so deeply that a great gash is yawning in its neck and the blood comes bubbling out, bright red. But despite that, he clearly hasn't cut through the blood vessels, for in Grit's estimation there's not enough blood flowing.

"It looks easier than it is," she explains. "You have to sever the oesophagus, the windpipe, the vagus nerve and the large blood vessels with one swift cut, so that the animal bleeds to death quickly. That's the reason why it's bad that the priests here aren't trained slaughtermen."

The ram thrashes about and resists, gets up on its legs and tries to bleat – but it can only mime bleating. Hanging out of the gaping wound in its neck, like the end of a pale garden hose, is the twitching windpipe, that is now sucking in an influx of blood instead of air while above it the ram's mouth is gasping in a futile search for air.

There's a bio-young policeman standing next to me. Immediately my pulse starts to race and I feel guilty again, but the guardian of the law is just watching the slowly suffocating sheep that finally collapses and lies down in its own blood. The policeman's gone pretty pale.

One of the grey overalls drags the sheep by its back leg across to a drain with a water tap. Suddenly the sheep stands up again, turning its blood-soaked head towards us. It opens its mouth again for a mute bleat, blood dripping down in viscous drops, then the zombie sheep drops down on its side again and starts waving its legs in the air, as if it was galloping along. It just doesn't stop.

"They're just convulsions," Grit says. "The sheep's dead."

"Listen," I say to the policeman, by now ashen-faced, "earlier on I reported to the police that a motorbike gang, looking for violence…"

At that moment one of the slaughtermen sticks a gushing hosepipe in the mouth of the ram, that's still thrashing its legs, washing its windpipe and oesophagus nice and clean, and the policeman spews up at my feet.

"Oh my God," I say, taking a step back, "can't they wait just a minute or two until the sheep's stopped moving?"

"It's dead," says Grit.

Clearing my throat, I turn to the policeman again. "Are you up to taking a report?'

He's still very pale, but he nods, then goes to get the hosepipe, rinses out his mouth and washes away his vomit into the drain.

I explain the matter and even coolly give him my particulars.

"Okay," Grit says, tugging at my sleeve. "I think it's about time we went looking for Elli."

So off we go. They're really direct these animal rights activists, no beating about the bush. I like that. I have a brief fantasy of a quickie with Grit in some storeroom or other where we've taken refuge from the rampaging Fat Rats, where it's cozy and warm while all hell's being let loose outside. Or in a public convenience. But first of all I have to find my worthless brother. We make our way through a disgusting, disgraceful hell on earth: men, women – true-young and true-old – and children are scuttling across puddles of blood and giving a hand with skinning and jointing the sheep and goats.

It's the little and slightly bigger kids who're always crowding round where a sheep or a billy goat's having its throat cut. Once I see a mother go over to her seven-year-old son, put her arm round his shoulders and quietly talk to him. I can't hear a word of what she's saying but her gestures, her demeanour, her concerned and gentle expression tell me that she's saying, something like, "You shouldn't be looking at that. Afterwards you won't be able to get to sleep again. Mickey Mouse's on television just now. Wouldn't you rather come home with me?"

But of course the seven-year-old reacts in the same way all little boys in his situation would react. "Noooooo!!!" he howls indignantly, wriggling out of his mother's grip and hurrying over to where another animal is struggling in mortal anguish.

Finally I find my brother right at the end of the abattoir site. He's kneeling on the ground in a brown djellaba, an ankle-length Moroccan gown with a pointed hood, but I still recognise him at once, with his bulky physique he stands out everywhere. Unless he decided to join the Fat Rats at some point or other. Then he wouldn't stand out, of course. Beside him is a man of considerably slighter build wearing what looks like a confirmation suit and round spectacles. He has a book in his hand – it's too fat to be *The Book of Irrefutable Knowledge*. To go by the gilt edging, it must be the good old Bible. Standing reverently around the two of them are various Disciples of St. John, four Randolphians in black – capes, studded jeans and heavy boots – and around ten lower-ranking brethren in plain black suits. The wives of the lower-ranking Disciples of St. John have a strange predilection for large-patterned floral dresses and shiny red high heels with round toecaps and an ankle strap. Some even have artificial flowers in their hair. The Randolphian wives express their bond with God by wearing historical dress in brown and grey with hems that trail through the mud. Bahro has clothed her highly pregnant body in dull black. There are beads of sweat on her little piggy nose. To compensate for all this personal humility, she has gone overboard with her children's clothes. Her daughters are dolled up in frilly pink, the boys are wearing light-blue velvet suits. The other children are also wearing these, but Babro's brood have clothes embroidered with hundreds of rhinestones.

There's a bound lamb in front of my brother, a very small one it would take a great deal of goodwill to call a ram. The show's about to begin.

"Abraham!" The weed in the confirmation suit cries or, rather, reads out.

"Here I am, Lord," my brother cries, completely absorbed in his role.

Now the candidate for confirmation, "Take now thy son, thine only son Isaac, whom thou lovest and get thee into the land of Moriah and offer him there for a burnt offering upon one of the mountains which I will tell thee of."

"Uwe," I shout, "Uwe!"

Clutching the terrified lamb under his arm, my brother stands up, annoyed. Eyes wide, the lamb stares into space.

"You dare..." my brother thunders, still in his Abraham voice.

"You have to get away..." I say. "There's a gang of rockers going to turn up any moment now. The Fat Rats – something like the Hell's Angels. They want to save the sheep."

"We're ready for radical animal rights people," my brother says, pointing to two fat-arsed cops at the back of the tent. They have batons and handcuffs hanging from their uniform belts.

"Not animal rights activists – Ingo Dresen!" I say.

"Ingo Dresen?"

My brother drops the lamb. Grit picks it up and unties its legs.

"Why didn't you say that right away. Let's get out of here quick."

He waves his household over, including the brats in pink and sky-blue, and declares an orderly retreat. Only the police stay there.

"You can come with us," my brother tells me graciously, "our bus is in Lagerstrasse, just beyond the television tower."

Grit puts the lamb in my arms. Small though it is, it must weigh at least two stone. And it doesn't keep still either.

"First of all we must find Elli and warn her," Grit says.

"Elli knows what's going on," I say, "she probably left ages ago."

"What has Ingo Dresen got against us?" Uwe asks as he hurries on ahead of his herd of almost fifty, with his own pastel-coloured brood and Babro, like a fat inkwell, immediately behind him. "Last year he wanted to join in with us. He said something about a broad Christian front and that he was now a Christian. However we did manage to put him off."

Carrying the traumatised lamb and with Grit beside me, I have to make an effort to keep up with him.

"Now you're seen as a heretic and he's after you."

"A heretic? Even the Pope said that the Abrahamic sacrifice is not contrary to the doctrine of the Catholic Church."

"You tell that to Ingo Dresen."

"What happened to your nose?"

"There's the police," Babro says from underneath her cowl. She points towards Feldstrasse and Heiligengeistfeld, where seven flashing blue lights have appeared. "Why don't we just go back to our tent?"

Female obstinacy, even among the religionists. But before

my brother can reprimand her, the infernal rattle and roar of motorbikes comes heading towards us from Sternstrasse. There must be a lot of them, really a lot. And they've coordinated their engine-sounders so that they're playing Rimsky-Korsakov's 'Flight of the Bumble Bee' – a violent and very loud bumble-bee flight that comes across more like the vicious buzz of steel hornets. But that of course means that it can't be the Fat Rats. The Fat Rats ride Harleys and hydrogen engines with drum-and-melody sounders just don't correspond to the retro spirit of a Harley-Davidson. And, anyway, Ingo Dresen would have set them to the 'Ride of the Valkyries'.

There they are, and there are a lot of them. At first sight they look clean and smart, truly civilised. The precise opposite of the Fat Rats. But despite their brand-new red-and-white bikers' outfits, their snow-white gauntlets and their shimmering silvery-white helmets, there's something threatening and vicious, even perverted about them, and despite their moderate speed, something disturbingly purposeful. Their bikes are hypermodern racers that consist almost entirely of wheels. Above the reflecting visors there's a large cross, a sword and a branch with leaves on their helmets.

"What does that mean – the sword and that branch on their helmets?" I ask my brother.

"The olive branch is the Christian symbol of peace," Uwe says, but he doesn't look at all reassured. They're only twenty metres away from us when they come to a halt and each one stretches his right arm to the side, at which an eighteen-inch iron chain drops out of his gauntlet. Then they actually start to pray. With their engines running. Hands folded – in gloves with iron chains hanging out of them.

"Those aren't angels of peace," I say. "They're bloodthirsty zealots."

Uwe's little herd turn on their heels as one and run back into the abattoir. Now my brother and his family are right at the back with me and Grit behind them. Me still carrying the lamb. All around us the startled Bible-bashers are pouring out of the tents, for now the arrogant rumble of the Harley engines can be heard from the other side. As I have to clamber over an overturned slaughtering block, I can even see the Fat Rats for a brief moment. Clearly they've divided in two and are starting to surround the former abattoir from both sides. "Close the sack," as Ingo Dresen would say. The Disciples of St. John are running all over the place, with no idea where to go to escape. They're trapped. We're trapped. Rounded up like a herd of cattle, we finally gather together in the middle of the former abattoir, while from three sides the Fat Rats and from the fourth the red-and-whites are bearing down on us on their bikes. Mothers clasp their children and squat down on the ground with them, men run to and fro holding their heads, panic stricken, some are crying while others run back to the tents to release the sacrificial lambs that are still alive. The fear of the Disciples of St. John has reached a degree which, in their desperation and willingness to submit, has something religious about it. For what has a religion, that feels daring when it disregards the odd law for the protection of animals, got to oppose the religion of violence that ignores every single rule?

And I'm stuck in this mess because I insisted on warning my crackpot brother. He's still standing there close to me, his outspread arms protectively round his family, his chin jutting out resolutely. Grit's still here too. I put the lamb in her arms.

"Quick, get away. Now! They're not after you. When they see the lamb and your animal-rights overall, they'll most likely just let you through."

Grit nods, takes a deep breath and heads off diagonally towards the bikers. She's allowed to pass unimpeded.

"Where's the police, then?" my brother asks.

The seven blue lights are still rotating all by themselves in Feldstrasse. Not a policeman to be seen anywhere at all. They probably just can't cope with everything that's going on. No officer in his right mind will get involved in a confrontation with these bike-riding berserkers. That's a job for the army.

And then it begins. Engines are revved up beyond the pain threshold and the Fat Rats – inspired by their longing for their former greatness and manliness, their sensitivity blunted by decades of training in violence on the computer and in real life – come hurtling towards us. I run off without even looking for my brother and his family. Now it's every man for himself. I'm quick and light on my bio-twenty-year-old feet that hardly seem to touch the ground. At one point I have to evade one of the chain-swinging red-and-whites – I duck down out of the way, then do what is almost a squat vault over some railings and take five steps at once as if I were weightless. All around me tents are collapsing, people running, children falling over and getting trodden on by those behind, but my every step is assured. When one of the women in floral dresses slips and falls down, I simply leap over without even touching her. It's the crowd scrambling along behind me that sees to that. The red-and-whites are driving up and down between the rows of tents, slapping the canvas with their chains and wrapping them round tent poles and running over anyone who gets in their way. A few of the Randolphians have pulled themselves together and picked up chairs and tent poles to knock the attackers off their bikes. Their sombrely dressed women, led by the remarkably fearless Babro, are throwing anything they can get their hands on – sacrificial vessels, tupperware and sheep's heads. But like knights of old, the red-and-whites are protected by their helmets. And there's not a single policeman anywhere to be seen.

What I do see, though, is Ingo Dresen. Without a helmet on he's driving at walking pace past the tents. I stop, mesmerised. He hasn't seen me yet. In his arm he's keeping a careful – you could almost say tender – hold of the grubby grey billy goat that's already looking round perkily. Behind him Fat Rats are following at a lumbering rat-trot. They have cans and are pouring petrol over the tents and debris. Babro screams at a lower-ranking Disciple of St John that he should do something. It's a chrono-young guy in an elegant, figure-hugging suit, hair slicked back and a Bible under his arm, who's just about to run off past us. Responding to Babro's scolding, he actually stands in the way of the Fat Rats, holding out his Bible towards them. Ingo Dresen simply drives past. The first Rat on foot knocks him down with one swing of the arm. When the young martyr tries to struggle up, the next Rat pokes him in the face with the flat of his hand. The Disciple falls over backwards. The Rat grabs him by his slippery hair and pushes his head down in the nearest pool of blood. Two other Rats with petrol cans stop to give the lad a few kicks in the ribs. Always alternately: right foot, left foot. They make unpleasant thudding sounds, but perhaps I'm just imagining I can hear them for actually there's far too much noise going on.

Ingo Dresen stops right in front of me, sticks his splayed legs in the sand and keeps his Harley stable solely with the strength of his trunk-like thighs while he lets go of the handlebars to stroke the billy goat's head.

"You're here? Good man. I knew I could rely on you."

"I… er…" I say.

"Most people have a weak point. Not me. But most people.

Forget it."

A sickening crunching sound – perfectly audible this time. I really did hear it. One of the Fat Rats has kicked the young lad in the face. He wipes his boot clean on the victim's suit. The Plague Trumpet tries to get up again but is pushed back onto the ground. Four Rats are kicking him now – face, ribs, face, back. He curls up, trying to make himself small, to protect his head as far as possible with his arms, but the four fat guys really lay into him now. It's like a dance. They throw their arms in the air to build up momentum then kick, and as they do so, they look happy, really happy. Not far away other Fat Rat foot soldiers are kicking a security guard who's also lying on the ground. Their faces too are glowing with the same unfettered enthusiasm.

"Bad men do what good men only dream of," Ingo Dresen says. Obviously he can see the look of horror on my face.

"The main thing is, you're with us again."

The four Rats further on have stopped kicking their victim. The Disciple of St John is lying on the ground, motionless. One of the Rats kneels down beside him and bends over his face. I assume he's going to try and revive him, then I realise what he has in mind. He bites his ear. He tears half his ear off with his teeth. It's stuck between his teeth, the blood's dripping down his chin and he rolls his eyes ecstatically. The other three whoop.

Suddenly a shout, "The fuzz!"

Indeed – a company of police is storming the site. Water cannons have drawn up all round and are shooting jets of water at the crowd. Beside them are three gigantic vehicles such as I've never seen before. They look like those huge combine harvesters – only in black. At a tantalisingly slow speed they roll across the area, flattening tents and motorbikes, and they look so terrifying it makes your hair stand on end.

"Jump on," Ingo roars in my ear but I stand there as if paralysed. The four Rats who beat up the young lad trot off. Fire flares up on either side. In a few seconds all the tents and debris around us are blazing. The air is suddenly so unbearably hot, it's as if it's about to burst into flames itself. The brave young Plague Trumpet is lying right next to a burning barrel and still not moving.

"Get on, will you," Ingo bellows, clutching the sacrificial goat to him with his left hand. Then, with a roar from the Harley-Davidson, he's off. Together with the billy goat. By now the whole place is burning. Police are approaching through the heat haze. In their dark, clumpy gear they don't look like human beings but like combat robots from a hostile planet. The flames are mirrored in their helmets and shields. I run over to the unconscious Plague Trumpet and pull the body with the smashed head, away from the fire. When I look up I see one of the police right over me. He raises his baton. I try to look him in the eyes, to make him see by my stupid naive expression that I'm one of the good guys, but all I can see is the blazing inferno reflected in his lowered visor and he too seems to see something other than my harmless look, for the next moment the baton comes crashing down on my head.

When I come to again I'm neither in hospital nor in the police station, I'm lying on a patch of grass. A paramedic's shining a stick of liquorice in my eyes. No, it's a pocket torch.

"Looking good," he says, gets up and simply goes on. How can he simply go on? I feel sick, I'm trembling and I've got a headache. I'm sure I don't look good. Grit's beside me. She gives me something to drink. From a saucer. The water runs down over my chin and neck. I'm still on the site of the old

Hamburg abattoir. It hurts when I swallow.

"Grid," I say, "wherd de lab, Grid?"

I must sound ridiculous. I'm speaking through my nose and it's swollen and completely blocked.

Grit points to the left and, after two unsuccessful attempts, my eyes manage to remember how to switch from close to distant focus and I see Ingo Dresen with several – seven, nine, whatever – Fat Rats. They're sitting on their motorbikes, at least those in front, with Ingo Dresen in the middle, of course. There's another row behind them. They all have lambs in their arms. One of them must be the one I gave to Grit. Ingo's the only one posing with a goat. And the stupid press photographers go along with this, photographing the touching picture of the hulking great guys holding the fragile animals so gently in their arms. Okay then, any woman seeing the picture is to think, they might possibly be violent, it's even quite likely that they've just been indulging in violence. But they weren't doing it simply for pleasure, but for a cause that is greater than themselves – and for the poor animals. I prop myself up on my elbows and look around. Still trembling. There are four ambulances parked here and one is just setting off, it's blue light flashing, and two more are just arriving. Something's running down into the back of my collar. I touch it and look at my fingers: blood. I feel higher up. There's an open cut on the back of my head. The paramedic presumably didn't notice that.

"Where's the police?" I ask Grit.

She dabs the bruise on my forehead and my nose with a damp tissue. My nose hurts like hell.

"They left ages ago. They say there's been more than twenty emergency calls – and that just here in Hamburg. And it seems to have been even worse everywhere else."

The Fat Rats are still standing around happily chatting, which presumably means they won't have to pay for what they did to the poor Plague Trumpet. I try to look at my old wristwatch, that has no smart functions whatsoever, but someone's taken it. No one's that poor that they don't possess something another person would kill them for.

"What's the time?"

I feel for my wallet. It's still there. I take it out. Someone's stolen the banknotes but the papers are still all there. And I sewed up most of the money in the lining of my jacket anyway.

"Just after five," Grit says.

Still carrying the billy goat, Ingo Dresen comes over. "I've always said Basti Bastard had a tough nut. How d'you feel anyway?"

"Dammit, I've got to get to the airport," I say through my blocked-up nose. "Otherwise I'm done for."

Grit looks surprised but Ingo Dresen says nothing. Apparently I've now become one of his friends, and he accepts what his friends say without question. It's somehow frightening how quickly that can happen. He puts the billy goat down and fetches his motorbike.

"I hope your flight leaves before half seven," he says. "I have this kind of premonition that the airport computer's going to crash at half past seven."

I get on behind him and, trying to keep some distance between his legs and mine, hold on to the back of the saddle. Pity I didn't manage to get anywhere with Grit.

27

Clouds, some clouds at last! I stare out of the window of the plane at the mattress, white as soapsuds, below us. I'm still trembling, still bleeding so that I've had to stick a large wad of dressing between the back of my head and the seat. After the plane spent two hours in the queue I'm just glad to have made it up into the atmosphere, supersaturated with CO_2 though it is, before the broad-front hackers' sneaky Trojans managed to put the airport computer out of action.

They almost refused to allow me on board because of the cut on my head. The woman at the German Buzzard check-in desk tried to make me go to the airport doctor first. When I started making a fuss, she immediately called two security guards but fortunately they agreed with me that the cut was nothing to speak of. I just had to take care not to soil the seat on the plane, they said, and it would be better to put me in a row by myself.

It's not just the effects of the police baton that are hurting, it's above all the recognition that the civilisation I knew and valued is in the process of dissolution. Society has become violent, has broken up into lots of splinter groups that will stop at nothing, and if anyone complains, they immediately call their bodyguards. Now we can see what a stabilising effect the repression of women had and how important it is to bring back that inequality. Civilisation can only be sustained if every man, however stupid, poor or incompetent, is allocated a woman whom he can tell what to do. Otherwise it's just violence and chaos.

However revolting I think Ingo Dresen is – I can't say how much I loathe him, that scum, that fat piece of shit – I can still sympathise with his desire to re-establish the old conditions. Naturally I don't want a state based on the crude fantasies of an Ingo Dresen, that have no place for human rights. But it wouldn't be a bad thing if a damper were put on unfettered feminism with its infinite egoism and the idea of men as beings that have to be re-educated. It would be enough for me if Ingo's broad front managed to destabilise this state a little – perhaps just to the extent that the fact that I locked up my wife and girlfriend in the cellar would be disregarded as a mere trifle. So that I can go back. So that I don't have to stay in Paraguay. What is there for me in Paraguay?

The gay steward with the Magnum moustache hands out little aluminium foil bags with Asiatic writing on them and totally oversalted nuts inside. I pull down the tray table from the back of the seat in front and rummage through my bag for the set theory exercise book and the toy cowboy, which I packed to calm me down and remind me who I am. Apart from school exercise books, the cardboard box in the loft also had a plastic cowboy swinging his lasso sitting on a crudely made, rather thin and faded horse. At one time it must have been brown. When I hold it in my hand I can immediately see the surprise bag in my mind's eye, it was blue and red, though I can't remember what was written on it any longer. What I can remember though, is the sickly-sweet smell of the puffed rice the bag contained. Revolting stuff that was even spurned by the hardened palate of the primary school kid I once was. What junk they used to feed us back then. I'm touched by the frugality shown by my generation – at least during childhood.

Of course, even back then the contents of the surprise bag were made of plastic, but if the population hadn't exploded and we'd remained modest in our demands, the world would probably not be about to end.

I put the horse and cowboy down on the tray table beside the oversalted nuts and switch on the compunicator screen in the back of the seat in front. It has four different games of skill on offer, two films glorifying violence and one romantic comedy, a music programme and the information about our flight. A news programme – no chance. It's a good thing I haven't got round to disposing of my egosmart. Now I can plug it in and – provided the broad-front hackers haven't disabled the whole communications system – find out what's been happening in the Bundestag. Are Olaf Scholz and his bunch of women still in power or has there actually been a coup d'état.

I put my earplugs in and select Top News for an up-to-date summary, after which I'll switch over to Newsnight to get more details. A young guy in jeans, a shirt with a snake print and an animal mood top that keeps on contracting and slackening off, contracting and slackening off, is sitting on the rounded edge of a pink desk.

"Hi there, guys. Our news starts with a sensational announcement: just half an hour ago Christine Semmelrogge, who was Germany's minister for the environment, the decommissioning of power stations and disposal of nuclear waste before she was abducted two years ago, has turned up again. A second woman is said to have been held together with her but her identity has not yet been revealed. Now there's a thing. Stay tuned, we'll get back to it. Okay then. At a meeting of the North Europe Council in Brussels the Sun-Cop Agreement…"

I pull out the egosmart plug and stare at my knees, not

daring even to look round. I've probably gone bright red. How did they get out? I chained both of them up, Christine to the kitchen island, Elli in the bathroom. I took away every spoon, in fact any small piece of equipment they could have used as a tool. I even removed the fridge so they couldn't take it apart and use some metal component as a key. I thought of everything. Everything! I feel sick, I'm sweating and shivering with cold and don't dare to look at the other passengers. Thank God I'm sitting by myself. I have to calm down. I have to calm down immediately. I have to hold my nerve.

I take the set theory exercise book and open the pages filled with childish writing in order to immerse myself in the clear truths of mathematics.

Every natural number has a predecessor and a successor. Exception: 1.

Let us choose any point on the number line (eg 5), then all the numbers to the left are smaller, all the numbers to the right larger (than 5).

I close the exercise book again and get the German Newsnight on my egosmart. This time, however, I don't run the news on the compunicator screen, but watch it on the smart's mini-display, still using German Buzzard's throwaway earphones. Good old Newsnight, and still with Hanno Petry.

"Good evening, ladies and gentlemen. Earlier this evening Dr Christine Semmelrogge, minister for the environment, conservation, the decommissioning of power stations and the disposal of nuclear waste, who disappeared in 2028, has turned up again. It is clear that she was held prisoner in the house of her divorced husband, Sebastian Bürger. Bürger is press officer for the Democracy Centre and it is suspected that he is on the run. We'll go over now to Inga Wenzel in Hamburg. Is there any more information, Inga?"

Inga Wenzel is standing by the garden fence of my parents' old house. It's my house and yet not my house. They've turned it into a crime scene: red-and-white tape, guys in white overalls, photographers and outside-broadcast vans, a white tent in the front garden and a few huge lights focused on the front door and glass bricks – the old cliché of the horror lurking behind the façade of normality.

"Good evening. No, Hanno, there's nothing much new to report. The police are keeping a low profile so as not to jeopardise the investigation in any way. Frau Dr Semmelrogge, who at the time of her abduction was regarded as a possible future chancellor, is in Eppendorf Hospital at the moment. Her condition is said to be good, given the circumstances. She is reported to have named her divorced husband, Sebastian Bürger, as the man responsible for her incarceration. There is still speculation about a second female person who was locked up in the cellar dungeon with her and whose identity is as yet unknown. Nor is it clear whether this person was another prisoner or an accessory to the crime. Now the search is on for Sebastian Bürger."

They've got me. One look at their computers and they'll see that I'm on my way to Paraguay. That is unless Ingo Dresen's hackers have managed to get their act together and finally destroy the airport computer. How is it that my wife is the lead story on the news? What's happened to the putsch in parliament? I watch Newsnight right through to the end: Sun-Cop agreement; disturbances at the Disciples of St. John's sacrificial feasts in Berlin, Hamburg, Dortmund and Wiesbaden. Forty-eight injured in Hamburg, even more in Berlin. The Conservatives' proposal of a childcare subsidy for children who are looked after at home instead of in a nursery school, with a double payment if it's the mother who takes on the task; a mass attack on the Hungarian Wall by refugees, at least four hundred refugees shot on the Indian Wall, twenty on the French. Another eighteen refugees drowned in the English Channel, a hundred and fifty off the coast of Italy, record high temperatures in South America, forest fires in Portugal and Greece, floods in India, sport, the weather. It's going to be clear and sunny. And that was it. No mention of an attack on parliament or even of an attempt to overthrow the government. No mention of any hacker attack on the Internet.

I have to sneeze and I can't stop. I probably caught it from Christine.

Now RTL news:

No news of any kind of putsch there either. However they do go into the bloodbath at the old abattoir in greater detail. From the Newsnight report you got the impression it was just a matter of masculine tussles. The whole nightmarish scene with screams, blows, blood, children crying, engines roaring, flames and tables being smashed was trivialised.

On RTL at least a few victims (sic!) covered in blood are allowed to speak before the picture of the tenderhearted Fat Rats with the lambs in their arms is shown. The rest of the programme consists entirely of the report on Christine. There are pictures of her with Racke and Binya standing outside Eppendorf Hospital and waving. And last but not least, a wanted photo of me is shown. It's a photo that was taken at the class reunion when I was standing beside Reinhard Hell, one of the two mummies. Reinhard's face has been pixelated – a great improvement. Some self-important snitch among my classmates must have gone to the police. I try to remember who took the photo. I suspect it was Rolf, but I'm not sure and try as I might, I can't bring it back to mind. On the photo I look as if I'm in my late thirties but I'm still recognisable.

After all my hairstyle hasn't changed. Covering the lower half of my face with a paper handkerchief, I pretend I'm blowing my nose and as I do so I look round on either side and behind me to see if any of the passengers are staring at me. So far no one is.

There comes an announcement over the loudspeaker. "Ladies and gentlemen, this is your co-pilot speaking. A minor technical problem with the air conditioning has been detected. It's not a cause for alarm but in such a case regulations require us to make a precautionary landing at the nearest airport. Captain Engelke will therefore take us down in Paris as soon as we receive the signal from the tower. If you have undone your safety belt, will you please fasten it again. We hope that the problem will be sorted out quickly and we can resume the flight as soon as possible. We will keep you informed of any further developments."

Irritated grumbling and the occasional groan in the rows in front of and behind me. All at once I'm quite relaxed. You have to know when you've lost. The gay steward and one of the stewardesses are standing at the front of the seats and looking as unobtrusively as possible at the rows of seats at the back of the plane, at me that is. Then, after a brief exchange, the stewardess disappears through the curtain to business class. Presumably the gay steward has to keep an eye on me. Pretending I misunderstand this and think he's trying to flirt with me, I lower my eyes then suddenly give him an intense look. The steward blushes. He probably thinks I'm a bit of a cutie – and only bio-twenty.

I switch on Top News again. After the pictures of Christine that have already been shown, Ingo Dresen suddenly appears on the screen. Yes, Ingo Dresen it is, but not because he's taken control of the army but because some TV woman wants to ask him about the Semmelrogge abduction case. The TV woman is a fat dame with short orange hair and a necklace of porous lava stones. Like in the Flintstones. Ingo Dresen's standing outside my house, the house with the crime-scene tape, talking to the TV woman; he brushes away a strand of greasy hair, with a silly grin on his face, as if he still had a lamb in his arms. It's the first time I've seen him show anything like embarrassment and it takes a while before I understand what's happened.

It was a mistake to give him the letter. But it was the last second before check-in and I handed him the crumpled envelope. There was no other way. Just before check-in. If it hadn't been, I would have posted the letter myself, of course.

"It's important," I told him. "It absolutely has to go in the postbox."

"Sure thing," Ingo said, giving me a comradely pat on the shoulder. I didn't doubt for one second that he'd post the letter but obviously he didn't. He must have torn it open while he was still in the airport and read it like a nosy old fishwife. And then he had nothing better to do than to briefly break off the revolution of enslaved manhood in order to liberate a woman from her dungeon. A romantic. Deep in his heart Ingo Dresen is a real romantic. Rides on his trusty Harley to Redderkamp, runs down the cellar steps, pushes the shelves aside and with feverish fingers enters the code he found in my letter.

I just can't bear to watch the way he postures in front of the camera. He's beaming all over his face, the noble knight rescuing the fair maiden, drunk with all the approbation and praise. He's not used to that. And he likes it, he likes being liked. Even someone like Ingo Dresen needs more love than he deserves. And who do people love more than a hero who has rescued a damsel in distress? To gain importance, that's what it's all about. Even if in order to do so you have to do the opposite of what you believe in. Even if it means you have to betray your own people.

"I headed over there at once…" Ingo says, "…definitely not a feminist, but there are limits…" he says. "…to Paraguay…" he says and, "…someone has to put a stop to his game…"

There's no solidarity among the weak. What is a friendship between men compared with praise from the lips of one of the truly powerful, that is of women? With Ingo Dresen, man's last bastion has fallen.

I shuggle across to Newsnight. A press conference has been arranged in the Hamburg Conference Centre. Christine is sitting between Günther Grothe, the head of the Hamburg CID and Chancellor Scholz, who has come specially from Berlin. It's devastating how old she looks but everyone behaves as if they don't notice. And Christine herself doesn't seem to be at all aware of it. She's really enjoying being the centre of attention. Whatever crimes she tries to saddle me with, these pictures show that life in the prepper room has clearly done no lasting damage to her.

A butch female journalist – moustache, cropped hair dyed black, green tweed suit with hot pants – asks in a voice dripping with concern how Christine feels and what the first thing she did after her liberation was. Christine hasn't learnt anything from her experience but is her old cocky self again.

"I took a shower. I took a very long shower and now I feel fantastic."

There's a huge round of applause as if that were a great achievement. No one seems to be bothered that she hasn't mentioned her children nor her new partner. I try to find Elli, but she isn't there. Where is Elli?

"Who is the second woman who is reported to have been with you?" a slim guy with an artistic scarf asks. "What's the situation with her?"

The head of CID asks them to respect the anonymity the woman wishes to maintain. "In all probability she is another of Sebastian Bürger's victims, but our enquiries have only just begun and this woman is in such a disturbed mental state that it could be weeks before we can question her."

He clears his throat. I don't believe a word the guy's saying.

Someone asks Christine whether she can imagine taking up her old position as minister again.

But of course she can.

Olaf Scholz interjects that he had never given up hope and that from the very beginning it had been agreed among the current ministers of both sexes that Christine would naturally take up her old position again as soon as she came back. Until Frau Dr Semmelrogge had had time to bring herself up to date, the ministry for the environment atomic bla-bla-bla etc would have a dual head. At this Gottrich, the poor sod of a minister who's now been yoked to her, assures everyone how delighted he is to see Frau Dr Semmelrogge back again, safe and sound, and that he is really looking forward to working with her.

It looks as if almost half the members of the Women's Party-Social Democrat coalition are there, all the bio-young female ministers with their tattoos and piercings, and the few male ministers they feel they still have to put up with. They clap and blubber, all these women, and embrace each other, for clapping and weeping is of course much more important than getting on with government business. It's probably their male secretaries who are seeing to that. In the middle of all the wailing and snivelling a male journalist asks if there's anything in the rumour that Olaf Scholz isn't going to stand for re-election but is giving up the post in favour of a woman.

Frau Kahl, the health minister, immediately snaps at him

that this was hardly the moment to go on about far-fetched rumours and the whole crowd of women falls into indignant muttering – they refuse to allow a factual question to stop them wallowing in emotion.

"This kind of rumour, which everyone not only suspects but senses can't be true…" Olaf Scholz begins when he can finally get a word in.

"Can you imagine being the next federal chancellor," the butch journalist bellows to Christine. By now not even the male chancellor is allowed to finish what he has to say.

Christine smiles. "At the moment I feel capable of anything."

There is a thunder of applause. Scholz is quick to join in. What else can he do?

I pull out the plug of my egosmart, take a deep breath and lean back. What a joke the whole business is.

I wonder what it will be like facing Christine in court. How much will she give away just to leave me in the shit? If she really is thinking of running for the office of chancellor she mustn't put too much emphasis on her position as victim and there are some details she would do better not to mention.

Suddenly there's a young woman standing beside me, possibly even chrono-young. "Excuse me, but could I borrow your smart? Just for a moment. Only if you're not using it yourself any more. They say Christine Semmelrogge's just turned up."

The steward gives us a concerned look and squares his shoulders. I hand the girl my egosmart with all its revolting apps and suites and cables and earplugs. "Keep it. It's a present."

"Are you serious? Surely you're not."

"But I am," I say softly. "Why should I bother with

technology that's going to be the focus of the first attack in the next war? Anyway, you're not allowed to use smarts in prison."

"Okay."

She goes back to her seat, two rows behind me. The others sitting in the same row bend over the smart so excitedly that they must be the true-young children of a pious family from a sect that doesn't allow smarts. The three of them swipe this way and that on the gadget, still awkwardly but with the instinctive astuteness of youth. They ought to listen to the leaders of their sect and concentrate on learning skills they're going to need when the electricity and water supply, cashless payment transactions and public transport have all broken down. At the time when I wanted to wander through the woods with Elli and hold up filling stations. But where is Elli? I need her so much now.

Where is Elli?

Dedalus Celebrating Women's Literature 2018 – 2028

In 2018 Dedalus celebrates the centenary of women getting the vote in the UK with a programme of women's fiction. In 1918, Parliament passed an act granting the vote to women over the age of thirty who were householders, the wives of householders, occupiers of property with an annual rent of £5, and graduates of British universities. About 8.4 million women gained the vote. It was a big step forward but it was not until the Equal Franchise Act of 1928 that women over twenty-one were able to vote and women finally achieved the same voting rights as men. This act increased the number of women eligible to vote to 15 million. Dedalus' aim is to publish six titles each year for the next ten years, most of which will be translations from other European languages, as we commemorate this important milestone.

Titles published so far:

The Prepper Room – Karen Duve
Slav Sisters: The Dedalus Book of Russian Women's Literature – edited by Natasha Perova
Take Six: Six Portuguese Women Writers – edited by Margaret Jull Costa

Forthcoming titles include:

Baltic Belles: The Dedalus Book of Estonian Women's Literature – edited by Elle-Mari Talivee
The Price of Dreams – Margherita Giacobino